What Everyone Is Saying About *Start Up Marketing*

"Nulman is a master marketer. This book is an absolute must for anyone who's serious about success. He makes marketing magical and fun and provides anecdotes and ideas that are a blueprint for success."

—Milton Lieberman, *Parade* magazine

"Nulman takes great care in empowering the small business person at all levels of marketing. His style is unusually friendly and magnetic."

—Stanley L. Robinson, Ph.D., P.E., retired international vice president, Johnson & Johnson

"A feast of remarkable insights from one of America's leading marketing experts."

—Irena Chalmers, consultant to Windows on the World and The Rainbow Room

"This is the first definitive book on marketing that offers pragmatic advice and tangible tools to success. Phil Nulman's insights and perceptions benefit every person in business today."

—Eugene Dalbo, national director of advertising, Boy Scouts of America

"Finally, a marketing primer that delivers real examples and principles that help people in business break through the mundane, the mediocre and the uninspired. Nulman's book is a gift to anyone wanting renewed, creative thinking."

—Ronnie Yeskel, CSA, casting director, *Pulp Fiction*

"This is an essential guide to marketing success. Nulman has helped us with virtually every start up marketing program we've done. Start Up Marketing is the map small business people need to find the treasure chests of success we all desire."

—Robert N. Page, president, Quick Chek Food Stores

Start Up Marketing

An Entrepreneur's Guide to Advertising, Marketing and Promoting Your Business

By
Philip R. Nulman

CAREER PRESS
3 Tice Road
P.O. Box 687
Franklin Lakes, NJ 07417
1-800-CAREER-1
201-848-0310 (NJ and outside U.S.)
FAX: 201-848-1727

START UP MARKETING

ISBN 1-56414-256-6, $16.99

Cover design by L & B Desktop Publishing & Printing

Printed in the U.S.A. by Book-mart Press

To order this title by mail, please include price as noted above, $2.50 handling per order, and $1.00 for each book ordered. Send to: Career Press, Inc., 3 Tice Road., P.O. Box 687, Franklin Lakes, NJ 07417.

Or call toll-free 1-800-CAREER-1 (NJ and Canada: 201-848-0310) to order using VISA or MasterCard, or for further information on books from Career Press.

Library of Congress Cataloging-in-Publication Data

Nulman, Philip R., 1951-
    Start up marketing : an entrepreneur's guide to advertising, marketing, and promoting your business / by Philip R. Nulman.
        p.   cm.
    Includes index.
    ISBN 1-56414-256-6 (pbk.)
    1. New business enterprises--Management. 2. Marketing--Management. 3. Advertising. 4. Sales promotion.   I. Title.
HD62.5.N85   1996
658.1'11--dc20   96-28856
                                                                          CIP

Dedication

To Elaine Yannuzzi, who made this book possible. Thank you for your love, time and attention. And thank you for being the consummate marketer and the finest counselor a writer could possibly have. Without your constant encouragement and positive energy, the manuscript would still be scraps of paper in a desk drawer. I cannot describe how grateful and fortunate I am to be able to call you my mentor and my friend. You are indeed an extraordinary gift!

Acknowledgments

To Joan for her enormous help, love and enthusiasm. I know you've waited a very long time to see the book I often spoke of become a reality. And thank you for trying desperately to keep Barrie and Samuel out of my hair for extended periods of time. I clearly could not have completed this project without your dedication and affection.

To my children Barrie and Samuel, who inspire and exhaust me every day.

To Mickey Gerber, my childhood friend and my devoted fan. Thank you for your passion and your help in so many different ways. Your computer expertise is only surpassed by your intelligence, warmth and love. You will always be one of my great heroes.

To Peter Schessler, a man who is a master of common sense and a marketer of practical solutions. You are indeed a great friend, and you remain a part of my success in more ways than you could ever imagine.

To my parents, Samuel and Sylvia. Even though you've been gone for a very long time, you are always in my heart and mind.

Contents

Introduction

The original title of this book was *How to Fly When Your Wings Won't Flap*. I had chosen this imagery based on the way most people approach starting or energizing a business: We begin as if we are standing at the edge of a cliff, uncertain if we have what it takes to make the leap to the other side. Will our wings carry us across or fold while attempting to flap?

Beginning the flight requires energy, effort and fortitude...and we must keep in mind that in every start up situation, a process takes hold as we move ahead higher and faster toward what we consider our destination. But as many philosophers have said, it is not only the destination, but the journey, as well. As entrepreneurs reach their goals, new ones are immediately established. In truth, we never stop flapping our wings—we just continue the journey and constantly change direction.

Starting a business, or making the commitment to start a marketing program for an existing business, is fraught with anxiety. There are, of course, expenses, fear of failure, burnout, frustration, worries about competition...the list is practically endless. Sometimes, though, it helps to focus on the potential joy instead of the possible misery.

It also helps to assume a leadership persona and see yourself as someone who can make the critical decisions necessary for a start up situation. If you've ever watched a flock of birds in flight, you've undoubtedly noticed that their flight formation closely resembles a perfect "V"—with one bird in the lead, closely followed by the flock. This pattern of flight is critical to the journey birds take each fall because it enables them to remain focused and fixed behind the leader and to achieve the greatest speed. Your goal is to attain the pinnacle position in your marketplace...leading the pack as your competitors flock behind. Because people form leading and following positions, your start up success depends largely on the position you assume relative to those around you. After all, it's *your* business life, *your* career and *your* vision that matter most. And how you get to the lead position depends on your ability to market your business, your service and yourself!

Most people don't know what marketing is, how to use it or what possible benefits can be derived from it. This book explores the power and possibilities of marketing. The system we call marketing is defined in simple, objective, practical ways—utilizing principles that have long helped large corporations succeed. This book breaks these principles down into an accessible form for start up marketers. It's like giving away a map to hidden treasures.

When you are faced with starting your business, kick-starting a professional practice or reinventing an existing business, you need answers, methods and a means of achieving greater success. This book illustrates how to be heard, what to say and how and when to say it. Whether you are creating a business or repositioning one, the book uses anecdotes, real examples and concepts that will help you along the way.

There are two issues you'll find addressed in almost every chapter: the issues of proclamation and identity—or who you are and how you get noticed. These are clearly the most critical aspects of marketing today. In order to create the proper perceptions in the marketplace, we must be heard and remembered. Therefore, it is vital that everything we do as marketers reflects the fact that breakthrough messages and ironclad identities are achieved. We do this by paying careful attention to what we say and how we say it.

This book gives you the tools you need to make marketing a powerful part of your business—perhaps the single most important element in achieving your success. You'll discover how a small restaurant achieved breakthrough brand identity, a distribution company created a new category of business, a tiny direct-mail effort became a national success...all using marketing principles illustrated in the pages to come.

Start Up Marketing shows you how to create a marketing plan, and more importantly, how to create marketing magic. Exercises, anecdotes and examples teach you what it takes to think creatively and which marketing messages will be heard above the noise. You'll discover the myths and the methods of media, with practical solutions to complex questions, as well as many real-life examples of what works best!

This book dispenses with the theoretical—combining the hard-hitting, practical information you need to outmarket your competition with the more passionate, creative systems that will give you an enviable position in your field. You'll discover how to become a brand in your own industry or profession, how to establish a unique selling proposition for your product or service, what aspects of your business are most exploitable and which marketing strategy is right for you.

I have spent more than 20 years in marketing. My experience incorporates launching major magazines and new product introductions, positioning both consumer and business-to-business products and working with start up companies far too numerous to mention. I have brought this experience to this book—not in an effort to create text, but to give you insights, secrets and substantial examples of how to make your business soar. I have spent my career creating marketing messages that break through the barriers of consciousness. Remember my 2 percent rule and you will be among those who are ultimately written about as major success stories: *98 percent of the marketing you see, hear and perceive is mundane, mediocre and boring.* Become part of the 2 percent who are seen, heard and responded to by taking advantage of the information I give you. Read every page and then reread it. And most importantly, use the many ideas and examples as models for your own success.

People want to drive in the fast lane and stay on the inside track. That's how I want you to approach your start up marketing plan: Keep your foot on the accelerator, even around the turns. This book will teach you how.

Fasten your seat belt. We're about to turn the key and start up marketing!

Chapter 1

What Business Do I Have Being in Business?

First, let's define marketing in exact terms. Then we can move on to understand how marketing can create the kind of magic that every businessperson wants in his or her life. Indeed, there is magic to be made if you follow the plan and use the "potions" set forth in the upcoming chapters.

Marketing, simply stated, is bringing goods or services to market. The image that comes to mind is the peddler pushing the wheelbarrow through dusty streets in order to secure a position in the "marketplace"—the arena where he or she can sell goods to customers who come to this central zone in order to procure whatever they need.

But that's only the beginning. This simple peddler needs to do more than just show up in the marketplace. If it were that simple to succeed, there eventually would be no room for any new peddlers in the marketplace. (Unfortunately, most people *do* simply show up to market—without a plan, without a goal, without a clue.) To be successful, the peddler must also post a sign touting (advertising) his wares. He must set prices, establish a format for displaying his products (merchandising) and do some personal selling (suggestive selling) as well. In some cases, he might be asked to demonstrate his product— even guarantee that if it fails or isn't up to standards, he'll be there the next week to make good on it. In short, he is creating value points, exhibiting his products in the best possible way and speaking to his customers about the features and benefits of his products or service.

If he does these things, what he's done is tantamount to modern marketing. He's gone to market, advertised, merchandised, promoted, demonstrated the sale and even guaranteed his goods. In spite of the myriad of changes in the way we do business, these simple, basic practices are still at work today in our higher-than-high-tech world. We're all still looking to market our products, our services or ourselves in the same manner as the peddler on the dusty road to success.

Marketing, stated more elaborately, is a system that includes a variety of methods, all designed to sell something. A useful metaphor for this system is a freight train. Thinking of the system as a freight train can help us get a sense of just how powerful and connected each aspect of marketing is to the whole plan. A marketing plan incorporates the methods of advertising, sales promotion, merchandising and public relations. Like a train of cars being pulled by a locomotive along railroad tracks, these methods trail behind as the essential "freight" connected to the marketing plan. And we rely upon the marketing "locomotive" to guide us to our destination—the goal we've established for our business. This consists of the elements that put you into motion to begin with, such as the ideal size of the business, the number of employees, the gross volume and where you see your success in the years to come. These are "destination principles," and you will be keeping them posted in your mind and on your walls for years to come.

Unlike textbooks and many other materials on building a successful business, this book is going to dispense with theory and stick to user-friendly methods of putting marketing to work for you. Let's face it: We're all selling something, regardless of what field we're in or what type of business we own or want to start. From products to services, the core issue is still *selling*! What sets us apart from the "clutter" that exists in the marketplace is our ability to stay on track, single-mindedly, until we reach our goals. The fact is that you *can* get there from here, if you keep focusing on the track in front of you, only looking back occasionally to see who's gaining on you.

As we move forward, we will discover many "sidetracks," but for now, let's concentrate on getting the train from the station to the destination.

Finding your vision

The first step for anyone in business who wants to implement a marketing plan is to ask the big, looming question, "What is my reason for being?" Most people don't have the slightest idea why they chose the business they're in, so when I survey clients who want to start or enhance a marketing program, I always begin with the question, "Why are you in business?"

The answers are usually cryptic: "To make money, what else?" or "It was my grandparents' business, then my parents'. Now it's mine."

The *real* answers are difficult to come by. But they must be extracted in order to begin marketing successfully. If you cannot answer this question adequately, what difference are you going to make in your industry? If your reasons for being seem shallow, it's time to create much more specific goals and to invent more significant contributions in the marketplace. You're about to start a business or fire up an existing one—why? Dig as deeply into your being as necessary in order to create at least a half-dozen good, original, identifiable reasons for the creation and existence of your business. And examine how they differ from the standard, superficial answers you might have given before.

Some businesses go about answering the question by developing "mission statements." You may have heard a great deal about these. Admittedly, they were innovative a decade ago, but now they're laden with clichés. The reason these declarations have lost their effectiveness is that people don't really understand why they're in business. The rationale behind mission statements is that they allow businesses an opportunity to reflect on their quest, but creating a mission for an unfocused business is nearly impossible.

So, instead of working on creating our own mission statements, we're going to think in terms of *vision*. It may almost rhyme with mission, but that's where most of the similarity ends. Your vision is more than your mission because it forces you to project imaginatively, intellectually and emotionally. In short, your vision is the ideal you have in your head. It represents the ultimate model of what you feel your business is or what you would like it to become. It must include specific statements and objectives that define why your business deserves to be a model for everyone else. Your *vision statement* is the most expansive, optimistic, imaginative, idealized set of sentences you will ever create. And you will constantly keep it before you...reaching to achieve every aspect of it every day that you are in business. Think of your vision statement as the eyeglasses you put on every time you enter your business environment. They make things clear and give definition to everything you do while you're working. They provide the focus that makes you live up to your own expectations. Your vision is your foresight.

Business demands that we be visionaries or we're certain to get lost in the crowd. But business vision is more than being able to focus. It requires you to be introspective and prospective. By looking inward first, you can begin to develop your outward vision. To develop your vision, you must answer the following questions:

• What is the philosophy of the business?
• What does that say to your staff, your customers?
• In what ways does it satisfy you?

• How would you like your business to be spoken of by your customers?

• What are the key differences you bring to the marketplace that others cannot or do not?

• What do you expect to happen in your industry in the next decade?

Remember, creating a vision for your business is more than writing some words on a page; anybody can create a few short paragraphs. What you must do to establish your vision is ensure that you commit your thoughts to action before you commit them to paper. Begin to establish goals for each aspect of your business vision, then write the essential points of the vision on a sheet of paper and refine it until you are thoroughly satisfied. Next, post it in front of you and everyone else in your organization as a constant reminder that you're all playing on the same team and that each member must contribute towards the fulfillment of the vision.

Who is your business?

A good exercise that will help you focus on your vision is personifying your business. By anthropomorphizing your business, seeing it as a person with distinct qualities that will benefit your customers, you can begin to understand it better and get closer to important issues we will explore later on.

Most people in business don't recognize that they're really selling the *benefits* of their products, not the products themselves. An old adage in marketing is that mattress stores are not selling mattresses—they're selling a "good night's sleep." You need to ask what aspects of your business create joy, ease, simplicity, comfort or satisfaction in people's lives.

Exercise

List 10 positive attributes that lend human traits to your business. What this does is create a business portrait that has tangible qualities, qualities you will utilize in your vision statement. You may want to choose from some of the following or add any that you feel are appropriate.

happy	sexy	creative
healthy	sincere	tall
slim	athletic	sensitive
vivacious	good-looking	empathetic
energetic	honest	communicative

Once you have chosen your 10 attributes, visualize these qualities in a person. Also choose a gender and an age for your business. You may base this on the existing nature of your business. Who are the important people on your team, how old are they and what do they look like? Be candid and honest. If you see your business as a frumpy old man, you've got some work to do on refocusing your image. Perhaps you see the business as an energetic teenager, a thirtysomething housewife, a dynamic downhill skier, a sexy senior citizen. What would you *like* your customers to perceive of you? Through this exercise, you are creating a *model* that will help you focus on the key selling attributes of your business. This model, or portrait, of your business has a look and an appeal that is definable, and it is the starting point for a process we call *visioning*. This model will allow you to rethink the synergy that exists between your company and your customer.

There's no "me" in marketing

Once you have your model, take a look at your business and see if the model fits the customers' needs, not your own. Remember, your needs *will* be met by giving customers what they want. Marketing is fulfilling the needs of the marketplace first and foremost.

When a chain of convenience stores needed to address the critical issue of customer service in order to elevate their image (both to their employees and the public), they asked me to create a mission statement for them. I asked the same questions that we're dealing with in this chapter:

- What is your reason for being?
- Where are you going?
- Who are you?
- What do you look like to your employees and your customers?

Further, I told them that in order to help identify their mission/vision, we would need to do some research into their existing identity. To help us obtain the information we needed to create a vision statement, we would develop focus groups—two separate groups of 12 to 20 people. In this case, a professional marketing research organization was employed to invite people who were existing customers and who had knowledge of competitive stores. (The customers were surveyed by phone in order to determine their worthiness for the research we required.) This group was exposed to a series of questions regarding the business, the products, the service and the value of the experience at the store. Examples of slogans, ads and new products were exposed to the group in order to gain a sample reaction to the client's business.

With this type of research, the client typically sits behind a one-way mirror in order to observe the reactions of the participants.

By the way, you don't need to spend thousands of dollars for your own focus research. I often recommend that individuals in business gather family or friends—you buy the donuts and coffee—and prepare a series of questions that will help you provide focus and establish your vision. Be bold, honest and vulnerable. Invite criticism, comments, suggestions and opinions in order to help you shape and reshape your business.

In this case, we were focusing on the issues of image, quality and specific product categories. From the focus groups, we learned that even though the company had a better image than the convenience store industry as a whole, the overall image was poor. People did not identify quality service and friendliness with this type of store. Bottom line: We needed to address negative associations head on. The company had to commit to satisfying the needs of the customer in a new and enhanced way.

The result of the research, and the consensus reached by everyone involved, was the development of a vision: TCD—Total Customer Dedication. The client was happy with it. The staff seemed satisfied. Plaques were ordered to go into every store. Quotes were hung in the corporate offices from company directors who espoused great things for the future of the chain. Everything seemed focused, except for one thing: What did Total Customer Dedication mean? It sounded great. It looked great on lapel pins, cufflinks, plaques, signs, clocks, blazer emblems, buttons and uniforms—but what did it mean to the customer?

And so we began to look for ways to provide the vision statement with a tangible, practical marketing plan. We learned from the focus groups that this particular convenience store chain was perceived as a middle-aged woman who drove a station wagon. She was amiable, average-looking, friendly, somewhat short and of medium build.

Nothing exceptional, right? Indeed, it was a model that didn't exactly include the target market or the goals and objectives of the company. The appropriate personification for the company's vision was a thirty-something, personable, sensitive, tall, athletic man or woman with striking good looks and a dynamic personality. So, training methods were employed to allow the company to move toward a realization of this vision. Remember: Your vision must relate to the needs of your customer. If you create a business that only meets your needs, you're out of business. The focus is always on the customer, which is why we do whatever is necessary to get to know the customer.

We learned from this exercise that the reason this convenience store chain was in business was to provide products and services that fulfilled the needs of today's busy families. This included fast, friendly service, fully stocked shelves, extraordinary values, greater variety than the competition, longer hours, shorter lines, fresh foods, private label brands—things that perhaps weren't even consciously noticed by customers but still significantly influenced their opinion of the store.

Thus, Total Customer Dedication became a usable, realistic vision statement, bought into by both customers and employees.

Making the most of what you already know

You already know a good deal about your business or your concept for a business. Being entrepreneurial really means looking through a window, focusing on what's out there, not on the dirty streaks on the pane of glass. If you take the knowledge you already have and apply it to a plan, you're gaining ground.

A simple method of assessing your strengths and applying them to your business is to identify five of your powerful points in business and five of your weak points. The goal is to transform the weak points into five new powerful points; the resulting list can be your "top 10" list of positive attributes.

Frank Simon, who attended one of my seminars, owns a flower shop. Frank was honest about his shortcomings. The reason was simple: His business was in trouble. This is his list:

Powerful points

1. Knowledgeable horticulturist.
2. Raises exotic flowers.
3. Exhibits unusual displays/bouquets.
4. Extremely creative designer.
5. Offers free consulting and advice on plants and flowers.

Weak points

1. Would rather stay in the back room than sell.
2. Shy around customers.
3. Doesn't cater to the clientele.
4. Doesn't communicate well with staff.
5. Isn't particularly personable.

Frank needed to develop a marketing strategy in order to bolster his sagging sales and remain competitive for the gift and celebration market, which had been captured by a gourmet emporium down the street. The emporium had a billboard on the way into town stating:

You can't eat flowers!
For a great gift of taste:
Barron's Gourmet Emporium

It was a small town. Everyone knew that Stan Barron, Frank's chief competitor, was positioning his store against Frank's Flower Shop. Frank needed to develop his current strengths and turn his weaknesses into renewed strengths. Frank knew that Barron's was well-known locally for (of all things!) its tuna fish. So Frank developed a retaliatory theme:

> *You can't win her heart with tuna fish!*
> *Stop and smell the roses.*
> *Frank's Flowers*

In addition, Frank began to come out of the back of the store and address the needs of customers. He greeted them, counseled them and began teaching floral artistry on Saturdays at the local community college. He also treated his staff differently, creating incentives and bringing in pizza twice a week for the six people he worked with each and every day. Within a month, each of his weaknesses was turned into a marketable power point. The moral of the story is: *Know thyself, change thyself, sell thyself!*

CPR for the small business

Whether you're looking to start a new business or put more power into an existing business, you need CPR—Communication, Perception, Response—to move forward.

Communication: not what you say, but how!

How we communicate is often more vital than *what* we communicate. Sound strange? Well, think of how frequently you see the words *sale, value, service, quality* and other overused, flat, forgotten marketing verbiage that no one truly hears or registers anymore.

A machinery manufacturer wanted to assure his customers (companies that bought his machines for use in various industries) that quality control was the highest priority within the company. A new marketing effort was necessary because one of the machines they manufactured had been failing and, after numerous attempts at fixing the problem, the manufacturer pulled the model out of the line. But the manufacturer's image was already tarnished, and the issue of quality had to be restored. Management wanted to run ads using the phrase *quality assurance.* They wanted to explain how careful they were at testing each piece of machinery before it left the factory. Their idea, however, was simply to use words that everyone had heard but that had lost their meaning long ago.

I told them that something far more powerful was necessary to regain market share and to build a credible quality base. The first thing we decided to do was to run an advertising campaign that communicated quality assurance and quality control without ever mentioning those words.

The ad featured the company's chief engineer—a man well-known in the industry—with his name and title included. His photograph was prominent, his face congenial and reassuring, his demeanor professional but friendly. The headline:

If you ever experience a problem with any of
our equipment, here's my home phone number.

The subheadline:

And by the way, we've just extended our
warranty from three years to six years!

The ad went on to briefly explain that they had doubled what the rest of the industry offered as a warranty. The phone number was real, and calls were forwarded to the chief engineer during work hours and accepted by him until 10 p.m. every night of the week. Seven people called after business hours in the first month of the advertising. All of them called to test the reality of the campaign. The company, of course, had built engineering integrity into their products, so the advertising was backed by real "quality" without ever using that much overused phrase *quality assurance*. By extending the standard warranty, the company put their money where their collective mouths were. But their communication had to be powerful—and real.

The response? Increased sales within the first quarter of the marketing campaign. This program became their new "reason for being."

Perception is reality

It's the oldest expression in marketing, but some clichés retain their authority. Think about it: What we perceive, we believe. Our perceptions become part of our reality, our thinking, our belief system.

Creating perceptions is more than a marketer's responsibility—it is, indeed, an obligation. Every day, we make decisions based on our own perceptions—perceptions that were created and communicated to us by companies looking to sell us something. Now it's our turn to alter others' perceptions about our businesses. Every business is in the business of designing perceptions.

When people look at an abstract painting, perceptions vary greatly. This is not what businesses want. We don't want subjective judgments, multiple interpretations or vague understanding. We want to impose our thinking on the customer in order to create a perception that leads to a response. This part of our CPR process is vital to our success, but we must keep in mind that perceptions must be based in reality because once we create a perception and market it effectively, it takes on a life of its own. You can only fool customers into buying once. If you create a perception and lead customers to your product, then let them down, you'll lose them forever. Remember the adage: We want products that never come back and customers that always come back!

Perceptive programming

We'll talk about branding later, but think about your own perceptions when it comes to the products or services in your life. Are you programmed to buy a certain type of soda, ketchup, lawn tractor, automobile? To a large degree we are led down the product path, and if we like what we try, we buy! No, we're not robots, but often we do react robotically. Why? Because to some degree, we've been programmed. This is what every business wants—small, medium, large or giant. Programmed perceptions create business realities.

Not long ago, I became involved in a business venture that complemented my own career in marketing. Two other friends in the marketing field joined me in creating a start up direct marketing company. The original concept was to create a selling proposition based upon a very specific image—that is, to create a line of products that were sold on the basis of the image they projected as well as the specific attributes of the products themselves. We knew that the qualities we communicated would be attractive to a small, selective market, and our goal was to match the image to the market, recognizing that the image statements and identity we created would be as significant in creating the sale as the products were themselves. We, therefore, created a product line that was perceived as mysterious, mythical, romantic and exceptional.

Our launch item was a bracelet that adjusted by sliding knots to expand or contract it. This style of bracelet originated from the Masai tribe in Africa and was sold to adventurers on safari with the myth that it would bring them good fortune. Originally made from the tail hair of elephants, the bracelets were worn with great pride and were immensely distinctive. We began to have these talisman-like products manufactured exclusively for us, then set out to create perceptions that would sell them. First, we knew that the African origin of the bracelet was a strong selling point. Second, we wanted to incorporate aristocracy, rugged individuality and an adventurous spirit into the marketing message. Thus, the company behind the bracelet was dubbed "Pendragon's." "Pendragon's" was chosen as the company name because it is steeped in medieval legend and lore. King Arthur was purported to be the illegitimate son of Uther Pendragon, king of Britain, and Igraine, the wife of Gorlois of Cornwall. We wanted a name that incorporated a mythical past in order to enhance the talisman-like products we were going to include in the direct mail offers. To further support the image and romance of the marketing, we employed a voice actress with a decidedly British accent to record our answering machine tape. She sounded lusty and sensual with a mysterious tone that became an integral part of the program to create the proper perceptions for our company and the product line. The bracelet itself was magnificent, handmade, unusual and high-tone, but the image associated with it was even stronger than its features and benefits. We ran small space ads in magazines that matched our upscale, slightly eccentric market—*The New Yorker, Mother Jones, The Atlantic.* The ads were headlined:

Out of Africa

An illustration of the bracelet surrounded the headline, with this copy underneath:

> *Years ago when tribal laws allowed, these mystical safari bracelets were woven from the tail hair of elephants. Now, we make them in gold and silver by hand using great care. The four knots slide to adjust to any wrist. Many adventurers return from safari with these bracelets instead of big game as their trophy. We consider those travelers to be the lucky ones!*

All of the appropriate information to secure an order was included—prices, sizes, address and phone number. The 800 number was answered by our mysterious British woman, who offered the history of the bracelet and combinations of silver and gold and explained that with every order came a booklet on the origins of this and other products that carried talisman-like qualities. She also explained (without being asked) that a money-back guarantee was in place for one year after purchase. (Removing obstacles from the selling path before they get in the way is an important step in creating positive perceptions.)

Pendragon's was on its way, with an initial investment of less than $10,000 total from three parties. Of course, the full-color literature sheets depicting the bracelets in sterling silver and gold also carried the air of mystery and romance. These promotional sheets were sent to customers who inquired through our advertisements. With an ornate dragon as a logo, the company was perceived as an international trader. The perceptions we created caused the desired results and response.

Our first ad in *The New Yorker* created a response of a little more $6,000 in orders. The ad cost approximately $1,900. The cost of goods (mail order requires about a three-time markup to make money) was $1,780, with packaging and postage totaling another $390. The net profit was under $2,000. In truth, it didn't matter what product we had chosen. The fact was that the product had appeal, but the perception of the product had been greatly enhanced by virtue of a marketing plan. In its first five years, Pendragon's has shown 20 percent-sales growth on this one item each year since the inception of the business. Again, we imposed our message on the market, choosing to utilize here in America what the Masai tribe had done in Africa.

Response: Why we're in business

We know who we are now. We've established why we're in business—to fulfill customers' needs in ways that others don't. If we can't say that's the reason and believe it, we're destined for mediocrity. Response is the effect of successful marketing messages, creating the desired reaction from customers. It's what happens when communication is designed correctly. Response is created by the images, ideas, benefits, features and real value we offer the customer. In the case of Pendragon's, the response continued to grow, and the customer base developed into a much larger group than we imagined. Why? Partly because we gave people enough of "the three R's" to make a buying decision.

The three R's of Response

Romance. We created an aura that isolated the product from its category. We did this by choosing a product that already had an adventurous spirit of its own and a history steeped in myth and mystery. We used what was intrinsic to the product (its own strengths) to build a selling statement.

Reality. The claims we made about the product's integrity were absolutely true. The metals were brilliantly polished, each bracelet was handmade, one at a time, and the craftsmanship was superb. The product was real, wearable and guaranteed to perform beyond the customers' expectations.

Research. We knew the competitive products in the marketplace. In fact, the chief competitor (a major purveyor of exotic goods based in New York City) had even claimed that he held the patent on the product. We sent our lawyer to investigate this claim and found that the patent had long since expired. So we built a better mousetrap based upon research into the few companies who offered similar products. And we kept our price points at or below all of those who offered a like bracelet.

Revisiting our reason for being

One of the primary methods of defining our mission/vision is to know the competition better than they know themselves. Out of your field of competitors will come many answers for you—through *modeling,* or emulating.

As consumers, we're bombarded by a neverending stream of images, statements, comparisons, ideas, boasts and offers. But when we take off our consumer hats and put on our business hats, we can study the marketplace and analyze what's really the *best*. Then, we begin to carefully and consistently build a portfolio of "examples." These examples allow us to draw comparisons and to focus on who's doing a superior job in any given industry. This permits the marketer to reference various issues from the competitive field...using the finest attributes from as many different examples as possible to help define a marketing position and strategy.

Let's look at the retail jewelry business for a moment. Anderson's Jewelers was a third-generation store. It sold essentially the same commodity products anyone would expect to find in a retail jewelry environment. But it wasn't enough to continue along with essentially the same sales from year to year. For one thing, inflation and competition were ever increasing. So Richard Anderson was looking for his "reason for being." The first thing he had to do was study his competition, taking two crucial steps:

1. Learn from what is being done well.
2. Learn from what is *not* being done well.

This is a simple procedure. Richard plastered his walls with the ad of every competitor in his marketplace. Guess what he discovered? If he covered the company logo and address on each ad, there was absolutely no way to differentiate one store from another (with only one exception). Out of 13 ads, 12 had absolutely no identifiable features except a name at the bottom of the ad!

Richard now had two powerful opportunities. First, he could use the message that had the most distinguishing features as a model upon which to improve. In this way, Richard was looking at the marketplace and choosing the best example of communicating, but going one step further. Essentially, he was creating his marketing identity by adding value to messages already in the marketplace.

The second opportunity was more significant. He had the ability to step out of the crowd and distinguish himself in a way that would ultimately become his singular "reason for being." The field around Anderson's Jewelers was filled with flowers of the same color. Richard had to appear as a blue iris in a field of white ones. He needed to stand out first before he could deliver his goods to the customer.

"Things as they are, are changed upon the blue guitar."

This quote from a poem by Wallace Stevens tells us that imagination is essential to change. Creative thinking can get people to see your business in a way that will make it more powerful, more potent (remember, the word "potential" comes from the word "potent"), more engaging to customers and more a part of their thinking.

What we often do as businesspeople, particularly small business owners, is look at what other business owners do and think it's sufficient to do the same thing. Giving your business the attention it deserves requires renewed thinking. Take a look back at your exercises. Rethink your selling propositions. These are the key issues that make your business unique. Your selling propositions define who you are and illustrate what makes your marketing position potent. They are your list of features, benefits and all of the specifics that comprise your marketing mission. Do your focus research around the kitchen table with friends and family, and look long and hard at what you can do that will attract attention to your business, career or venture.

The blue guitar is a symbol of change. Strum it often enough and you'll begin to hear the harmony of creativity.

Final analysis

By now, your vision statement should be closer at hand. The vision statement is a capsulized version of a larger plan. You will leave this chapter with the ability to complete the following sentences, not in vague, general terms—but with specificity and clarity.

I am in business to:

1.

2.

3.

4.

I alone offer the consumer of my products or services:

1.

2.

3.

4.

My 10 most exploitable strengths are:

1.

2.

3.

4.

5.

6.

7.

8.

9.

10.

You now have a model, a vision and an understanding of the marketplace you're in, your competition and yourself. Now you're ready to move on to the next phase of your marketing agenda.

Chapter 2

You Are What You Do

There's a saying that image is everything. There's much more truth in that statement than you might think. Groucho Marx's cigar became a symbol to an entire generation. So did George Burns's use of the same prop, a device whose original purpose was to keep him from laughing at his own jokes. The image of Frank Perdue and his chickens is burned into our memories. Orville Redenbacher took his popcorn (a commodity item) and raised our awareness with qualitative differences conveyed through the use of his "corny" personality.

Many years ago, I interviewed for a creative position with a large advertising agency. The creative director was a flamboyant woman who smoked a pink pipe. I sat with her for more than an hour, left the interview and remembered only one thing: *the pink pipe.*

She puffed on it during our conversation, tapped it in the ashtray, gently blew smoke from her pursed lips. I was seduced, entranced and forever left with a picture of this pink pipe in my mind. Later on, when relating this story to industry peers, everyone who knew her said, "Oh, you mean the lady with the pink pipe." This simple device had given her personality, authority and memorability. It became for others the singular, identifying symbol of her.

We all need pink pipes. Businesses are trying desperately to discover which issue, element or device can hook into the marketplace and reel in customers.

Businesses have personalities, too

The toughest thing for a small business to achieve is personality. Even though you would think that personalization is easier among small businesses, the small business has to first overcome critical obstacles—money, media exposure, monumental messages, image! There are two ways to succeed in business and in creating a business personality. One is to be very rich, buying impressions and creating image with frequent messages in the marketplace. The other is to be much, much smarter than everyone else in your field. The goal of most small businesses that don't have deep pockets is to make every dollar count, every word count, every message count. We have an opportunity to create powerful impressions, compelling imagery and a bold identity, if we're smart enough to remember that no one forgets the woman with the pink pipe—no one!

When people are their own businesses

Occasionally people are literally their own business. Professionals such as doctors, lawyers, dentists, consultants, accountants and engineers are all in the business of selling themselves. Their image, then, is closely tied to their personality, and vice versa.

Take the political consultant who is renowned in the Democratic party. He's bright, well thought of, with a national reputation. When candidates need information or campaign work that requires communicating through traditional media or mail, they call him. No client has ever been to his office (thank goodness, because it is the antithesis of what one would expect). He drives a beat-up sport utility vehicle and wears worn jeans, sweatshirts and sneakers without socks. He reads newspapers at traffic lights and dictates into an old hand-held recorder. His image is that of a highly "independent" professional, but he can afford that image because his reputation is already in place. Most businesspeople cannot afford nonconformity because acceptance is hard enough to come by, even when they play by all the rules.

Imagine yourself, then become you!

According to American Heritage Dictionary, image is a *mental picture of something not present or real*. Because image is our own creation, our own device designed to stimulate the imagination, it is our responsibility to pay careful attention to the image we impose upon our business. Marketing begins in the mind. We've modeled and created portraits. Now we need to imagine who we'd like to be. We already know that businesses have personalities—the question now is how we establish these personalities and what we do with them.

Exercise: A marketing and image drill

The dentists of a large practice had as their goal a continuous flow of patients to their offices. They previously used a myriad of methods of obtaining new patients, such as flyers, ads and mailers. And when we met at their offices in the waiting room, I asked a simple question: "What is the personality of the practice?"

No one had a clue, because there *was* no personality to the practice. Each of the dentists and staff members gave me a different answer, and each, indeed, had a different personality. One was cold. One was friendly. One was aloof. One was informal. One was downright frightening. My first piece of advice was to unify the personality. Remember, once you've established a business or professional personality, you can develop your image. Until then your message remains muddled.

I also asked these questions:

1. What happens when a patient arrives?

2. How long does a patient usually have to wait?

3. What distractions do you offer the patient who's waiting?

4. Who greets the patient when the dentist is ready for him or her?

5. What does the dentist first say to the patient when he or she is led into the operating room?

6. What does the dentist wear?

Let's start with just these six. The answers were typical and thoughtless because none of them confronted the primary concerns of the patient. You don't need to be a rocket scientist to know that one of the first issues for anyone going to a doctor or a dentist is *fear*! Even for those who don't mind, being comforted is a process that goes a long way—particularly when someone is about to put their hands into our mouths.

Answers to the questions:

1. When the patient arrives, the receptionist asks for the person's name and insurance information and asks the patient to wait in the waiting room.

2. The average wait is 20 to 30 minutes.

3. The only distractions are magazines and a box of old children's books in a small basket on the floor.

4. A dental assistant comes into the waiting room to get the patient. The assistant is dressed in surgical whites with a mask hanging from his or her neck.

5. "Hello."

6. Both male and female dentists wear washed-out blue
   scrubs, goggles, a mask, rubber gloves and plastic splash
   guards attached to the sides of their goggles.

Then I asked who was in charge of marketing the practice. I was instructed that the office manager (a pleasant woman) placed ads and kept track of responses.

What's wrong with this picture?

Common sense dictates the answers. However, common sense did not prevail in the 20 years that this practice had survived. The reason they hired me was to address the issues facing the practice today—keen competition, new insurance options and an aging patient base. They needed to insure their future, and a professional marketing program was necessary.

I asked them what image they thought they enjoyed in their community. The responses were rather banal: "We're well respected, we've been here a long time." "People seem happy with us, they come back." "Nobody seems to complain."

I asked: "Have you ever asked your patients what they think of the experience, the relationship?"

"What relationship?" one of them replied.

That was the crux of the problem. The practice couldn't possibly convey an image because none of them understood that as we prepare for the first decade of the 2000s, we are all in the *relationship business*. Every business has a relationship with every customer—*this* is image! Even though dentists don't frighten me, I want *comfort marketing* to take place from the external communication (checkup reminders, ads, fliers) to the visit.

Here's what I told them: Every patient who walks in the door must be greeted in the same manner. Your mission/vision statement must be kept right in front of the receptionist. She must memorize it, live it, speak it, eat it and drink it...

"Good morning, Mrs. Jones. Nice to see you. You'll be seeing Dr. Jane Wilson this morning, right? Can I get you a cup of coffee or juice? Please help yourself to today's newspaper or a magazine, or if you'd prefer, there are headphones attached to the CD players so you can listen to some music while you wait."

I told the members of the practice that they should send their office manager to trade shows. I mentioned the Variety/Merchandise Show, The Gift Show and The Toy Show—all at the Jacob Javits Center in New York City, since their practice was only an hour away from New York. Once there, the office manager should buy a supply of children's videos, games, toys and giveaways. The waiting room furnishings should be updated, made much more friendly and made to look comfortable and inviting.

Further, no one, I repeated, no one should come into the waiting room to greet the patient except the dentists! And they should greet patients by first name—offering their first name as well: "Good morning, Doris. I'm Bob Arons, and I'm the dentist who will be working with you today." Notice, he didn't say working *on* you today. Of course, if it's not a new patient, then the dentist will simply greet them in the waiting room with a pleasant hello. Next, I told the dentist not to put on scrubs until he or she walks the patient into the operatory. My suggestion was that they wear tennis shirts and casual slacks. It's more work to slip on a scrub-top for each patient, but it sets a strong precedent and creates a far more casual, far more friendly *relationship*.

They listened intently. They didn't like what I told them, mostly because they were less interested in their patients' "pain" (the issue that patients are most concerned about when visiting dentists, according to research studies) than they were with their own habitual behavior and convenience. But I wasn't there to make them feel good about themselves—rather, to make their new patients feel good about them.

In the final analysis, the "image" we created for this group was far warmer, more engaging and more human than before. They took some of my ideas and abandoned others, but the impression they left in the marketplace was more successful and the results were stronger than any in their history. This new personality was communicated in mailings, advertising, in person and even in phone conversations with existing and prospective patients.

How do you turn an electrical plug into a silk purse?

Making inanimate objects come to life is no small task. But image-building has to take place regardless of the product or service. Today, it's increasingly important to study your product and then step back from it. Look at it objectively, stare at its qualities and think about what it does for the customer, not what it is!

An electric plug is, in and of itself, simplistic, mundane, even boring. It has two prongs and a plastic housing and attaches to a wire. Why would anyone take notice? The marketing dilemma facing Branin Electrical Supply was decreasing market share. Their prices were competitive, their distribution was fine and their sales force was adequate, yet competitive companies were taking more and more of the market share.

The task before them was formidable. They needed to discover why their piece of the pie was decreasing and what could be done to stop the erosion and increase sales. After we examined the advertising, sales promotion, public relations and direct marketing, we discovered that nowhere in their communication was anything that offered the customers comfort, excitement and innovation. Nowhere did they illustrate any benefit to the customer except to show photographs of the product with a catalog number and price. Their own customers didn't notice their message, and potential customers couldn't possibly find it among the clutter in trade magazines and mail.

They needed energy. They needed to take an electrical plug and literally plug into some current. So we created a program called "More Current!"

This simple two-word program was supported by a host of new and renewed opportunities for the customer. More Current! meant newer colors, styles and shapes, and it meant that issues that were otherwise taken for granted were now revisited with vigor and with bold statements about the depth of the company. The products themselves were animated—taking on personalities that conveyed energy. The company was seen as being plugged into the 90s and beyond! They were no longer selling electrical plugs; they were in the energy business.

The enthusiasm that this created allowed the research and development people to begin working on energy saving plugs and new, innovative technologies that could be brought out in the future. The marketing director admitted that after looking at the same product for 15 years, he had lost sight of its potential.

The image of the company went rapidly from that of a tired, dusty (though reliable) supplier to a supercharged marketer. Remember, true marketers can develop a plan and sell any product based upon image-making. The key is always to begin with a credible product that lives up to its own image.

Writing your own ticket

Many people approach business the way they approach stepping onto a merry-go-round. They climb aboard, they hand over their ticket and, as long as they keep riding, they are content. The problem with a merry-go-round is that while you may be content with the ride, you're not getting anywhere.

The reason businesses don't get anywhere has to do with the fact that they don't properly employ the use of image, visionary thinking and the ability to make an impression. Impressions are image-associated communications that remain part of the public's consciousness.

The impression we make in business is identical to the personal impressions we make. What would you like to see when you look in the mirror? More hair, less chin, finer features, a softer expression? Well, only personal grooming professionals can help with that. But remember, your business does have a "physical image" as well as an invented one. So you must start by looking at your sign, your building, your offices, your parking lot, especially if your customers come to see you.

Think about your business image. What does it mean to your customers? Recognize that you need to "re-image" your business every five to seven years. If you don't, you run the risk of losing your customer's attention. Image is everything! And when you fine-tune your image, you make your customers stand up and take notice.

Automobile companies fight for attention. If we really think about it, automobiles all do the same thing. They run on four wheels, get us from here to there, keep us warm in the winter and cool in the summer. Sure, some have tops that go down, others have sunroofs, some are long, others are short—you get the picture. But aside from features and benefits (every product has them), cars essentially do the same thing. The way we buy into one particular kind of car (or anything else) has a great deal to do with image.

Your image: Love it or leave it!

You're going to live with your image for a long time. People will remember it, long after you've decided to change it. And images aren't always created by you. Think of cases in which rumors circulate about a business or in which product tampering has occurred. These become part of the business's image.

Image creates attitudes. It elevates the business and keeps it top-of-mind. It can be applied to quality, style, design, speed, sex, value, exclusivity, eccentricity. In short, it sells products that would otherwise be passed over.

Think about your own business or business idea. What images do you associate with it? Use the simple list on page 36 to help you define your own image. Simply check off the words that apply to how you would like your customers to perceive your image.

Check off up to four, and list them in order of importance. Remember, this is based upon what you would like your customers to perceive of your business.

___ warm	___ emotional	___ honest
___ cold	___ intellectual	___ romantic
___ thin	___ comprehensive	___ sexy
___ chunky	___ energetic	___ sensitive
___ sensual	___ with-attitude	___ compassionate
___ solid	___ compulsive	___ caring
___ flamboyant	___ loose	___ stoic
___ amusing	___ organized	___ cool
___ sincere	___ easy	___ funky
___ serious	___ formal	___ familiar
___ silly	___ casual	___ caring
___ spiritual	___ real	___ creative

You can begin to build your image base from the four concepts you have chosen. Suppose you're in the optical business and you're targeting teens. The choices above would be fairly simple—*funky, cool, sexy, silly*. If your target market was designer-oriented adults in their 40s, you'd likely choose *creative, sincere, romantic, caring*. From this, you'd begin to shape an image that will ultimately become part of your business's exterior, interior, cards, signs, ads, brochures, commercials and personal appearance. Consistency is as much a part of image-building as anything else. It will keep your image intact and help you begin to "own" that portion of the marketplace.

Make your day

Clint Eastwood could easily sell security systems, but we wouldn't want him to take on his Dirty Harry persona to sell lawn furniture. Matching the right image to the right message is imperative. When we look at the image of a car transforming into a panther with its sleek, muscular body, bolting ahead in great strides, the image of speed and power—of sensual, sophisticated prowess—smacks us right between the eyes. Automobile manufacturers recognize who buys their products and why. So matching the image to the market is your task, as well.

It would be inappropriate for a store that sells perfume to create a "quality" image. People don't think about quality as a selling proposition when they make a decision to buy perfume. Imagine the owner of a perfume company getting on television to talk about quality control in his factory. Who cares? We take for granted that the product is not going to peel skin from our necks—we want to know what it is going to do for our own image, our own lives, our own relationships. When we buy based on image, we're fulfilling our own needs and our own fantasies.

When Tylenol was tampered with, Johnson & Johnson stepped up to the bat and hit back with concern, sincerity of tone and solutions. The chairman didn't back-pedal, become defensive or attempt to explain his way out of the dilemma. He simply took responsibility—financially, morally, legally and ethically. This was a case where a company stood behind its image and, even in the face of great adversity, enhanced it when the incident could have destroyed it.

It is important to live up to your image once you create it. Therefore, you must create it based upon your ability to support it. And as the old saying goes, *Use it or lose it!* Your business image must be part of your everyday vocabulary. It must relate to everything you say and do about your business. It's your new lapel pin. It's the logo on the back pocket of your jeans. It's your new hairdo. It's the new you.

Chapter 3

Positioning: Comfortable or Compelling?

Did you ever see a blue fire truck? How about a silver school bus? I haven't either, but I'm sure if I did, I'd take notice. We're all creatures of curiosity. (That's why we're so often caught in traffic because of rubbernecking, not obstructions.)

The way we convey our unique identity is through a market position that causes others to take notice. If there is one truism in all of marketing, it's *positioning*. Think of the way you position yourself in different situations. If you sit on the beach, your body language is different from how you appear in a business meeting, which is different still from the way you sit at a basketball game. You establish a position that relates to the specific event in which you are participating. This position is part of your individual image and identity. If you wear a sports team shirt to every game, you are establishing your identity in that situation. If your beret is your hat of preference when you drive your sports car, that is your position in that situation. The position you assume in a specific circumstance identifies you to those around you. It becomes your image.

Try as we might, we cannot gain a better notion of how to increase market share and develop strategies that will ultimately lead us to success than *positioning*. Our greatest desire in business is to increase our market share. The concept of *ownership* means that what we gain in market share, we keep—unless we do something very foolish. Ownership, therefore, means tucking those customers into our business, maintaining the business through "relationship" marketing and proceeding to build our business base by establishing a market position and gaining more attention than our competitors.

When you do what's unexpected, you get more than you expected

We all expect to see a red fire truck. It's part of our belief system. When that very object appears with different attributes—color, style, size—we take notice. Giving your customers what's unexpected, creating messages that are unforgettable and offering opportunities that people are unaccustomed to being offered—these all add up to increasing awareness. Our business messages deserve to be heard. Our job is not to keep people complacent, if by keeping them complacent we continue to offer them what everyone else is offering them. We need to make people aware of, in very short order, our marketing position or USP (unique selling proposition).

But first we have to get their attention. It's like the story of the man and the mule. When asked why he hit the mule over the head with a stick, the man replied, "I just wanted to get his attention." We gain attention by creating impactful messages. These messages may consist of unusual words, phrases or graphics. They may include large, bold typography, photographs, vibrant colors and designs. You know what makes you stop and read, watch or listen. Because it is imperative to pose our proposition with elements and issues that are different from everything else around us, this becomes a formidable but unavoidable task.

Getting attention isn't enough. Once we've gotten the customer's attention, we need to establish identity. Identity begins with the creation of a marketing position. This position defines your business relative to the competition. Think of it as your fingerprint. Ideally, it should relate only to you in ways that your competitors cannot readily copy. To be sure, once you've entered the marketplace with a USP, your competitors will be right behind. The way to outsmart the field is to be first and to be looking over your shoulder constantly. The establishment of a position puts your competitors on notice that you've created a marketing identity that leads the pack. What we want, as marketers, is *proprietary inventory*. This refers to our ability to own and protect issues, identities, products, services that relate to our company alone...at least for a time. When we establish our own warranties, personalized products, image, customer service policies and personalities, we are on our way to establishing *proprietary inventory*.

If you were to define your strongest attribute and have it printed on your shirt, that would be your slogan or position statement. Start up businesses as well as existing businesses need to establish a position statement that tells the world where you stand in relation to your competitors.

Again, position statements are typically thought of as slogans. We're all familiar with slogans—we hear them, see them and sing them all the time. What a truly great slogan does is differentiate the business so quickly that we know who the business is before we are told. This identification creates drama and keeps customers connected to the message.

Exercise

1. What can you offer your customer that nobody else is offering?
2. Look at the field of competition, and take three issues that presently pertain to your company alone.
3. How can you remove obstacles that the competition places in the way of selling?
4. What value-added service will help build your position?

An example

Sometimes your marketing position must be created in reaction to the marketplace. A good example of this is the travel and adventure clothing company that manufactures "the world's best outdoor hat." This hat is $45.00, but it includes a lifetime guarantee. Plus, it was designed to repel water and block UV light and is unshrinkable and machine washable. The company's position statement is:

Our return policy: We want you to return!

Their position is clearly defined. I don't know of another company that has adopted this philosophy of doing business. They're smart. When they started out, they sold their hats at trade shows, boat shows and outdoor shows. I bought one as a gift for my uncle. That was 10 years ago. He still wears it, and it hasn't worn out.

No matter what hat we wear, we're all consumers!

Take a moment to think about how your life is divided. Ostensibly there's the professional you and the personal you. Interestingly, business owners forget the fact that everyone is a consumer. If you're selling medical products to doctors, you're going to use appropriate language, graphics and tone, in keeping with their doctor mentality. The mistake that businesses make is that they tend to forget that a doctor shifts from doctor mentality to personal mentality hundreds of times a day. While it's true that medical devices appeal to his professional side, the communication techniques we employ in marketing don't have to be boring, serious, profound or completely technical.

Great positioning, indeed great marketing, recognizes that there is a crossover from one consumer mind-set to another. Thus, we can employ similar thinking to engage, entertain and inform the professional person who is also a private person.

Helping the contractor construct his position

If you haven't looked through the classified ads in the newspaper lately for a home improvement or home remodeler, take a look. The weekly papers have little boxes (classified display advertisements in bold) that contain the contractors' advertisements. I'm always astonished to see so many ads that look alike, sound alike, have no position relative to one another...and make it impossible for the consumer to make an inquiry or a decision.

One of the contractors, a deck builder, attended a seminar I gave at a metropolitan area hotel. After three hours of speaking, the seminar ended and the contractor came to ask me questions. He didn't understand why his marketing plan didn't work and why he had such a pitiful response to his advertising. I didn't understand why he didn't understand.

"Don't you want the consumer to see your message?" I queried.

"Of course I do. That's why I'm here."

"But you didn't hear what I was saying for three hours," I replied.

"What do you mean? My slogan is: *Decks our specialty!*"

"What does that mean?" I asked.

For 15 minutes we played badminton. He hit the bird back over the net, and I kept smacking it right back at him. Finally, I pulled out a newspaper and asked him to pick out his ad. It took him 45 seconds to find his own ad in the local paper. Once he found it, he admitted that it looked pretty much like all the rest in the paper. He was merely part of the shopping list. In fact half of the ads carried the same *deck* message.

Consider your customer

If nothing else, consider the poor customer who wants to use your services. If you don't care about your own image, market position or message, at least give the customer an opportunity to make a decision.

And so I asked the contractor, "What do you think consumers think of people in your industry?"

"I don't know. I guess they're concerned about the fly-by-night operations—you know, guys that don't show or don't finish the job...that sort of thing."

"Okay, then," I said. "Why don't we begin there?"

In truth, the contractor hadn't a clue about which path to take toward a marketing position. And he shouldn't have had one—it's not his business. I don't have a clue about building a deck, either. So I applauded him for coming to the seminar and gave him a position to begin his campaign, plan and strategy: *Remove the customer's fear.* Thus, the small square ad carried a new message:

If you're considering having work done on your home...
You'd better do your homework!

That was only the very beginning of a marketing position. To construct the marketing plan, we needed to hammer this position home with a "mix" of methods. The first order of business was to build a testimonial portfolio. Second, we needed the ability to offer financing through a finance company or bank. Next was a series of *guarantees*. One guarantee was that the consumer would get a quote on the job within 24 hours of inquiry. The next guarantee covered workmanship, craftsmanship and completion...*in writing*!

The company then invited the public to do their homework— contact the Better Business Bureau, the local chamber of commerce, the Builder's Association, the local trade association and a host of other credible sources for affirmation of this company's services. By inviting potential customers to do their homework before having work done on their home, this company established a marketing position, and the marketing materials carried this "slogan" prominently.

When we challenge the customer to notice us for reasons of reliability, credibility and integrity, when we give them compelling reasons to respond, when we break through the clutter with meaningful messages...we're marketing! Until then, we're just in the marketplace without justification.

Chapter 4

Stalking the Big Idea

Having a "Big Idea" to work for you is something any size company can do—from the sandwich shop to the muffler store to the insurance agency to the local bank. The Big Idea is something we all desperately want for our businesses, but it doesn't always come in one fell swoop. The Big Idea is the ultimate set of selling propositions for any business. It is the quintessential piece of communication that transcends specific offers, promotions or advertising. It provides constant focus and establishes the smartest system of setting a marketing tone. The Big Idea is the trendsetting standard for any given industry. It comes along only now and then...and can be the singular reason for start up success. Remember *Pizza, Pizza*? *Have It Your Way*? *Coke Adds Life*? *Please Don't Squeeze the Charmin*? *Let Your Fingers Do the Walking in the Yellow Pages*? These are all Big Ideas.

Sometimes the Big Idea is established in stages—slowly but surely, we evolve into recognizing that we've created a lot of little ideas that add up to a Big Idea. The absolute magic in marketing occurs when a business recognizes the series of ideas or even a single idea that has the potential to catch fire. Let's explore the concept of a Big Idea. Think about marketing ideas that are memorable in your life or experiences with businesses that have left you impressed.

You've heard of extreme sports—how about extreme service?

One of Nordstrom's big ideas is what I like to refer to as "extreme service"—making the customer's life easy, pleasant and relaxed and making customers feel important. The way that extreme service works is best exemplified by a story that has been circulating in advertising and marketing circles for years. Here's how it goes:

A man walks into Nordstrom. He is looking for a particular pair of sneakers on sale. Upon fitting him, the salesperson regretfully informs him that his size is out of stock. The man is mildly disappointed and prepares to leave. The salesperson stops him and asks if he would be willing to wait five minutes. Puzzled but willing, the customer waits. Soon after, the salesperson returns holding a box of the same exact sneakers in the correct size. He fits the customer and apologizes for the wait. The curious customer inquires how the salesperson found the correct size...only to be informed that, rather than risk losing a customer or disappointing one, the salesperson ran to another shoe store in the mall, found the sneakers in the correct size, bought them and honored the sale price. What's the Big Idea? Extreme service just won that customer for life.

Stew Leonard's (a gigantic food store in Connecticut) was renowned for extreme service and extreme selection. Stew related in a speech how he learned about customer relations early on. A customer returned a carton of milk to the store, complaining that it had turned sour. Stew smelled the milk and simply commented that the milk smelled fine. The customer flew out of the store without even arguing for a refund. Stew Leonard lost the customer forever...and calculated that if a customer who shops for a family of four spends about $125 per week in the supermarket, he just lost $6,500 over the next year. Stew related the story because it was a turning point in developing the Big Idea: The customer isn't always right, but he's never wrong! From that day on, the Big Idea was customer service, with an extraordinary amount of time and energy being spent on making the shopping experience "fun and easy," even to the point of creating merchandising displays of cows mooing in the milk section!

Turning a local gourmet shop into a national institution

Elaine Yannuzzi was a real estate speculator and an entrepreneur. She and two partners purchased property in a semirural/suburban section of New Jersey. They built a speculative building of approximately 6,500 square feet and couldn't find a buyer or a tenant. The building sat vacant month after month. Out of desperation, Elaine decided to create a store in order to save the building—not exactly the traditional way of beginning a business. In Elaine's case, the business was created to fill an empty building in an attempt to recoup her investment. The business began as a fancy food store with crafts and bargain kitchen and household accessories. Because of Elaine's natural business acumen, Expression unltd. soon became a destination for people wanting to take a drive into the country and experience a very unusual retail environment. Elaine studied models of similar businesses in New York City, Atlanta and San Francisco and did her homework on unique methods of merchandising and esoteric product selection—fancy vinegars, oils and spices. And as the store evolved, it gained a prominent reputation among both serious food shoppers and the general public. In fact, Expression unltd. became a model for many stores.

The way Elaine built her business was through dedication, research, hard work, creativity, innovation...*and a Big Idea!* The Big Idea was really multifaceted. First, she was prompted to add an extensive cheese department to the store. Then she managed to buy huge shipments of Brie (a very popular semisoft French cheese) at big discounts. Because she was willing to buy carloads, she had a decided price advantage that allowed her to own the cheese market in the entire metropolitan area. And she did own it.

The Big Idea was to fuse her own personality and identity into the selling proposition for the store. And so, Elaine Yannuzzi became the focus—indeed, the Big Idea:

> *The Big Cheese really knows her cheese!*
> *Elaine Yannuzzi is full of beans!*
> *Elaine Yannuzzi minds her own business!*

The ads included a photo of Elaine with the appropriate product at hand. The product was cheese, coffee and gourmet foods, but the Big Idea was the "real product"—Elaine Yannuzzi herself. By marrying the person to the product, customers felt a great sense of confidence and an overwhelming trust in the business. For Elaine, it meant minor celebrity status, which had a distinctive downside—lots of customers wanted to meet Elaine and have her personally help them with product information or selection. This nuisance was minor, though, considering the energy that was now in play.

Ignorance is bliss?

You walk into a store and see a sign that says *charcuterie*. The case is filled with some identifiable and some nonidentifiable products. You recognize sausage and salami, but there are lots of things you clearly don't have experience with—exotic pâtés, unheard-of smoked fish, imported spreads and a selection of caviar with way too many syllables to pronounce. Intimidating, to say the least.

Remember, marketing dictates that we remove obstacles from the sale. Even when we need to create illusions, we must be forever cognizant that explanation follows illusion. Elaine *educated* her customers without being patronizing. Each product had a descriptive sign—poetically offering serving suggestions, use and taste description. In addition, she sampled every conceivable type of cheese—from unknown imported products to better-known domestic cheeses. Her intention was to elevate the customer base to appreciate unusual, finer foods without scaring them away. It worked. Expression unltd. became perhaps one of the best-known gourmet food emporiums in the country and won industry recognition. Elaine became a member of the editorial advisory board of *Family Circle* magazine, won numerous awards in the specialty food industry and has lectured throughout the country. A career was born out of an empty building and a single idea...a Big Idea!

The Big Idea can have a small beginning

Who put pizza delivery on the map? Who offers "pizza pizza"—a concept of doubling the sale with each customer? Remember when we talked about modeling? Well, each and every one of us has a shot at a Big Idea for our business, regardless of its size.

The Big Idea begins by exercising our imagination and, like positioning, allows us to tear through the common business fabric in our own community. Consider the law firm that was looking for a Big Idea. It had 16 partners and 12 associates, a big payroll and very little focus on new business development. Like every other law firm in town, it wanted to be noticed. But how and what would bring it attention? This simple exercise was a beginning, and it ultimately led to the Big Idea.

1. What are the hot issues in your industry today?

2. What are the most notorious issues in your industry today (those getting the most notoriety from the press or the marketplace)?

3. Is there an area of your business that you or one of your co-workers is "expert" in?

The hot legal issues in the workplace were sexual harassment, employee complaints, discrimination, gender equality and advancement. These were issues identified by the law firm. The notorious issues were clearly sexual harassment and discrimination. Two of the partners had expertise in these areas of law. The Big Idea was emerging. It became "The Workplace Bill of Rights"—a document designed to look exactly like the Bill of Rights, detailing the rights of workers with specific language, clauses and issues. It was developed into a poster, cards and a mailing program. The mailing was designed to be sent to union halls and associations. Further, it was developed as a promotional and public relations campaign designed to create an image of public service for the law firm. Indeed, it was a public service concept as well as a Big Idea for furthering the marketing of the firm.

Jack Stanford was a limo driver. He liked the work and loved the independence. But, like many people, Jack believed he could make more money by owning his own limousine service. When we first spoke, I encouraged Jack because he showed a great deal of entrepreneurial spirit. And Jack was already exhibiting some big ideas that would ultimately earn him great success.

For example, Jack noticed that most executives were stressed on their way to the airport for several reasons. The experience itself (even for the seasoned business traveler) was often harrowing. Delayed flights, traffic on the way to the airport, connecting flights, baggage hassles...the list is endless. Jack had a great solution to alleviate his customers' anxiety. First, he guaranteed that his service would arrive on time, or the trip was free! This alone instilled trust. Second, the limo had the daily newspapers, coffee, cappuccino, pillows, blankets, an outlet for laptop computers, a cellular phone for the customer...and a selection of New Age music for meditation or relaxation. The customer was treated like royalty. He also handed the customer a Limo-Line, a toll-free number that the customer could call 24 hours a day for return trip cancellations or changes. And again, he reiterated the guarantee: *on time or free!* Word of mouth helped Jack build his business, but he utilized a strong program of marketing to local businesses explaining his Big Idea services. In four years of incredibly hard work, Jack has acquired a fleet of 12 vehicles—some stretch limos, some vans, some sedans. He has gone from a driver to an owner/operator to a mid-sized business entrepreneur. And every time he has a new idea, he tests it with his customers.

Jack's success came about as a result of being perceptive and curious. He was never afraid to sound corny or even old-fashioned. He was only afraid of not trying to stay fresh and innovative. His innocence turned out to be his most successful trait, because he never permitted anyone to be cynical or edit his ideas until they were tested. And he spent most of his waking hours jotting down new thoughts and methods of making his company more successful. He was filled with "firsts" and was eager to try each one. Jack had all of the traits of the entrepreneur...and you can, too.

Chapter 5

Emotion and Reason: The Heart and Mind of Marketing

Examine the following list. For each item, jot down an "E" if the decision to purchase the item would be based upon *emotion* or an "R" if the decision would be based upon *reason*.

____ motorcycles		____ aluminum siding	
____ computers		____ life insurance	
____ automobiles		____ cellular phones	
____ real estate		____ barbecue grills	

Let's begin with this short list. Marketing works because the marketer appeals to the heart or the mind of the customer, and sometimes both. This exercise will illustrate the primary and secondary processes that produce purchase decisions. Primary processes represent decisions based primarily (up to 80 percent) on either emotion or reason as the key ingredient in creating a response or producing a purchase decision. Secondary processes represent decisions based upon far less significant reasons for a purchase response. For example, when people buy batteries for their flashlights, the primary process that takes place is related to reason, not emotion. The decision to purchase is primarily a practical one, making logical issues like value, quality and convenience—as opposed to emotional issues like romance, adventure and desire—the key selling propositions.

Purchase decisions are rarely based 100 percent on emotion or reason. There is typically a 20 percent variable in deciding upon a specific product or service. This 20 percent is the secondary process that kicks in once the buying decision has been made. The 20 percent factor relates to pragmatic comparisons such as cost, quality, reputation, rebates, reviews or critiques. These issues sway us to choose between manufacturers, suppliers or retailers, but they do so only after the primary decision has been made—the decision to purchase that category of product or service. Occasionally, we will refer to the 20 percent factor as "strong secondary" because the secondary issue is more significant in certain purchases than others.

Motorcycles. (E) Motorcycle manufacturers do not expect logic to dictate purchase decisions. The primary process in seducing a customer to purchase a motorcycle is *emotional* (some might even suggest *irrational*). The reason is that motorcycle buyers are already pushing the envelope. Later on, in Chapter 14, we'll discuss the major trends of today that address the schizophrenic nature of our society when it comes to purchase decisions. But for now, suffice it to say that both motorcycle manufacturers and retailers know that their customers want to feel the wind in their faces, the sound of cylinders, the excitement of speed, the rush of pulling up to a crowded restaurant on a modern-day stallion. Buying a motorcycle is a gut issue, and until it comes to comparison shopping, no other principle is represented. Once the primary decision has been made and a motorcycle manufacturer or retailer has won the heart of its prospective customer, there are qualitative decisions to be made, such as which type of motorcycle to purchase and from which dealer. These represent the 20 percent factor and incorporate the reason process.

Computers. (R) Reason dictates computer purchases. Eggheads and novices alike want to be informed and convinced and to exercise concise comparative thinking before making a purchase. Both the original process (to buy a computer) and the comparative shopping are reason-driven.

Automobiles. (R) Primary; (E) Strong Secondary. The second largest purchase for most families is the automobile. The decision is primarily based upon practical principles with strong emotional overtones—particularly for younger and male shoppers. The family automobile is first a necessity, then a luxury. The rational reason for buying is to have reliable transportation with good economy. The features and benefits are weighed carefully, then the bells and whistles are debated. If you were a car dealer, and a 20-year-old man with a ponytail and earrings walked into the showroom, would you steer him to the sedan or the two-seater?

Real estate. (R) Primary; (E) Strong Secondary. For years, real estate agents told sellers to put vanilla extract in a pot of boiling water, bake muffins, put out flowers or spray perfume on the furniture before potential buyers showed up. These techniques simply create a more inviting atmosphere. Remember that our hearts and minds work together. If we enjoy the sensory experiences and associations that come with pleasant smells, then we are more susceptible to buying. The smell of muffins baking in the oven, for example, creates an emotional response. It brings back memories of family, childhood and nurturing experiences. This is a marketing tool designed to make emotion part of the selling feature of a home, and it works very well. In similar fashion, many stores will incorporate scents and sounds into the selling environment in order to put customers in a better frame of mind to buy. We are emotional beings, and we respond to stimuli in significant ways...even when the primary motivation to buy is based on reason.

Even though most homes are sold based upon the kitchen and the master bedroom, the primary decision is a practical-rational one. Location is paramount, then the number of rooms, lot size, taxes, neighborhood conveniences, and then such things as the romance of the view, the circular drive, the two fireplaces. Real estate businesses must understand that the rational-emotional mind-set has to be addressed with marketing savvy, tools and finesse.

Aluminum siding. (R) Home remodeling is based upon reason. Though people delight at the sight of a freshly painted facade or a newly carpeted room, the primary motivator is reason. Price, color, style, durability, quality, warranty, reliability of contractor, completion time and cleanliness of crew are all the factors that are utilized in marketing this product/service. This is essential in the marketing strategy of an aluminum siding contractor. These contractors must remember that they are battling for the consumer, based upon the logical comparative assessment made by a homeowner with a wide menu to choose from in selecting a vendor.

Life insurance. (E) Primary; (R) Secondary. Fear! It's the key factor in buying or selling insurance. You can't hold insurance in your hand. You can't do anything with it. You're paying lots of money in the event something happens. In a sense, you're betting against your own life, health and happiness. Insurance is sold by creating statistical fear, and statistics are what drives insurance risks and rates. It helps us to understand marketing principles if we recognize that everyone is afraid. Offering people reassurance is clearly worth something. Insurance policies are shopped on a comparative basis, but the strong primary reason used in marketing this incredible "intangible" is the fear of the unknown event.

Cellular phones. (R) Primary; (E) Secondary. This is a perfect example of an almost perfect split. Cellular phone marketers (both cellular service companies and retailers) use reason to sell to the business user. The features and benefits of cellular phones for the businessperson include convenience, time management, cost savings, accessibility and service. These are all credible issues for the heavy user who uses the phone to enhance and increase his or her business. Thus, the marketing emphasis in the promotional literature, advertisements and commercials will relate to price, quality of sound, business deals (that might otherwise have been lost) being made on the car phone and the ability of offices to reach people for key decisions within seconds.

The secondary market for cellular companies is the social user. This market receives a different message. The primary selling proposition to the light user is *safety*. For this reason, you'll see advertisements, commercials and literature that depict a woman sitting by the side of the road late at night in the teeming rain with a flat tire. If she had a cellular phone, the message implies, all would be well. This is a good marketing strategy because safety is, indeed, a strong secondary marketing objective.

Barbecue grills. (R) Primary (E) Weak Secondary. Barbecue grills don't sell well in winter (even in warmer climates). When spring arrives, people begin to fantasize about being outdoors and the great American tradition of barbecuing becomes top-of-mind. So marketers (both manufacturers and retailers) of barbecue grills take advantage of the practical issues first, focusing on features such as grill size, automatic start, cover with glass window, thermostat and nonstick surfaces. We make our decision based on features, benefits, price, promotions (free grill tools with purchase) and guarantees. Part of the marketing effort, though, is the idea of spring and the romance of being back outdoors. In a sense, even though we are responding to practical issues, we are aware that the product is closely associated with *feel-good* thinking.

Pushing the right buttons

You're in a dark movie theater and the handsome, devilish hero has just taken a bullet in the heart. Suddenly you feel as though *your* heart is breaking. Then the music starts in, causing you to shake and covering you with chills, and you depart from the movie feeling strung out, rung out and totally though temporarily weakened. You've just had a cathartic experience. It's what every screenwriter, author, composer and, yes, *marketer* wants.

When interviewed by William F. Buckley, Leslie Fiedler, a noted literary critic, stated that what every writer wants is to remove the reader from the present place and time and take him or her to

"Another Place"...just for a while. And he said that popular culture (I include advertising and marketing in popular culture) does this better than any other genre of the culture.

Like filmmakers, we want people to react to our messages in ways that keep us in their memories. So we take great care to identify *why people buy* our products. What we want as marketers of products or services is to use emotional messages and rational messages when the situation calls for them. Understanding when to employ either reason or emotion is a critical choice in our marketing strategy. For most of us, our products possess qualities that allow for the use of emotion, reason or usually both, even though we must maintain a primary and a secondary strategy as discussed in the beginning of this chapter.

We design our selling messages to tap into customers' psyches and stay there. That's what successful marketers do. And that's what we're going to do to increase market share.

You've gotta have heart

Ben & Jerry's started as a very small ice cream shop. The revolution (not evolution) of the company began with sincerity, principle power and a unique sense of *community*. The reason this example is "revolutionary" in the marketing hemisphere is that the company made an incredible commitment to marrying the business to social responsibility. To Ben Cohen and Jerry Greenfield, community represents the entire country. Their vision was to create a company where people were considered as important as profits. And they did.

To begin with, a percentage of profits is continually contributed to such causes as the preservation of rain forests. Further, the company has opened stores in urban areas with specialized training and employment of homeless people...turning poverty into profitability. This is the sense of community that Ben & Jerry's brings to the marketing arena. It is a very unique vision that has resulted in enormous success for the principals, employees and customers.

Marketing research suggests that community is a vital issue for companies focusing their energies on the first decade of the 2000s. Making people feel good about purchase decisions is what *moral marketing* is all about. It uses rational selling propositions while touching people with issues that affect their emotional lives. Getting the customer to invest in you (not just literally but emotionally), which is what every customer does every time he or she buys something, can be greatly strengthened when there's another reason to buy from you instead of your competitor. Whether you choose to give a percentage of sales to a charitable organization and make that part of your selling platform, or simply donate to your favorite charities, today's customer wants a sense of sharing. It makes everybody feel better about buying. Whether you run a dry cleaning establishment or a car wash, an investment firm or a hot dog stand, the issues are the same.

The connection between marketer and market is made stronger when the issue of community comes into play. It's as simple as putting local charities' canisters in your store or posters on your window, or doing something like the following, which is one of the most creative examples I can think of...

The winning ticket

A local clothing store on the main street in a rather small town had a great idea to establish community. The store owners' association was constantly troubled by the difficulty that patrons had parking. This particular owner decided to combine the marketing of her business with a community gesture. The idea was ingenious. She created a promotional flyer that was designed to look like a parking ticket—same size, color and style. Then she sent her staff out into the street regularly to feed the meters that were just about to expire. The "ticket" was placed on the windshield of the cars that most likely would really have been ticketed. It read:

> *Your time was just about to run out...*
> *So we ran out to feed the meter!*
> *Now that you have a little more time,*
> *Stop in and visit us!*

The community loved it. The other business owners loved it. The idea used community to market the business, and the results were splendid. The store created traffic, publicity and goodwill...and everyone benefited.

Never lose sight of your customers. They are your most important community.

Working at networking

We recognize that the customer is our community. We must also recognize that "referral sources" or networkers are also part of our community, a vital part. I strongly suggest that you investigate local networking organizations. They're listed in business-to-business phone directories and often run ads in business journals, newspapers and magazines. Typically the number of people in an organization can run from 10 to 50. Networking can range from informal meetings among peers to formal groups designed specifically to impact on others' businesses within the group, utilizing a two-pronged approach. First, networking groups provide third-party leads (each noncompeting member becomes a sales agent for another) and second, companies do business with each other directly.

True networking groups provide strong leads to the members. And the categories range from interior design firms, chiropractors, insurance agents and banks, to auto body shops, printers, accounting firms, photographers and attorneys, to florists, realtors, computer software firms and caterers, to auto leasing specialists, mailing list companies and jewelers—every conceivable category imaginable. If you can't find one that you can join, begin your own.

The regular interaction among members keeps your needs in motion. Don't be afraid to make your needs known. If you have a specific need to gain entry into a company in order to market your goods, ask! It's likely that someone knows someone who can provide you with a reference to use in connecting with the prospect.

Camaraderie with other businesspeople is a big part of your future community. I have gained valuable business leads and have developed profitable business relationships from my association with a networking organization. It's like having a team of salespeople at work for you— every day, reaching out into the community, recommending your business whenever appropriate.

The customer needs an excuse to buy

Let's give our customers an excuse, or permission, to buy our products or services. That excuse might be indulgence, reward, health, sanity, compassion, satisfaction.

What we're doing when we offer the customer an excuse to buy is removing all of the negative feelings that might be associated with the purchase. For example, if we're selling triple-fudge chocolate cake, we might want to establish all of possible reasons for indulging in this delightful dessert...such as a list of 10 tension-producing events that have occurred during the past week, with a message to the customers that they're justified in indulging themselves:

You've had a hard week of work. The mortgage is
due. It's almost time for your dental checkup.
The dog has fleas. The roof needs repairing. The boss
is in a lousy mood. The kids are climbing the walls.
The windshield on your car has a slight crack.
Your mother-in-law is on her way to visit.
That salad you had for lunch stunk.

It's okay to give yourself something really great once
in a while. You deserve it!

Of course, this concept works just as well in the sale of exercise equipment as it does in the sale of chocolate cake. If the excuse to buy includes health benefits, better looks and greater sex appeal, then the cost of the product can be more easily justified. If you tell the customers that indulging in a specific piece of exercise equipment will give them a body that they've always dreamed about and allow them to feel better, then you're offering an excuse or permission to buy.

By giving them permission to buy, by offering creative reasons and establishing a creative platform, you can dispense with all of the logic that produces skepticism and allow the customers to see that we're all only human. And being human, we occasionally need someone to tell us that it's okay to splurge—provided that we're not putting ourselves in real danger.

In truth, sometimes customers need to be cajoled and reminded that it's okay to think with their hearts.

Chapter 6

Getting Closer to Market

I'm always surprised to find that most business owners, regardless of the size of a business (with the possible exception of Fortune 500 companies), approach marketing with fear, ignorance and frustration. Fear is a great motivator, provided it decreases once the system gains momentum. Ignorance can be overcome with guidelines, and frustration never ends until you retire, maybe! Business owners typically think of marketing in terms of getting behind the product and pushing, often uphill. And if you're like most of them, you see yourself with arms outstretched, struggling to get this giant ball over rough terrain, through treacherous jungles and up steep slopes.

Pull—don't push

From now on, you're going to begin to look at your marketing objectives from the top of the hill, not the bottom. You'll see yourself on the other side of the jungle, in the clearing, not in the treacherous bush. What you must do is visualize your marketing program from the success end backwards, where you can have the distinct advantage of envisioning what your success will look like. You may see your products scattered throughout the country (representing greater distribution), or people waiting in line to buy your product or service or come into your store (representing greater market penetration), or your message on billboards, cable TV, radio and in the hands of your customers (representing increased exposure), or bright, bold graphics and logo (representing a powerful new image).

Also look at your business from the customer's side. When you identify customers' needs, wants and expectations first, you begin pulling your marketing program through instead of pushing. Remember the saying about the mattress store? Well, it's the *advantage you provide your customer* that begins the marketing process. By thinking of your product from the customer's perspective, your marketing is tuned to the needs of the marketplace.

Something old, something new

Randy was the second-generation owner of a 50-year-old hardware distribution company. His father was an extremely conservative man who didn't believe in marketing or advertising. He even had a dislike for salespeople. Essentially, the business grew in spite of itself, to a point. Sales of $9,000,000 had been flat for several years. At the point of stagnation, Randy looked for help. Randy was like a patient who doesn't see a doctor until he has a problem, reaching out for all the help he could get.

The first question I asked Randy was, "How do you survive 50 years of business without having a plan?"

"I have no idea," he related honestly.

Incredibly, the company had not reprinted its catalog in more than four years. Its dedicated salespeople were desperate for a catalog from which to sell. For four years, they simply used the manufacturers' literature in a three-ring binder. Astonished, I asked why. The answer was a shrug of the shoulders first, then the explanation: "We thought we could save money."

I asked for a list of weaknesses and strengths and the company's own perceptions of its customers. The admitted weaknesses included insufficient inventory, slow delivery, poor customer service and a complete lack of identity or sales penetration in regions of the country where dedicated salespeople didn't travel. Sales representatives (independent sales agents who carry a multitude of products in their line) were completely unsuccessful in penetrating the territories not covered by the dedicated sales force.

I reviewed the direct mail literature, trade advertising (their customers were hardware stores, carpenters and construction people) and their promotional tools such as literature, sales promotion booklets, fliers and advertisements. They possessed neither a marketing position nor a strategy. A half of a century into business, and they were looking to reissue themselves—indeed, *reinvent*—themselves to the marketplace.

A further complication was competition that had been far more aggressive in pursuing the market. Randy had seen his market share decrease by almost 9 percent in three years, due to competitors taking bites at his customer base. It's difficult for most business owners to realize they must constantly look over their shoulders. Randy didn't know that the market was slipping away until the fiscal review—when the accountant indicated that there was trouble.

The first order of business was to get information—not to create new artwork, a new style, a new position, a new strategy, but simply to get the information we needed to develop a plan. To get this information, I asked:

1. How do your customers see you?

2. Who is the customer? How well do you know your customer? When was the last time you surveyed them, inquired about their needs, communicated with them after a sale?

3. How is your competition reaching the customer? Is price the driving force? What about reliability? Has the competition discovered your weaknesses? When was the last time you offered something exceptional to your customer?

4. Have you lived up to expectations in the marketplace? Where's your vision? What kind of innovations have you incorporated during the past five years?

5. Are you dysfunctional? Do you lack information about your own industry trends? Have you overlooked your customers' pain (problematic issues that have caused them concern)? Have you enabled your customers to make an easy purchase?

6. Have you provided line extensions? What have you done to increase the customer's profitability? What can you do to sell more? Are you postured to win in the marketplace?

7. All business strategies need to change. How have yours? Where's the focus? Who's your customer going to be tomorrow? What can you do to change?

8. What demographic issues have affected your business? Are superstores killing the independents? Have small hardware stores been taking it on the chin because of comparatively small inventory?

9. How has the product mix changed? What shifts have occurred in product sales and why? Has the "do-it-yourselfer" market shifted? What are the top 25 performers in your line?

10. Can you win customers back? What's it going to take to make them feel better? How much money will it take to regain a customer? How much revenue was lost in losing a customer?

The interviews with the salespeople began, and their complaints were heard by management. Part of their problem was the history of conservatism at the company—particularly under the direction of Randy's father. The "spirit" of the firm was always rigid, uninspired and conventional. This was a major source of frustration for the sales staff. They were stifled. Even when they suggested creative approaches to increasing business, the cost factor kept them from being entrepreneurial. If, in fact, the sales staff didn't have inspiration to sell from the management side, their task was enormous. So, what did the salespeople need? First, they needed some independence and flexibility. They also desperately needed to be supported—financially, emotionally, creatively.

All 10 questions were answered to the best of everyone's ability. We tested some of the answers and began to develop a strategy. But we made one surprising discovery: Primary competitors had already developed their own pitch based upon Randy's company's weaknesses. The competitors had been smart enough to isolate the hot spots and draw customers away, particularly in two areas: inventory and customer service. By positioning themselves as "heavily stocked" with quick turnaround and "consummate customer service," these companies began to erode Randy's business.

Back in the game

One thing working against Randy's company was the inability of any of the top management people to *schmooze*. For those of you unfamiliar with the term, *schmoozing* is another word for *rubbing elbows, making conversation, networking, socializing, nurturing*. The chief competitor knew the importance of schmoozing, and he practiced it regularly. He met with customers, sales representatives, buyers, plant maintenance people, building managers...and maintained relationships that benefited him.

Randy, however, was not comfortable doing this. So we chose a "replacement schmoozer" to perform this most important task. Fortunately, the fellow chosen liked to play golf, enjoyed socializing and truly had a good time talking to people. He was already working for the company as a salesman and had a fine record of success.

The company also joined industry trade associations, after having allowed memberships to lapse for many years. The president of the company admittedly loathed personal or "relationship" marketing, but he understood the importance of it, particularly for one segment of the company's customer base—buyers for hardware store chains. The designated schmoozer developed a game plan that included attendance at specific events, a letter-writing campaign to customers with premiums included in the packaging, a series of seminars for customers and distributor sales groups, a new technology newsletter—everything necessary to get Contract Hardware back in the game.

Customer service also cleaned up its act. Each employee who dealt with customers indirectly or directly was given a five-point checklist and a strong incentive and disincentive plan. The checklist, shown below, was laminated, and company policy mandated that it be placed in front of every person who had any contact with a customer or dealer representative. The checklist:

1. Always answer the phone by saying: "This is Contract Hardware. I'm Mary, and I'm here to help you."

2. In response to any problem whatsoever: "No problem."

3. Beyond the problem phase or order phase of conversation: "Do you have our newest literature?"

4. "May I send you an invitation to our next seminar, titled *Software Solutions in High-Tech Hardware?*"

5. "How may I help you further?"

The incentive plan was simple. Because daily diaries were kept, it was easy to track customers' inquiries, problems or requests. A survey was sent out to each person who called customer service. There was an incentive for the customer to fill it out and return it in the postage-paid envelope. If the survey signaled that the customer felt positive about his or her dealings with Contract Hardware, the customer service representative was given points, redeemable for money or gifts. If, on the other hand, the survey suggested a negative experience on the part of the customer, the customer service representative received a disincentive—points that affected his or her raise during the biannual review.

The inventory problem was overcome by restructuring debt with a new bank and freeing cash flow to pay for new stock (specifically for the 50 top-selling products).

The company was readying itself for reentrance into the marketplace. It created new advertisements, a new logo and a new position statement. A mission/vision conference was held, with every employee in attendance (except vital phone order-takers). The company actually recast its bait into the waters and began to slowly reel in the old and new customers. Within two years of the reemergence, Contract Hardware was up 27 percent in sales and had entered six new markets.

So significant was the change that industry trade publications ran stories on the second half-century of this 50-plus-year-old company, which had successfully gotten back into the game...when the game was almost over.

Chapter 7

Bucket Marketing

Visualize the marketplace as a large field. Spread out across this green field are red buckets, orange buckets, blue buckets, brown buckets, black buckets, white buckets, gray buckets, yellow buckets. Now, step back and put on your binoculars. Focus on the red bucket. In it are products that are specific to that area of the landscape (the marketplace). Now continue focusing on the other colored buckets, recognizing that each has different products filling it...products that pertain to the local environment in which they are marketed.

Today's marketplace, even on a local level, is multifaceted. What I mean by "bucket marketing" is marketing that addresses the issue of market segmentation. There exist many variables within the marketplace, however large or small. If we don't recognize these differences, we lose our ability to connect the product or service to the customer. If the red bucket has blue bucket products in it, the customer who comes to the red bucket will be disappointed. There will be no reason to buy.

In a very real way, marketing dictates that we are all things to all people, if we're in a broad-based commodity business. (We'll discuss the opposite theory, exclusionary marketing, in Chapter 8.) Why? Because we're in the business of satisfying the needs of the market, not our own. So if a certain segment of our market is Hispanic, we speak Spanish, carry products that appeal to Hispanics and get to know the culture, nuances and selling opportunities. If another segment of the market is Hungarian, we'd better know our way around that culture as well.

Customer withdrawal

Once a customer disassociates himself with a business, his next stop is a competitor's business. Not only does the first business lose the customer, but it runs the risk of losing everyone associated with the customer. Word of mouth still plays a mighty important role in marketing. We can't afford to fill our buckets with the wrong merchandise because our potential loss is far beyond one customer.

Filling your bucket

Quick Chek has 100 stores in the nine northern counties of New Jersey. As with any successful chain, the stores look alike, the signage is the same and the logo, the merchandising and, for the most part, the experience are the same. So customers know what to expect as they drive around the state. The same thing is true of our expectations when we visit a McDonald's. We expect to find hamburgers, fries, soda. But if you take a careful look at many of the nation's most successful chains, you'll notice variations that correspond to each market segment or "bucket."

Within the Quick Chek chain, each store has its own unique characteristics (however slight or subtle). That's because each store has its own community, and each of these communities has its own needs and wants. While 95 percent of the product mix may remain the same in most of the stores, there's a 5 percent variable that focuses on the community. If the neighborhood is Portuguese, it would be nonsensical to carry a large line of Polish delicacies. Bucket marketing is as simple as looking at the marketplace, recognizing its variations and catering to what's common and uncommon about the "bucket."

Bucket marketing doesn't stop with product or service offerings. It has to do with communication, personnel, recognition of ethnic holidays, symbols and sensitivity to the "face" of the business on the part of the customer. If you're in someone's neighborhood and you're not sensitive to the needs of the neighborhood, you'd better get out of town before you're out of business.

Take a careful look at where you are as well as who you are. Businesspeople often overlook the enormous diversity in our culture because they take a singular look at who comprises our culture. One of my clients sells products to customers in a dozen countries overseas. Each piece of literature must be translated into 12 languages, with rough copies of the translations sent to the customer representatives who are native to each culture. The reason for this is simple: Before we checked with the local marketplace in the foreign countries, we discovered colloquial differences in language that were, sometimes, highly offensive to the overseas customers. Sure, we were translating the English into the correct language, but we were using the incorrect tone, nuance and style. So, we often appeared too formal, too flippant, too smug...too stupid!

The differences in our marketing field are not confined to cultural variables. They include situational, lifestyle and personal changes as well. The world is filled with huge buckets, but so is our own backyard. Fill each bucket with the correct products, expressed in the appropriate fashion, and you can own your field full of buckets.

Being customer-driven doesn't mean driving yourself into bankruptcy!

Since 1990, more than 100,000 retail businesses alone have declared bankruptcy, and the outlook, according to Management Horizons, a division of Price Waterhouse LLP, is that the figure will be exceeded over the next five years. Every aspect of the retail community is expected to be affected by a downturn in the economy.

The marketplace is fickle. Herb Kleinberger, Chairman of Management Horizons, a corporate management firm, suggests, "Retailers must rationalize their customer base, and effectively fire customers who don't meet their sales and profit requirements. Through relationship marketing, retailers will get more personal with customers and court only the ones they want to do business with. They'll incur 'an intelligent loss of business.' "

This means that business owners have a responsibility to assess their customer base. Knowing the customer is critical. As we near the year 2000, it's an absolute imperative. If we discover that the customers we're attracting through our marketing efforts are not making us successful, we need to disconnect from the "relationship" that exists between the business and the customer base and redefine that relationship. Becoming more personal with our customers is tantamount to knowing them better, caring for them better and relating to them better. For example, if we attract a customer who is only driven to our business because of price promotion, perhaps we can't afford to own that customer anymore. If that's the case, we must return the customer to the marketplace and pick another one.

Maybe McLuhan was right

When Marshall McLuhan said "the medium is the message," a lot of people didn't understand exactly what he meant. But when we look at our own businesses, *where* we communicate dictates *what* we communicate. If we've built a business based on price cutting, we own a certain customer and we've excluded another. When businesses fail, often the underlying cause is "customer isolation." By isolating our customer, we're isolating our message.

Proactive marketing means being a pro who's active

Relationship marketing requires proactivity. It means you have to get off the chair and into the community, sponsoring fund-raising events, sports activities and local charities. It also means that you have to take an active role in the customer's life (the bucket). If the signals that the economists are suggesting are correct, only the proactivists will survive. According to Carl Steidmann, chief economist for Management Horizons "In the next 5 years, 70 percent of teens will come from one-parent households. They'll be tougher customers for retailers to deal with because they'll be less educated and will have suffered from a breakdown in traditional family."

If your bucket includes teens, you need to understand the issues that affect their lives, situations and relationships. For example, the issues of time, convenience and saving money will be critical. These teenagers are the sons and daughters of baby boomers, who have produced a generation of young people who demand immediate gratification. These teenagers have been taught to demand value and quality. They are a far more savvy group of consumers than any generation before.

None of your business?

Your customers are your business. The research suggests that as we head toward the year 2000, we have to listen to the marketplace. We have to foster the following in the marketplace:

1. Credibility. When we become part of the customers' culture, we become a credible part of their business. Recognize that you must constantly reinforce your worth to the customers by referencing your own success and by including any issues of recognition or notoriety that you have achieved. Your importance as an integral part of your industry will bolster your credibility with your customers. When you keep yourself tied to their business, in personal and in business ways, you're certain to stay in the loop. Credibility is achieved by consistency. It's hard work to maintain all of the specific issues that keep business relationships vital...but it's necessary when there's so much competition ready to do whatever *they* can to build a credible base with your customers.

2. Belonging. We're all looking for community. The relationship between business and customer is a special kind of community. Break down whatever barriers, perceived or real, that exist between you and your customer. Make the customer feel closer to your business through personal selling, relationship development, birthday cards, first names, letters and a nonstop program of communication that's nonobtrusive and informal. Develop a customer database that maintains customer profiles and pertinent information coupled with a "red flag" system that highlights your calendar when customer issues need attention. We must constantly remind the customer how important we are in his life and how committed we are to his well-being. The integrity of this relationship is critical to success, and the customer will not "break up" with you without good cause.

3. Excitement. There has to be energy in any relationship. If your business doesn't maintain a certain level of energy, the luster wears off and the vitality decreases. If you run a supermarket and you don't remodel, you risk losing the customer. If you run a shoe store and you don't have the newest stock or displays, you risk losing the customer. If you're selling insurance and you don't have the latest computerized comparison sheets and color charts, you risk losing the customer. If you own a restaurant and the menu doesn't change or new specials aren't added regularly, you risk losing the customer.

4. Sensitivity. Never allow the competition to beat you at anything. Remain totally reactive (as well as proactive) by keeping careful tabs on the competition. Never let a customer convey that your competitor down the street is 20 percent less expensive than you are and has a better service guarantee. Remember, if you're not sensitive to the marketplace, the marketplace will not be sensitive to you!

5. Equality. Don't ever let your customers think that there are differences in the way you treat them. From pricing to payment terms to discounts to incentives to private mailings to public offers, maintain equality on every level—unless there is a specific program in place that relates to volume purchases or payment terms.

Chapter 8

Sometimes You Have to Play Hard to Get

My 5-year-old son knows he's not supposed to put his hands in the fishbowl, yet he goes for the goldfish time and time again. He knows it's prohibited behavior, so it becomes primary behavior.

Recently I was expelled from a large, prestigious networking organization for poor attendance. Even though I had intended to disconnect from the group (because of scheduling, travel and philosophical differences), I was furious that I was the one being rejected. So furious, in fact, that I began to mount a marketing effort to the board of trustees, designed to have me reinstated. It wasn't until after my presentation to the board and their vote to reinstate my membership that I stood back and asked myself why I had bothered. Hadn't I gotten exactly what I wanted? I knew the attendance rules. I consciously made a decision to break the rules, knowing full well the consequences. Yet, I was maniacal in my need to be brought back into the group. My sense of community was shattered. Now I'm back and I feel more comfortable, but I may not stay.

Remember that person you wanted more than anything else in high school? The more he or she rejected you, the more intense your feelings became. Then, after two years of wooing him or her, you finally went on a date...and it was just "okay"! What happened to the fireworks? Where was the magic? Why didn't the sky explode?

The point is that this basic aspect of human psychology—*we want what we're told we cannot have*—is, in certain situations, perhaps the most powerful marketing tool we have available to us.

"Nothing's as pretty in your hands as it was in your head."

—Starbuck, character from *The Rainmaker* by N. Richard Nash, American playwright

We work hard to gain new customers. We want to give them the best product and price, the best experience. But sometimes we need to look at exactly who our customer is in order to fulfill his or her needs. We also need to look at who our customer *isn't*. Communicating in an exclusionary fashion becomes a powerful method of targeting our market. By telling the customer that our product isn't for everyone, we define exactly who it *is* for. Yes, we are excluding certain people from our selling theme, but by doing so, we are defining and focusing on our true customer while we create an air of exclusivity that is a powerful motivator for prospective customers. This may sound cynical, but it's not. It's a significant tool that creates the desired image, position and definition for our business-customer relationship.

"I don't care to belong to any club that will accept me as a member."

—Groucho Marx

Bob Peters owned the largest racquetball and fitness facility in the metropolitan area. As an ex-owner of a large manufacturing firm, he had deep pockets and a personal obsession with fitness. When he sold his manufacturing firm, he put all of his time and attention into succeeding in this mammoth fitness facility. The problem was that his weekends were essentially packed, his early mornings were full and his early evenings had plenty of people. He really couldn't accommodate more people during the peak periods and weekends, so he couldn't grow this multimillion-dollar business. Bob wanted and needed nonprime-time general memberships. But he needed to give people an incentive to join and use the place during underutilized periods. What did Bob do? He decided to tell the world that he didn't need their business. The advertisement in the major daily newspaper stated:

> *Magna Spa & Fitness thanks you for your enormous support. Our facility is forced to close its memberships due to unprecedented demand. We will be accepting names for our waiting list on a first come, first served basis! Again, thank you for making this the most successful facility of its kind!*

Within six weeks, more than 1,000 people signed up for the waiting list. Of those people, the owner was able to sign 400 to a "limited membership," maintaining their status on the waiting list for a full-time membership. For now, the new members had access to the facility only during weekday daytime hours. Exclusionary marketing worked. Bob told people that he didn't want to dance anymore, and the public filled his dance card anyway.

When businesses want to be perceived differently, often messages that exclude rather than include are the most powerful.

"It is far safer to be feared than loved."
—Machiavelli

Often, we are the victims of our own sense of comfort. After all, being comfortable is a great deal easier than being anxious. But in marketing ourselves, anxiety is something we will necessarily encounter and create. We need to understand the methods necessary to make it work for us. No one ever said that changing our business behavior leads to comfort, but then, comfort doesn't lead to success.

Andrew Schwartz has a customer, named Gabriel, who provides his company with a great deal of business. Andrew sells solvents and polishes used in the manufacture of silverware to Gabe's company, a manufacturer of tableware. Gabe is a middle-aged man in this third-generation manufacturing firm in New York City. He is, by all measures, very successful. He belongs to the most prestigious country club in Westchester County, travels internationally, lives in an exclusive community, wears the finest clothing and dines in New York's best restaurants weekly. For almost a decade, Andrew had been nothing but solicitous, humble and exceedingly patronizing to Gabriel, and Gabe was always quick to take advantage of the vendors who served his company.

Apparently, Gabe felt some misplaced resentment toward those who made money from his firm. His ego and personality demanded far more attention than most people could realistically offer. Andrew did everything right in his business dealings with Gabe, but once, only once, he forgot to send a get-well card to Gabe after he'd undergone gall bladder surgery. Gabe never forgot what he considered a gross act of insensitivity. Andrew's dilemma was clear. He needed to maintain the business relationship because of the amount of dollars it represented to his company. But Gabe had little respect for Andrew, and the relationship was already in jeopardy. Andrew was in a tough place. Not only did he need to regain Gabe's respect, he needed to attempt to increase business as Gabe's company grew. He also needed to establish "limit-setting."

Altering behavior is part and parcel of jockeying for position in the business world, and Andrew needed to market himself and his company to Gabriel in a way that solidified the business they did together. The first step toward limit-setting was for Andrew to back off slightly and establish an identity that would command more respect from Gabe. In order to do this, Andrew looked at the bottom line. The worst-case scenario was that Andrew would lose Gabe's business (about a half-million dollars per year). But if the relationship didn't change, sooner or later, Andrew was likely to lose the business anyway. Upon weighing his options, Andrew decided that exclusionary marketing was his only option to keep Gabriel's company a customer.

Toot your own horn first, then ask your friends to toot, too!

The first order of business was for Andrew to gain attention. So he gathered articles about his company that ran in trade journals (kept in a company scrapbook), photocopied them and asked an "insider" friend within Gabe's company to show them to Gabe at an appropriate time. Next, Andrew had an existing customer (and friend) call Gabe, presumably for a business reference regarding Andrew's company. During the phone conversation, this "friend" dropped some other references given to him and mentioned the incredible accolades related by other industry people about Andrew and his company. Gabe's perceptions of Andrew began to shift, however slightly.

You've got to look the part

Next came the "Don Johnson" look. Andrew started to show up for meetings in linen jackets, pink shirts, no ties. The change in attire, in the "look," was accompanied by a change in attitude, demeanor and even the way Andrew displayed his product line. He now had a new case, a sharper display and a new business card, logo and presentation folder. It was a significant shift in posturing the person and what the person represented to Gabriel's company. Gabriel *had* to take notice and connect Andrew's appearance to the image of the company he represented.

Andrew's memos, phone voice and general presentation were more powerful, more creative and better positioned. He used bold headlines in his letters, highlighting different selling propositions. He mentioned industry functions, dinners and speaking engagements that Gabriel was connected to through their common industry association. Gabriel was more interested in Andrew, and Andrew's business was becoming more valuable to him, perceptually. Indeed, Gabe's perceptions about

Andrew were beginning to change. Because Andrew had friends within Gabe's company, he was able to track the success of his program. It was working better than he thought. As Andrew became more independent, he became more desirable to Gabe. In fact, Andrew began to receive golf invitations (which he politely declined). Andrew was more aloof, more elusive, more attractive. And business was stable.

The plan continued. Andrew sent Gabe information and literature about his competitors, alluding to the fact that they had contacted him because of his expertise in the industry. He also sent Gabe numerous articles about the competition (culled from industry papers, magazines and newsletters). Gabriel began to see Andrew as a valued ally who could conceivably become a powerful adversary.

In spite of all this image-altering, there was a final confrontation that signaled the ultimate change in direction for these two businessmen. It took place in the cafeteria of Gabe's company on an occasion when Andrew was making a sales call. Gabriel, a most boastful man, was entertaining a young woman from another company as Andrew just happened to walk past them. Since Andrew also knew her, Gabriel referred to him by saying, "Lisa, you know Andrew Schwartz. He used to sell us chemical supplies."

Gabe's need for control and power, coupled with leftover resentment, was behind this attempt to humiliate Andrew. It would have been totally out of Andrew's new character and business personality to retreat without an appropriate response. Andrew's retort was swift and pronounced.

"You know, Gabe, you may be right. The word is that your chief competitor wants to cut an exclusive with us. And by the way, they outspend you two to one."

Andrew was prepared to lose. The worst that could have happened was a break in the business relationship—or that the relationship would continue in a dysfunctional fashion, in which case Andrew was destined to lose anyway.

When Andrew walked out the door, he was certain that he had lost a half-million dollars in sales. Yet, when he arrived at his office, there was a message to call Gabe's administrative assistant. When Andrew called, the assistant related the message that Gabe was out of the office (not wanting a direct confrontation) but that he wanted to apologize for possibly offending Andrew in front of a mutual business associate.

She further related that Gabe had meant no harm in his comment and that it was just his way of teasing. In truth, he had a history of far worse abuses that had gone uncontested. But Andrew had done some limit-setting, some image changing, some exclusionary marketing... and he regained the respect of a valuable customer.

In essence, our businesses are always tied to ourselves. The business takes on the personality we create for it, and we become what our businesses are thought to be. By suggesting that what you market is valuable, and reinforcing those suggestions in a myriad of ways, we become valuable. Your business is not for everyone, and by narrowing your focus, you are expanding your horizons.

Choose me, please!

Remember in high school when teams were being chosen on the softball field, or when the cheerleading squad was being selected, and you were terrified of being left on the sidelines or selected last?

Why are certain individuals or businesses chosen and others overlooked? In part, it's because most people don't know how to invite acceptance and popularity. Businesses don't become "popular" by accident. Marketing carefully crafts a business's worth. The magic is knowing when to employ which tactic—exclusionary messages, brand imaging, aggressive or passive behavior, relationship marketing, social selling or publicity.

Most people in business don't realize we're in the entertainment field. Advertising (we'll get to that aspect of marketing soon) first looks to entertain. If we don't get the customer's attention, we don't get heard. You already know what delights people in your business. If you don't, then go back to Chapter 1 and begin again. The most powerful marketing begins from a firm, confident, well-established foundation. Remember, your business needs to be reinvented every five to seven years. You need to operate from a position of strength, even when the economy, the competition or the rest of the world is protesting.

I once used the economy and the specific industry as excuses when a client reported stagnant sales. She said something I will never forget: "I don't care what the hell the rest of the industry is suffering from. We're going to succeed."

She absolutely refused to hear excuses. And I was motivated to come up with solutions. I did. And I kept her as a client.

Whether you're marketing yourself to a customer, a partnership, a networking organization or the general public, the rules are the same. You need to control the situation from the outset. Your hands must be tightly on the reins in order to steer the team on the course to success.

If you're in a service industry, you're literally marketing yourself as well as the product. I have never met an insurance salesman who was caustic, nor have I met a stock broker who insulted my choice of ties. For those of you in service fields, the following "bites" are based upon marketing principles throughout this chapter.

Make sure your datebook is filled

Recently, I was finishing a presentation to a prospective client. The president of the company explained that his choice was between my company and one other. He wanted to visit both offices before making his decision.

"Let's set a date now, shall we?" he said.

"Certainly, how does next week look for you?" I replied.

We both pulled out our datebooks. Mine is leather with a sailboat carved into the cover. His was engraved with his initials. He flipped his pages to reveal a very busy schedule for the upcoming week. I flipped my pages to reveal an even busier schedule. He looked at my pages. I looked at his pages.

"Shall we try the following week?" he queried.

"Good idea," I replied.

He flipped to the following week. I flipped to the following week. His schedule was pretty clear; only one day had something written in it. My schedule was fairly full; only one day was blank. He looked at my schedule. I looked at his schedule.

"Looks like Thursday is best for you, huh?" he said.

"If that's convenient for you, that would be great," I answered.

We set the date. Some of my "appointments" were notes to myself. Perish the thought that I would expose a datebook that exhibited that I was free for the next month! I appeared busier than he was, though I was entirely accommodating.

Be unavailable, not unobtainable

You've been trying to reach a business prospect for two weeks. She's finally returned your ninth call and your feelings have turned from eager to anger. It's clearly not the right time to accept the call. First, you're not prepared with a script that will enable you to maintain your esteem and gently suggest that it's been exceedingly difficult to reach her. Second, answering the phone on the first take makes you appear far less valuable than she is. What you do is have the screener (voice mail, assistant, receptionist) explain that you're on another call and you've got still another one waiting—and you're en route to a meeting within minutes. Have the screener ask the caller when the convenient time would be for you to return her call.

You've done two important things: You've established a successful, independent identity, and you've allowed the anxiety to shift slightly from your side to hers. When the appropriate time comes, wait 10 minutes past it and return the call. If she is not there or doesn't accept the call, simply state that you'll try again tomorrow. Don't give her the opportunity not to call back again. You've got to maintain control, and keeping the call-back opportunity in your hands is the only way to do it.

A little distance can go a long way

You established a business tone a long time ago. People know what to expect from your company. But that hasn't exactly gotten you off the ground. Establish a slightly different business posture. Reflect before answering questions, and allow yourself the luxury to get back to people instead of giving them answers immediately. You're about to change the harmony and establish a new tune. You can do this without being offensive but by remaining a bit distant...just enough to draw the customer in.

Remember, too, that aloofness usually creates the kind of subtle anxiety we spoke of before. By holding back, you're actually drawing in. When the customer who's ignored you for months finally asks you to lunch, refuse. Then you can suggest that you'd like to get back to him or her when your schedule permits. When a customer asks for information or an opinion, suggest that you'd like to take some time to reflect, gather information and get back to him or her expeditiously. You're going to begin to draw the customer in by keeping him or her at bay for just a little while.

Recently a client of mine accepted my suggestion to meet on some issues that were of interest to me regarding his company. He told me he would call me Tuesday morning to establish a mutually convenient time. Tuesday morning came and went, so did Wednesday. I asked my assistant to call him and leave a message indicating that I would be tied up the rest of the week, but that I was very interested in getting together to discuss the subject that we spoke about recently. This accomplished two things: It reminded him that we had spoken, and it established my interest but not my anxiety. He made the appointment from that message.

Yes, we have no bananas

When a department store was advertising its food department, the owners wanted to attract an upscale, gourmet-oriented clientele. They couldn't possibly have cared about selling $8 tins of imported oatmeal, but it was intriguing to use this product as a hook. Thus, I consulted with them in the creation of a full-page newspaper ad that included an illustration of a tin of oatmeal. It read:

No silly cereals sold here!
If you're in the market for silly, sugary snacks,
don't bother coming to us.
We leave that stuff to the supermarkets.
But if you're looking for a magnificent way
to begin your day, sow some wild oats.
At $7.99, that's about a dime a bite...and worth it!

Guess what? They actually sold out on imported Irish oatmeal.

But that wasn't their goal. In fact, it didn't even pay for one line of type in the ad. But something interesting happened as the campaign evolved. With marketing efforts concentrated on customers who were more appropriate for the product lines in the store, increases in gross dollars occurred. Sales were up and profits were up, because the "right" customers increased in numbers, even though overall traffic was down. Before exclusionary "target" marketing, the store had attracted many customers who were far too intimidated by imported goods and who were not really in the market for such high-priced products.

Exclusionary messages created the right tone to attract the right customers—those who were interested in the specialty foods offered by the store. By creating a message that told customers what not to expect, the store actually pinpointed the customers who would be most likely to buy.

Interestingly, some companies' goals actually include a *decrease* in sales. In these cases, exclusionary marketing is used to cause a drastic drop in gross sales volume—in an effort to enhance profitability. A computer firm, for example, recently established a sales objective to bring it from $29 million to $17 million in sales per year, with a 51-percent increase in profits. By eliminating the sale of hardware (an accommodation to clients that represented little or no profit) and targeting corporations that required highly sophisticated software consultation instead, the company would greatly decrease unprofitable sales.

When the sales department heard about the plan, they almost collapsed in unison. But when the strategy was carefully explained, they understood the sense it made. By telling customers what it *didn't* do, the company brought far greater focus to what *it* did do. The bottom line: It decreased the sales volume and created a much stronger profit picture!

Chapter 9

Some Personal Marketing Tips

Accouterments spell success. Remember what we talked about in Chapter 2—how image impacts everything we do? Appearing important bolsters our business personality. Think of your briefcase, appointment book, pen, automobile, business wardrobe, hairdo and watch as solid investments in business marketing. A Mont Blanc pen is, in a sense, money in the bank, because it bolsters your image. People still identify material goods with success, and customers want to deal with successful companies. A Mont Blanc pen is a simple symbol of success. It identifies you as someone who does well in business. An Armani tie or scarf costs less than $100, but, in truth, either is worth 10 times that much because they create powerful perceptions. And as for the $150 that's supposed to go into the bank at the end of the month, place it in your pocket. As superficial as it may sound, people associate money with business savvy. As a marketer, you want to employ every means possible to prove your worthiness...which may include flashing a roll of bills in order to appear as though you have earned the rewards of successful business dealings.

We judge others by symbols of success. Remember, you are establishing a marketing identity and are inviting positive intrigue.

Stop and think about your own perceptions of people with whom you do business. What are those perceptions based upon? How do you make judgments about people? Is it from first impressions about their appearance, car, cuff links or other accouterments?

Every month for six years, Clarence Simms was visited by the same salesperson, Jim Morrow. Jim would see Clarence in his office to sell him stationery supplies. Clarence had come to take Jim for granted, until one day when they left the office at the same time. Clarence noticed Jim walking toward a 944 Porsche in the lot. Jim quietly got in the car, fired it up and took off. Clarence took a giant step backwards. He has not looked upon Jim in the same way since that day. The relationship has shifted. It has new life, energy and respect. Why? Because Jim is now perceived as successful, and Clarence has new respect for him. Superficial? Absolutely. Jim didn't change; Clarence's *perceptions* about him changed.

Corporate "war"drobes

War has become a popular metaphor for marketing. Interestingly, some corporations are paying careful attention to not only the demeanor of their corporate sales and marketing people, but their appearance, as well. Their "uniforms" are now carefully analyzed. Appearance consultants are more plentiful than ever before, and businesses are finding that they must carefully address the issue of wardrobes and appearance when entering the so-called business battlefield.

The concept is to refresh the "corporate" look on a regular basis... keeping tabs on trends. This entails changing aspects of appearance such as hairstyle and style and color of clothing at least every quarter. The idea is a good one because it recognizes the importance of keeping the messenger as fine-tuned as the message.

Know more about their business than they know themselves

I have a friend who sells magazine space for a business publication. His clients are industrial firms. Harry works very hard at knowing his markets (various industries) and his clients. In fact, what impresses me about Harry is how much more he knows about his customers' industries than his customers know. Harry has made it his business to understand their business in substantive ways. He never uses the information to make clients feel ignorant, but he carefully weaves industry statistics, data and news into the sales and marketing effort. And he always leaves them with magnificent little "bites" of information that give them an edge in their own marketing. Harry is not a salesman—he's a marketing professional in every sense of the word.

You're in business to provide a product or a service to someone. Make it your business to get the information they need to make an informed, intelligent buying decision, and make sure you have the accurate data before they get it from someone else.

Recently I was shopping for a car. I had narrowed my choices by virtue of magazines, personal preferences, referrals and economic and practical considerations, and I was ready to be further educated on specific models. When I went to the local dealer, I was prepared to buy, and presumably the dealer was prepared to sell. Well, I was only half right. The salesperson approached me with a cordial greeting. The conversation was truly unbelievable.

"Are you interested in any particular model, sir?" she asked.

"Yes, actually, I am interested in this vehicle," I answered.

"Great. Would you like to test-drive it today?"

"Well, before that, let me ask you a few questions."

"Certainly, sir."

"Does it come standard with keyless entry and leather?" I asked.

"I'll check on that for you," she said. "Did you have any other questions?"

"Yes," I said. "Is this a six- or an eight-cylinder?"

At this point she walked around the vehicle and checked the dealer information sheet. "I believe this is a six-cylinder, but I'll have to see if this car comes with an eight-cylinder."

I wish I had tape-recorded the conversation. She didn't have one single answer to any of the rudimentary questions I posed. She was, to use a popular expression, *clueless*!

How could anyone work as a marketer of products without understanding the very basics of the product? It was senseless. After a few more volleys with this pleasant salesperson, I sought out the sales manager and shared my frustration. He defended the young woman's naïveté, explaining that she was new. He made a calculated mistake, a critical marketing error: He defended a weakness in his own organization! Businesses should support their staffs—it's even appropriate to defend an associate if the customer attacks for personal reasons or is unjustified in criticizing an employee—but a business should *never, ever* defend an indefensible action.

The dealership lost all credibility with me, and they forgot a golden rule of marketing: *Know thy product*. In truth, I knew more about the product than the marketer, so if I were totally sold on buying that model automobile, I might have simply tried to get the best price. But since I was still shopping, I needed service first.

In business, you must know the subject. You must be the informer, not the informee. The difference between being the marketer and the customer is knowledge. Never let the customer know more than you do.

The maitre d' should know your name

Yes, it's an old cliché. But the amazing thing about clichés is that many of them still hold true—and this one does especially.

For many businesses, social interaction remains an essential part of the marketing program. Many companies, large and small, have a line item in their budgets for golf outings. In fact, there is a company that organizes seminars that actually take place on the golf course. Two golf pros founded a company designed to teach businesspeople how to do business during golf. A lot of business is still done over the breakfast, lunch or dinner table, as well. It's useful to carry our images into the social selling environments.

One of the most popular restaurants in my company's area has received national attention. It's difficult to get a reservation, particularly for a Saturday night. So difficult, in fact, that when a client of mine requested that we meet for dinner, I couldn't get a table until 9:30 at night, four weeks in advance. Needless to say, I was embarrassed that I had no clout in my own backyard, so to speak. But I also vowed not to let that occur again. So I went to the restaurant for lunch on a Tuesday (a slow day) and sought out the maitre d'. In keeping with the image and tone of the restaurant, he was appropriately aloof. I told him that my office was just a few miles away and that I planned to entertain clients at his establishment. I also explained that I would greatly appreciate any considerations he might suggest in order to accommodate my customers. Further, I asked if I could be afforded some personal attention upon arrival in order to appear more important in front of the clients.

I handed the maitre d' a giftwrapped box and told him that I considered this to be the beginning of a mutually prosperous relationship. He looked slightly stunned. When he opened the box, there was a small crystal sculpture engraved with the logo of the restaurant. It looked like a small Emmy award. Of course, my business card was enclosed, as well.

He shook my hand and told me to call him personally whenever I needed to make a reservation. And he assured me that I was now a preferred customer and would be treated accordingly. I didn't offer him a bribe. I offered him an opportunity to make me feel important. This is, of course, reverse marketing, where the customer is marketing the company. His response was professional. He appreciated the crystal and the significance of the customization. He placed it at his station, and it has remained there ever since. I, too, have remained there ever since—not on top of his desk, but in his *mind*, which is the goal of marketing.

Use your middle name or make one up

You've been Paul Smith for far too long. You're about to undergo a metamorphosis. From now on, you're never going to be plain, old Paul

Smith again. Your new name is Paul Austin Smith. This establishes you with more importance than before and begins to invite inquiries from those who've known you forever. Businesses change their names, logos and alter their identities every so often. It's good business to add a new dimension to your person and company.

Recently, I was asked to create an image campaign for a telephone company that sold local and long distance service. The object was to create a new identity—enabling the customers to see an evolution, not a revolution. The change had to be more transitional than radical. Therefore, the logo was modified to appear more contemporary. The color of the stationery was changed, and the company's brochures and sales literature sheets were all updated to refresh the look. What emerged was a company that looked revitalized, not acquired. The company's central message of service and simplicity wasn't replaced... just embellished with stronger language and high-tech references. The company changed its wardrobe, brushed its hair, polished its shoes and reentered the marketplace with a more pronounced identity. It was perceived as a player again.

Here's another example of shifting a business posture. A 60-year-old firm needed to reestablish its marketing appearance because of increased competition and a look that was not contemporary enough to compete with new competition. The company had maintained the same logo and slogan since it was founded. The company was heavily invested in its corporate look, and there was great equity in its name and graphic identity (logo). Substantial fears about creating the new marketing personality were that customers would perceive the company to have changed hands or relinquished control to another firm, or that the present administration was out of control. These concerns were mostly exaggerated, but there was enough sensitivity on the owner's part to keep the changes modest, though definitive.

My suggestion was a slight modification in the logo. We italicized the letters so that they were more forward-moving. Further, we created an abstract symbol that gave a more high-tech impression. We also altered the colors. Thus began a break in a 60-year-old tradition. The customers were responsive and inquisitive, delivering many accolades to the sales staff. The employees of the company were equally enthusiastic and revitalized. A slight addition in the slogan and some spit and polish, and the transformation was well under way.

The science of negotiation

You're in a tough spot. You desperately want the client or customer to choose your idea, your company, yourself. You've got the right widget to satisfy the customer's needs. But he or she wants a *win* situation, instead of the proverbial *win-win*.

Where do you go? First, you relate the litany of positive attributes that make you the clear choice for this customer's business. Second, you offer acknowledgment that this customer's business is worth bending for, but you have so many commitments that are positioned more profitably that you can't accept his or her scenario. However, you can offer a compromise, but only if a commitment is given within 24 hours. Everyone wants to feel victorious in business or any relationship. They want to feel as though their needs come first. You can offer the customer that feeling, but only if he or she is willing to act quickly. Win or lose, you're going to get your answer and move forward or move on. Get the commitment based upon a compromise that appears to give the customer almost everything he or she needs. Remember, you haven't said no. You've said yes—with options.

Greetings from your neighbors

Bob and Janet were living in their house for six years. They had a home-based business selling personalized gifts, greeting cards and invitations. Bob was an investment banker who helped Janet during the evenings and weekends. He helped with trade shows, wedding and social showcases and was very supportive of Janet's efforts. The business showed a profit after 15 months and generated $160,000 in sales during its second year. Bob and Janet aggressively marketed the company.

One of the best opportunities for them to increase their marketing efforts with little or no investment was within their own community. But for reasons beyond their understanding, social interaction was not forthcoming. They attended church functions and township events, but relationships that could have resulted in both social and business interaction didn't develop.

They decided to create a marketing plan with two goals in mind. Goal one was to meet as many people as possible. Goal two was to expose their home-based business to the many people in their community who would likely use it.

They compiled a list of 15 couples they knew as acquaintances. The purpose was to expose Janet's dynamic product line to friends in the community. They created a group name, an agenda and an identity and sent out questionnaires to the people on the list. Their cover letter stated that for ease, convenience and comfort for all who would participate in the establishment of this social collective, they would limit the number of interested parties to 20. The letter further stated that criteria for inclusion would be a prompt return of the questionnaire and the level of interest expressed in the return form. Bob and Janet would select those couples who showed a greater interest in a group that would combine social and business interaction.

In the mailing, Janet explained that she would reward anyone who gave her leads. The incentive would be elegant personal stationery for the person or persons who provided her with simple word-of-mouth introductions. Exactly 10 couples showed up to the first gathering. Coffee and cake were served, and Janet's wares were spread out for everyone to see. That first evening, six of the 20 in attendance left her with names and phone numbers of people to call. In each case, Janet had a name to reference when contacting these new prospects. This method of marketing has become her primary way of getting new customers.

Janet used a variety of companies as a model for her own business. Certainly, the idea of inviting people to a home in order to create a social selling environment is not new. There are many success stories related to this type of marketing. But Janet initiated her marketing efforts by establishing a social setting within her own community. Because she was first in the local marketplace and her products were exceptional, she now owns the market as far as her product line is concerned.

Chapter 10

Media Advertising: Time to Shout!

The media—small, medium and large—have the statistical data you need to begin a media program. Many businesses don't realize this research is already done for them. Newspapers, radio stations, magazines, billboard companies, direct marketing firms and mailing list houses all have demographic information that allows you to target your audience.

Let's say you own a store that sells compact discs on Main Street. You just opened, and you're in need of advertising. What are the key issues in deciding what approach to take?

- Where do I advertise?
- How do I say it?
- What do I advertise?
- How much do I spend?
- What do I say?

To answer some of these questions, we draw upon issues already covered in previous chapters. Now you will be able to apply these principles to create an advertising media strategy.

Some background on media

Most start up companies have primary, secondary and tertiary markets. This occurs when they establish priorities for their customers. The primary customers usually will account for the lion's share of the business. The other segments of the market may or may not be worth spending media dollars on, so for now, we will concentrate on your primary market because it represents the largest return on investment.

Trade associations have the information you need to make intelligent marketing decisions. If you take the time to contact your own industry's associations, distributors and manufacturers, they will supply you with industry statistics. Suffice it to say that you will be looking to reach the largest number of your potential customers at the lowest cost. First, understand that *CPM* means cost per thousand (the dollars necessary to reach 1,000 listeners). *Reach* and *frequency* relate to who you're reaching and how often you reach them. You will begin making decisions based upon the available media and the data they provide for you.

Let's begin with the local weekly newspaper and the daily newspaper. As soon as you contact them, they will send a sales representative to see you, at your convenience. This person will enable you to make an informed decision because they will present you with a *media kit*. This portfolio of material will illustrate cost per thousand and reach. They will also offer incentives to achieve frequency. These incentives encourage you to commit to an amount of lines or number of advertisements you will use during the year. The larger the commitment on your part, the more discounts you achieve. The information in the media kit will include the contracts, the readership profile, which includes age, income, home ownership, product preferences and possibly even ethnic breakdown, education, number of children in household—everything you need to make an informed decision.

If you're selling CDs, you may already know your "best customer." Let's assume the customer is between the ages of 18 and 34 (a typical demographic group). The customer has some discretionary income and spends money regularly on music. The customer profile also includes musical preferences (you base your inventory on what sells to whom) and what incentives are recognized as successful by the industry (record promotion companies can help you with this). As you shape your customer profile, recognize that your advertising must reach your largest customer group and must also convey specialties that exist in your store, such as jazz, blues, rock 'n' roll, rap or classical. You'll be drawing from the information on positioning in Chapter 3 in order to define your advertising message.

The media kit will be your research tool. Now it's time to make some decisions regarding the questions we raised above. You're going to do a comparative analysis of the available media. And you'll examine the relationship between cost and cost benefits. You'll also examine the quality of the editorial environment in which your advertising will appear. The editorial "well" is the quality of the stories, the level of readership and the overall impressions made by the specific medium you're considering. If the weekly paper is poorly perceived in your community, or if its existence is solely based upon coupon and price promotions, it may have a limited value to your business and you may only consider it as a promotional vehicle during sale periods.

Aside from the quality of the medium under scrutiny, you consider the other advertisers who appear in the paper. Examine them closely to see if your competitors are advertising in the paper, and ask questions. The media sales representative will know who the advertisers are, how often they run ads and what kind of responses they've had.

Aside from media representatives and the use of various media kits, the primary resource for obtaining media information that includes circulation, demographic profiles, frequency, rates, editorial objectives and format is a publication called *Standard Rate and Data*. You can find this in the reference section of your library, or contact the publisher, SRDS, L.P., at 3004 Glenview Rd., Wilmette, IL 60091; 708-256-6067 or 800-323-4601; fax: 708-441-2264. It is divided into volumes that include consumer publications, trade publications and broadcast media.

One of the sources for valuable information regarding media for specific market segments can be obtained from the United States Institute of Marketing. Their reports include everything from retail newspaper advertising to casino advertising to airline advertising to insurance marketing. The Institute has been researching high volume advertising since 1954 and is in the business of selling reports that offer statistical data on the most effective media and messages in various industries. Their toll-free number is 800-627-5384 for information on and prices of their marketing reports.

Media mix

You are awakened by your clock radio. In addition to the news, weather and traffic, you receive advertised messages. You shower, dress, pop a bagel in the toaster, turn on the TV and wolf down your breakfast. The first commercial message you receive is on the side of your juice container. Then you see the same product on the television while you're eating your breakfast. You get into your car, turn on the radio and hear a commercial for the very same product. And just when you thought you were safe, you get onto the highway...and there it is on a giant billboard. Now you're at the office, and you take five minutes to read your morning paper, and it's there, the very same product. You hear it on the radio, piped into the office. You go out to lunch—it's there on the side of the bus. You head for the restroom, and, believe it or not, there's a poster in the privy. On the way home, you see and hear the same product advertised again.

Finally, you're convinced you need the product in your life, so you go to the store, and the display prominently reinforces every other image you've received. Just as you get the product, you realize you've been "gotten." It's okay—it happens to all of us.

Simply stated, the purpose of a media mix is *getting to the customer!* One medium reinforces another. True synergy is in effect when we expose our message through a variety of media in order to make the most lasting impression. Remember, we are looking to own our part of the marketplace. The budget will dictate how much of a mix we can accomplish. We'll prioritize the available media and make intelligent choices based upon the relationship between the number of impressions and the cost. Our goal is to communicate to customers in every walk of their lives.

Fragmentation

Before we embark on the media planning process, let's talk about the difficulties of purchasing media today. During the 1950s through to the 1970s, media planning was relatively easy. There were a few television networks, radio stations, billboard companies, newspapers and magazines. Today, the media possibilities are limitless and audience fragmentation is mind-boggling. We're faced, even on a local and regional level, with a much more difficult task. Where and when do we find our audience? Our customers are in cars, at offices, on the Internet, watching one of hundreds of cable channels and new networks, listening to local and syndicated radio programs, playing interactive computer games, involved with CD-ROMs or electronic messaging, modems, fax broadcast services—the list is building daily.

Let's face it, we're deluged with messages every minute of every day. Rather than being in the Information Age, I believe we're in the Information Overload Age, and it's to both the detriment and benefit of businesses. The opportunities to communicate with the world from our laptops is overwhelming, but who are we reaching, and at what cost? And how do we know who's doing what and when?

The logical place to start is to look at the media available to us, trade or consumer, and develop a strategy that matches the media to the message.

Media budget

The simplest way to create a marketing budget is to look at a percentage of sales or projected sales as a budget guideline. The American Association of Advertising Agencies (405 Lexington Ave., New York, NY 10174; 212-682-2500) publishes, by industry, average percentages used as marketing budgets by literally every classification of business. If your industry averages 2 percent of gross sales as a marketing expenditure, you will want to use this amount as a guideline to get started in your marketing efforts. So, if your gross annual volume is $300,000, your target media budget will be $6,000, using others in your industry as an example.

Important: First, remember that a new business requires a jump start, so you may want to either front-load your advertising or increase the percentage above the industry average. Front-loading means that your first quarter of promotion will be the heaviest (it pays to begin a campaign with larger print ads or more frequent communication materials in order to gain market presence). Second, your budget must include not only the cost of advertising space (newspaper, magazine, radio, TV, direct mail, billboard) but the cost to produce, print and mail materials.

Here's a useful way to look at media budgeting: If your business is making $1 million per year, is it worth your while to hire an employee to communicate to your customers for, say, $25,000 for the year? And could that person achieve the kind of communication that you need? Probably not. A $25,000 *marketing budget*, however, can buy you a lot of activity—advertising, direct marketing, telemarketing, trade shows. Isn't it worth the price of a moderate-level employee to beat the bushes with good communication materials?

Your budget should be fixed on an annual basis. This does not mean that you won't make changes during the course of the year. When shifts in the marketplace occur—increased competition, price wars, rising cost of goods, media opportunities, special promotional offers—you may need to change the rules and increase or decrease your spending appropriately. You may also want to take budgeted dollars from one quarter (December, January and February represent the first quarter if you are doing business by calendar year) and shift them into another part of the calendar.

You should, however, always have a plan in place. Everything you do in marketing is a function of budget. Without it, you'll lose control of the program, and the results will be marginal, at best.

Approach your budget as if you were hiring a person, and you will be able to justify the costs easily. Remember, marketing should not cost you money; its purpose is to *make* you money. But as the old saying goes, you've got to spend it to make it. Intelligent marketing begins by appropriating dollars to programs. You've got to make every dollar count, so plan your strategy well in advance. Take advantage of every prepaid discount you can or prompt-payment media plans that save you several points. You can also command better positions in print media when you plan far in advance.

Newspaper and magazine

Your print media selection process will incorporate 12 points:

1. Editorial quality.
2. Relative cost per thousand (reaching your demographic group at the lowest comparative cost).
3. Frequency. Is it a daily (newspapers only), weekly or monthly?
4. Other advertisers.
5. Ratio of advertising to editorial.
6. Clutter (number of ads on the page that inhibit the chances of yours being seen).
7. Special sections that relate to your product or service.
8. Availability of color.
9. Pass-along readership (how many people actually read it).
10. Does publication support advertisers editorially?
11. Placement of ad.
12. Special services offered by the publication, such as free production of advertisement or merchandising of ad (includes sending copies of your ad to your customers free of charge).

Many publications, especially weekly newspapers, operate on an unspoken *quid pro quo* basis. While it is not a published policy, often newspapers will run a story on the advertiser's company with the commitment of an advertising schedule. This ties the advertising to editorial in a way that grants the message more exposure and greater depth of credibility.

Choosing to advertise in a particular newspaper or magazine is dictated by your overall budget as well as the cost per thousand. Therefore, even if a daily newspaper delivers your target audience at a lower CPM than the weekly, but costs six times more, you may sacrifice the cost per thousand in order to afford the advertising. Generally speaking, weekly newspapers or "shoppers" cost substantially less than major dailies, though on a cost per thousand basis they may not be competitive because of much fewer readers.

For the most part, your customer will shop where the messages that interest him or her are plentiful. For this reason, you must study the media to determine the "type" of advertisers in the paper. Based upon the advertisers in the newspaper and information contained in the media kit provided by the newspaper's salesperson, you will determine where your customers are. For example, a recent survey by the *Atlanta Journal* pointed out that 58 percent of inquiries at auto dealers were the result of newspaper and magazine ads. Why? Primarily because people in the market for an automobile rely upon an environment that contains a lot of automobile messages—the car and classified section of the paper!

In some cases, the media environment is primarily advertising. Depending again upon your customer and your product, this may not be a drawback. If your business appeals to a younger market (teenagers, for example) you need not rely upon outstanding editorial. If your target market is upscale men and women, age 40-plus, editorial quality becomes a much more important issue.

Can't see the forest for the trees?

Because clutter is a big factor in determining the viability of an advertising medium, it pays to look at the where your advertisement is placed. ROP means run of paper. This means that your advertisement will appear anywhere between the covers as opposed to running in a specific section or a more prominent position. It's to the newspaper's advantage to sell you this program. However, analyze your own reaction as a consumer of the newspaper. Particularly if it's a free shopper-style paper, is the clutter too overwhelming for a smaller ad to be noticed? If this is the case, it may be worth a premium to have your ad placed strategically. Many newspapers will allow you to choose your placement (upper right hand page, far forward, is the traditional favorite) with the payment of an additional fee. If the clutter is enormous, it's wise to consider this option. If not, then you can deal with the competitive clutter of the pages by designing a "stand-out" ad. Obviously, the use of color, borders, bold typefaces, photography and illustration can help combat the clutter factor.

Another important element in evaluating the newspaper is *readability*. Is the newspaper readable? Is the printed reproduction acceptable? Are the photographs clear? Does your ad concept fit into the format of the surrounding environment?

Special sections

Most newspapers have sections and most magazines have special issues ostensibly designed to create synergy between editorial and advertising. Notice in your own community how often the newspapers will notify you, as a businessperson, of an upcoming section covering *fashion, catering, outdoor activities, music, electronics, boating* and *automobiles*. The editorial design corresponds with a major effort on the publication's part to get complementary advertising. This works to your advantage, particularly since the section or issue will be read more carefully by customers interested in your product category. In some cases, you may become part of the editorial story if you're involved in something special or unique or offer an unusual service to the community you serve.

Pass-along readership

Both newspapers and magazines will offer you what they refer to as RPC (readers per copy). This is the number of assumed readers of each issue of the publication. For example, if the newspaper or magazine is retained in the home or a business environment (like the waiting room at a chiropractor's office), then an estimate is made on the number of people who actually read each single issue. For magazines, readers per copy is used to dramatically increase the number of impressions (people seeing your advertisement) advertisers will receive. In the case of newspapers, the issue of readers per copy is weaker, because newspapers are typically discarded daily or weekly. It's good for you to understand, though, that the publication's advertising sales pitch to you will likely include the issue of RPC. Remember, it is not guaranteed or paid circulation; it is only guesstimated and cannot be audited or incorporated into your media strategy.

Free production and merchandising

Almost all newspapers will produce (physically create) your advertisement for free as part of an incentive to gain your business (this usually does not apply to magazines). But in most cases, the creative product offered by the newspaper is extremely limited. The medium merely provides you with a service to give you an advertisement—not a strategy, position, identity or campaign. For this reason, I suggest strongly that you utilize all of the other resource information provided in this book to create all the necessary elements you need before you allow your message to be exposed. Magazines and newspapers will also "merchandise" your advertising. In the case of magazines, they may offer you mailing list services, send a copy of your advertisement to parts of their subscription list and offer other "value-added" incentives to become an advertiser. The most beneficial form of merchandising is the publications' mailing list or a program of mailing your material to their list—paid for, at least in part, by them.

Of course, before you decide to use newspapers or magazines, an examination of the other available media is vitally important.

Radio

The most interesting story I've heard about radio comes from a seminar I attended at the Radio Advertising Bureau, the industry's trade association in New York City. One of the speakers was relating how a very famous advertising mogul insisted that every radio creative meeting be attended by artists as well as copywriters. In fact, each radio script had to be storyboarded (a process that details in single frames the action and words used for a television commercial). This visual representation had to be done for each radio commercial that was developed by this particular Madison Avenue agency. The reason was simple: Radio is the most visual medium available to advertisers since radio commercials have the best opportunity to create vivid imagery in the minds of the consumer.

Aside from the creative aspects of this powerful medium (we'll talk more about how to write a radio script later), radio delivers a targeted audience at a relatively low cost per thousand. In the United States today, there are more than 9,000 stations and literally dozens of programming formats that range from heavy metal to classical to religious to all-talk. Radio is particularly useful in reaching teenagers because, traditionally, they are not heavy users of other forms of media and are dedicated to specific musical formats. They can be isolated by carefully selecting specific stations that are dedicated to music that appeals to their demographic group. The same holds true for the mature market. Typically, the older population segment is less divided among the media they use regularly, and they, too, tend to tune into radio as a primary means of receiving entertainment and information.

Statistics from the Radio Advertising Bureau indicate that more than a half-billion radios are in use in our country. Even in the cluttered media environment that exists today, people listen to radio...at home, at work and, primarily, in the car.

Studies also show that radio listeners are "station loyal." This means that there is far less "surfing" with radio than with television. This is an advertiser's dream because it means we can tap into our market with a good degree of confidence that we'll be reaching them. This is why the demographic profile of the customer is especially important when choosing the stations to which you will devote your advertising dollars. The match between market and station is significant.

We also need to understand the time of day that people listen to radio. It's no mistake that the prime time for radio listenership is called *drive time*! Although drive time varies from station to station, it consists, for the most part, of morning drive time (5 to 10 a.m.) and afternoon drive time (3 to 7 p.m.). If they could, radio stations would stretch these designations so that the entire day was drive time because they get such a big premium for this day part.

Because radio is "car driven" (pardon the pun), you want messages that are memorable, don't impart too much information and distinguish your business quickly. Like billboard, radio allows you to get to the customer during times when shopping decisions are made, and you can influence customers to "drive" right to your business and buy. According to the Radio Advertising Bureau's statistics, consumers are far more influenced to buy within 30 minutes of a commercial radio message than any other medium. Billboard runs a distant second, followed by TV, then newspapers, then magazines.

Radio has a more cumulative effect on the customer. Unlike print, radio requires far more frequency to invoke a response—it enhances impressions that are made by television, print, outdoor and other media. The synergy that's created between radio and other media works to your distinct advantage, creating a cumulative effect. The frequency of messages and the "visual transference" (hearing what is seen in broadcast or print) reinforces the message with customers.

Your choice to advertise on radio should be based upon the demographics of the station and the cost of drive-time commercials. The typical formats are either 30 seconds or 60 seconds. I highly recommend utilizing the 60-second format because you will pay about a 30 percent higher premium than for the 30-second commercial—thus getting twice the amount of exposure for a third more money.

Unlike most print media, radio rates are highly negotiable. Rate cards display published rates for commercials during different parts of the day, but you need to negotiate parts of the day, frequency contracts and rates before you assess the value of the station to your marketing efforts.

The station will probably attempt to sell you ROS (run of station) ads because they require no commitment to broadcast your commercial during any particular time. This is not to your advantage. You will need to negotiate for a mix of drive time and midday. The station may use *overnights* (announcements broadcast from midnight to 5 a.m.) as an incentive to get your advertising, but these are mostly throwaway spots that can't be sold anyway. They are of no benefit to you. Begin your negotiations by asking for an abundance of drive-time spots in your program. The station will offer you a *grid* that will scramble the time slots. There is some economic benefit to buying one of the station's packages, but you'll be getting parts of the day that don't always reach your audience. So, ask for specifics regarding when your spots will run, even within the designated part of the day. Drive-time spots that begin as early as 5 a.m. or as late as 10 a.m. don't deliver the same audience as those running at 7 a.m. or 8:30 a.m., so insist on tighter time constraints regarding your commercial schedule. The station sales staff won't like you, but you're looking to maximize your dollars, not accommodate the media. Also, be sure to ask for *air checks*, which are actual tape recordings of the broadcast that include your commercial message, providing you with proof that your advertisement ran correctly (also known as "proof of performance"). They will ensure that the commercial is being read properly (if it's read by disc jockeys or on-air talent as opposed to having been prerecorded), and they indicate the time of the commercial as well.

Choose the personality as well as the program

Talk radio has become a booming business. The on-air talent runs the gamut from shock jocks to right-wing reactionaries to ultraliberals to sometimes hateful voices. Remember, you are sponsoring the type of show you advertise on, and there are risks. Examine your feelings about your customers, and assess whether they would be listening to the type of show you're considering. Obviously, if you own a pet shop, you're going to choose to run your commercials on the Saturday afternoon pet show. If you own a gardening supply store, you're sure to sponsor the gardening hotline show.

Occasionally, you may be tempted to set reason aside and run your commercials based upon your own likes and dislikes...choosing a format or on-air personality you personally enjoy. If you choose to sponsor programming on this basis, you're wrong. Remember: You are not necessarily the customer, and when a program exists that complements your product or service, you should certainly include such programming in your advertising schedule.

You are not your own customer

My clients often tell me what they like to read, listen to or watch. I listen intently only because I'm interested in them as people, not as media planners. If you allow emotion to dictate your selection of media, because of personal likes and dislikes, you're making the wrong decision. Frankly, it doesn't matter what you prefer; it only matters what your customer prefers, and most often the two are not the same.

Again, as a sponsor, you can choose either to associate or not to associate with a particular type of programming or personality. To some degree, you will be classified as supporting the editorial content of the show, much in the way you support the newspaper or magazine in which you advertise. This is a dilemma when the radio show that reaches your audience with the greatest efficiency is controversial enough to "turn off" certain segments of the market. It's a business decision that you must make only after you've weighed the downside, and the downside is that your advertising may have more negative impact than positive.

Play it safe, sponsor the weather

Special segments of radio shows are sold to advertisers. You can become a sponsor of the weather, traffic, lottery results...and this allows you to mix 60-second commercials with 10-second announcements and tags. Tags are one-sentence bursts, such as:

Today's traffic report is brought to you by
Today's Generation Tapes and Compact Discs,
located at 323 Main Street in Madison.

You'll discover a host of choices available to you once you begin to invite the stations into the bidding, so to speak.

Rate the stations

Arbitron is a company that tracks the ratings in the radio business. This data is compiled in diaries that are sent out to homeowners throughout the country. In your own community, people are keeping track of their listening habits and entering the information into these diaries. The samples are analyzed statistically, and ratings are applied based upon the statistics, which include the number of people in an audience and station preferences. It is, at present, the most widely used system for establishing comparative audience figures, and you will use it to determine which stations deliver to your audience most efficiently.

When you set out to buy airtime for your business advertising, ask the following questions:

1. What are the average quarter-hour estimates (estimates of the number of people listening to the station for five minutes during a one-quarter-hour segment)?

2. What are the GRPs (gross rating points—average quarter hour rating multiplied by the number of commercials) of the advertising program being suggested?

3. What is the cumulative rating (total number of different people listening to the station during different parts of the day)?

Asking these questions will not only demonstrate your serious intent and that you're well informed but will help you assess the comparative value of each station in your market.

Radio offers you an opportunity to buy into the broadcast mentality at a low cost per thousand. You are going to create lasting impressions, and you will be perceived as a viable entity in your marketplace if you include broadcast as part of your media mix. People like radio because it's the most portable means of receiving broadcast communications, and it invites the imagination to run as wild as we want.

Cable television

Virtually any business can now be on television. The cost of local cable advertising is low enough to attract even very small businesses. Cable television has grown so fast and so furiously that it is now a staple in the marketing and advertising plans for both local and national advertisers. Statistics from the industry indicate that there are more than 11,000 cable systems bringing programming to more than 60 million households. With wired television in all but 35 percent of homes nationwide, cable television is a most cost-effective medium. It is estimated that more than three-quarters of the households nationwide will have cable television by the year 2000.

If you stop to think about it, cable television has brought electronic advertising to local businesses that would never have been able to advertise on traditional broadcast television. Almost all of the homes in the United States receive at least 30 channels. Because cable is still considered relatively new to the advertising community, less than a quarter of the industry's revenue is derived from advertising. The rest of the income comes from both cable and premium program fees.

Cable provides you with a targeted approach to reaching your customers because you select cable systems that include specific communities, ZIP codes and local markets. Thus, you can concentrate your marketing efforts on those areas that represent your best opportunities. You may choose to advertise on certain cable companies based upon the demographics of their communities. The media kit you receive from the cable company will define the market it reaches. Study these packages carefully, choosing cable systems that reach your customer.

While cable stations as Nickelodeon, TBS, CNN, CNBC, Lifetime, USA and ESPN—just to name a few—are offering some innovative programming, cable television is a long way from reaching the maturity of broadcast television, particularly with regard to national advertising. If you have a product that's sold nationally, the biggest cable networks combined can only deliver 60 million households. If you were to advertise on NBC, CBS and ABC, however, you'd reach 35 percent more households. So advertisers will use cable to *augment* a marketing program, not as a primary means of producing results. But cable television does offer local and regional advertisers a good selection of stations that deliver targeted consumers. For example, Nickelodeon owns the preteen and teen market in various parts of the country. The programming is very specific and represents a wonderful opportunity to reach these consumers, from a widespread campaign to a very local one.

For most small to medium size businesses, cable television is worth looking at. Remember that the movie channels do not currently accept advertising. However, there are 25 cable networks, which include:

Arts & Entertainment	MTV: Music Television
Black Entertainment TV	Nickelodeon/Nick at Nite
The Cartoon Network	Nostalgia Television
CNBC	Preview Guide Channel
CNN: Cable News Network	TBS Superstation
Comedy Central	The Learning Channel
Country Music Television	TNN: The Nashville Network
The Discovery Channel	Turner Network Television
E-Entertainment TV	The Weather Channel
ESPN Sports Network	USA Network
The Family Channel	VH1
Headline News	WGN Cable
Lifetime Television	

Choosing the program

People watch television for a variety of reasons. When considering its significance in your media mix, recognize that television is extremely personal. It reaches its audience in the most intimate settings imaginable—the home, the bedroom, the den, the kitchen, the kid's room, even the bathroom. Because television uses sight and sound, it is a complete medium—powerful enough to move us to tears, create uproarious laughter and bring families together. It is a staple in the American diet and a marketer's dream come true.

Television offers us another unique opportunity in marketing our products—*demonstration*. We can educate, excite, make offers and demonstrate the benefits of our product. We can *show* the results of a good night's sleep on the mattress, or the good business sense it makes to use Ace Messenger service, or the security and comfort of dealing with the local insurance agency. Remember, we are imposing our messages on the prospective customer using real images, people, motion, music—the same elements great programming uses to entertain and move you. We want our marketing message to be equal to or greater than the programming. That's where the magic is!

Outdoor advertising

Outdoor advertising began during prehistoric times when cavemen carved messages on rocks. Posting public notices goes way back to the days when messages were communicated on stone facades and tablets. Much later on, poor souls trekked up and down avenues wearing sandwich signs. *Eat at Joe's* was one of the more memorable sandwich sign messages from the 40s and 50s.

Today, outdoor advertising consists of billboards, banners, flatbed trucks carrying full-size billboards, transit advertising on buses, subways, shelters and stations, planes trailing banners, blimps with messages tattooed across their bellies...well, you get the picture.

Nationwide, about $1.5 billion is spent annually on outdoor advertising, a relatively small figure compared to the amounts spent on other media. However, it is significant, because as technology advances, outdoor advertising will increase in popularity and viability. Also, as technology increases the number of channels and stations available to the consumer, the resulting fragmentation will cause more interest in less "cluttered" media environments, such as the outdoors.

Traditionally, I recommend outdoor advertising as a complementary program to radio, TV, direct mail and print. Remember our discussion about media mix? Outdoor is a secondary medium and works well in concert with another medium as the prime communicator.

The top 10 outdoor advertising categories by revenue are:

1. Retail stores.
2. Cigarettes and tobacco (excluded from broadcast advertising).
3. Restaurants, hotel dining and night clubs.
4. Automotive.
5. Beer.
6. Financial.
7. Resorts and travel accommodations.
8. Radio stations.
9. Real estate.
10. Physical culture (hospitals, health spas, diet/nutrition).

The top 10 outdoor advertising categories by revenue growth:

1. Retail stores.
2. Restaurants, hotel dining and night clubs.
3. Automotive.
4. Financial.
5. Gasoline and oil.
6. Life and medical insurance.
7. Liquor.
8. Passenger travel.
9. Beer.
10. Real estate, brokers and developers.

Source: Competitive Media Reporting

The revenue percentages of various methods of outdoor advertising are as follows:

Top 1 percent:both bench and mall advertising

2 percent: airport advertising

4 percent: supplemental forms

5 percent: bus shelters

6 percent: transit

8 percent: sports stadium

12 percent: in-store

23 percent: 30-sheet posters

34 percent: bulletins

Source: Outdoor Services, Division of Western Media, New York, NY

Let's begin with billboards: Location, location, location!

Your goal in choosing outdoor advertising should be to define the best locations and work hard to get postings on billboards. Traffic studies by the billboard companies will tell you how many impressions each board receives. This, coupled with "riding the boards" (driving past each prospective billboard location, a process that is mandatory for selecting the right billboards), will lead you to a correct decision.

Many billboard companies offer a rotation program that utilizes a number of locations during your schedule. This way, your message is placed on different roadways, offering you a mix of consumers. If you're determined to have your message posted on one specific billboard, you can negotiate the terms with the company. Not long ago, I was offered a billboard located just outside of the Holland Tunnel on the New Jersey side for one of my clients. This message would be seen by commuters during the afternoon and evening hours and would be the first impression they received upon exiting the dark, dismal, cavernous tunnel. The cost was, of course, based upon the traffic count and was appropriately expensive. The client declined and the opportunity was lost. A billboard location such as this one doesn't come along very often; it tends to become a staple for larger advertisers.

Because you have a three-second window of opportunity to capture your audience on billboard, be certain that there are no obstructions, trees or buildings blocking the view. Also, ask the following questions before placing your order:

- Is the board illuminated for night-time viewing?
- Are there Traffic Audit Bureau circulation figures for the boards you're considering? (This bureau verifies traffic counts.)

- Who was the previous advertiser (if the board is vacant)?
- Is it a poster or painted board? (Posters must be printed at additional costs. Ask for the cost of the painted message.)
- Are there any special effects available, such as digital lighting, three-dimensional graphics or fiber optic messages?
- Will the billboard company help design the board, and at what cost?

The trade association for the outdoor industry is the Outdoor Advertising Association of America (OAAA). This is a national association that includes some 600 outdoor advertising companies. You may contact OAAA at:

Outdoor Advertising Association of America (OAAA) Headquarters
1850 M Street NW
Suite 1040
Washington, DC 20036
202-833-5566

According to the association, 70 percent of outdoor advertisers are small and local businesses. This is significant because it points to the economic viability of outdoor advertising for community-based businesses. Because you can pinpoint locations and create super graphics (large messages), outdoor works well for the local business.

Almost every conceivable category has a place on America's billboards. Public service advertising exceeds $150 million per year. You've seen billboards touting everything from seat belt safety to political and public issues to crime prevention to American Red Cross messages and so on. The travel and tourism industry relies heavily upon billboard advertising to direct people to specific locations—to "tease" people who are long-distance bound. South of the Border, a veritable cornucopia of fast-food and tourist shops, motels and assorted amusements, begins teasing the I-95, Florida-bound travelers 50 miles or so before they finally arrive. The billboard messages are silly, humorous and downright ridiculous. If you've ever traveled the Northeast corridor, you're likely to never forget this very creative use of billboard advertising.

According to the Federal Highway Administration, 390,000 traditional billboards can be found in the United States. Almost all (46) states allow outdoor advertising, and revenues exceed $1.5 billion per year. These are impressive statistics, particularly because a large portion of advertisers consists of small and local companies. Billboards do influence our decisions, particularly those of the traveling public. We make our choices by brand and image, price and location...and billboards deliver these messages very effectively.

Some key terms for evaluating your outdoor program

Gross impressions: the total number of times that customers within your defined market are exposed to your message.

Gross rating points: a term also used in broadcast; the number of impressions a media program delivers as it relates to a percentage of the population. For example, one rating point represents coverage equal to 1 percent of the target market.

Reach: who receives the message from the media. The percentage of the public that is being made aware of your advertising claims.

Frequency: the number of times the target market has the opportunity to witness your advertising message during a defined period of time.

Traffic audit: the Traffic Audit Bureau's assessment of traffic counts for use in determining impressions for specific outdoor media. Usually performed every three years.

Cost per point: the cost to deliver a single rating point based upon a specific media schedule.

Co-op advertising: cost sharing by the manufacturer, distributor or dealer. This applies to all media purchases.

Violator: an add-on message, typically identifying pricing or special promotions, appearing primarily in the upper right triangle of a billboard.

Daily effective circulation: those who have the opportunity to see your outdoor message during an 18-hour period.

Coverage: percentage of the market that the message covers.

Some more pointers about billboard advertising

Before you make a decision to use billboard advertising in marketing your business, make sure you can create a message that is powerful and can be perceived in three seconds. Every message can be condensed to accommodate the billboard medium, but you must not make the mistake of trying to be all-encompassing.

One of the most memorable examples of billboard advertising was a motorcycle company's ad. The billboard used a photograph of a motorcycle roaring up the highway, with a primary focus on the broken white lines that divide the road. The headline was: *Tear along the dotted line.* This was truly a great idea, except for one thing. I remembered the concept but forgot the manufacturer of the product. The message is retained because of its powerful creative proposition, not its powerful selling proposition. When you use billboards, you must remember that the sale has to be made in an instant. Product identity is critical and sometimes that means compromising your creative delivery.

If this billboard had used the manufacturer's identity in a more prominent way, the likelihood is that the concept would be cemented to the product—inseparable and memorable. For example, *Ride a Kawasaki...Tear along the dotted line!* Even though this requires three additional words, it provides the product name before the concept— strengthening the selling proposition.

One of the billboards I created for a food store focused on a freshly made, ready-to-go chef salad. The concept was to promote a light lunch for people in a hurry. The headline was: *Lite wait.* The photograph showed a splendid-looking chef salad with an attractive price point. The message incorporated a double meaning, highlighting both convenience and low calories. The striking photograph and quick, playful headline created instant identification with the advertiser and represented the kind of products that could be found at the store.

Transit advertising: Moving messages and messages that move

Follow that cab! Stop that bus! Everything that moves now carries an advertisement. Busses, taxis, hot air balloons, planes, blimps and places where commuters congregate to wait for public transportation, such as train stations or bus shelters, all carry messages. It's all part of the world of transit advertising, which has some distinct advantages. The cost is relatively low. The CPM is most affordable. The creative possibilities are limitless. Any size business can take advantage of local transit advertising opportunities within its marketplace. But most smaller businesses never think about transit as a medium for their marketing program. It's worth thinking about!

I attended a New York Giants game last season with my daughter. The Metropolitan Life blimp hovered overhead during the entire game. The stadium was near full, and everyone kept looking up, then down, then up, then down. We'd all gotten the message after the first pass (of the blimp, not the game), but we kept looking up. Outdoor advertising is intriguing. Its method of delivering the message is creative.

Quick Chek wanted to concentrate its efforts on one particular location during a grand opening week of promotions. The marketing director asked me to develop a strategy that would focus on one store in a chain of 100. I hired a company that secured a billboard to a flatbed truck and followed the course I designated. The sign advertised the grand opening, phone and location of the store and kept roaming through the neighborhood for four days. The sales and traffic reflected the efforts of the moving billboard. We reached just the people we wanted in the community. Sure, we could have posted a billboard on the highway, but it would have reached only 25 percent of the "right" consumers.

The arena of advertising

In addition to traditional outdoor billboards, aerial advertising, shelters and transit, another popular forum for business advertising is sports arenas. Now, you may be thinking, where am I going to get the budget to buy advertising in a major sports arena? Well, I'm not just talking about big league scoreboards. I'm also referring to little league scoreboards right in your own community. They are available for businesses to advertise on, and their impact is enormous among local residents. What if your message was on six or more community little league stadiums surrounding your business location? How about supporting a local team by providing uniforms with your company's name on them? Combine this with placemat or menu advertising in local restaurants, and a small business can begin to "capture the market." Regardless of the size of the advertiser, the principles remain the same. If you can't afford the Super Bowl, try the "Mini Bowl" right in your own neighborhood.

Clearly we've come a long way from walking with a sandwich board up and down Main Street, but the theory is still the same. Outdoor advertising will become a valuable part of your program, provided you follow the rules on creative communicating that we'll cover in Chapter 12.

Direct marketing: It's no longer just mail

Until a few years ago, direct marketing was essentially synonymous with direct mail. Not anymore. Today, direct marketing is any form of communication directed to a specific customer through a variety of media, with the purpose of giving the customer the ability to order by mail, phone or computer or in person.

Direct marketing is the fastest-growing form of marketing communications in the world today. It breaks through all the barriers of media and delivers the message in the most targeted, focused manner. Direct marketing utilizes mail, freestanding inserts (the fliers placed in newspapers), marriage mail (multiple message mailings delivered in a single envelope), radio, television, billboard, online services, interactive television (which will be far more viable later on), database marketing, telemarketing, shopping networks, videocassettes, audiocassettes, infomercials, documercials, magazines, newspapers, catalogs, 800 and 900 telephone services...the list is mounting as quickly as technology permits. The bottom line, however, is to focus on the customers in a world of ever-changing methods of reaching them. We must maintain the integrity of the message regardless of how it is delivered. The messenger may be electronic, but the message is still from one group of human beings to another.

Because direct marketing is so focused, you can reach your target market with little or no waste. This is significant because with traditional mass marketing, we often reach large numbers of people who cannot possibly avail themselves of our product or service, primarily because they are not in our service area or it's not convenient for them to travel to a location. If you want to target consumers in one county but the media reaches three counties, you enter the program knowing full well that two-thirds of your audience cannot take advantage of your business offer. Therefore, the higher costs of direct marketing must be weighed against the higher amount of waste in mass marketing.

Remember, with direct marketing, you are communicating with your customers in a more personal, detailed manner, because you have chosen them both demographically and psychographically. One interesting statistic illustrates the importance of the use of a "P.S." in direct mail. It also illustrates how critical it is to keep your selling propositions bold and quick to reference. A review of more than one million direct marketing pieces showed that a P.S. can increase returns as much as 8 percent if the message communicates an outstanding feature or benefit.

In the case of direct mail, you know who your customers are, literally. You know their names, ages, incomes, family status, genders, lifestyle traits, attitudes, opinions, personal habits. This information allows you to communicate in an intimate fashion. Direct mail, done correctly, is perceived by customers as personal, even when they know it's not.

The subscription prescription

When I was working for *McCall's*, part of my responsibility was to create subscription offers, inviting people to subscribe to several publications. The first was a lifestyle publication that targeted "TNT"—The New Twenties, which consists of males and females between the ages 20 and 29, married or single, with no children. A headline that was used was *TNT...they're dynamite*! The magazine *Your Place* was designed to appeal to every aspect of this market's lifestyle—home, food, recreation, sex, relationships. The first subscription letter that I wrote to The New Twenties went like this:

You say you want to be a star...someone who can juggle three oranges while riding a two-wheel bike...build a house and find love on a warm summer day.

You say you want to be the greatest lover, explore your inner self, earn a good living, plan a beautiful future, fulfill your fantasies and make the best tuna fish sandwich this side of the Mississippi River.

You say you need time to be alone...and time to spend with someone who can share your thoughts, feelings and maybe your life. Perhaps you're not quite sure what you want to be in 10 years or, for that matter, who you want to be tomorrow.

***Now, there's a magazine that deals with your life**—your problems, passions, dreams and realities. In fact, this magazine is so totally devoted to you that it's called* Your Place.

We're not about to offer you the moon...or even a 1-in-10-million chance of winning a car...all we're offering is help, humor, information, insight, fun—from the super serious to the absolute absurd. Your Place *takes you, shakes you and lets you go...to be whatever you want to be.*

Your Place *is for men and women who like life...and everything it has to offer...films, poetry, music, food, sex, love, money and more. It's not just a magazine...it's a way of living, relating and experiencing new things.*

Let Your Place *into your life...you'll be amazed at all you have in common!*

The letter spoke to the potential subscriber in a tone of voice that remained personal as well as promotional. Also note the use of bold letters—a simple device that draws attention to one of the essential selling themes. The issues raised in the letter were common to the target market, designed to establish a sense of community with the audience. Indeed, the publication itself was edited by people in their 20s, a concept that was utilized in reaching advertisers.

Since my responsibility was not only to promote the publication to subscribers but to advertisers as well, we used a theme that hit a high note with the advertising community. We created a powerful promotional brochure with the cover statement: *We have met the readers...and they are us!* The contents of the brochure included a primary message that connected, in an intimate way, the magazine and the market. This was an important message for the community of potential advertisers because it bolstered the issue of credibility. If the magazine truly understood the market because they were one and the same, then the editorial product would be more easily accepted by the reader.

Advertising revenues are based upon the number of readers and the quality of the reader. In this case, people in their 20s were a most attractive market, because they spent lots of money on themselves.

The second magazine we launched was *Working Mother*. This direct mail letter was sent to target advertisers:

What has 30 million feet, moves freely in and out of the house and gathers lettuce?

*The answer is today's working mother, a very special audience of **more than 15 million** women with children under the age of 18 in the house. These women have needs and problems unlike any other group. The working mother is leading a dual existence—coping with kids, home and family in addition to her job responsibilities. In short, she needs help.*

*By now, you've probably heard that **help is on the way.***

This vital new publication represents a breakthrough for both readers and advertisers.

*It's designed to help her cope...and to provide you with a market of women **who make major purchases as well as everyday buying decisions.** She is greatly concerned with her appearance and performance—on the job and at home.*

Please pay particular attention to the rates for our first issue. I'm certain that you and your media staff will concur that the price, medium and market make Working Mother *an irresistible buy.*

For both publications, we had incredibly targeted markets: subscribers and advertisers. Both were launched with great support from the advertising community and, in the case of *Working Mother*, the audience.

Your Place was a brilliant idea and was positioned against a magazine called *Apartment Life*. We did a mailing to key advertisers, simply looking to create some name recognition. We offered premiums to this highly targeted list of advertisers for correctly counting the number of times *Your Place* appeared in the brochure we mailed out. The response was overwhelming because the premiums (record albums and cassettes) were attractive, the promotion was *fun* and the target market (media buyers and planners) was interested in such a targeted medium. We achieved a 40-percent response to the mailing and had phone calls, letters and memos from some of the most powerful names in advertising—touting the creativity of the mailing piece and the high level of name awareness we had created.

But the problem with *Your Place* was lack of consumer promotion. So, we had 54 advertising pages (I was told this was the most successful launch in consumer magazines relative to ad pages) but not enough readers. The subscription letter you just read was one of very few messages that reached out to The New Twenties. I was sorry to see the magazine go, but the point is that direct marketing—whether to consumer or trade markets (subscribers or advertisers)—can take on a personal tone and communicate in a far more connective way than other media.

Knock, knock. Who's there?

We're aging (we hope gracefully). According to recent census statistics, the U.S. population is getting older and better. According to census data, the 44-and-under population will grow by less than 3 percent by the year 2010, while the 45-and-older group will increase by almost 59 percent.

Marketers need to know where the population is in order to develop strategies that will succeed. The mature market has become one of the most sought-after by businesses with appropriate products and services, mostly because it is growing so rapidly. People are living longer and staying healthy. Look at products offered to this market—all kinds of exercise equipment, travel packages, recreational programs, fashions. We are living in a different world today. It's important to recognize how quickly demographic groups are altering their behavior in response to new information, technology and geography.

Study your customers' needs and changes in their lifestyle. Recognize that before you develop your direct marketing program, you must develop your customer profile carefully. Your future depends upon the future of your customer. If you're in a start up mode, consider the population shifts, growth and changes before you decide on a product. Remember, direct marketing is driven by the market, not the product.

Getting personal

Direct mail can ask for the order. You can appear more vulnerable because there's no one else watching. So, you have the unique opportunity to communicate creatively—one on one with your customers—telling them why they should consider your product. You can even talk about their lives in ways that other media approaches don't permit. And you can appeal to their emotions in a specific, personal way.

The New Yorker had a subscription renewal mail-order program some years ago. After about two or three mailings inviting readers to renew their subscriptions, they sent a postcard that stated: *Come back. All is forgiven!* I received one of these postcards, and it was accompanied by a wonderful illustration—a small male caricature with a sad expression on his face—that actually made me feel guilty. In fact, I felt so personally connected to the message that I renewed my subscription.

This is an example of direct mail done well. What you, as a businessperson, want to derive from direct mail is the establishment of a connective bond to the customer.

Direct mail requires margins

Typically direct mail requires high margins (gross profit or markups). The standard formula for marketing a product direct to the consumer is three times cost. The cost of media exposure, packaging, postage and fulfillment requires reasonably high margins to be profitable. Furthermore, if the product is easily available at retail outlets, it dampens the mail-order appeal. Suffice it to say that direct mail works wonderfully for a product that is less price sensitive, with a higher margin and smaller distribution in the marketplace.

Database marketing

The major shift in pointing direct mail advertising toward the future is the advent of database marketing. Database marketing is a system of maintaining customer data accurately on a computer. It imposes certain controls into our direct mail system. It is imperative that we recognize the importance of continuity in direct marketing. Today, population shifts, job changes and lifestyle changes all result in radical changes in the geography of our direct mail customers, and their attitudinal changes also affect our success.

It isn't enough to develop a one-shot approach to direct mail anymore. For one thing, it doesn't work. And even if your first attempt was successful, you wouldn't want to stop there, would you? Database marketing establishes systems that permit direct marketers to repeat successful offers and to eliminate failures. By maintaining information about who buys and what sells, you can develop a comprehensive program for repeat sales and increase the efficiency of your program.

If we view our customers with priority, we have prime prospects, nonprime prospects, present prospects, past prospects and future prospects. We need to know:

1. What our prime prospects are buying and want.
2. Why our nonprime prospects are not buying enough.
3. What our past prospects bought.
4. What our present prospects are buying.
5. What our future prospects want.

It is imperative that we have a process that eliminates nonprospects (those who have not bought after repeated sales efforts). Catalog companies do this by updating their lists constantly. The cost to reach the right people is the same as the cost to reach the wrong people. Database marketing helps us find the right customer. By organizing the responses to your mailing and comparing them to the original list, you will immediately identify who has not responded. Then and only then can you analyze your failures and your successes.

For example, Pendragon's Unordinary Adornments maintains the following information (data) on a direct mail customer:

Robert Josephson, 41 years old, married, two children under the age of 16.

Address: 15 Montrose Court, South Miami, Florida. Lived at same address for seven years.

Purchased: Gold Safari Bracelet   July 9, 1991
           Sterling and Topaz Cat Pin   Sept. 18, 1991
           Sterling and Gold Safari Bracelet   Dec. 1, 1993
           Sterling Posey Pin   May 3, 1994

Upscale neighborhood, *vip zip* (very important person ZIP code)

What do we know about Robert Josephson from our data? First, we know he has the disposable income to purchase our products. Second, we know that he buys our products. Third, we know that he likes our products because there are no "return" notations in our database. Because he is a regular customer, we will keep updating his data in order to keep him as a customer. He will receive every mailing that goes out, every catalog, every special promotion. Robert Josephson will be a prime prospect. Further, when we pursue a telemarketing program, Robert Josephson will be targeted as a top priority. He is, in fact, a preferred customer.

This modest example illustrates what we need in order to be in the direct marketing business. At a recent Direct Marketing Association seminar, a keynote speaker stated that there is no such thing as direct mail alone anymore. We are in an age of synergism. Direct mail without telemarketing or another complementary promotional tool is like rowing with one oar.

I believe this is true. Database marketing is a method of fine-tuning our customer and prospect list. It is a valuable, even imperative, tool in direct marketing today. But no one element of direct marketing works alone. Database marketing works because it keeps focusing and refocusing on our customer, redefining the terms under which we can maintain communication and gain responses. You need to do the following before creating your database.

1. Find out who your customer is. What information do you have regarding the customer who represents the best profile for your product or service?

2. Maintain constant customer communication through mini mailings, postcards, surveys, query letters and incentives.

3. Prospect for new prospects. Your current data will offer you insights into developing new customers. You want customers who are close in type to existing customers.

4. Always look to excite your customers with generous offers for preferred shoppers. Use a gift certificate offering a percentage discount, free shipping and handling or a complimentary giveaway with their next purchase. Regardless of how upscale your offering is, even top earners appreciate recognition and value.

Database marketing is simply developing the means to keep customer information, contact and priorities in place. It allows us to be much more efficient in our mailings, choice of media and creative approach. It's not without cost, though, and depending upon the size of your business, it may be wise to get professionals to get you online. Computer consultants are ideal candidates to help you get a program started.

Before you lick the stamp

It's imperative to analyze your product to see if it qualifies for direct mail.

1. Does the product fill a need not widely present in the mass marketing arena?
2. Does your offer really *offer* something special?
3. Can you achieve a minimum of a three-time markup?
4. Are you ready to fulfill promptly?
5. Do you need to inventory the product, and at what expense?
6. Have you tested the product with friends, relatives, co-workers?
7. Is the price point (cost to the customer) realistic and attractive?
8. What competitive products exist and at what price?
9. Do you have a reliable source of supply?
10. Does the product have the potential to be proprietary?

Remember that you're asking customers to give you their credit card numbers over the phone or to send you a money order or check in order to receive a product they haven't touched, smelled, held or examined. That's a lot to ask, isn't it? Therefore, credibility is a key ingredient in putting your program together. If the product fills a need in the marketplace because it is unique, has added value, is not easily available elsewhere and is perceived as being realistically priced, then you've begun to address the credibility issue.

What about your offer? Does it make sense? Are you providing the customer with good reasons to buy? Have you addressed the issues of product integrity, quality, guarantees? Direct marketing offers must-carry guarantees in order to be credible. If you have endorsements from celebrated customers, associations or business bureaus, you'll want to use them. One direct marketer I know has sent his products to many celebrated people with a self-addressed stamped envelope asking for comments that he can use for the products' promotion. He has a list of celebrities who are happy to receive this high-end product and who have become endorsers. This type of strategy builds instant credibility and greatly enhances your offer.

Recognize that direct marketing businesses don't have traditional overhead. Your rent is your advertising budget and the costs of packaging, shipping labor, fulfillment, telephone staff, credit card machines (they cost more for mail-order operations because banks want additional security and higher percentages) and 800 or 900 numbers.

There is good justification for the product selling at a minimum of three times cost, and if you fall below it you run the risk of losing money or operating on a very small margin. Once you've established that your selling price is competitive with similar products available at traditional stores (or through trade suppliers), or that there is no direct competitive product easily available elsewhere, you're in business. If you are having the product manufactured for you, then establish price controls and firm delivery dates by contract. Your supplier can make you or break you, so always have a backup manufacturer (divide the business between at least two suppliers).

Personal note

When I established my direct marketing business, I had only one supplier (manufacturer) for a primary product. After three seasons of successful selling, he wanted price increases and longer lead times. I accommodated him on both requests. The beginning of my fourth season, I ran short of this particular product and had $15,000 in advertising scheduled over a few short weeks. After leaving numerous messages for him, I began to panic. To begin with, I had put my company's future (it was three months before the holiday selling season) in his hands, and he wasn't returning my calls. After days of phoning him, I finally got him on the phone, only to discover that he was suddenly unhappy with our arrangement. Even though I had a contract, by the time we got to court, my direct marketing company would have been in bankruptcy. And while it's true that this firm is not my primary means of support, it is a successful venture and one that I truly enjoy. Besides, I have commitments to people who place orders...and who, in this case, were waiting to receive the products.

Fortunately, we both compromised. I gave in to what I considered blackmail by paying more for each product, and he promised to deliver the product. Right after the holidays, I ended the relationship with him and lined up three new suppliers who provided me with competitive pricing and guaranteed performance.

The worst-case scenario for an entrepreneur entering a direct marketing business is an interruption of goods. The only viable way of ensuring a continuous source of supply is to have options. This means developing relationships with at least two, preferably three, manufacturers or suppliers of the products you sell. Otherwise you run the risk of having advertisements running, customers ordering and nothing to ship.

Fulfillment simply means that you need to create a program to receive, package, ship and track the product. There is no way of knowing how much you will sell from your first advertisement or mailing. So, you need to be prepared for the best-case scenario. Let's assume your advertising message appears in a magazine with a circulation of 100,000 readers. Anticipate that you will receive a 1½-percent inquiry response of the total readers, if it targets your best possible prospects. Remember, if your message is designed for direct sales (giving all the information one needs to make a purchasing decision) then you'll receive orders and inquiries. If, on the other hand, your ad is designed to get the reader to respond for more information, such as a catalog, sales sheet or phone follow-up, then you'll only get inquiries.

If you receive 1,500 inquiries—representing a 1½-percent response of 100,000-plus readers (remember that more than one person reads a single copy of a magazine)—some industry experts will tell you that you can expect between 10 percent and 15 percent sales from the 1,500 inquiries. I will tell you that the conversion from inquiries to sales is more likely to be 3 percent to 5 percent, particularly until you have fine-tuned your program. If this seems small, consider what would happen if you opened a shop on Main Street, put out a sign and waited. How many people do you think would respond on the first day? Also, if you average 75 sales at $200 per sale with a three-time markup, you've done pretty well.

Direct mail requires the same investments that any other business requires. Can you hit a home run when you first step up to the plate? Possibly. But you're more likely to hit home runs after you've stepped up to bat a few times. The two things that will lead to home runs are frequency of message and customer satisfaction...and both take time.

The likelihood is that you will need to inventory the product based upon the projections I have outlined. If you have a supplier who will ship to you on an as-needed basis, you're lucky. If not, then double your anticipated sales for the first venture into the marketplace. You're in this for the long haul, and sitting with inventory is far less costly than losing sales because you have no goods to ship on a timely basis.

By a captain, you're no captain

When I bought my first boat, I proudly displayed it to my aunt. I was delighted to be wearing a nautical outfit complete with a captain's hat. I asked her what she thought of her nephew the captain. She responded:

"Phil, by you, you're a captain. By your brothers, you're a captain, by me, you're a captain...but by a captain, you're no captain!"

What do you really know about your product? Are you able to answer customers' questions adequately? Can you be perceived as an expert? In truth, you must be perceived as an expert or you shouldn't be in business. Knowing what you're selling is as important as knowing how to sell it. A great many people entering direct marketing do so because they want to create an easy business to operate from home or as a sideline to their existing livelihood. In theory, it sounds great. But in practice, it can be a disaster if you don't play by the rules.

When I first began my direct marketing venture, I learned everything I could about jewelry. I was already fairly well-versed in the industry because I had many clients in the field. I practiced answering customer questions. I read all the material from the Gemological Institute of America on carating, gram weights, gems and stones, and diamond quality, and I asked a lot of questions of people in the profession. I spoke to jewelers, manufacturers, customers. When I felt competent to answer the customers questions, I ran my first ad. I was really glad that I had taken the time to educate myself, because I was deluged with questions about our products. In some cases, I had to refer to materials or mentors in order to provide proper answers. I learned two things: (1) that you must have a product or products that withstand the scrutiny of the public eye, and (2) that you must be expert enough to know what you don't know and then find out.

Direct mail businesses require the same concentration of customer service and patience that any business does, only more so. When you're face to face with someone, it is far easier to win them over or settle problems. When you're distanced by mail and phone, you're unable to display your expressions. So you'll encounter all kinds of people—many of whom begin the relationship on the premise that they are being cheated. Credibility, therefore, is the single most important element you must address in creating your program.

Testing, one, two...

Before you know how to sell direct, you must do what the most sophisticated direct marketers in the country do: *test*. You are not only testing your product or service (services sell just as well as products through the mail on a direct basis), but your creative message as well.

The way you establish a test is by running your ad in the highest priority publication or mailing to the highest priority list—on a small scale. If the publication you choose is national, investigate regional editions to test your ad. If you're mailing a piece of literature or catalog, then choose a region to test before you go national. You will discover through the test who is buying and what geographical areas yield the best responses.

I have found through testing media that Pendragon's products sell to a very specific customer whose demographic and psychographic profile is rather eccentric. The first series of ads demonstrated an audience of people between 30 and 50 years of age, 60 percent female, 47 percent professionals (doctors, lawyers, accountants, professors), living primarily in western and southern states, extremely well-traveled, high-income, frequent mail-order shoppers.

Upon surveying our customers, we also found out that most of the professionals were physicians. We also learned that 65 percent of our customers had been to at least one of the African nations and had some knowledge of the origin of our products. In addition, our customers drove foreign automobiles, dined out of the home at least twice a week and were involved in adventurous leisure activities such as skydiving, skiing, parasailing and boat racing. This information was captured by offering the customer an incentive during our test advertising stages. The incentive was simple: Fill out a simple survey and receive a complimentary gift (a silver chain that cost about $6). We sent the surveys to a random group of customers in order to control our out-of-pocket expenses and almost every single customer surveyed returned the form. So, for less than $1,000, we were able to retrieve enough information to fine-tune our next test. Once we had established who our customer was, we went national. We have maintained the same marketing program developed from our test every year since our inception.

It's all in the list

There are thousands of sources for good mailing lists. Begin by consulting your yellow page directory or business-to-business phone book. You can also use list brokers (people who can get you any type of mailing list you need). The costs will begin at about $60 per thousand names on disc or labels. We'll discuss creative strategies later, but suffice it to say that mailing labels have long lost their impact. Suppliers of mailing lists tend to fall into two categories, generalists or specialists. The general mailing list company provides a wide spectrum of mailing lists for both residential and business mailings. The specialist company will focus on one particular market segment such as new homeowners. This type of company will deliver to you a list of new residents who have moved into a community within a month. They compile the list manually so they're considerably more expensive than standard offerings. These names are culled from deed and mortgage recordings on a regular basis. The list company literally sends staff to municipalities in order to make copies of these recordings. This type of list is extremely valuable to any business looking to develop customer loyalty before new residents have begun shopping for the products and services that will become staples in their households. Of course, a business owner can choose names by ZIP code in order to ensure a match between the demographic profile of the customer and the product being marketed.

You can also develop your own mailing list based upon the type of business you own. In fact, with a good software package, you can spend the time necessary to create a database using directories and your phone. You might begin by researching at the library or contacting local organizations. Take a look at:

- Association directories.
- Classified listings.
- Consumer phone books.
- Church and synagogue membership lists.
- Municipal records.
- Human resource departments of corporations.
- Industrial directories.
- Business-to-business directories.
- Directories of manufacturers.
- Specific organizational directories.
- Trade directories.

This is a laborious task but a necessary one. The directories will list business name and/or personal name as well as the addresses. Once you have determined the criteria for selecting your customer, enter the information. This is the beginning of your dedicated mailing list, and it can be merged with other list sources as you develop them.

Begin with an ad or a mailing?

If you're looking to begin a direct marketing effort, there is an essential decision you face. Do you begin by exposing your offer through advertising first and developing your own mailing list, or do you begin by mailing your message to prospects? There is no simple answer. Much of it depends upon the product, the market, the offer. Of course, doing both is always preferred, but most companies cannot afford a direct mail effort and a direct response advertising campaign at the same time.

Therefore, I suggest that you develop a media strategy first, testing markets through advertising rather than mailing lists. Typically this will be more cost-efficient and will also provide you with a good mailing list because each customer represents a future prospect for additional sales.

Your advertisement can also offer the product on a direct sale basis or a catalog for more information. You must have an 800 number (they're inexpensive) and you should establish an account with the major credit card companies in order to process orders over the phone. In my experience, 95 percent of your orders will ultimately be placed by phone with the customer providing you with a credit card. Once you've tested the media with advertising, you have a good sense of your customer and the product's appeal. You are also in the process of developing the most valuable mailing list available: real responses to your offer!

I only want people with six toes on their left foot

It may not be a long list, but if you make socks that have six toe compartments, you'll find a list. Seriously, lists have become so refined, so specific, that you'll discover that almost any audience you can dream of can be reached with a targeted mailing list.

In addition to the two associations listed below, many states have direct marketing associations, and these organizations can provide listings for the states that offer these services:

National direct marketing associations

Direct Marketing Association, Inc. (DMA)
1120 Avenue of the Americas
New York, NY 10036
212-768-7277; fax: 212-719-1952

Largest and oldest trade association in the direct marketing industry. Provides conferences, lectures, seminars, programs.

Direct Marketing Educational Foundation
1120 Avenue of the Americas
New York, NY 10036
212-768-7277

Sister organization to DMA. Assists in providing information on direct marketing at the university level. Answers inquiries, provides speakers.

Many large companies such as Dun & Bradstreet have mailing list divisions. A very good source for mailing lists is magazines. Most publications will rent a one- or two-time use of their mailing lists or sell them. This is beneficial, particularly if you have had success reaching your customer through an advertisement in a specific periodical. If the publication is reaching your audience, utilizing the subscription list for your own mailing may be to your advantage.

Renting a list

Mailing lists are leased for specific uses for an agreed-to number of times. They are also available with or without phone numbers, titles and specific names (heads of household, officers of companies). You must know the rules before you obtain a particular list. List companies control usage by "seeding" the list—placing "control" names within the list in order to monitor the usage. If you intend to use the list more than the contracted number of times, negotiate with the list house. Otherwise you run the risk of being charged for unauthorized use.

The company list

If you're mailing to corporations, businesses or specific companies by category, you'll need to reach the right people as well as the right companies. Begin by selecting the companies based upon the number of employees as your criterion for mailing. This information may prove more valuable than gross sales in determining the viability of the prospect because sales figures alone can be deceiving. There are many companies that have gross revenues that seem attractive but few employees. Choose businesses that fit your model, and be certain to get the right names within the company. Office mail is not likely to be forwarded unless it is of significant importance. The only method of overcoming this problem is through telephone inquiries to obtain the correct name and title of the target customer. Though time-consuming, it is worth the trouble, and the result is a much higher return on your investment. Much of this work may already be done for you by the mailing list company, but in some cases it may be necessary for you to get on the phone and verify the information.

A clean list

Ask how often the mailing list house updates the list. The biggest problem with mailing lists is datedness. If a list has not been cleaned recently, more than an acceptable 3 to 5 percent of what you mailed will be marked "return to sender."

Newsletters

Generally speaking, there is no medium more boring than the newsletter. However, if composed with brevity, clarity and creativity, the newsletter is an ideal method of staying in touch with your customer.

Newsletters are also useful direct contact tools for nondirect market-ing businesses.

In the case of your direct marketing program, the newsletter for-mat is ideal for continuing communication. Once you've established a direct link (a purchase), you have a responsibility to maintain contact with the customer. The newsletter can offer the customer information, insights and new ideas regarding the products, lifestyle or customs that appeal to them. And newsletters read like newspapers, so there is a degree of editorial integrity associated with them. They also point to your company's credibility and professionalism. The newsletter must adhere to certain criteria:

1. Be brief.
2. Use bold headlines.
3. Offer insight and information.
4. Don't commercialize or promote.
5. Be authoritative (you're the expert).
6. Invite letters, comments and inquiries.
7. Announce upcoming events, products or issues pertaining to your shared interests.
8. Use photos whenever possible.
9. Reiterate mission of company.
10. Keep bulleted editorial statements in personal tone (first person).

The primary benefit of the newsletter format is to establish your company as professional and to remain ever-present in the customers' mind. Top-of-mind, continuous communication is the best possible way to retain your customer base. My suggestion is to begin mailing the newsletter quarterly (one issue every three months). Four issues is sufficient in order to maintain the connection that is desired be-tween seller and buyer. If you have news that is worthy of more fre-quent communication, then send out a special supplement and note that it's an *extra*!

Newsletters become more customer-friendly when they include the customer in the news. Invite letters, comments and suggestions from customers. By publishing these, you're inviting the audience into the community, so to speak.

Make your statements count

Consumer statement stuffers arrive with almost every credit card bill we receive. Business statement stuffers (or package inserts) are sent not only with bills but are stuffed into product shipments. It's a system that should be in place and on automatic pilot every time an order is shipped or a bill is sent out. It creates an opportunity to announce upcoming promotions, discounts and incentives, special orders, seasonal selling opportunities and a personal dialogue.

There are two great reasons for using statement stuffers. Number one is to get your bills noticed and paid. You can do this creatively if you put your mind to it. Number two is to create an ongoing dialogue with the existing customer base regarding your company. You are paying for the shipping and postage anyway, and a simple, dynamic statement stuffer will not add to your printing costs. You can, of course, include a business reply card (the postage is prepaid by you, but only for those that are returned) to facilitate responses.

Catalogs

The nature of catalog advertising is changing rapidly due to technology. However, catalogs will still be a viable sales tool for a while. At the library, you can find the *Directory of Mail Order Catalogs*. This large reference book will list catalogs by category.

One of the simplest ways to begin a direct marketing program is to put together the same package you would submit to infomercial companies (see the section "Direct response television: Snake oil or salesmanship," pages 118 to 124) and send it to catalog companies that offer products similar to yours. The advantages are obvious: You have no up-front costs if the catalog company accepts your product. You simply establish pricing and wholesale the product to the catalog house. You no longer own the "image" of the product—the catalog company can depict the product in any form it desires since it paid for it—but you also don't incur the expenses of marketing your product directly.

About 50 percent of adults in the United States make a catalog purchase annually. Catalogs have become a smart shopping alternative for dual income families. Because catalogs tend to specialize, they provide options—both in merchandise and pricing—to traditional "store" shopping. Manufacturers and distributors use catalogs to sell directly to consumers. Catalogs are also used as a sales promotion vehicle and are left behind after a sales call for reference and ordering. But because the traditional sales call has become costly, we are seeing more and more catalogs being placed on Web sites so businesses can access information and place orders through the Internet.

Traditional catalogs, though, are still a viable business option. If you're a manufacturer selling to distributors, your catalog is your lifeline. If you're distributing products, your own identity and product line will be represented by your catalog and sales literature.

Though there are many advantages, one of the major disadvantages of retail catalogs has been the increased costs of paper, printing and postage. This has lead to reduced revenues and less than competitive pricing in certain categories.

Specialty mail-order companies such as J. Peterman, The Sharper Image, Hammacher Schlemmer and Banana Republic (while it was still positioned as a purveyor of adventure and expedition apparel) are just a few examples of companies that offer a specific type of product line not readily available in the retail marketplace. They also have distinct personalities that set them apart in the marketplace. In fact, J. Peterman made such an indelible impression with his catalogs—through stylized artwork, copy, even the size and paper stock—that he's featured on the prime-time show *Seinfeld*. Most of the universe simply offers products and services. *Innovative* marketers (there are very few) offer opportunities, adventure, entertainment, pleasure, excitement, benefits and image.

Before you develop a catalog (business or consumer), think long and hard about what makes you respond as a consumer. Don't do anything that falls short of your own expectations just because the category of catalogs has long been considered mundane. Follow the example of the ones that stand out. Develop a philosophy of doing business on a direct basis that gives customers much more than simple information—give them an experience!

Direct response television: Snake oil or salesmanship?

It started shortly after television entered our lives. Maybe you watched it on *The Honeymooners*: "Can it core a apple?" (a classic misstatement by Jackie Gleason). Or you may have seen it on *I Love Lucy*: "Vita Meta Vegamin." Or you may have been channel-surfing and suddenly found yourself drawn into a "program" all about a miraculous mop. Or how about hair you spray from a can? Juicers? Teeth whiteners? Fishing lures? Automobile polish? Cookware? Vacuum cleaners?

Incredible as it may seem, direct response television—the forum for advertising such products—is the fastest-growing direct marketing industry today. The advertisers even have their own trade association, the National Infomercial Marketing Association. (You can contact the association at 1201 New York Ave. NW, Suite 1000, Washington, DC 20005; 202-962-8342; fax: 202-962-8339.)

I attended a conference sponsored by NIMA where most of the major companies in the infomercial industry gathered to share information and discuss trends. Interestingly, the primary concern at the meeting was the issue of self-regulation, particularly since the government is hovering above these companies, ready to strike. (The Federal Trade Commission has been involved in the follow-up of consumer complaints for years. They have introduced regulations that prohibit companies from making unsubstantiated claims.) Indeed, there is an enormous image problem in the infomercial industry. And it is well-founded. Up until very recently, many of the sales claims were exaggerated or even fabricated, and litigation, fines and government intervention were the norm. Today, NIMA is attempting to remedy the credibility problem with networking, communication among members and a more sophisticated approach to marketing.

It is an industry with enormous potential and power, with sales of more than $1 billion predicted before the year 2000. It represents marketing opportunities for manufacturers, inventors, patent-holders, even small entrepreneurs. Of course, it must be approached with reason and caution. Infomercials are presented in a variety of formats. Primarily 30- or 60-minute programming is utilized to create an information-demonstration selling agenda for a product or group of products. There are almost always at least two pitch-persons. One does the actual demonstrating, the other plays the "devil's advocate" by taking the audience/consumer side with questions designed to confront the demonstrator. It is carefully orchestrated and, often, brilliantly acted. And it does represent a mighty powerful method of selling.

Methods and the madness

There are two basic methods of making infomercials work for you. The first applies to smaller individuals or companies with an attractive product. The major infomercial companies (available through NIMA) will simply purchase the product from you. Most often they will create the proper packaging, add a bonus (to sweeten the direct offer) and take care of everything from media buying to production to fulfillment. You simply sign a contract to supply the product at an agreed-to price and relinquish all control thereafter, maintaining only your profits. The critical issue here is that infomercials require at least a five-time markup. Therefore you must be able to deliver your product at an extremely attractive price in order for it to have appeal to the customer and to keep it competitive within the marketplace.

Most of the money made in the infomercial industry is, curiously, not from direct sales through television. Most of the dollars are generated from the eventual retail distribution. Here's how it works: A product runs successfully on an infomercial program. It usually lacks retail distribution. The infomercial creates identity, product awareness and demand. It establishes success within the marketplace—enough success to warrant retail distribution. Then, the companies such as As Seen on TV come into play. This company (there are others like it) creates the opportunity for retail distribution of the product using the infomercial success to merchandise it at store level. You may have seen this in mass merchandising environments (large retail outlets such as Kmart, Wal-Mart, Sears). Now the product has all of the elements necessary to succeed at the retail level. It has had the benefit of television exposure, customer awareness has been created, brand identity has resulted from the media blitz...it's ready for retail sales. Remember, you are simply the supplier, but you've invested nothing to get the product launched. Infomercial companies have selection committees that will evaluate your product and determine its "saleability" as an item for sale on a direct TV basis. If they think it will sell, you will begin the negotiation process.

The other method is to create a partnership. In this scenario, you will both share the investment and the rewards. Suffice it to say that this requires a great deal of up-front money. Even in the test stage, the infomercials that may just run in Dallas, a popular test market, are expensive to produce. This scenario is not for small concerns.

If you're thinking about submitting your product to an infomercial company, consider the following:

1. Is the product highly demonstrable?
2. Does the product offer a promise?
3. Is the product available elsewhere in the marketplace?
4. What value-added elements can the product provide?
5. What credible issues or endorsements can accompany the product
6. Does the product add joy and satisfaction to the customer's life?
7. What guarantee can accompany the product?
8. How often will the product be used by the customer?
9. Can you provide quality assurance and consistency?
10. Does the product appeal to all regions of the country?

Infomercial marketing is, perhaps, the most exciting form of direct response advertising, with the possible exception of the Internet. But because the Internet is in its infancy stage, direct response TV is the most dynamic means of direct selling. However, you must pay careful attention to certain issues when considering direct response TV.

Safety may sell, but not on TV

You can't sell fire extinguishers on infomercials. You can't sell mace guns on infomercials. You can't sell burglar alarm systems on infomercials. Why? Because the product's use is filled with negative imagery. There's no immediate gratification. It doesn't make you feel good about yourself, and it only works in an emergency. Don't try to sell emergency-driven products on direct TV.

I feel better having given you that vital information. Now, what *does* sell? Lots of things.

Self-improvement sells on TV

Richard Simmons sells. Recently I attended a conference where Richard was a speaker. He was marvelous. To begin with, Richard Simmons is the most sincere individual I have ever listened to in a business setting. He is vulnerable. He is successful, personally and professionally, and he is completely nonjudgmental. As a marketing professional, it is easy for me to see why Richard Simmons has become his own brand (we'll discuss branding in Chapter 15). Just as Kleenex has become the first brand name we associate with tissues, Richard Simmons is the first name that comes to mind in the world of weight reduction and fitness today. He has used the infomercial format with creativity and compassion—introducing the concept of hope to viewers around the country.

The premise, the promise

The best infomercials deliver a *premise* and a *promise*. When the premise is plausible and the promise attainable, there's magic. Let's stay with the Richard Simmons example for a moment. Simmons's premise is simple: Lose weight, tone, get healthy! His promise is his own personal commitment, caring and compassion. And they're real. We believe because we see the demonstration—the before-and-afters, the testimonials, the emotion. Personal change is difficult, but it's probably the most powerful premise for direct response TV because it holds the most promise. And while it's true that a great many people will buy the product and just put it on the shelf, those who use it and succeed become the best examples a marketer has.

Do-it-yourself direct TV

Infomercial companies purchase a combination of cable and broadcast (nonwired TV) to deliver their messages. They have a sophisticated test market system in place and an equally sophisticated fulfillment program. This is not to say that businesses cannot create a direct response TV program on their own. The infomercial format allows businesses to purchase programming time, instead of advertising time, from television stations. There is a vast difference in cost. It would be cost-prohibitive to purchase 30- or 60-minute blocks of time at advertising rates. However, programming time is affordable enough for many businesses to begin an infomercial campaign, particularly on cable television. Some stations will orchestrate a deal with a marketer on a per-inquiry basis. This means that the station will charge the advertiser based upon the response. While the number of stations that will operate on this basis is more limited, it is wise to inquire about a per-inquiry arrangement in order to get your infomercial marketing started.

As long as you know the rules and study the infomercials that are currently running, you will understand how the format is used and what categories are most attractive to customers. Think of the categories that are dominating the airwaves today—cosmetics, hair care, fashion accessories, car care, diet, exercise, vacuums and household appliances, juicers, fishing lures, health care, vitamins, real estate, successful selling, making millions—each one of them holding a premise and a promise! One of the earliest and best examples of a huge infomercial campaign was "Where there's a will, there's an A"—a program incorporating creative methods of teaching children to read—featuring television actor John Ritter. Statistics indicate that the program has generated more than $70 million in revenue to date and is continuing to rack up sales.

Today, almost all TV stations accept infomercial advertising. The power of the medium and message has caused major advertising agencies to form separate divisions dealing exclusively in direct response TV (DRTV).

Documercials

A distinction has been made between infomercials (designed to elicit a direct sale via an 800 number or mail-in address) and documercials. Documercials deliver a story, not a hard sales approach. These 30- or 60-minute "documentary-style" programs are designed to deliver a non-promotional, image-oriented message. If a company can present itself well within a traditional 60-second commercial format, think of the possibilities that exist within a 60-*minute* format.

The documercial allows for great artistic freedom—a car company can use a "slice of life" approach to introduce a new model, a resort can present its community with romantic, sentimental overtones. The documercial sells the concept more than the specific product. It addresses lifestyle issues, features and benefits, planting a seed for future sales because its message focuses on how the product will impact one's life without referring to "a deal." The products that are most popular in this forum of marketing include automobiles, real estate, motorcycles, boats and other high-end offers such as vacation time-shares.

Small businesses are less likely to promote their products in a documercial than an infomercial simply because a documercial shows no direct relationship between its message and the sale. Therefore, the return on investment is far slower and more cumulative. And the infomercial production companies are not interested in partnering with advertisers on documercials because of this absence of direct sales and immediate profits. The small business owner, therefore, is ultimately on his or her own if choosing to produce a message using this format.

Because the documercial promotes a product's image instead of asking for a specific response, in order for a small business to benefit from this format, it would likely produce a program about the company, the product and the unique qualities and attributes that set them apart. The typical format would be 30 minutes, and, in the case of small businesses, it could run on cable rather than broadcast stations. A documercial can also be produced and mailed as a video news release. A small business can effectively demonstrate its wares through the documentary format on VHS cassettes mailed to prospective customers. This would enable the business to avoid the higher costs of buying cable television time, which requires great frequency (multiple showings in each market) in order to be effective.

Armchair shopping

The same process for selling your product or service to an infomercial company exists when you look to sell to one of the home shopping networks. Home shopping is exploding. Depending upon what you're selling, you can submit a product to any of the home shopping network companies by mail, or you can find out which days they have "open houses" where you can show up for an appointment. In either case, recognize that major retailers are already using home shopping networks in order to market goods. And celebrities are finding outlets for endorsing products on television shopping channels. In a relatively short period of time, home shopping has gained credibility and acceptance among all levels of American consumers.

As we become more accustomed to watching shopping channels, our buying habits will go through evolutionary changes. What's interesting is that home shopping appeals to all market segments, in every region of our country—high as well as lower income, males as well as females, young as well as older. Granted, there *are* regional differences (remember bucket marketing), but every corner of this country responds to the concept of shopping at home.

If your product fits one of the categories of home shopping—such as jewelry, fashion, crafts, literature, appliances, household goods, sports and recreation, just to name a few—you should begin by developing a cover letter, product illustration or photograph (don't send a sample until it's requested), pricing information, turnaround time on orders, unique aspects of the product, present market share, patents or trademarks, information on competitive products in the field...and what I call a *product power pitch*. A product power pitch is a simple four-part presentation:

1. Describe the product as if it is the only one in its category.
2. Give key selling propositions concerning why it will sell well on television.
3. Create an identity for the product by naming it.
4. Tell why middle America wants it.

Put these power points on a standard 8½" x 11" piece of stationery and mount them on a 9" x 12" piece of colored poster stock. Mail your information to the home shopping station in a large envelope so that the material is flat. Include your cover letter, product illustration or photo and power pitch. Be certain to follow up with a phone call, and be persistent. The selection committees take time to respond, and unless you know someone within the organization, you need to be noticed. Also remember to keep your profit margins as tight as possible because, as in infomercial advertising, the markup must be high for the TV shopping channel to make money.

The shopping channel will give you lots of statistics regarding the viewers. This information will give you a good sense of the audience and its buying patterns. Suffice it to say that almost half of the shoppers are married and equal percentages of professionals and blue-collar workers comprise the mix. About half of the market is Caucasian with the other half comprised of Black or Hispanic shoppers.

Because people are channel-surfing, products that appear on home shopping channels must be striking in presentation. If your line of necklaces don't sparkle, shine and shout, you're out. So be certain that your product fits the medium. Don't try to force the medium on your product. It doesn't work.

Audio and video direct

The downside to using audio and/or video presentations to market direct is the *cooperation factor*. We are asking the customer to do several things in order to get to our selling message. Provided the packaging is compelling (boxes always get opened), the recipient must open the box, take out the tape, find a cassette player or VCR, place the tape in the machine and sit back and watch. Unless the subject matter is important enough to the customers, you're asking them to do a great deal in order to uncover the message. Therefore, I strongly suggest that you measure the market relative to how important your message is to them before you consider the use of this medium.

Also, when using audiotapes as a primary means of communicating, consider using a professional for the voice-over work (narration).

Not only does it sound better, but, in some cases, it is wiser to have someone speak for your company, rather than create the sales message yourself. Unless you're in a service business where your identity is critical to the central selling theme, a professional will add a whole new dimension to your audio or video marketing. Recent statistics indicate that direct marketing with videocassettes yields a response that exceeds direct mail by about 2½ percent. This means that the visual program creates more excitement among prospects than the static medium of print mail. Analyze the costs and the return on investment before you allocate dollars to any one specific method of direct marketing.

Recently I received a very professional direct mail package from an insurance agency. It was boxed in a white corrugated shipping container with a strong selling message on the outside. I opened it because I never overlook packages, even when I know they're promotional. Inside was a beautiful presentation that included a videotape and a brochure. I popped the videotape into the VCR and sat back to enjoy what I thought would be a unique presentation—considering the creativity and care taken in packaging the pitch. The disappointment came suddenly. Two minutes into watching the video's host, I was convinced someone had sold this poor guy on the idea of using himself to market his product. Wrong move! To begin with, he had a pronounced speech impediment that made it difficult to follow the monologue. And he was obviously reading from a TelePrompTer or cue cards. I was incensed. The video marketing company had convinced a small business professional to do a *big* promotion—packaging, custom brochure, smart presentation...everything was great up until the actual sales message! I was angry with the marketing company, not the businessperson. He obviously had followed the marketing company's direction, taken its lead and convinced himself that these so-called professionals knew what they were doing. And they did, except when it came to the most important aspect of the marketing effort: the video itself.

You're not a businessperson—you're a movie director

In a sense, marketing with videotape is very similar to the infomercial genre. The best ways to use video for direct marketing are to keep it lively and interesting and to incorporate as many credible endorsements into the program as possible. If you're central to the selling theme and you're presentable, you certainly can consider appearing in the video. If, on the other hand, you don't possess the stage presence required to perform professionally, you may want to relinquish the role to another spokesperson. Remember, it's important that your video be captivating enough to keep people interested and get them to respond.

There is no specific formula regarding the length of the presentation, but a three- to five-minute video is usually an appropriate running time unless you're producing a training or demonstration piece. The video represents an opportunity for you to market your business, position it and communicate the features and benefits to a captive audience. Once the prospective customer places the video in the VCR and turns on the television, you have a marvelous opportunity to capture them. The key concept here is to be compelling:

1. Use fast, frequent cuts. Don't allow the camera to stay on a single subject for more than 15 seconds.
2. Provide short testimonial sound bites from real people expressing themselves honestly and nonpromotionally.
3. Address the customers' needs, not your own.
4. Be creative and utilize colorful graphics.
5. Take advantage of both the video and audio elements of the medium by coordinating appropriate music to camera movements. You don't want to appear static.
6. Identify your strengths in the first minute.
7. Remain focused on your key selling strengths, statement or position.
8. Continually come back to your spokesperson as the coordinator of the information contained in the video.
9. Don't be afraid to tell the prospect that you want his or her business. Use powerful visual expressions in asking for the order.
10. Close the video with the information the customer needs to respond—your company name, a specific message, address and phone—and be sure to repeat the unique selling proposition when summarizing.

Packaging the video is as important as the program itself. Your package must excite the prospect in the same way that video covers get you to rent a specific movie at the video store. Think about what makes you choose an unknown movie. The graphics and copy are designed to sell the movie to you in 10 seconds. The same issue applies to direct marketing your own video. Use the movie videos as your model. Begin with a title, a short burst of language about how much the customer will learn in a brief period of time and what that can do for the customer! You want the prospect to rip open the package and be in a receptive mind-set.

If you're selling your banking services to a businessperson in your community, you want them to see you as an innovator, a customer advocate and an enabler, if you will. The video cover should make the points that break the barriers typically associated with your industry. You know the stumbling blocks already (if not, you certainly should), so utilize them to create counterstatements regarding how you have overcome them. Small businesses need to feel important and less intimidated by banks. They also need to know how you can help them with as little risk as possible. Focus on their pain and anxiety, and create a merchandising message that eliminates their fear. For example:

> *You are three questions away from*
> *a no-hassle credit line!*
>
> *#1. What is the name of your company?*
> *#2. How many years have you been in business?*
> *#3. How much do you want?*

From this point, you'll offer a brief biography of your business, highlighting your accomplishments, the very same kinds of accomplishments that will enable the prospect to see his or her success tied to a partnership with your bank. Right now, you're not a banker, you're a movie director. You're selling the prospect on viewing the video. You'll get to his or her specific banking needs later. First, you must entertain him or her.

Entertaining is really the first order of marketing and becomes a key issue in direct marketing. Because videos are, in effect, associated mostly with the entertainment industry, we want to take advantage of that perception and create entertaining images. That's why we model our video after commercial television rather than business videos. If we use most business videos as a guide, we are doomed to fail. Yes, that's how bad they are.

The same rules apply to audio presentation, except that you will not have to deal with the visual elements. This is both a plus and a minus. The positive aspect of audio is the imagination factor (take a look at our section on radio), which allows us to create imagery that captures the attention of our target market. The downside is that it lacks the visual element to reinforce the selling theme.

The audio presentation, like the videotape, also asks customers to do more than simply read a postcard, letter or brochure. It requires that they find a cassette player, put in the tape and fire it up. Once you get them to do all of this, you have exactly 10 seconds to capture their attention and hold their interest. If you don't engage them within the 10-second time frame, you have lost them. This principle applies to everything you do, but unlike using printed material, you will never get them to go back to the cassette unless you entertain them from the word *go!*

For high rollers only

The most compelling direct marketing video and audio presentation I have ever seen was delivered by a tuxedo-clad messenger who arrived in a limousine. He was delivering a package to a client of mine, a builder. This particular builder was a well-known customer of an Atlantic City casino. The marketing people at this casino devoted large sums of money to enticing high rollers to special events. I was seated in his office when the messenger appeared. He asked to speak to my client and was ushered in by the secretary.

"Sir," he said, holding out a box, "may I present this special offer to you compliments of the management of our casino?"

As soon as he finished speaking, he was gone. We were left staring at the box, wrapped in shiny silver paper with glorious red ribbons.

"Unwrap it," I said.

"Why?" he shot back.

"What do you mean 'why'?" I asked.

"I already know what it is," he said cynically.

"Are you kidding? I'm your marketing guy. I want to see what's in there," I insisted.

"Here, you open it," he offered.

I unwrapped the package to reveal a box of truffles and a video. As soon as the box was opened, believe it or not, an audiotaped message began to play—from a tiny microchip automatically activated by the simple flip of the cover of the box. The taped voice belonged to a casino executive, who spoke personally to my client. He invited him to a special evening affair that included a limousine to the casino from his home in northern New Jersey, a suite complete with champagne, dinner and show tickets. I was astonished. My client was amused but had been the recipient of this type of direct marketing effort before.

"Will you go?" I asked.

"Of course. Wouldn't you?" he said.

When I stopped to think about the expense the casino executives had undertaken to get my client to their hotel, I was at first surprised. A few moments later, I realized how little, in the scheme of things, they had actually spent. Let's say the messenger and limousine cost $250 and the package itself another $200. Then let's assume the casino's target customer spends tens of thousands of dollars minimum per year. If you think about it, even a custom, targeted, direct marketing presentation such as this yields an incredibly high return. The video portion of the package included a short direct-to-the-customer, personalized invitation, complete with fast-paced images of the casino floor and inviting personnel welcoming the honored guest. Suffice it to say the message was loud and clear and produced the desired result. My client went to the event and reported to me some weeks later that he left an appropriate amount of money at the gaming tables. At least he had fun.

Now that you've heard the message, read the book

You cannot rely upon audio presentations alone in direct marketing. Companion literature is a must. Your brochure, sales material, flier or letter must support the premise of the audio message. This means that the same tone, style, language and personality must come through from tape to print. If you entertain and excite your customer with a voice (or voices) and imagery (remember, you're going to use music and sound effects as well as a melodic voice), then the same sensibilities should be in play in your printed message.

The purpose of the material you send along with the audiocassette is to invite the customer to listen, thus the packaging is critical. Further, you want the customer to retain something tangible about your company. The brochure is a leave-behind (something that's left with the customer and retained by him or her) that allows the prospect to refer to your sales message long after the audiotape has been discarded and forgotten. Dynamite graphics and a short, entertaining/ informational audio message accompanied by an equally inspiring brochure will prove a mighty performer, but remember: *You've got 10 seconds to live or die!* So don't forget that your message isn't as interesting to anyone else as it is to you. You are not the customer. Test the speech, the music, the mood and the sound effects with as many people as possible. Anyone who will listen should be surveyed. You are creating a long commercial, and customers need to stay stimulated and turned on...or they will turn you off.

Direct marketing wrap-up

Direct marketing does not exist in a vacuum. It is an integral part of an overall marketing effort and should be considered as a major element in the development of a media strategy. Direct marketing can pinpoint customers more powerfully and personally than any other method of employing media. It can be expensive, and the more specific your needs, the greater the cost, but it is far less wasteful than other targeted approaches of marketing. Consider the costs and keep in mind that you are in complete control of your universe. You have control over the reach and the frequency (who receives the message and how often), as well as the selection of your prospects' demographic and psychographic profiles (who they are and what they think). This means that your assessment of the target market must be true. You can establish this through the kind of market testing we spoke of earlier.

Sales promotion: A lot more than calendars

The term *collateral materials* refers to virtually everything that carries your advertising or sales message—newsletters, brochures, letters, fliers, even calendars and postcards—in short, everything that is collateral to media. Sales promotion is the part of your program that assists and supports the sales effort by promoting the sale in a variety of ways. Sales promotion materials are often used in personal selling— across the desk, in meetings, presentations and seminars. In retail marketing, sales promotion can be comprised of incentive offers, too.

The relationship between advertising and sales promotion can be illustrated by the following chart.

Advertising responsibilities:	**Sales promotion responsibilities:**
a. creating identity	a. creating choices
b. creating position	b. creating action
c. creating demand	c. creating buying

The two activities work closely together to produce a sale. Sales promotion activities involve delivering the sales message to the customer in a more personal, involved fashion. Advertising softens the marketplace by imposing messages designed to infiltrate the consumers' consciousness. Sales promotion delivers on those messages in ways that answer questions and bring the product closer to the customer.

Promoting the sale

Recently I created a marketing program for a large technical company. The company was well known in other industries but relatively unknown in our new target market. The advertising positioned the product line and created a bold identity for the company. All of the mechanisms were in place to bolster the image and brand identity and carve a niche in a new market with a host of premiere products. I opted to utilize the company's equity in other arenas in order to lend immediate credibility to our cause. By referencing other markets, I was able to illustrate how the manufacturer had dominated these industries and how the same qualities and commitments could be applied to the new markets.

The first opportunity to present our wares was at a national trade show. The booth design was reconfigured to support our new identity and supergraphics (large color photos mounted on the booth) were employed to draw attention to our selling proposition. In addition, we created a sales promotion presentation that consisted of an automatic slide presentation that used a synchronized sound and slide show shown from behind one of the booth panels (this is called *rear screen projection*). The announcer took the customer through the six-minute presentation with aggressive graphics, energetic music and a truly scintillating script. The presentation was dynamite because it held the attention of the audience by creating enough tension with each slide— setting the customer up for the next slide. It created a choice, because the customers chose the booth, drawn in by the sales promotion message. It created action, because the customers wanted to get closer to the product and needed more information. It created buying, because the customers were given all the information necessary to place an order.

The supplemental (collateral) materials consisted of a brochure detailing the company history, product performance, list of references (current customers), features and benefits, technical support services and pricing. The third element was a simple three-ring binder flip chart that allowed the salesperson to reinforce the slide show message by highlighting and reconstructing the most salient points. And because this was a small, personal presentation, the salesperson and customer were now seated two feet from each other. The sales promotion could be delivered in an intimate setting with opportunities to discuss each aspect of the product pitch.

Sales promotion supports advertising and vice versa. The idea is to use advertising to build selling opportunities. Once awareness has been achieved, sales promotion can take over and create the sale. *Advertising brings the bodies to the door. Sales promotion opens the door and closes the sale!*

Sales promotion also involves the use of premiums and incentives. Trade promotions often include contests in which leading salespeople can win a trip to an exotic destination, such as Hawaii, for selling more than the next person. These types of sales promotion programs are generally costly, but have proven to be performance producers for many companies.

Point-of-sale or point-of-purchase (POP) sales promotion is part of the process of selling called *merchandising*. POP selling exists in virtually every industry—from plumbing supply to wholesale distribution to retail to automobile dealing. Most of us are all too familiar with point-of-purchase displays in retail stores such as supermarkets. They are often placed at impulse points, such as the checkout counters, where people congregate and wait. Research has indicated that merchandise displayed at the payment area in stores has a much better chance of selling than in the aisles. That's why you see so many magazines, candy, gum and sodas within easy reach of the cash registers. The displays are essentially indoor billboards that fight to gain the customers' attention in the clutter of store interiors. They are another part of your media mix and reinforce all of the other marketing efforts. And point-of-sale materials often create quick response by offering immediate gratification.

This type of sales promotion is not limited to print displays. The use of in-store broadcast is, indeed, a form of point-of-sale messaging. How often have heard over the loudspeaker while you were shopping: "Shoppers, hurry over to our fresh fish department where you'll find lobsters on sale for $7.99 a pound, but only for the next 10 minutes"? The message is usually repeated every two minutes with a new countdown. In addition, in-store radio programming has arrived and represents unique opportunities for promoting sales. We're already finding video monitors on shopping carts, video presentations at the deli counters, big screens in the super hardware and housewares stores—all demonstrating products on sale. Sales promotion is everywhere. It's part of what you must believe in if you want a complete marketing effort.

Sales promotion, then, consists of all of the materials you can use in promoting a sale:

- Slide and sound presentations.
- Flip chart presentations.
- Leave-behind literature.
- Video presentations.
- Premiums and incentives.
- Point-of-sale material.
- Coupons/mail-in rebates.
- Product samples.
- Event marketing.
- Trade shows.
- Contests.
- Discount programs.

A small sample about sampling

Expression unltd. was one of the country's best-known gourmet emporiums, and I would like to return to the subject for a moment.

132

Elaine Yannuzzi, the founder and president, introduced a tremendous cheese department at the suggestion of a friend, the late Sol Zausner, who was renowned in the dairy business and the head of Zausner Foods. Sol convinced Elaine to make a huge commitment to stocking a large variety of cheese (some quite esoteric) at a time (early 1980s) when most of the immediate market ate Cheese Whiz and American cheese. Elaine created a cheese department. She bought freightloads of brie and had enormous success offering huge discounts on wheels of brie. Famous folks from renowned New York suburbs (known for some of the richest pockets in the nation) came to Expression unltd. for the magnificent "wheel deals." But even these folks weren't buying the more unusual cheese she offered. Elaine knew why. The reason was intimidation. So she began a sampling program that, by conservative accounts, cost more than $100,000 per year. She created trays of cheese labeled with suggestions on serving, cooking, when, where and how to eat, etc. Some people came to her store to eat a meal of samples, but she didn't mind. In fact, she encouraged as many people as possible to sample. And she sold tons of cheese as a result, as well as tons of crackers and breadstuffs. The sampling program was costly, but it was a powerful sales promotion tool that allowed even the most sophisticated consumers to preview the product before committing to the purchase.

Today, there are companies that will create sampling programs for your product. It's expensive, but it has proven to be a most successful method of launching a new product or removing inhibitions in the marketplace.

Event marketing

You, as a businessperson, should take a careful look at what events can do for your business and think about the benefits of associating your name with a spectacle that captures TV, radio and print coverage—because it's news as well as entertainment.

The NJFOB (New Jersey Festival of Ballooning) is one of the largest hot air events in the United States. It is held during July at an airport about one hour from midtown Manhattan. The three-day event includes the launch of an enormous number of hot air balloons at dusk, a large display of antique automobiles, children's activities, row after row of vendors offering everything from balloon-related products to a wide range of foods, gifts, crafts, jewelry, clothing and artifacts, and booths for insurance companies, real estate brokers, investment firms, charities and community groups. There are concerts, airplane rides and photo opportunities...and it's covered by the network news, magazines, newspapers and radio stations. And you see some of the most famous corporate names on the balloons themselves. Is it only for the rich and famous companies? Absolutely not. In addition to the larger corporate sponsors, there are loads of small businesses who take advantage of associating themselves with the festival by promoting their products or services at the event. These sponsorships are important—not only to the owners of the balloon festival but to the businesses themselves, who are selling to the substantial crowds who attend the event. They are also selling themselves to other businesses. Typically, considerably more than 100,000 people are physically present at the festival, but that's just the beginning, because the news coverage and the brand identity that accompany the sponsorship can promote a small business way beyond the three days.

Event or sponsorship marketing is on fire because almost all companies can benefit from associating themselves with issues and activities. It broadens their selling appeal and produces an amplified effect that enhances the image of the companies involved. Because of the increasing appeal of this type of marketing, it is sometimes difficult to get involved in sponsorships. The auto racing world is a prime example of how companies create event marketing as part of their mix. Major auto products manufacturers, gas and oil companies and battery companies all look for opportunities to sponsor teams. It's a natural method of reaching their target customers—in a way that is adventuresome, exciting and real. Unlike advertising messages that supplement programming, event marketing takes place in the context of the event itself. Thus, when you see a bright red car whip around the bend with the logo of a motor oil product larger than life on its side, you're seeing the product in an environment filled with people who are keenly interested in the sport and the products relevant to their passion—in this case, cars. Fans are watching the race, aware that the machine and the sponsor are in it together. Can you see the decals as the car turns the corner of the track? Or notice the sleek machine during a pit stop? Or catch sight of the car when it comes by your town on a promotional tour?

Do you get the implication that if the race car team uses that particular product, it must be *great* for *your* automobile?

According to statistics, more than $4.5 billion is now spent on sponsorships annually—for tennis matches, football games, concerts, festivals, baseball games, auto races, arts events and more. What you must remember is that event marketing reaches from international communities (such as the spectators at the Olympics) to local and regional communities. Events are events wherever they occur...and, if your market is within the audience of the specific event, then you can benefit greatly by becoming a sponsor.

What event marketing does for your business:

1. Provides associative/synergistic image-building based on the type or nature of the event. An example of one plus one equaling three.
2. Builds identity to target audience in a highly credible fashion.
3. Allows you to gain valuable public relations.
4. Permits you to be perceived as a benevolent member of your community.
5. Creates loyalty among event enthusiasts.

Event marketing offers your employees an opportunity to become involved in a hands-on approach to promoting the business. Employees should be encouraged to participate and attend the events to which you're aligning yourself. Because of the nature of event marketing, employees become greatly excited by the association of a smaller company with a larger issue or event. I have clients who sponsor hungerthons and festivals that benefit a variety of charities, taking advantage of media tie-ins, and the employees are very much a part of the process.

According to statistics from IEG Sponsorship Report, event marketing is broken down into the following categories:

- Sports: 65 percent.
- Entertainment: 10 percent.
- Cause/charities: 9 percent.
- Arts: 6 percent.
- Festivals: 10 percent.

Important notes

Suffice it to say that, like any other single element in a marketing program, event marketing should not stand alone. It works in concert with the rest of your program and should be considered part of your media mix if an appropriate opportunity is present.

You must choose the event based upon your business requirements, not your personal interests. Remember, you are not your customer. So select an event that is appropriate for your business and use your head, not your gut. Also make sure you have a written contract that details your rights and obligations—particularly as they relate to your ability to be an exclusive owner of a category.

You need to promote your participation in the event to your customers, so don't engage in a sponsorship unless your budget permits you to take advantage of ancillary activities that will enhance the event marketing. You cannot rely upon the event management team to include your message in their marketing communications. You need your own plan and your own ability to sell your participation in this activity. Without the ability to market the event, your results will be less than satisfactory.

Up, up and away

The primary sponsor of the New Jersey Festival of Ballooning is Quick Chek Food Stores, a chain of more than 100 food and food/pharmacy stores. Because this company is a client of mine, I have participated in Quick Chek's association with a variety of events, charities and causes over the years. When they became a corporate sponsor of the balloon festival and received top billing—"Quick Chek's New Jersey Festival of Ballooning"—I was concerned about the association mostly because of a simple, practical issue: the weather! For 362 days each year we planned for this event. We created promotions, tie-ins, advertising, public relations—all contingent upon three days of weather. Balloons don't fly in rain, lightning storms or strong wind. I knew, of course, that the festival owners were protected by insurance, but what about my client? Let's assume that the weather prohibited the event from happening? What then? Would 362 days of planning be in vain? The answer was, probably. Was the event tie-in worth it? The answer again was, probably.

In reality, the event has gone off without a hitch each year. Yes, there's been some rain or drizzle, but nothing that would prohibit the sponsorship from continuing. Still, one wonders about the ramifications of associating with a festival that gets rained out. Clearly, my client remains less concerned with the weather than I do and is heartily committed to continuing the sponsorship.

Sponsoring events gives companies the ability to test new products, launch new ideas and network. It creates enormous equity in brand identities and inflates (pardon the pun) images profoundly. But choose your event carefully. Define your goals and strategies for becoming a sponsor. Define your needs. Pinpoint what you will gain from this association. Think about your customers and whether you can reach them with this event. Explore how your involvement in this marketing effort could spiral. Then climb aboard, and sail up, up and away!

The agony and ecstasy of public relations

Dorothy Parker once said, "I hate writing, but I love having written." That's precisely the way I feel about the entire subject of public relations. I hate doing it, but I love having done it. The reason I hate it is that I'm used to dealing with the hard issues of marketing. As a marketing person, I dictate *what* is marketed, to *whom* and *when*, *where* and *how*. Public relations, on the other hand, denies me the privilege—no, *the right*—to control my universe. It's like ice-skating in March...you know there's some thin ice out there, but you don't know where. I like the control of marketing—knowing exactly when my clients' messages will be disseminated and being able to choose the language, style, graphics, tone and overall theme of the communication. In every other aspect of my life, I exhibit no traits of being a control freak, but in my professional life, I admittedly am one.

Public relations is nonpaid promotion. It requires us to put our message into the hands of the media with no controls at all. At times, it also requires that we expose more than we would like to about our business. I remember an incident that occurred during a marketing campaign for a large multinational company that had gone through some slips and slides in the past decade. I had an opportunity to place a feature story about the company with a noted magazine. This represented an opportunity to express a message in a way that would be unsurpassed by any other form of promotion. I contacted the marketing director and told her with great exuberance that I had made a contact that would result in a feature story. She was equally excited. Two hours later she called to tell me to kill the story. The president of the company didn't want to run the risk of the publication getting a hold of some old information and referencing it. He was so afraid of risking the exposure of some old closeted skeletons that he passed on this enormous opportunity. In a way, I understood his concern. Public relations runs a fine line between being an asset and a liability.

Trade talk

Business-to-business publicity lives by different principles than the consumer press. The adage in trade P.R. is "Ink is ink." Indeed, some people believe that any publicity is better than none at all. That's probably true in trade circles because rarely will trade media run the risk of offending an advertiser or potential advertiser. The relationship between editorial and advertising is much closer in trade publishing than it is in consumer circles. Articles often support advertising.

Your goal in business-to-business public relations is to have press releases run as often as possible, covering every interesting aspect of your company. You can begin with new product releases, which should always be accompanied by a photograph. Then, of course, every personnel shift or change should be supported by a press release. Any conceivable occurrence should be considered for publicity. Remember, you are talking to your own industry or to industries that can use your product or service.

For example, if you are creating publicity for your accounting firm, consider where major clients come from. What are your specialties? Who is likely to respond to a firm your size? How well-known is your company in the industry you're targeting? What unique strengths do your partners have that can be exploited in industry publications? I suggested to a large accounting firm that it run advertising and offer publicity releases to a medical journal.

Why? Because several of its partners were extremely well-versed in handling problems specific to medical partnerships, practitioners and health care facilities. Publicity material drawing on these strengths were created. The response was significant because the article was informational, credible, readable, honest and nonpromotional. In fact, the only references to the specific practice were the name and title of the author (one of the accounting partners) and one reference to the name and location of the firm.

A prestigious insurance brokerage company had a partner who was extremely knowledgeable in the graphic arts field. In fact, he was so well-known in the printing trade that he became an expert on insurance matters for a regional segment of the industry. He became a "media source" and was called upon to elaborate on the various pitfalls of insuring printers. The publicity and advertising targeted the trade with intense spirit, and he developed into a *brand* for the graphic arts field. Thus, when graphic arts companies needed insurance or insurance information, they automatically called upon this firm.

An expert is someone who is quoted

A friend of mine who is a nationally recognized consultant in political and association circles made this statement to me recently. It's true. But the big question is, how does one *become* an expert?

Public relations works beautifully when you become a source for both trade or consumer information—someone who is called upon for sound bites and quotes and referenced as an authority, a specialist, a mentor! This doesn't happen magically. It requires hard work, commitment and dedication. It begins with correspondence to the media, which must be continuous and unrelenting. Your first order of business will be to send a letter to local editors. In addition to the standard introduction, you should include quotes from a variety of people about yourself, referencing your strengths and accomplishments. Be sure to use real names, companies and credible quotes. Don't overinflate the statements! Too often, testimonials are weakened by exaggerations such as "Mr. Jones is the best accountant in the United States today." Keep it sane and believable!

Professional practice

Professional practices, organizations and associations require a bit more finesse when it comes to promotion. Solicitation needs to be more subtle. Public relations, therefore, is a preferred method of communicating because it is perceived as noncommercial. The purpose is to gain your prospects' attention in a way that appears to be based completely upon third-party interest. The information needs to look like news, not advertising, creating a greater level of comfort for doctors, dentists, lawyers, accountants, engineers, architects—all of whom have not had long histories of seeing their peers promote.

As the rules for this type of promotion have evolved, professionals now have the ability to both ethically and legally create advertising. But advertising has remained shaky ground for many in the professional arena. The preferred venues are still public relations and subtle information-giving methods such as targeted mailings, referral communication materials, cross-promotions with other professionals, seminars and networking.

How to become a media source

If you're in a mainstream business, you need to do all of the same things as professionals, but you need not be concerned with the perception that you are commercial. Public relations can make you an expert if you have something new to say or a new way of saying it:

1. Write an article about your industry without mentioning your own business. Speak about the concerns that are common to everyone and elaborate with authority, citing examples that support your claims.

2. Begin a letter-writing campaign to the trade press editors who are responsible for your area of expertise.

3. Write a short press release covering initial subject matter.

4. Send an audiotape to area radio stations of a staged interview between a staff member (moderator) and yourself.

5. Create a press kit that includes all of the above materials and a photo of yourself mounted on a professional resume.

6. Create a library of reference materials that can be called upon for adding integrity to your claims.

7. Offer to speak at industry gatherings, trade shows and professional associations.

8. Subscribe to (and consider listing in) *Experts, Authorities and Spokespersons,* a yellow page type of publication that lists speakers and authorities by category. (I've included the Washington, D.C. address and phone number on the next page.)

9. Create a press event for your company, inviting prospects to attend a party with refreshments, entertainment and information. You are the keynote speaker and will be distributing valuable resource material to attendees.

10. Contact local cable television talk shows and include information on your specific areas of expertise, awards and previous press coverage.

The next time you pick up your newspaper, trade magazine or professional journal, stop and think about the stories you're reading. If there's an article in the health section of the paper regarding a new method of reconstructing hips or knees or replacing joints, and a local orthopedist is quoted, how do you think that particular doctor happened to become the expert referenced in the story? By accident or design? Bingo, if you said "design." Public relations is usually so subtle that readers have no idea that almost every quoted source in both consumer and trade articles comes from a public relations effort.

The goal for business owners and professionals is to become a source for stories. Get yourself quoted often enough so that your name and identity become synonymous with your area of specialization.

Good P.R. doesn't live by words alone

I know of a college president who prides himself on being a magician at creating public relations opportunities, not necessarily in the traditional sense, but rather in the "relationship" sense. He has been known to offer his preferred parking space for a month to a faculty member who has exhibited some form of excellence, has reached a goal established by the college or has been nominated by peers for an act of kindness. The parking space is the incentive, but the ensuing publicity in the school newspaper and the faculty journal is what it's really about.

This particular president looks for every opportunity to motivate his staff. Thus, he offers awards and rewards for virtually every conceivable activity. So, for example, if 92 percent of the students in a particular class achieve A grades, the professor is awarded a plaque in the "hall of achievement." Then, of course, the faculty member is taken to lunch, written about in an interoffice memo and reported upon in the faculty journal.

In addition, the student newspaper prints it as a publicity release. It also goes on the professor's permanent record, and the credit for this academic achievement is given to the teacher, not the students. It works. It's a public relations program designed to invite and incite excellence. And often all it takes is the issuance of a publicity release. So, let's learn to write one.

How to be an expert, authority or spokesperson

A marvelous reference book called *Experts, Authorities and Spokespersons* is the verified source of media interviews for virtually every possible topic. I stumbled upon this book by accident many years ago, and I have been a big fan of it ever since. Because it is sent to the news media to be used as a sourcebook for speakers, experts and authorities in various fields, if you are included in it, you become a recognized spokesperson in your area of expertise. It is requested by national news media, including the major networks, cable TV stations, radio stations, newspaper editors, magazines, national newsletters, celebrated journalists...the list goes on and on. The top 10 states for the 14th edition in terms of requests include Washington, D.C., New York, California, Virginia, Maryland, Illinois, Florida, Pennsylvania, New Jersey and Texas...all major markets.

Most recently, 10,794 copies of the 14th edition were mailed to major media companies and individuals. It is a marvelous publication for the entrepreneur who is in hot pursuit of publicity and yearns to be considered an industry expert. The topics include money management, manufacturing, business, telecommunications, family, retailing, the environment, motivation, computers, education, counseling...every conceivable topic.

For information about being listed in this media source directory, contact:

Broadcast Interview Source
2233 Wisconsin Ave. NW
Washington, D.C. 20007
800-YEARBOOK
Web address: http://www.yearbook.com

There are both reference listings and display advertisements available to individuals who wish to be included in this directory.

How to prepare a press release

Writing a press release is quite simple. Unlike the more creative process of producing an ad, publicity requires a more straightlaced approach. Here are the basic elements in a consumer or business-to-business press release:

- **Date** (day, month and year of publicity being issued).

- **For** (name of company being publicized).

- **Contact** (name of person who can be contacted if more information is required).

- **For Immediate Release** (or date you would like the story published).

- **City and state of business being publicized.**

- **Headline** (offers primary news objective).

- **Subheadline** (optional, reinforces the headline).

- **Text** (the story in concise language—maintaining editorial style and integrity).

- **Closing** (pertinent information regarding address, phone and anything else that gives the reader necessary data).

Use your letterhead to create your press release. Be sure to double space, leaving sufficient margins. You are issuing facts, not opinions. The headline should get right to the point. An example appears on page 143.

The subheadline and text should always immediately support the headline. So, get right to the point and provide the reader with a string of sentences that gives the necessary information. Tell who, what, when, where and why the incident is occurring and, whenever possible, use quotes from the insiders of the story.

Remember that regardless of the reader (trade or consumer), the issues are essentially the same. The press release is a news offering—so don't cloud it with superfluous statements.

Say it, then say it again

Whenever you engage in a publicity effort, you must remain dogged in pursuit of your goal: *media coverage*. I have seen stories published because of aggressive marketing, not only newsworthiness. The nature of publicity is such that it is incumbent upon you to get to know editors by phone, letter or fax, sending creative packages about your company...whatever it takes.

Sample Press Release

Date: September 12, 1996
For: Techno-Forms International
Contact: Jim March, 800-555-4334
For Immediate Release
Dayton, Ohio—

Techno-Forms International to Merge with Comquest Corporation
New Company to be Called Com-Tech Global Industries

Dayton, Ohio—The President of Techno-Forms International announced today that the company would merge with Comquest Corporation of Indianapolis, Indiana. The merger will bring together two leaders in digital printing to form a company with far greater ability to handle national and international clients.

John Pallini, President of Techno-Forms, will assume the leadership role in the new company. According to Mr. Pallini, "The merger will allow our new company to compete in the global market and to invest in the advancement of new technologies that will ultimately strengthen our research and development capacity. This will produce more economic methods of high-speed, high-capacity digital printing."

Com-Tech Global Industries will build an additional 23,000 square feet in Dayton, Ohio, and will move Techno-Forms into the new facility. The merger will result in the hiring of more than 100 technical people—in addition to those staff members who will be moving from Indiana.

For literature on the new company and its capabilities, contact Jim March at 800-555-4334 or fax your request to 800-555-4287.

When I lecture to professional groups on professional practice promotion, the most-asked question relates to how to get press coverage. Again, because professionals are more sensitive to being overtly promotional, publicity is an attractive method of being heard. On one occasion, a dentist came up to me after the seminar and mentioned a litany of issues that he felt might warrant publicity for his group practice. Of the 17 issues he referenced, I only heard two. First, I heard him say that he was in practice with his two children—both dentists. Second, he said that his own background included training and teaching that made him one of 14 practitioners in the country who were certified in a specific area of dentistry. Two stunning statements for a marketing consultant to hear. The press release went out the very next day:

A Family of Practitioners for Your Entire Family

Only 14 dentists in the U.S. are certified to perform implant dentistry...one of them is in your own backyard!

Both headline and subheadline drew attention to the interesting, newsworthy, distinguishing factors that readers would find compelling. The text immediately supported these statements, offering readers insight into a family of dentists, one of whom was nationally recognized. The fact that this story had human interest and unusual appeal and cited a noted professional in a local environment contributed to its acceptance as an article. The newspaper (a large daily) sent a reporter to get the story. After three hours of interviews, a full-page article was published, and the practice was the focus of regional attention. Of particular interest to the readers was the story of a father and two children—all of whom attended the same dental school and ended up practicing together.

Our purpose in creating the press release was not to see it published as written, but rather to get the attention of the editor and create a dialogue. This is a good lesson to remember. Most often, what you write will not be published without changes, a new slant or an interview in order to get to the real story. Use the press release to tease and excite an editor. Give information, but make sure you provide as many unique aspects to the story as possible. The news media wants factual, honest information, but they also want readable copy.

Many companies spend a great deal of time and energy developing editorial relationships. A wonderful win-win situation is developed when the editor relies upon a qualified source to provide insight, counsel and information that can be used in the development of a story.

When an enormous international dairy, located in Denmark, wanted to launch a wide range of cheese products in the United States, we created a relationship with trade and consumer editors by making them aware of the products and the company. We did so by mailing press kits to the media people, including samples of products, literature, ad reprints and an invitation to a large press event at the most famous Scandinavian restaurant in New York City. This event coincided with a trade show that took place each summer.

The evening was planned with great care and everything we did pointed to the culinary artistry of Denmark and the magnificent cheese products to come out of this beautiful country. A magician incorporated the products and the Scandinavian theme into his performance— photos were taken and there were contests with prizes that included trips to Denmark. The buildup to the event included highly creative mailings with gift tie-ins such as clocks, a road atlas, watches, aprons, umbrellas—all coordinated to the theme of a specific letter (for example, the clock mailing contained a letter headlined, "Isn't it about *time* you tasted Denmark?"). Key food editors at publications (both national and regional) received these theme mailings once every 10 days for 40 days. Relationships that worked for everyone developed. When a particular editor had an article idea or wanted to round out a story idea for the holiday, a dialogue ensued and my clients' products were referenced in the piece. Individuals at the cheese company became consultants to the editors—offering information, research, statistics, marketing trends—and the result was an ongoing rapport that resulted in lots of great press coverage.

Good public relations can result from good human kindness. Many companies remain in the public eye by a continuing association with charitable relationships. The peripheral benefit is that a company is well thought of. This type of benevolence works on many levels. Companies that create goodwill often become the focus of articles, documentaries, interviews and features that focus on the positive side of corporate America. Small businesses have grabbed the baton, as well, with programs that give something back to the community. Choose your association with a benefactor, and don't be afraid to toot your own horn. Creating good news is refreshing!

As a businessperson, you've got to be willing to work the press. Editors are people. They respond to news of all sorts. Get to know the appropriate editor and be obsessive about sending out press releases. Don't overlook any possible tie-in or announcement. Be creative in approaching your subject matter. Think about the benefits to readers, and remember who you are addressing. Publicity is, after all, public information.

So don't write about private events that will be construed as promotional. Don't send a major daily newspaper a story about your company picnic. It's inappropriate. The same story might very well be interesting news for your local weekly or the shopper. By the same token, don't send strong news to the weekly. Keep the important issues going to the larger media. And remember, if it looks like news, acts like news and sounds like news, it's probably news!

Chapter 11

The Passion Principles: Unbridling Your Creativity

Make some heat. Create some noise. Ruffle some feathers. Shake things up a little—no, a lot. Light a flare in the crowded marketplace, then step back and watch everyone watching you. It's called *getting noticed,* and it requires more than catchy headlines or colorful graphics. *It requires passion!*

The Passion Principles are the heart and soul of marketing. They are the creative ideas, the power that propels products through the rough seas toward the promised land. They are ultimately responsible for the success or failure of services, people and products. This chapter will include the principles as well as the creative process. You will learn how to write an ad, a brochure, a radio script, a television script and just about anything else that might become part of your marketing plan. It's time to take a look at how we conduct business and what creative marketing entails. The Passion Principles also include a variety of compelling notions designed to make your marketing efforts dynamic, different and distinctively your own.

Fasten your seatbelts...we're about to take off

Sit back. Relax. Prop your feet up on the ottoman. Unbutton your top button. You're about to change the way you see things.

Fold your arms in front of you. Comfortable? Good. Now, fold them with the other arm on top. Uncomfortable? Good. Change is tough, isn't it? Changing the way you do things is difficult, at best. It's why so few people actually change. And it's why so few businesses make changes about the way they do business.

Change often involves pain as well as passion. It requires that you see things differently—even if you've been seeing the same way for 50 years. Marketing is about change. It's about massaging our systems—reevaluating the way we do business, the way we see business, the way we create business. Companies who don't change usually don't survive the changes in the marketplace. Imagine if you made buggy whips and didn't see the changes coming. What about typewriter companies? Adding machines? Turntables? You get the idea.

Once you've decided that change is necessary and that there might be a better way to do business, you're ready to digest the Passion Principles. But first, let's begin by looking at the way you think. Creative thinking is really about changing the way you see things. It's about looking at the same issues as well as new ones with rose-colored glasses or sky blue glasses or pink glasses. It's about taking off the gloves, removing the blinders, breaking through the ruts, creating new paths to success.

Great marketing is the way you see your business once you've seen your customer. When one of the founders of Blockbuster Video and Boston Chicken was interviewed, the question posed to him was, "Why did you get into the rotisserie chicken business?"

His answer was absolutely brilliant. He stated, "Rotisserie chicken? Who says we're in the chicken business? We're in the multiunit franchise business. We just happen to be selling chicken."

This, by the way, is the same man who is now creating a used car dealership network on a branded basis with warranties, credibilities and endless opportunities! There are millions of used cars in the marketplace, yet no one has thought of creating a national dealership chain with the kind of identity that this venture will entail. This is breakthrough thinking...and it happens far too infrequently in business.

Your job is to begin to look at things from a different angle. The logical place to start is with your existing business. Every business has bad habits. We sustain them because we haven't thought of or acted upon ways to improve them...until now. We're about to break the bad habits and create new opportunities.

Begin at the beginning

It's 8 a.m. Monday morning. Your staff meeting is about to begin. The eight people in your company are seated at the conference room table. Everyone's tired. Everyone's a little anxious. Everyone's more than a little ready for their second cup of coffee. This is where your week begins...right here in the Monday morning meeting. Usually your first order of business is to review projects and make sure everyone is where they ought to be. Then, you check off the status of each assignment and confer about billing, problems, priorities, emergencies. Then you might chat a few moments and dismiss everyone to their duties.

What's wrong with this scene? Nothing if you're totally happy with your present success. But change begins at the beginning, and our beginnings are Monday mornings. The first issue in creative marketing is marketing to your own people. Your most valuable asset is your people. They make the product or the service salable, or they contribute to inhibiting the sale.

8 a.m. Monday morning. The coffee pot's full. The bagels and condiments are on an inviting tray. You begin by applauding the past week's successes. A job that was done well. A new client. A large sale. A cost-saving measure that was introduced. A valuable suggestion from someone who's usually withdrawn and quiet. A staff member who created a new way of looking at an old problem. Any excuse for piling on the praise should be incorporated into your plan. After all, you're about to begin a marketing program that's designed to market your business to your own people. It's a logical place to start. Most businesses don't encourage creative communication among team members, even if they are forward-thinking enough to have adopted a "team" philosophy.

Remember, every time you assemble your staff, you're conducting a sales and marketing meeting. By thinking of your own people as the customer, you are forcing yourself to constantly think about how you conduct business, how you market your product, how you are perceived. Following the Passion Principles, we will begin creative exercises that will illustrate to you how you can alter others' perceptions of your business by becoming "the Pied Piper." But first, the Passion Principles. These principles are an integral part of the creative marketing process.

Passion Principle #1: The Four A's

The Four A's—Acknowledgment, Achievement, Accomplishment, Admiration—constitute Passion Principle #1. Collectively, they are your four reasons for being, and they should remain an active part of your overall marketing effort.

How do you acknowledge excellence? How do you mark achievement? How do you recognize accomplishment? When do you communicate admiration? I'm not just talking about incentives for making sales or a bonus at the end of the year. I'm speaking of a real commitment to keeping people connected to a common goal. The number-one motivator is acknowledgment or recognition. Sometimes it's as simple as remembering birthdays or anniversaries or acknowledging people because they're innovative. We tend to reward busyness, not innovation. But in truth, *busy* isn't necessarily *profitable*. Seventy percent of employees don't speak up because of fear of reprisal. If your team is afraid to push the envelope because they might be perceived as off-base, you're missing marketing opportunities every day. A situation that involves fear in the employee pool leads to a lack of extra effort. By putting passion into play in the workplace—you're inviting and inciting positive responses. Remember, people feel nameless and faceless without acknowledgment. It's hard to get good ideas from invisible people.

Your employees are your customers

One of my clients wanted to motivate its sales force. We discussed the usual incentives—money, electronics, trips. For the most part, they work rather well. But like everything else in business, they're subject to the *three-year itch*. I tell my clients, "Every three years, you have to change policies and procedures. You have to take a look at the way you do business with your own people...then scratch, refresh and reissue."

Well, the incentive plan we were discussing was almost four years old. It had gone almost a year beyond the three-year itch. So I asked the president of the company what he knew about each of the key sales managers and members of his field sales staff. After all, there were only 17 of them. He didn't know nearly enough about any of them and only a little bit about six of them. First, I said, we're going to get to know them. Each one of these individuals has a different interest and each one will be motivated in his or her own way, but we won't know any of this until we know them.

We spoke to the people who worked with them. Then we spoke to the people who worked for them. Then we spoke to each of them *about* each of them. Then we conducted personal interviews—social interviews called The Up Close & Personal Plan. The human resources manager conducted these sessions as though they were first interviews. In fact, many of them had not been interviewed with such intensity when they were first hired. We were careful not to intimidate them by establishing certain ground rules. We told them:

1. The Up Close & Personal Plan was only for key producers. (This put a positive spin on the process.)

2. The process was designed to create a more cohesive team.

3. The information was to remain completely confidential (between employee and employer).

The interview consisted of questions about their family life, recreational life, hobbies, automobiles, homes, spouses, children, parents, background, aspirations and problems. Essentially, we were looking for their pain and pleasure.

The result yielded a great deal of information that was put into a plan. The plan was to create individual incentives based upon individual preferences, lifestyles, needs and desires.

In one case, we sent a specific salesperson's spouse a dozen red roses each time he hit quota. We had learned in The Up Close & Personal interview that his wife was passionate about roses. This was part of the company's way of keeping the commitment to the four A's.

Another member of the sales team was an avid canoeist. She was acknowledged for her performance by receiving an Old Town canoe, purported to be one of the finest made. She was not only surprised but truly moved by the very personal nature of the gift and the fact that someone had taken the time and interest to focus on what made her happy. Her total commitment was greatly reinforced, and she was more motivated and more loyal than ever before.

Passion Principle #2: The power of possession

The saying is that possession is nine-tenths of the law. The real question is, "Who owns what?"

Auto dealers can drive you crazy and Realtors can put you in the nut house

There are two major purchases for most families: a house and a car. Amazingly, most Realtors and car dealers have never made a study of marketing. Imagine that. Houses and cars cost more than anything else we purchase in our lifetime. Yet, in both cases, the marketers of these commodities have little or no marketing experience. Now, while it's true that many individuals do a credible job, these industries don't pay nearly enough attention to training people how to market... or if they do, there's little evidence of it. I use these two areas of business as examples because they represent huge amounts of money to the average consumer.

The customer falls in love with a car. The power of possession is in the hands of the car dealer. But the dealer doesn't know how to use the power. Why? Because no one has taught the dealer the simple rule of possession. If you're a car dealer and you have a product that a consumer wants, all you have to do is deliver it. Right? *Remember, you don't want to own the car—you want to own the customer.*

Remember, the car dealer has the product the consumer wants. The manufacturer spent enormous sums of money to get its message into the consumers' consciousness, and it worked. Now there's a customer who wants possession of the vehicle, but the automobile dealer has ownership. What the automobile dealer very often doesn't see is that what's necessary in transferring ownership is simply giving the key to the customer. By giving the customer the power to start the car, so to speak, the dealer is taking a passive, rather than aggressive, role. Traditionally, car salespeople were taught to pressure, cajole, even stand between the customer and the exit. But what does the customer really want? The customer wants to feel in control...so give the customer the keys!

The hard sell makes selling hard

The average consumer shopping for a car thinks that price will drive the sale. In truth, price is only one of several issues. If you own the dealership, consider that your industry image is poor. Don't feel badly because you've undoubtedly been part of the problem, not the solution. For many years, car dealers have contributed heartily to creating the worst image in commerce. Why? Because they, too, thought the deal was in the price. When you shift the emphasis away from the price (acknowledge the deal and the value) and begin to give control to the customer, the issue of price becomes secondary, not primary. The business owns the product. Good marketing creates demand. Demand produces desire. Now you've got a customer who desires your product. You're halfway home. Don't blow it by trying to maintain control.

Put the customer in the driver's seat

When I purchased my first new car, a bright red Pontiac Firebird with a four-speed manual transmission, I was armed with the traditional belief that I would have to fight with the dealer to gain control. After all, it was the dealer who had what I wanted and only money stood between us. So I went to several area dealers to get the best price. The most conveniently located dealership was the last I visited. The salesman was an older fellow who was extremely pleasant. I went in, expecting an adversarial scene. Instead, I was met by someone exhibiting peculiar behavior. He was very nice, not in a patronizing way, but in a decidedly sincere way.

He began by telling me the pitfalls of the car I wanted, offering alternative models. He mentioned the less-than-average rating by *Consumer Reports* magazine. He also suggested that the gas consumption was relatively poor. He even suggested that I test-drive it in rainy weather before I made up my mind. Then, after all was said and done, he told me that if I was sure about the car, it would be wise to wait the two months for the new model to come out because it would have better features and the resale value would be higher. He gave me control. We never talked about price until later. He also told me that, while he would always try to match the best price, he would give me, in writing, three things that created additional value. One was a free loaner program. Two was delivery of the vehicle to my home or office (long before this was done). Three was two free simonize applications during the first year of ownership. Next, he took me to the service manager and introduced me. He showed me around the service area and walked me through the parts department. I didn't ask for any of this, but I was sold. He put the power into my hands and made the sale an easy experience for me. When it came time to discuss price, he was $90 higher than the lowest price I had gotten from another dealer. I couldn't bring myself to negotiate. Why?

Because he had prenegotiated by giving me value I had not requested. And he never attempted the hard sell. He never dangled the keys, he just handed them to me and said, "Drive!"

Saturn is one company that broke the mold. It established a system of selling and a marketing plan that reinvented dealerships. It invited the customer in. It nurtured the customer with a concept of family membership. It created a cult. It issued a strong statement to the rest of the car universe: *We're going to be better because we recognize the problems associated with our own industry.*

Possession is more than ownership. It's capturing the marketplace with tentacles that rock, cradle and move people. Saturn knows this, and it has redefined automobile marketing by creating an identity that strongly resembles community and friendship. It acknowledges that it has a strong brand. It also acknowledges that you are special for recognizing this. You possess each other.

You're on third base and you're going home

Developers, Realtors, builders and even homeowners can all learn from the same experience. In the case of a home, the keys open the door to even larger dreams than those associated with a car. Home ownership is, after all, part of the great American dream. But often both the seller and the buyer see the experience as competitive rather than cooperative. So, obstacles are placed in the path of the sale. If you see the power differently and establish a dialogue with the customer even before he or she arrives, you're beginning to transfer the authority to the buyer (after all, they're making the decision to buy). Remember, everyone's scared. Buying or selling a high-ticket item creates more tension and anxiety than buying or selling a pack of gum. But the principles are the same. You've got a product you want to sell and someone else wants to buy.

You've already heard about Realtors putting vanilla extract into a pot of boiling water, baking muffins, using floral aerosol sprays, making sure there's a fire in the fireplace, keeping the kids out of the house when prospects are walking through, uncluttering closets, keeping the verticals open so the sun shines in and on and on. That's all part of merchandising and it certainly has its place, but the real marketing of a home or any high-ticket item comes from the contact and conduct of seller and buyer. And it has to do with the power of possession.

When my friend wanted to sell her home, she created a marketing strategy. After all, she said, "Wouldn't you want a marketing plan for a $350,000 business?"

Of course, she was right. Marketing real estate is a business even if you're selling your own home. So, after many failed attempts of marketing the home through Realtors, she set out to create the most dynamic marketing program possible. The cornerstone of the program was to differentiate her product from all the other homes for sale in the area. None of the Realtors had developed a strategy. Together, we did. Her idea (a brilliant one) was to market the home as an estate sale with ads in the classified sections of *The New York Times* and *The Wall Street Journal*. Because her mother had recently passed away, the home was, in essence, being sold as an estate property. In truth, estate sales have more panache because the perception is that they're being sold cheaper.

Further, the property was quite prestigious but couldn't be seen from the street because of the lush foliage, trees and bushes in front of the home. Anticipating the problem, she had enough of the obstruction cleared in order to "frame the home" from the approaching roadway. Because it sat high on a hill, the presentation was remarkable. Next, she loaded the opportunity with features and benefits. She included many items that would normally be part of a negotiation process, giving the buyer the choice of taking them or leaving them. She also created a brochure for prospective buyers. It detailed the history of the house, the property, the community. It offered information about the school system and hospitals and included articles touting the community as one of the most desirable in the Northeast. Restaurants, libraries, recreational centers, parks, banks, important local businesses were all listed and critiqued. It was magical. She had given the buyer the power to buy. Each prospect had the resources to make an intelligent decision in addition to a passionate decision. She made it easy, and it was. The third couple who looked at the house bought it. My friend got her price, and the buyers got theirs.

Personal selling played a key role, as well. The seller sat down and discussed each issue of concern, removing each obstacle whenever possible. She modeled her marketing method after Nordstrom's. The answer to each reasonable query was "no problem." And both parties came away feeling like winners. The seller acknowledged that she wanted to sell, and the buyer expressed keen interest in buying. The only real issue was the transference of the possession. The marketing program had done its job—it attracted the customer. The customer now had to be made to feel in control. The seller gave the buyer that control when she acknowledged her interest in satisfying the buyers' needs without deeply compromising her own needs. When the buyers asked if they could bring family members to see the house, or if they could take measurements, bring carpet swatches, floor tiles...the seller went beyond their requests. She offered to introduce them to the neighbors. She even left the house so they could experience each room at their leisure. She gave them the authority and the control they needed to feel like owners before the papers were final.

Passion Principle #3: Creating quality experiences

In *The Incredible Power of Cooperation*, Kaoru Ishikawa states, "Why fight among yourselves when you can unify and win?" Winning isn't about one party being on top and one on the bottom. It isn't knocking out the competition or taking advantage of the customer. It's *about unification*. It's about marketing that truly makes a difference to both parties. It's about establishing guidelines that lead to success. It's about taking care of the customer. It's about discipline. And remember, don't fall in love with the product, fall in love with the customer! A marvelous example of this type of thinking takes place at the Disney Corporation. Disney's four disciplines are listed in order of priority:

1. Safety.
2. Courtesy.
3. Show/entertain.
4. Efficiency.

Does Disney have to market these concepts? The answer is a resounding no. The reason is simple: Disney owns these disciplines. It has created an identity that is synonymous with each of these noble issues. Disney equals the quality experience.

Decisions are easy when values are clear. The marketing decisions made by an organization are quite simple once a philosophy has been established. You are a marketer. You're in business to succeed. That means you're in business to have others succeed, as well.

You know how it feels to be a customer. Have you ever walked away from an experience feeling cheated? Have you ever felt taken advantage of? Have you been angry during or after a business transaction? Have you felt as though you and your feelings didn't matter one bit to the seller? In order to be a better businessperson, you must first place yourself in the position of the customer, your own customer. Ask yourself these questions:

1. Is this a quality experience?
2. What could make this better for me?
3. Do I feel important?
4. What makes the experience positive or negative?

If you understand how the customer feels—really feels about your business—creating a quality experience is not hard. Business owners often get stuck in unconscious incompetence, otherwise known as "the rut." This occurs because we listen to our past, not our future. If you are in business, you do business by rote. It's like rowing without using the strength of your legs. You've been rowing with your arms for so long, your legs have weakened. Then someone tells you, "Use your legs—you'll go faster," and all of a sudden, you're moving with much greater efficiency.

The genesis for creating the quality experience begins with awareness. Awareness is followed by discipline. Discipline is followed by change. W. Edward Demming, founder of the Total Quality Management movement, states, "I'm not here to answer your questions. I'm here to question your answers."

When you create positive perceptions, approximately one-third of the people affected will relate the experience to others. Interestingly, bad news travels farther. More than two-thirds of the people affected by a negative experience will happily relate that experience. The lesson: *People love to trash!*

Does everyone in your organization consider themselves to have customers? Or are the customers only customers to the sales staff or the owners? Our goal is to have each member of your business connected to the customer, if not directly (actual contact), then emotionally and intellectually. If a person who does word processing or filing for your company keeps the customer in mind and is constantly reminded of the importance of the customer, his or her performance will be far more directed. You can enhance this experience by creating incentives that affect everyone on the staff—not just those directly involved with the customer. Make the people who are in support positions become directly affected by the efforts of the entire company and directly affected by the customer!

There is a hotel chain that goes to great lengths to create a quality experience for its customers—all of its customers. But like any business, the hotel chain is aware of its most important clientele—the business traveler. So, when you, the guest, get out of your car, and the valet takes your bags, he or she will say something such as, "It's so good to see you again. You were here not long ago, weren't you sir (or ma'am)?"

The valet has scoped you out. You look and sound like a business traveler. And it's a good bet you've been to the hotel before.

"Yes, as a matter of fact, I was here about a month ago," you say.

"Good to have you with us again," comes the reply.

Just as you are within earshot of the check-in counter, the clerk says, "It's so nice to have you with us again."

Huh? How did that happen? How did they know to make you feel so important? It's really quite simple and quite brilliant. The bellhop tugged on his ear as he approached the check-in counter. That signaled the clerk that you're a regular customer of the hotel, and as such, you're about to be made to feel very important. That's the beginning of your quality experience at that particular hotel. Your business depends upon total cooperation when it comes to company spirit. If the person who's out front gives your customers the wrong signals, the results can be disastrous.

There's a moment of truth. It takes place so quickly that you can hardly notice it. It's the tough tone of voice on the part of one of your customer service representatives. It might be a flippant remark from one staff member to another. It could be a wisecrack you yourself as a business owner make to one of your sales staff. It may be a bit too much attitude toward a difficult customer. The moment of truth comes quickly. So, remember the four possibilities that exist in conducting business:

1. Negativity. You're about to drown.

2. Indifference. The boat's taking on water.

3. Positivity. You're really starting to sail.

4. Magic. You're going to win the cup.

You're always marketing—from the moment you open the door to your business until the moment you close it behind you at the end of the day. You're marketing to your own people, your customers and your future customers. Negativity strangles the marketing process. Indifference makes it near impossible to achieve any of your goals. Positivity means you're on the right track. Magic means you've gone way past what you have to do in order to achieve results that exceed and delight both your customers and yourself. Make some magic...create quality experiences and hear the register ring!

Take another look at the quality experience you're offering your customers. Does it contain some magic? Remember, that's your goal. It's a marketing imperative. Use the following checklist to get closer to a quality experience. Remember, you can't have all the answers unless you know all the questions.

Quality experience checklist

1. Do you review your product or service relative to continuing improvements?

2. Do you give your customer enough information to fully benefit from the product?

3. Do you guarantee the product?

4. Do you establish win-win guidelines?

5. Does the product pass rigid tests?

6. Do you constantly review competitive products in order to stay ahead in the marketplace?

7. Is personal service a critical issue?

8. Does the entire team play by the rules?

9. Do you ask the customers what makes them happy?

10. Do you give the customers three things they haven't asked for?

Most customers leave because of poor service and poor experiences. The cost of a poor experience is great. The cost of winning customers back is even greater. A quality experience begins from the second a customer is made aware of a product or service. This is where the marketing effort either succeeds or fails. *Remember, you never get a second chance to make a first impression.*

Why banks fail

Actually, I'm not referring to bankruptcy—I'm referring to the failure to win customers over. Why would an institution that holds your mortgage, car loan, savings account, vacation club and college fund treat you poorly? That's a good question. Many banks teach tellers to be staid, not personable. They want to be perceived as authoritative. It's quite puzzling. I recently met with a bank officer in order to express my anger about the way I was treated at a particular branch. The teller only created obstacles, providing no solutions to a problem with a third-party check—in spite of the fact that I was known to the bank personnel. Instead of creating a quality experience for both of us, she couldn't see beyond the boundaries of bank policy. It really wasn't her fault. In truth, she wasn't given the flexibility and authority to market well, and she was justified in being cautious. She simply wasn't trained to use discretion in order to create a quality experience. Discretion, in this case, would have been to acknowledge that I was a frequent customer—holding multiple accounts in the bank. The bank manager didn't even offer an apology, only an explanation. Explanations without empathy toward the customer do not create quality experiences. I was finally able to cash the check, but it didn't feel good. And the bank lost my loyalty. The bank is now vulnerable because one of its assets is looking at the bank's competition. If you've never experienced a similar teller tale, you're in the great minority, I assure you.

Being violated at the Division of Motor Vehicles

Have you ever heard of unconscious incompetence? Well, it's alive and well at the Division of Motor Vehicles. It's not that I expected to be treated well or to have a quality experience while getting my license renewed. But I was truly surprised to be treated with such complete indifference. After all, I'm a customer, right? Wrong! The reason I wasn't treated like a customer was because the people in the motor vehicle business don't perceive the relationship to be seller/buyer-oriented. They believe that their service is a privilege, not a right (have you ever heard the term "driving privileges"?). Thus, the experience is nonquality-oriented. They never learned that when it comes to marketing a product, you need to be an educator, not a predator.

We never want our customers to be waiting in long lines. Truly innovative businesses create quality solutions to this problem. One restaurant owner I know brings a tray of appetizers to those in line. He offers complimentary soft drinks and never leaves the customers, and the customers never leave the line.

The quality experience begins in the mind of the customer

Customers have different expectations based upon their experiences. I didn't expect to be treated so poorly in the bank, but I fully expected a poor experience in the Division of Motor Vehicles office. Expectations are issues for both you (the business owner) and the customer. When they are in synch, the experience is the same for both parties. Anticipating what the customer wants and giving him or her more are essential to creating a quality experience. Creating a product with features that don't meet but rather exceed customer expectations is part of the process as well. When you exceed the need, you are truly making marketing memorable for the customer. Insisting on quality standards for both products and the people who sell them is another essential. The customer is, after all, always the customer.

What a way to start your day

Many years ago there was a coffee shop near my office. The owner was an affable fellow who gave a free lunch to kids with all A's on their report cards. He also had a free lunch drawing for local businesses each week. He had daily specials and delivered food to offices. He seemed to be attempting to market his small business.

The problem was Sally. Sally was a long-time employee who, for reasons unknown to the clientele, had soured. She had become caustic and confrontational. It wasn't a pleasant experience having breakfast there anymore. So, I told Jim, the proprietor, that Sally was a problem and that I thought he might want to try to correct her behavior toward customers. Jim explained that he'd talked to her, but it didn't seem to do any good. I suggested to Jim that he had a choice to make. He could either spare Sally's feelings or lose his business. He chose to lose his business.

When you exceed customer expectations and produce a delightful experience, you are setting a standard that your staff and your customers come to expect. Putting out fires is part of an imperfect system. Eliminate the source of fires before they get out of control and require extinguishing. The quality experience requires you to be SMART:

> Specific. Establish realistic goals. Remove obstacles that impede the sale. Do not tolerate negativity from anyone involved in the marketing process.

> Measurable. Quantify your objectives. Write down your goals. Make sure that every aspect of your goal-setting agenda is clearly defined and precise.

> Agreed upon. Create a document that details your agenda. Be certain that all of the essential issues are outlined and mutually agreed to by you, your staff and the projection you have of your customers' expectations.

> Realistic. Be honest with yourself. Be sure your goals are realistic, obtainable and accessible.

> Time frame. Treat each issue relating to your quality experience program with a deadline. Examine the way you do business now. If you commit to delivering a product to a customer by a certain deadline, then treat the delivery of your quality experience program in the same manner.

"None of us is as smart as all of us."
—Roy Disney

Checklist for creating a quality experience

1. **The Quality Experience succeeds** when everyone in your company participates. In creating any part of your marketing plan, you should always incorporate collective thinking.

2. **Focus first on the needs** of the customer, not on the needs to cut costs.

3. **Change is a necessary component** of success. Those who refuse to change cannot be part of your future.

4. **Create committees, but call them teams** (there's more spirit associated with teams than committees).

5. **Pay careful attention to any suggestions** from customers or staff. Post the most valuable ideas where everyone can see them. Celebrate innovation among anyone who cares enough about your business to make a suggestion.

6. **Constantly reward your people** for outstanding contributions.

7. **Any innovations or information** that is considered important should be sent to every staff member by memo. Wrap the memo in a ribbon!

8. **Explain carefully why each aspect** of your *quality experience program* is vital to everyone concerned with the company. Make certain that it is perceived as more than just another attempt at increasing productivity.

9. **Assume leadership and make sure** every top manager is involved in the process. This is a trickle-down program.

10. **Post progress reports** that show sales trends. Encourage a team spirit with a common goal.

Recently I heard an interesting statistic: 95 percent of new ideas offered to management from staff members are treated negatively. You're in business to succeed. I must reiterate this point. If someone, anyone, cares enough about your business to make a suggestion, it's incumbent upon you to treat it with great respect. Love it or leave it, but treat it with affirmation and appreciation. One final word: A quality experience is not only the way to do business, but it's free!

Passion Principle #4: The Peter Pan Principle

"I won't grow up."
—Peter Pan

Many years ago there was a book titled *The Peter Principle* that talked about people reaching their own level of incompetence. That's not what this is about. This is the Peter Pan Principle, and it's about maintaining the curiosity, energy, objectivity and innocence of childhood.

More than anything else, marketing requires thinking. The thinking stage of your business marketing plan is the most important because it's where you begin to set your sights on the bull's eye. Typically, we think about our business the way we think about ourselves.

The essence of the Peter Pan Principle is to remember what it was like to think "clean"—unencumbered by our history, our successes and failures, our patterns and habits. Children approach things with an amazing degree of wonder and freshness, unlike adults who have way too much business baggage to think fresh thoughts. So, the purpose of this principle is to get you to begin thinking about your business with a new perspective.

Exercise

Here's how to begin. List your top 10 business objectives on a sheet of paper. Next to each of them list 10 better business objectives—better because they are more attainable, more creative, more profitable, more service-oriented, more compelling. Engage as many parties in this activity as possible—your employees, friends, spouses, children...*especially* children.

Then compare the way you've been doing business with the new ideas. Now, look at the rank of each part of your objectives list. Are they prioritized by rank? If not, prioritize them. Establish deadlines for each objective. Total Quality Management illustrates a four-step process in implementing programs: *plan, do, study, act*. You are in the planning stage until you have agreed that your new objectives are fixed. Remember, you've been doing things the same way for a long time. Now, you're wiping the slate clean and beginning to reorganize your thinking.

Shakespeare wrote, "There is nothing either good or bad, but thinking makes it so." Don't think that you're correcting mistakes—you're rethinking and reinventing your business in order to make it better. In Zen, there is a belief that regardless of our surroundings or states of consciousness, our minds are always working. When we sleep, our cognitive processes are still very active. Therefore, Zen meditation teaches people to clear their minds of thoughts in order to rest and reevaluate. The Peter Pan Principle of marketing suggests that you clear your mind of past methods of doing business and concentrate on resting first, then on reevaluating your approach to the way you conduct business.

Exercise

This is a simple exercise based upon a process called projection. You've undoubtedly seen Microsoft's position statement: *Where Do You Want to Go Today?*

Well, I'm asking you: *Where Do You Want to Be in Three?* Three years, that is.

Concentrate on a clear picture of what your business will look like in three years. Put yourself in the picture. See those individuals whom you feel will be with you, or describe those who are new to your organization. What do they look like, sound like, act like?

1. Has the business grown in numbers, size, profits? How much?
2. What is the physical structure of the business, the same or different? Do you have a bigger office? What does it look like?
3. What line extensions have developed? New products or services?
4. How have the changes affected your life professionally or socially? Are you projecting yourself as a member of the country club?
5. How much more money are you making?
6. Which of the goals established three years ago have you achieved? Which ones haven't you achieved?
7. What are you doing differently from three years ago?
8. Are you spending more or less time at work?
9. Are you working harder or more productively?
10. Have you retained all of your customers?
11. Are gross sales up or down?
12. Are profits up or down?

By projecting yourself three years from now, you have helped to identify your goals and what motivates you to achieve them. Projection does something else as well. It helps to clear your mind and think about your business and yourself with more innocent, unencumbered thoughts. What you want is to reevaluate, reinvent and reissue your business every three years.

Raising the business

In a way, businesses are like babies—they need to be raised, nurtured and guided. Sometimes we forget who's rocking the cradle and who's *being* rocked.

A friend of mine runs a third-generation business. His grandfather founded the company and his father built it. After his father passed away, Roy took over. It's a relatively simple operation—a parts distribution company for the refrigeration and air-conditioning industry. They bring in products, warehouse them and sell them to installation and repair people. Not too complicated, right?

Roy wasn't really trained to be a people person. He was ostensibly a loner who worked to live, not an entrepreneur who lives to work. He had no great passions, though he liked to golf. His business was unexciting, uninspired and mostly run by virtue of its past, not its future. Roy was unchallenged but reasonably content. Then something happened. Roy became a father, and suddenly his needs changed. His wife stopped working. His income was cut in half. His expenses increased and understandably so did his need and appetite for money.

Roy had never marketed his company. He didn't have a clue as to how to improve his situation. Sure, he had run some ads occasionally, but he had stopped thinking about his business a long time ago. And he had never really understood who his customers were. He had their names and phone numbers, addresses and account information, but he had no idea who they really were.

I convinced Roy to adopt the Peter Pan Principle. After all, he had not taken a long, hard look at his company in years. Now, his own needs were causing him to be more motivated. The question, though, was: Where would Roy find inspiration? Inspiration clearly was not his strong suit.

Roy had never recognized his role in the business. The staff consisted of four people—a secretary, a bookkeeper and two warehouse packing and shipping people. They all did their jobs with little or no interaction except to take orders from Roy and pick up their paychecks at the end of the week. Roy knew very little about their lives outside of the office.

I asked Roy to create his business from scratch. We began with a blank piece of paper, answering:

- What would the business look like?
- Who would be running it?

- What kinds of products would it include?
- Who were the leaders and who were the followers?
- What services might be part of its selling proposition?
- What would his office consist of?
- Who was his customer?
- How much money would he like to make?

Roy spent two weeks in this rebirthing process, completing the picture. He thought about his business as if it didn't exist. He began to think clean. And through this exercise and his reaching back to innocence and a guiltless past (children don't feel guilt until they're taught it), Roy reinvented his business. First, he hired a new secretary. When he began to "fantasize" about his new business, he realized that his existing secretary didn't look, act or sound anything like his ideal. In reality, she was a detriment for years, but he had no reason to change the situation until now. Next, he created a more economical, part-time arrangement with his bookkeeper. Not only did he save money, but he was able to create a new position for a part-time telemarketer. He reinvented his warehouse staff, as well, providing them with incentives for timely shipping. He bought them uniforms and picked up the lunch tab every Thursday. He saw his business as new—a startup—and *he* became the founder, not his grandfather.

Within two years of the rebirth, Roy's sales increased by 22 percent with an increase in profits of 31 percent. He also redecorated his office, brought in a new product line and created a small but profitable direct-mail business that reached other distributors. Roy was not only a new father to a daughter, but a new father to a business.

Passion Principle #5: KCBY—Keep Competitors Behind You

Want to drive people crazy? Succeed wildly! I don't espouse treating the competition as the enemy. I promote the idea of treating the competition as the jealous friend. There's a huge difference. Modeling is a marvelous part of the marketing process. We look at what exists and use it as our model to improve upon. By constantly focusing on the playing field, by watching the trends and avoiding the fads, by taking what's good and making it better, marketing magic occurs. The idea is not only to be first, but to be first, second and third. The "me-too"-ers are always nipping at your heels, so learn to run faster.

Wallpapers To Go has a *You Gotta Love It* guarantee. It tells the customer to take the wallpaper home and keep it for a while. Buy it, and if you don't like it, return it, and get your money back. This establishes a tone and a position that quickly outsmart the competition. It takes a positive approach up front and delivers on its promise.

Holiday Inn in Orlando, Florida, has a remarkable program that allows parents to travel far more comfortably with children. It specifically targets the leisure traveler, offering parents privacy and convenience and giving kids an opportunity to have fun. The "kidsuite," as it is called, features a private playhouse that functions as a kid's bedroom with fun themes throughout, a separate room for adults and a mini kitchenette. The kid's playhouse/bedroom sleeps three with a bunk bed and twin bed and has its own television, video player and video game, radio cassette player, clock, fun phone, table and chairs. This concept targets the prime Orlando vacationer: the family. The kidsuite program is a fine example of KCBY because it's a first and because it addresses the primary objections that parents with small children have about traveling—crowded rooms, bored children, a single television for the entire suite. It's a classic example of problem-solving. By designing a program that keeps children within the same walls as the parents, but separate, Holiday Inn has created a comfort level within a "parent-friendly" environment. And by giving kids what they want to be happy and to stay out of their parents' hair as much as possible, Holiday Inn has readdressed the issue of a "kid-friendly" environment.

Does your business anticipate trends? Do you constantly condition yourself and staff to think of four new ideas per week? Do you exercise control (a negative inhibitor), or do you encourage uncontrollable behavior (the kind of creative thinking that needs to be toned down, not up)?

Keeping competitors behind you requires you to outthink them. This, of course, requires a regular review of their marketing materials. Know them and you know yourself.

Sometimes the simplest elements deliver the biggest results.

Letting people go

Bobbi's restaurant began as a simple luncheonette on a very busy street in a Connecticut city. She wanted to grow her business. So, she hired a very good cook. She dressed the place up. She improved her menu with more innovative, timely offerings, such as low-fat foods, turkey burgers, special salads. Business was brisk, but Bobbi knew she had lots of competition within a three-block radius. So, she never stopped looking for ways to KCBY.

Most restaurants in the area actually posted signs reading: *Restrooms are for customers only!* Not Bobbi. She posted a huge sign in her window stating: *Restrooms are for anyone who needs them!* Did this invitation cause problems? In fact, she could barely discern any situation when it was obvious that people came in only to use the restrooms. What did happen was that more people came in—some, she suspected, to use the restroom—but they ended up buying a container of coffee at the very least.

She had fresh flowers on every table. She brought crayons and coloring books to children. The wait staff wore buttons that said: *I work for you!* She didn't miss a trick. When her staff received their paychecks, there was a note attached to each check each week. It simply stated: *from the customers!*

Bobbi has a great deal of fun running her business. And she makes a great deal of money doing it. Her hobby is keeping the competition behind her by constantly challenging them. And when she sees something that she feels is innovative, she creates a marketing strategy to improve upon it. It's an obsession, and that's what passion is all about. Bobbi looked at the universe around her business and decided that she would do certain things exactly opposite her competition.

Encouraging creative thinking among your company members is an integral part of the Keeping Competitors Behind You principle.

The way it crumbles

I have a good relationship with a particular car dealer. I've leased several cars from this business, and I continue to do business with them because they are consummate marketers and I respect the way they conduct themselves. They do something very interesting after each transaction. They send the customer a tin of cookies. Now, in and of itself, that's not such an innovative piece of marketing, but the cookies come from Gimmee Jimmy's. This particular company is owned by and employs mostly deaf bakers. When the tin arrives, the card from the automobile dealer, thanking the customer, is just part of the package. Most of the literature (with the permission and approval of the auto dealer) promotes Gimmee Jimmy's. This type of promotion incorporates several issues of marketing:

1. Relationship marketing—maintaining a personal connection with the customer.

2. Cross-promoting—using one marketing message to introduce another.

3. Morality marketing—communicating business values or unique qualities that include not only product information but illustrate the benefits that affect a specific group of people.

4. Direct marketing—getting into the customer's home or business with a message.

5. Premium marketing—using, in this case, a consumable product offered free as a thank-you or as an incentive.

6. Publicity—including, in this case, a reprint from *Fortune* magazine in the package.

The article offers the customer an amazing insight into the company that has produced the product. In this case, Gimmee Jimmy's is shown to be a company that cares a great deal about its own people and its customers. Jimmy Libman himself is deaf, as are nine of his 12 employees. The story tells us that the bakers go wordlessly about their work, directed by a panel of colored lights flashing on a wall above them. A green light means a customer has entered the bakery. An orange light tells the bakers that the cookies are ready to be taken out of the ovens. Red is for the fire alarm. White means that a special telephone with keyboard and screen, used for communication between deaf workers and the outside world, is ringing. To ensure that employees look at the panel of lights above them, a blue strobe light under a counter flashes—bouncing off the walls so it can be seen from any point in the room.

The concept is amazing. And the automobile dealer's use of this gift from this particular company is ingenious. As a consumer, I am delighted to be the recipient of these great gourmet cookies. As someone who celebrates ingenuity, I am equally delighted to be made aware of an entrepreneurial venture that is owned by and employs physically challenged individuals. The dealership and the bakery are practicing the Passion Principle of Keeping Competitors Behind You. Both companies have acted in such a way that the synergy makes one plus one equal three. I am now a customer of both businesses...and a loyal one.

Huddle before every game

Evan Cummings runs a paper company. Every Monday morning he holds a staff meeting but calls it the ROCK—Roundtable of Competitive Knockouts. The purpose is to employ collective thinking to frustrate the competition. This acronym appears on the agenda that sits on the desk of each staff member every Monday morning. Evan loves to run the meetings himself. He begins by inviting anyone to issue any statement, thought or opinion, but in order to ensure that people speak without inhibitions, each person can either communicate the thought verbally or on a piece of paper, then fold the paper and toss it into the middle of the conference room table. Evan then shuffles the papers to protect anonymity, but people *can* claim their suggestions if they want. Then Evan begins the next stage of the meeting by reading each suggestion or comment aloud. The purpose of this exercise is to draw people into the center of the business and particularly to create heat for the competition.

This not only encourages creative thinking, but it asks for outrageous thinking. By getting your people to "think out of the box," you're asking for advice from everyone and allowing each person to express him- or herself without fear of criticism or retribution. Ask your people how they see their role in the development of the business and how they see the customer. Ask them how they see the competitor. And ask them how they see making the competitor go nuts. By including everyone in KCBY, you are motivating people to focus on a common opponent, and motivation is where marketing begins.

Dean R. Spitzer in his book, *Super-Motivation*, suggests that most organizational structures sap the energy out of employees. He further suggests that office politics and procedures make people feel inept and encourage mediocrity. Spitzer tells a marvelous tale about motivation. A group of ruffians is throwing rocks at an old man's house. The man begins to pay the kids to throw the rocks, gradually lowering the payment until the kids quit. It simply wasn't worth it to them anymore.

If keeping the competitors behind you is a game, if it's made to be fun and the rewards affect each and every one, then every Monday morning will begin by throwing darts at the bull's eye. Remember, no matter how fast you're going, there's someone gaining on you. Keep your foot on the accelerator and keep looking ahead. But keep your other eye on the rearview mirror.

If you keep the customer delighted, you'll keep the competition frustrated. Remember the adage: *The best revenge is happiness.* Innovative behavior requires promiscuity in the workplace. No, I'm not talking about sex, but rather an openness to all ideas designed to improve your customer relations and make your competitors grind their teeth.

Chapter 12

Creative Communication!

Admittedly, "creativity" is an overused word. But so far, nobody's been creative enough to come up with a better one. So for now, we'll use it.

Marketing without creativity is like brushing your teeth with your finger. It seems like you're doing something, but nothing really gets cleaned. Yet, most businesses do just that—market without creativity.

The 2% solution

It's known that 98 percent of what you see, hear, feel, taste and touch is dismissed as quickly as it is perceived. Think about it: How many messages are retained? How many pieces of communication become part of your thinking?

Most of us use a minimum of 30,000 words per week—5,000 of which have more than one meaning. There are 600,000 words in the English language. Sound astonishing? It is. Yet with all the words we have available to us, with all the words we use, we still have trouble communicating. Remember the adage "It's not what you say, it's how you say it"? Well, we're about to spend some time on how we say what we want to say.

Important note: Not every business owner will become a creative marketer. Not everyone can write copy or create concepts. Certainly not everyone can think visually or design graphics. But once you recognize the importance of this process, you will be better able to direct this type of activity for your business, whether you enlist the services of an advertising agency, a freelancer, a friend, or you attempt the creative work yourself, you'll have better tools and a far better notion of what it takes to think creatively.

Everyone remembers what Dirty Harry says

When Dirty Harry said, "Go ahead, make my day," an entire nation (make that *world*) remembered that phrase. I've heard it thousands of times, from people in the media to people in the street. It really wasn't what he said, it was how he said it.

Effective communication is broken down in the following manner:

- Words: 7 percent.
- Tone: 38 percent.
- Nonverbal: 55 percent.

Look, attitude and language greatly enhance the communication process. If a speaker were to deliver a speech without coming out from behind the podium, without the proper voice inflection, without the appropriate gestures, it would be just a speech. But if the same words are spoken by someone who exudes energy, enthusiasm, vigor and vitality, someone who looks the audience in the eyes and has posture, performance skills and an attitude, the same speech can be absolutely electrifying.

Words and pictures comprise most of creative marketing. Sometimes we use one to the exclusion of the other, but mostly we use them together. Remember, even if we're marketing in print without the use of accompanying graphics, or on radio or with audiocassettes, we're creating visual imagery. Language, when used effectively, is, by its very nature, visual.

What's in a word?

They say that seeing is believing. If that's so, then why do we miss most of what we see and hear? The reason is that most of what we see and hear—indeed most of what's communicated through media—is mediocre at best. How many vital messages have you retained in the past week, day, hour? Which marketing communications have captured you, and how many have you acted upon?

Well, the next logical question is: How much marketing information have you disseminated that has the potential to be retained and acted upon? Creativity is the make-or-break component of the marketing process. If you can't get your message seen, read, heard and acted upon, you're better off taking the money you spent on marketing and taking a vacation to Hawaii. Truly, so many businesses rest on their laurels, assuming that simply communicating, advertising, sending out fliers, running radio commercials and mailing brochures will result in a return on investment.

Words are, collectively, the magic wand of marketing. They cast spells and tell stories, but the right choice of words either moves people to act or bores them to tears. Think about the following words. Do they have meaning? Do they cause you to react? Do they say something to you in a new way? Are they compelling?

- Values Galore.
- Sale.
- Quality Merchandise.
- Bargain.
- Bonus Dollars.
- Money-back Guarantee.
- Spectacular Buys.
- Stupendous Selection.
- Giant Warehouse Sale.
- Tremendous Savings.
- Once-in-a-Lifetime Opportunity.
- Sensational Service.

What do these words mean? The answer is: very little. When you see them, you're witnessing a marketing program that is usually based upon the principle that if you repeat your message often enough, someone will listen. The truth is that misuse of words, lack of creativity and poor execution account for huge sums of money being wasted. It's been proven time and time again. Small marketing efforts that employ strong creative concepts and a brilliant presentation outperform much larger programs that are mundane. Size doesn't sell unless it's accompanied by a truly innovative, dynamic, compelling, spirited, even explosive, performance. This can be accomplished by shifting the way you think and flexing that portion of your brain that is nonanalytical, nonlinear.

Let's say you're running a sale ad for the installation of gas barbecue grills. Your competition begins each spring with ads that tout "Celebrate Spring With Savings," "Spring Into Value & Economy"—words that, by virtue of overuse, have no meaning. How can you communicate these ideas and still be heard? By forgetting the standard nomenclature and concentrating instead on creating statements that are attention-getting and proprietary to your selling proposition. For example:

Our competitors charge you an arm and a leg...
We stop at the wrist!

You can still introduce the specifics of the sale, tying in the theme with accompanying words and perhaps a graphic statement such as a wrist turning a wrench! You've just conveyed the exact same message as your competitor—*sale, value, economy, percentage off*—but you've done so in a way that has said it without the use of overused words, words that ultimately no longer have value themselves. This is creative communication because it uses an alternate means of saying the same thing. Clichés become clichés because they're said time and time again without being enhanced. When they *build upon* the acceptance of a phrase or statement already in peoples' collective consciousness, clichés and double entendres have a valid place in marketing communications.

When I was looking for a direct-mail approach to solicit liquor advertisers for a major magazine, I wrote a headline that simply stated:

Guess who's pouring into our publication?

Then I listed the major brands that were already signed up as advertisers. I got prospective advertisers' attention immediately by creating a double entendre and relying upon language that had already saturated our thinking. But I used the language in an enhanced way that would make people take notice of something they were accustomed to hearing but not with this particular message.

American humorist Garrison Keillor once said, "Sometimes you have to look reality in the eye and deny it." It's a good thought. And it relates particularly well to creative marketing. When you look at your business, recognize that there are two ways of seeing it. First, by viewing it as it really is and what it represents: income, opportunity and, hopefully, enjoyment. Next, view it as a caricature with exaggerated features and a funny voice. Stretch the business. Reshape it. Enjoy denying the realities. See the possibilities of expanding the way you think about your business.

Recently I was asked to consult on a mailing program for the American Sugar Growers. The purpose of the direct marketing effort was to convince corn growers to form an alliance with the sugar growers and demonstrate to the corn growers that they were facing a 25-cent reduction per bushel in revenues because of foreign subsidies supported by certain powerful leaders in Congress. It was our job to alert the corn growers (some of whom were unaware of the subsidies or the amount of their product that was used for sweetening soft drinks) that they faced such an economic downturn. The idea of using a well-known cliché—a line from a children's song—came about because it perfectly fit our cause. The headline of the mailing piece was simply:

Guess who doesn't love you a bushel and a peck?

When you flipped the cover, the advocates of the subsidy appeared. The basic message of the copy was: Even though you may believe that these are your heroes, they're in favor of reducing your revenue by 25 cents per bushel of corn. On the accompanying panel was a chicken scratching at feed, which happened to be corn. The headline:

When they're done...all you'll be left with
is chicken feed.

The use of clichés created compelling messages, reissuing these phrases as purposeful selling statements. In this case, we were selling a proposition designed to create action; we wanted the corn growers to recognize the threat, read the information and respond. The concept and the copy clicked. The message was easy to understand and relate to, and they couldn't ignore it because it was interesting, provocative and entertaining. When we give our audience a reason to applaud, when we offer them an opportunity to respond because we've presented our case in a novel fashion, we succeed.

Register your reactions

Discover your creative universe. Make a study of the way things are communicated in your own life, your own community. For the next two weeks, study the marketing messages around you. Listen intently to the radio commercials, watch the television commercials for mood, imagery, dialogue and music, look at every ad in your morning newspaper, pay attention to the billboards and register how many messages are memorable, moving and interesting and how many might cause you to respond. See if my assertion is correct. Remember, I've told you that 98 percent of what you see, hear, feel, taste and touch is forgotten. Our goal is to recognize why the 2 percent succeeds and to create marketing messages that fall into this tiny but powerful category.

Sometimes you have only seconds to succeed

Before we look at the construction of an ad, let's look at how little time we have to stop the reader. The best illustration of this is outdoor advertising, where we literally have a few seconds to gain or lose the reader.

In order to illustrate this, I will list some headlines and concepts that I have used on billboards for a chain of convenience stores selling sub sandwiches. The campaign was created in order to provide credibility to the sub program and to offer a unique service story. As you recall, we have to catch the drivers' attention instantaneously—providing them with enough information to create a reaction, but not an accident.

The goal was to tie the product to the person making it in order to highlight quality and service without using the obvious words. Further, we developed a training program that "certified" the people making the subs. Then we created a "brand" called Submakers to support the premise. The billboards depicted pleasant-looking people holding sub sandwiches and displayed the following messages:

Introducing Sub Humans
People Behind the Product

The Sub Servants
Promising You Great Service

The Sub Commandos
Combating High Prices

The Sub Committee
A Team of Sub Specialists

The Sub Compact
Luxury Features, Economy Priced

8 Mega Bites
A Low-Tech, High Flavor Experience

Designer Subs
Design One for Yourself

Three-word headlines were the common thread of this billboard campaign. The accompanying graphics were simple, bold and connected to the headlines. The campaign was supported by in-store signage, radio ads and banners hung on the front of each of the 100 stores. The results were impressive. The program developed into one of the most profitable programs in the history of the company.

The New Jersey Lottery entered into a co-op arrangement with this same company (Quick Chek), producing billboards that presented both the lottery logo and the convenience store logo in a co-op promotion. The headlines were:

It's a Win, Win for Everyone!

You Might Get a Quick Chek

The Dream Machine
(accompanied by photo of lottery machine)

Think Big
(accompanied by photo of little ticket)

The Green Grocer
(accompanied by photo of currency in shopping cart)

Fresh Bread
(accompanied by photo of stack of money)

It Could Be You

The Buck Starts Here

Somebody's Gotta Win

Picture the Possibilities
(accompanied by photo of man in hammock by tropical
sea)

In addition to illustrating how quickly we must get the customers' attention, these examples represent a billboard *campaign*. A campaign maintains a similar look, type style, composition and tone. While the headlines and visuals change, the overall impression is the same, so that ultimately the customer recognizes the advertiser without looking at the logo. This is significant for small businesses, which most often overlook developing a campaign strategy. The campaign develops a theme by creating messages that look the same but contain a slightly different perspective with each new ad.

For example, when a prominent local jeweler was looking to develop a campaign strategy that differentiated his business from numerous competitors, we looked at the marketplace and the research. The jeweler's primary customer was a man or a woman in his or her early 40s—decidedly upscale, polished and sophisticated. This customer's disposable income was among the highest in the nation, and his or her appreciation for jewelry and gems was pronounced. The campaign strategy was to select models that looked like this kind of customer and to maintain this identity throughout several years of advertising, based upon the strategy's success. The couple were depicted in various poses with headlines and copy that concentrated on the relationship between them and barely focused on jewelry at all. We had decided that what we were really selling, in essence, was "relationships"...and the jewelry itself was the result of the emotional connection between the people depicted in the advertisements. By focusing on people rather than product, we broke the mold of the traditional retail jeweler, offering customers a look at themselves in a very attractive way.

This ad was part of the campaign:

If Love Is a Game...
Why Not Start Winning!

(Photo of handsome couple against dark background.
They are involved in a frivolous, playful conversation
with a chess board in the foreground of the ad.)

Some people call it the game of love.
For others it's more of a mystery.
But, no matter where it comes from or why it occurs,
it's the driving force that changes lives.
At Simms, you'll find exceptional gifts of love. The
kind of jewelry that wins over hearts and minds.
Take a look at how the game should be played.
Simms...The Exception

The ad included a small inset photograph of two pieces of jewelry. There were no prices, no listings, no percentages off. The force behind the message was *relationships*—the real reason jewelry is purchased. Thus, the product itself played second fiddle. We wanted people to recognize that Simms was selling relationships.

The campaign also included the following follow-up ad:

When Desire Is Stronger Than Reason

(Photo of couple in formal attire dancing; diamond
necklace is in foreground with a $24,000 price tag.)

There are times when we must throw caution to the
wind. When thinking is more dangerous than acting.
For these times, Simms has a special collection of
extraordinary, breathtaking jewels
set in gold and platinum.
They're Not for the Faint of Heart...But They
Are for the Heart.

Again, "relationships" powered the ad. The use of a high-priced, high-profile necklace supported the claim and the selling proposition. What were we selling? Desire!

The follow-up advertising in the campaign also included:

You talked about a weekend away...
but then a weekend ends in two days!

(Couple walking together, embracing. The inset
photograph included a few pieces of a gold collection.
The copy talked about the lasting value of jewelry and
the fleeting memories of a vacation.)

A long time ago, she said
three words that changed your life...
Now it's time to change hers.

(Photo of couple loosely embracing with inset shot of necklace and earrings. The copy spoke of how powerful three words can be...and how words aren't always enough to convey feelings. For these times, it said, magnificent jewels can demonstrate love.)

Turn the act of giving
into the art of giving

(Photo of same couple. She is placing a ring on his finger. The copy explained that, at Simms, giving is more than a gesture, it's an art. No specific jewelry was advertised.)

I convinced this particular business owner not to use jewelry as the selling feature in his advertising by showing him a poster of competitive jewelers' ads with their names and logos covered. I then asked his group to identify the jewelry stores. They couldn't—because every ad was exactly the same...and each of those business owners had decided that simply depicting some items and prices would drive business. They were marketing to themselves. Not only was the mediocrity pronounced, but so was the "me-too"-ism. Every single jewelry store in the local market (about 10) did what every other store did. They decided to be in the commodity business, while we decided to create a *business personality*.

I created another ad for a jewelry manufacturer who was intent upon promoting *quality*—one of those words that doesn't have an impact on us anymore. So, we depicted a beautiful woman in the foreground of the ad, looking wistfully off into the abyss, while in the deep, dark recesses of the room was a jilted lover, forlorn as he glanced out the door he was about to use in leaving. The headline:

Our marcasite jewelry...
it lasts longer than love

The quality message was beautifully performed by the people in the ad...and we never mentioned the word "quality." The ad had an edge that was appropriate for the market: young women in their late teens and 20s. At first some members of the company felt the message was cynical, but as a selling message, it created the type of tension and brought the kind of identification to the jewelry that was needed.

Not everyone loves *The Honeymooners*

Larry Olsen owns a pancake shop. He took my advice and used imagery and imagination in refining his creative message. He runs ads, sends out fliers, buys radio time and even produced a cable TV commercial. Larry loves *The Honeymooners*. So much so that he has every episode, including the lost episodes, on video. So, everything he does relates to his passion, *The Honeymooners*. The store has several TV monitors in it, constantly playing *Honeymooners* episodes. His commercials use characters and lines from the show. His ads depict the *Honeymooners* apartment. He's in love with what he loves. The problem is that Larry never thought about what his customers love. His creative vision came out of his own pointed preference. In fact, many of Larry's customers are far too young to remember *The Honeymooners,* so they don't get it. Larry claims he doesn't care...it fulfills his creative need. This is a classic mistake in marketing. Larry loves *The Honeymooners* more than he loves his business. It isn't that this creative venue will cause him failure—his pancakes are good, and his message is consistent. However, the campaign will not return the investment nearly as well as it should.

Love is like a red, red rose

Every business has its own language. You're accustomed to the words, style, syntax and order of your business language. Probably too accustomed. Look at what you've done and attempt to create a simile or metaphor using the language through which you've communicated your business so far. You can look to many models for help. Hemingway was a master of the metaphor and loved to use simile in his work. One of his short stories was titled "Hills Like White Elephants." In the story, Hemingway's characters repeated the simile often, as they stared out at the hills. As readers, we saw the hills as the characters did, as white elephants—trunk to tail—connected across the horizon. Ask yourself how you could describe your business in another way—a way that says the same thing differently.

Take a product or service feature that is promotable. Now, compare it to something else, using "like" or "as." Or simply make the comparison using whatever words you like. Out of this exercise comes creative propositions that can be developed into headlines, visual concepts and creative programs.

Rubies as hot as fire. Sales techniques as explosive as dynamite. Home cooking like mother used to make. Service that's as sharp as the edge of a saber. By comparing, you begin to think visually...and it helps to focus on what you're selling. As we know, we're not selling the ax, we're selling the stack of chopped wood. Thus, if you use simile and metaphor, you can allow yourself to see the other side of the sale, so to speak.

It's not creative unless it sells

David Ogilvy, a noted guru in the advertising industry since the 1950s, made that statement a long time ago. It remains one of the most quoted lines in the annals of marketing. It holds such profundity because of a mistake commonly made by some companies. The mistake? Making the message much more interesting than the thing being sold. This has happened all too often, and the results are disastrous. For one thing, customers remember the message but not the product. For another thing, the message often could be applicable to many similar products, so customers are dazzled by the creative approach, but the specific application remains cloudy.

Exaggerate

A good creative tool is to focus on exaggeration as a method of communicating. Recently a colleague of mine handled a political campaign. He needed to distinguish the opposing candidate from his client. He knew that people pay little or no attention to a number 10 envelope (standard business size) and a letter. And as much as he preferred to create only positive communication, he knew that pointing out the shortcomings of the opponent would focus positive attention on his client. His use of exaggerated marketing as a creative tool included the design of a soda can with the opposing candidate's face in the center. The candidate's name was the brand, with the word *lite* under it. The can copy included:

> *The Soft Drink that Never Satisfies!*
> *All Fizzle, No Pop*
> *Same Old Tired Flavor...Less Substance!*
> *New Ideas? Never Had 'Em, Never Will!*

It also included copy on each side of the can:

> *For Best Results, Keep on Ice Another Four Years*
> *Packaged and Marketed by Special Interests*
> *Caution: Self-serving*
> *Imitation Flavor*

This message could not possibly go unnoticed, having been mailed to the voting public on a container that looked exactly like a can of soda. In direct marketing, one surefire way to get your message opened is to send it in a box, in an oversized envelope, as a telegram, as an invitation, in a mailing tube, in a cereal box—the possibilities are endless. In this case, the *can-didate* depicted on the can was so powerfully positioned as being *lite* that the presentation and the proposition were imprinted in the minds of the voters.

Occasionally, the use of exaggeration requires you to look at your business comedically. But, I must warn you that the use of comedy in marketing is difficult. If you're not really funny, then you fall flat on your face, like a stand-up comedian who faces a dead silent audience after the joke's been told. So, use exaggeration in a way that stresses your strengths and reinforces your selling message.

Many great ads use humor, but you're not playing to a late-night audience, so your approach must be witty, not caustic...funny, not offensive. Remember that you're putting yourself in the spotlight when you create your advertising, and if it's funny and positive, it can sell. If, on the other hand, the humor is shocking, you'll be selling to an empty theater.

Think about the obvious uses for your product or service and extend them beyond belief in order to make your point. When you watch a sneaker commercial and the athlete jumps 30 feet in the air, or a car sprouts wings and flies over the ravine, or a truck, unable to cross from one mountain to another, pulls them together, you're witnessing the use of creative exaggeration to make a marketing point. It's effective because it's memorable, and the intrinsic qualities of the product being sold are presented in a strong fashion by the use of gross exaggeration.

The first self-promotion piece I created for my own business stated:

> *If an ad agency needed an ad agency,*
> *they'd come to us!*

The copy then went on to elaborate that we truly believe our product is so superior that other advertising experts should be using us. Exaggeration? Sure. But the point we were making was reinforced by stretching, and by stretching we reach new heights.

Remember: You always want to start with a strong, simple, engaging image. You can begin to exercise your creative muscle by looking at your product or service and considering which of its aspects are most presentable. You want to have a conversation with the customers. You want them to understand that you've done something special and that you're willing to prove it. You want them to say, "Whoa!"

Years ago, my brother related a story to me. He was walking on the boardwalk with his girlfriend and her brother, who had an unusually large nose. A couple of adolescents were leaning on a bench by the railing dividing the boardwalk from the beach. My brother overheard one of the kids say to the other, "See that man over there? He has a bad case of nose."

Yes, it was an unkind statement. But it could have been said in many ways, the most likely being: "Look at that man with the big nose." The point is that it was said in such a way that it created a memorable experience for my brother and me—not because we approved of what was said, but because of the *way* it was said.

The rites of research

A little research goes a long way!

Before we begin to discuss the practical methods of creating advertising messages, let's look at some of the trends and research that enable us to create.

A friend of mine believes in humor. He also recognizes that in his speeches to associations, as an authority on fund raising, he *must* be funny, or he'll soon be forgotten. His research consists of a library of joke books and articles on humor. He has even, on occasion, hired a comedy writer. There are, of course, good resources for any subject matter, including humor. One of the newsletters my friend receives is the Funny Business Newsletter. It consists of an ample supply of humorous quips, quotes and anecdotes and includes an almanac of jokes, stories and quotes. You can get information about this particular newsletter by calling 800-915-0022 or writing to Georgetown Publishing House, 1101 30th St. NW, Washington, DC 20007. This and many other sources can be found at the library.

To research the material or the genre you will employ in your communications, there are vast libraries of reference materials that cost little or nothing to use...and make the greatest difference in your delivery and your credibility. Even with the research material available to us, we all shoot from the hip. Sometimes it works; other times we end up shooting ourselves in the foot. Understanding human nature and the way people act is a good foundation for creating our messages.

Often I hear people say, in response to ideas, "We've tried that—it didn't work" or "The boss won't like that idea." Then, of course, there's the old "We've been doing it this way for 20 years, and it's worked pretty well." You've probably also heard the expression "If it ain't broke, don't fix it." This statement really should be: "Fix it before it breaks." Preventive marketing requires us to look at the changes that are taking place around us on a continuous basis. One way to do this is to study the marketplace—on our own or through others. What do people want? Why do people buy into certain propositions and ignore others? What makes one product outsell another? Which industries are bound for glory in the next 10 years? The answers are hard to come by, mostly because there are so many factors that go into building success.

Research suggests that we are all afraid. Most of us are afraid of the unknown. Many are afraid of failure. Some are afraid of success. What are your customers afraid of? Can you identify their fear and use this knowledge to provide answers and solutions that help them overcome it?

Remember, we are selling promises. Therefore, we need to distinguish between thoughts and dreams. We are constantly thinking, but dreams are more fanciful and fleeting. We, as marketers, want to capture dreams, bottle them and offer them as part of our message. We want to tap into the attitudes, concerns, fears, aspirations and values of those who are potential customers. We want to understand their behavior as well. Major consumer research studies offer us some insights into human behavior, some of which can be instrumental in the development of a creative approach.

Do we want truth? Do we even know what truth is?

Truth. It's an incredible word. But what does it really mean? Is your truth the same as your customers'? What objective issues support your claims? In marketing, truth is a function of attitudes and behaviors. It is the prevailing belief. Is it true that Fed Ex can always deliver overnight? Is it true that you'll really get your money back if you're not satisfied? People buy into these "truths" because of the establishment of principles that didn't necessarily exist before. We are a culture of promisers and promised, but what we really want as businesspeople is to establish truths that people want and believe.

But what people *say* they want and what they *really* want are often at odds. This paradox must be studied before the creative marketing process or message is delivered to the marketplace. People say they want adventure, and at the same time they claim that their primary need is for personal safety. People say they want to focus on cooperation instead of competition, yet they maintain that one of their key desires is winning. People claim that they are more tolerant, yet reactionary behavior is at an all-time high. Confusion has entered the marketplace. The government wants less government. The private sector wants more support. The Republicans want what the Democrats used to want and vice versa. People are moving, shifting, divorcing, changing jobs, changing lifestyles, changing attitudes and behavior. Who are they? What do they really want? Where are they headed? And where is the truth?

Research suggests that while companies believe that their customers want traditional issues such as value, service, quality and variety, customers are saying that what they want is an "experience." They want an adventure—which can mean simply that they want something different than what they're presently experiencing. This is one reason that health clubs are proliferating. Most people who join health clubs don't use them nearly as often as they thought they would. In fact, health club marketers understand that they can oversell memberships because, while people have good intentions and are motivated by a desire for wellness and fitness, they don't follow through. People want the premise and the promise that come with the "experience" being touted by health and fitness facilities.

Security is also a big issue. Consumers want to feel that they are buying from someone who knows what he or she is doing. They also want to feel cared for and safe. It's a critical issue and one to which marketers must pay attention. What are you offering your customers that makes them feel secure? What do you possess that will allow them to feel safe in their "experience" with you?

How can we give people the "experience" they want? We have to pay careful attention to the division between what people say and what they actually feel. We're responsible for paying attention to our customers and their concerns. If the major trends point to the need for a "live for today" attitude, but people also have the need to plan, where does that leave us? In essence, we have to communicate what people want to hear and need to hear. We have to show them the extreme but deliver the mean. For example, if we're marketing pools, we may want to communicate the availability of the 20-foot-high diving board...knowing full well that backyard bathers don't buy it. By making the more extreme aspects of the product noticeable, we are offering excitement without risk.

The lifeguard's whistle

You jump into a pool. It's crowded. There are lots of kids splashing, and the incessant sound of the lifeguard's whistle is causing you to reel. If you're like me, you begin to fantasize about cramming the whistle up the nose of that 17-year-old, well-tanned, blond-haired, blue-eyed golden boy. I want to put a stop to the shrieking, shrill sound of authority. I reject authority.

But wait—there's a part of me that actually wants the lifeguard to be there, just in case I need him. After all, I'm not as young as I used to be, and I'm getting awfully tired after a few laps. And I'm content that he's perched high enough to keep an eye on me flailing away in an attempt at aerobic exercise.

We're constantly battling between what we say and what we feel or need. Surveys by the nation's leading research firms illustrate that 50 percent of those polled fantasize about doing something they know they wouldn't actually do. This is really quite astonishing. If half of the people out there are daydreaming about parachuting out of an airplane, knowing full well that they wouldn't actually do it, then where does that leave us? Do we appeal to people's fantasies or realities? If winning is really what matters, do we appeal to their egos? If being part of a community is what really matters, do we appeal to their sense of fairness?

The truth is that all the surveys and all the research have left us with lots more questions than answers. But we can make certain assumptions about the marketplace. First, people are insecure. Second, people are in need of an "experience." Third, people need to dream. Fourth, people want an element of danger in their lives, but they want to know that they are safe. As marketers, we can fine-tune our research with focus studies, exit interviews, phone surveys, intercepts... or we can read about major trends from major research groups. The bottom line is that we need to be noticed and we need to offer *the premise and the promise* in every piece of communication we produce. In essence, we must make our customers feel good about the exchange by being sensitive to their needs. Make your customers feel safe, but also offer them an adventure. This approach alone will stimulate the creative process. Whether you're selling flight simulators or vertical blinds, there's a creative way to promise security and offer adventure.

Research reveals the reason for the renegade

Why do we love outlaws? What is it about the tale of Jesse James that fills us with intrigue and a sense of romance? It's because we constantly suppress our own desires and fantasies. Why are pirate tales so popular? What made Westerns such a big part of our popular culture? Adventure and excitement. We live vicariously through the renegade. We see these cultural outcasts on television, in movies, in fiction, in newspapers, on the news. If they're not committing heinous crimes, we secretly want to emulate them. Who are they? They're the people who live romantic lives. People who set standards. People who have vision. People who appear fearless. People who ride off into the sunset, never looking back.

We go to the circus because there are people doing what we wouldn't possibly do. We buy tickets to the fights, hockey games, extreme sports...looking for ways to live vicariously, seeking thrills and getting as close to the edge as we possibly can without falling off ourselves. Our goal in marketing our businesses creatively is to become our own heroes, to distinguish our businesses in ways that make other people take notice. Much of marketing research today focuses on visioning.

Who are your heroes? What did they do that was noteworthy? How can you use pieces of our culture to create messages for your company? I have used quotes from novels, movies, short stories, plays and poems in marketing. I have drawn upon character traits for posturing many marketing campaigns. I have turned to what I have found provocative in order to flex my creative muscles. You have to alter your perceptions before you begin to alter the perceptions of others.

We've talked about modeling. Motivational speaker Tony Schwartz says, "If it works, copy it." Look at what you find compelling, outrageous, inviting and intriguing. Think about how great communication convinces you to act. Learn from it, because for many businesses, the cost of hiring professionals may indeed be prohibitive. Establish your guidelines in a way that makes creativity possible.

When most people buy their first house, it's a dream come true. But the initial feeling is fear, not joy. People see the payments, not the pleasure. They feel the anxiety, not the luxury or pleasure. See your business without its problems. Clear from your mind the obstacles that get in the way of creative thinking. See your own business's benefits in outrageous ways.

Marketing meditation

If you sell surfboards, see your product taking a surfer past the horizon to the Orient. Watch the sun set on your logo, glistening at sea. Witness the ultimate pleasure your product provides.

Ask yourself who you want to be tomorrow, and where you want your business to be. Consider how anything is possible. If you can dream it, you can convey it creatively.

Exercise

An exercise that is particularly valuable is to focus on your business as it exists today. Use your imagination to give your business a new shape, color and sound. If you're a distributor of electronic parts, create a TV commercial in your mind in which you're selling your company's products to your customers. Create a script, and use techniques such as closeups, music and known personalities to enhance the selling proposition. Divide your paper into audio and video, writing both dialogue and a description of each shot in your TV spot. Create the slogan, and cast the commercial with real actors—people from public life, not your own circle of friends. This meditative exercise allows you to see your business, perhaps for the first time, as a company that has a message for everyone.

Of course, if your product is for the general populace, create a script that generates visceral responses, producing emotional reactions, prompting action and creating positive anxiety. Let's walk through this exercise together. I often write commercials for products that are not in my client roster. I do it for fun and to exercise my creative thinking. Recently, I wrote a commercial for *The Wall Street Journal*.

I was reading this particular paper when I decided to do some marketing meditation. I closed my eyes and began to envision *The Wall Street Journal*. I thought about how frustrated I am when it's rainy and I unwrap the plastic bag to find my paper waterlogged. I rant and rave and promise myself that I'll contact the delivery person and threaten a lawsuit, at the very least. Out of that thought, I envisioned *The Wall Street Journal* being delivered on a rural road. A truck roars past a farmhouse—creating a great deal of dust in its path. The driver hurls the paper onto the front lawn of an old colonial home with gray wooden shutters and an old wooden porch in the front. The paper begins to blow away like a tumbleweed, as an elderly woman in a plain, old frock hurries after it. She runs and runs as the paper continues to blow into the dirt road. Just as she approaches the road, another truck is seen barreling toward the paper, which is now stuck in a tire track from the previous vehicle. The woman, with only seconds left until the truck runs over her *Wall Street Journal*, leaps into the road, tumblesaults several times, narrowly escaping death. The paper is in her hand and the truck has sped by her, causing dirt to fly in her face. She looks at her *Wall Street Journal*—the camera zooms in on this contented subscriber holding her paper close to her heart. These words appear on the screen, superimposed over the final shot: *Without it, you're out of it!* Then, there's an extreme closeup of *The Wall Street Journal* logo...fade to black.

By using the image of an old woman doing a miraculous physical stunt to save the newspaper, we're employing humor, exaggeration, overstatement and fantasy to make a very important point: *Without it, you're out of it.* This commercial is not real. *The Wall Street Journal* didn't hire me to write it. But it's extremely valuable to me because it allowed me to do some mental aerobics to keep the creative process going. It's my job to find creative solutions to marketing...and using any product with which to exercise is perfectly valid. The only downside is that nobody paid me for creating the idea.

In the movie *City Slickers*, the main character's wife tells her husband, who is going through a midlife crisis, "Go out and find your smile." It's just six words, but it evokes an enormous range of emotions.

And it speaks to all of us. Every business provides customers with something that they need or want. So identify what your business provides, and go out and find your smile. We need to experience passion on the creative side of our marketing. The difference between drama and drudgery depends upon it. Remember: We are looking for the mind-body marketing connection—capturing our customers' minds and hearts.

A novel by William Goldman entitled *Soldier in the Rain* depicts the profound friendship of two men. Each time they depart from one another, there is a special exchange. Eustis Clay says to his friend, Maxwell Slaughter, "See you later, Maxwell." His friend, the more paternal one in the relationship, always replies in the same fashion, "Until that time, Eustis, until that time."

These words—"until that time, until that time"—convey the intimacy of the characters' relationship and also create an intimacy with the reader. Businesses must recognize that the words they place in the market are the dialogue that drives their business.

Probably the most famous copywriter today is Tom McElligott, who started an agency called Fallon, McElligott in Minneapolis. I've read that Tom will sometimes spend a month on an ad headline—he's obsessive and a perfectionist, but this illustrates how critical words can be in conveying our message. One of the many, many brilliant campaigns for which Tom is renowned was for a spaghetti sauce. The ad features the Mona Lisa on one side of the page and a decidedly bloated Mona Lisa on the opposite side. Each Mona Lisa is holding a bottle of the sauce in front. The caption under the Mona Lisa we all know reads: *traditional*. The caption under the fat Mona Lisa reads: *chunky*.

The beauty of this advertisement comes from many elements—first, the association with an Italian icon, and second, the brilliant execution that ties so wonderfully to the concept of two kinds of sauce. The ad is memorable, funny, friendly, provocative, compelling...and considering that so many competitive products simply show a jar and a coupon, it's light-years ahead of the rest.

Many years ago, I created advertising for a large electronics manufacturer. My initial task was to create concepts for two products. The first was a microcassette recorder. It could easily fit into the inside pocket of a man's suit jacket. Or it could fit into a purse, a shirt pocket, even a vest pocket. The market was young executives. I began to think about the product and the person—connecting them in my mind. What were the fun benefits of the product? How might it be communicated comedically? What would appeal to people who would be recording meetings, conversations, seminars, classes...perhaps even surreptitiously?

Woody Allen was extremely popular at the time. So, I began to focus on a Woody Allen type of character (a nebbish) who was attempting to impress a beautiful girl with his spy-like appearance. The headline was: *For super spies and other guys.* The ad was produced for magazines. The company loved the concept because it focused on the product in a creative, memorable way, pointing out the features and benefits of the recorder, but in an environment that was playful, fun and entertaining.

The second product was a scanner that allowed the user to listen in on police, fire and ambulance calls. It was a voyeur's dream come true. The market was primarily male customers aged 18 to 34. They were pre-"techies" who loved the idea of tuning in to "forbidden information." The concept was to depict a youngish crowd of men with devilish grins on their faces, tucked away in an attic listening to the scanner. The headline: *Hear the news before it's news.* It was perfect because it conveyed exactly what prospective customers wanted—a tool to give them information that was secretive, proprietary and exciting. The ad invited them to get a jump on the rest of society, the rest of their community. It appealed to their sense of intrigue in a way that allowed them to feel special. The ad went on to articulate the "reason to buy," the qualities and warranties, the credible information that closes the sale. But the concept stopped them from turning the page.

We as marketers must pay careful attention to the world around us. We must always remember to create appealing propositions that are directed to the customer, not the marketer. We have to maintain a dialogue with our customer, personally and professionally. When we tap into what people are really thinking and feeling, we can create communications that work. Otherwise, we're talking to ourselves.

Sharing: A simple solution to understanding

Share groups are everywhere. Almost every conceivable industry has formed these vital associations. One of the many I'm familiar with exists in the convenience story industry. Groups of industry people get together on a regular basis to exchange information. In a sense, this is the most formidable forum for getting ideas and creating agendas. If your own industry doesn't offer share groups, contact the trade associations and inquire. These roundtables will provide you with more insight than you could possibly get on your own. You can then use this research to "focus" on your message and create the kind of compelling communication materials that are critically necessary to compete in the marketplace.

Often, businesses—including manufacturers, distributors, retailers and service industries—invite panels of customers to attend forums. Discussions include:

- Critiquing new products or new product ideas.

- Experiential exchanges about products or services.

- Sharing information about market conditions or changes in the marketplace.

- Exchanging stories that have led to successful sales or failed approaches.

- Feedback about promotional and advertising programs.

Consider establishing these types of meetings. Maintain the membership in **each group** through frequent communication. These seminars provide **opportunities** for your own customers to voice problems or frustrations and enable your customers to interact with your seniormost people in addressing issues that are vital to all involved. Le Tip, a prominent networking group, is listed in the business-to-business directories. It has groups in many different parts of the country. You can also find networking groups through your trade associations. Power Leads, another group, meets weekly in various communities and typically hosts meetings of noncompeting business participants with about 10 to 25 people per group.

Unleashing creativity through competitive intelligence

Finding out about your competitors is a formidable task. You *can* post their ads, mailings and messages on your bulletin board and study them. But there is a more sophisticated method if you're willing to pay the price. Special companies can provide you with the information you may need to formulate a marketing communications program. One such company is the renowned Find/SVP. This company, started in France, can, for a monthly fee or an hourly rate, provide you with virtually all of the information you could possibly want or need to launch a campaign or develop a strategy. The company is comprised of consultants in every imaginable field of commerce—from consumer products to industrial and technical fields, from health care to finances, from telecommunications to publishing, from importing to transportation. No, I'm not writing an ad for them. But you can utilize these types of companies to provide you with cutting-edge data that includes markets, industries, laws, management techniques, product development, competitive movements and on and on. You can access this information by phone, and the costs are now in line with small businesses' budgets. Find/SVP (625 Sixth Ave., New York, NY 10011; 212-645-4500) may prove to be a valuable part of your information gathering program.

Now, on to the creative process and how to apply it to practical selling themes.

Chapter 13

Making Your Communications Compelling

Marketing and advertising works when it touches people. It works when it solves problems and reduces fear. If we communicate in a way that makes people feel good about what we're selling and enables them to buy, we're on the road to successful communication. What do you know about your product? Do you know what problems it solves? Do you understand what it does that touches people's lives? Is it something that people need or want? How often do they use it? What can be said about it that makes people smile, laugh, cry? We establish the creative selling proposition by looking at these questions.

What are the five best possible selling propositions for your business? Let's use a motor yacht as an example in this exercise. The product is a 32-foot, twin-cabin, twin-engine boat. It sleeps six, has a galley, two heads, a dining area and a main salon, and it comes equipped with luxury features such as a color television, VCR, stereo with CD player, speakers throughout the cabin and lavish appointments. We need to focus on five propositions that will enable us to form a creative strategy:

1. It's like having a waterfront home.

2. It offers the freedom of moving from a horizon of skyscrapers to one of palm trees.

3. It's a family vacation.

4. It offers escape and adventure on the high seas.

5. It's fast enough to blow your hair behind your head.

Which of these issues is the most important? Well, in a recent survey, most people responded to the idea in number one and in number three. And while many loved the notion of escaping on the high seas in a fantasy of adventure, most families who bought a luxury boat spent a great deal more time in the marina than in the ocean. But the appeal reaches out to the sea, and the fantasy is a powerful part of the selling proposition.

Exercise

List five key propositions for your business. Look at who your customer is and consider what's important to him or her. From this list, you will uncover a vital part of your creative communication program.

Again, the premise and the promise

What are you selling? What is the premise? Where is the promise? Does your product lend itself to a humorous approach, a humanistic approach, a high-tech approach, a serious approach? Begin by doing the following exercise. It's called *writing your own review!*

Here's how it works. Create a movie review of your business. Use adjectives, accolades and critical remarks, as though you were reviewing an objective entity. Writing your own review is the first step in rewriting your business script and in creating compelling communications. Use the following format:

Name of company
Star performers
Supporting players
Past plot lines
Friends
Villains
Heroes
Moral of story
Years in business
Key selling features and benefits
Quotes from key employees about the business
Quotes from key customers about the business
Major accomplishments
Major successes versus competition
Goals and objectives for the future increases in revenue
Decreases in revenue
Outstanding achievements during the past five years
New ideas and programs that have been implemented
Weaknesses
Strengths

Give your business a rating. P is for poor. M is for mediocre. G is for good. E is for Excellent. O is for outstanding. I is for incredible.

Now, write a review for your chief competitor. Use the same criteria, and be as open and honest as possible. You will be comparing your company review with your competitor's in order to uncover the creative possibilities in communicating against the competitor.

Creating new realities

Before we begin the nuts and bolts of creating advertising, let's review how we, as marketers, create new realities. Let me begin by asking you the following question: *Does Jurassic Park really exist?*

My answer would be simply: It does now! Since its creation by the filmmakers, Jurassic Park exists. It's a place in our culture, our history, our arts. It has changed the landscape. As businesspeople, we want the very same thing to happen—creatively, you are looking to build a place for your business that becomes a reality for your market. While your message and your new reality will not likely affect the entire country or world the way *Jurassic Park* did, it will impact your specific market in much the same way the movie impacted the general public. This is a creative goal. We are making images when we make messages. We are filming our story and editing it for our customers, so that they will see exactly what we want them to see.

Not too long ago, I created D'artagnan Snellingwood, a character I have used in specific marketing materials for my clients. D'artagnan is a rogue, an adventurer, always pushing the envelope. Unlike me, D'artagnan will say and do outrageous things. And like the Jolly Green Giant, Elmer Fudd, Popeye or any fictional character, D'artagnan has a unique identity. He has become a new reality in a commercial campaign that I am proposing. The reason for his creation? As a marketer, I can put words in D'artagnan's mouth that couldn't possibly come out of the client's mouth. As a fictional character, D'artagnan can be outspoken, even outrageous, without causing the client embarrassment. For example, this character endorsed a dry cleaning establishment by claiming that it was so fast that it cleaned and pressed his suit before he got back in his car. I can create a persona that speaks for and about the business I represent, without risking the criticism of appearing too egotistical and self-serving. D'artagnan is removed from the realities that presently exist. Thus, he becomes an alter ego for the business, a new reality. Any time you use a fictional character, voice or place, you are creating identities that become part of your culture.

Unlike *real* celebrity testimonials, the creation of a proprietary program identifies your company through a character that couldn't possibly appear elsewhere for someone else. There is a decided advantage to beginning a program such as this.

When Channel Home Centers first introduced Wally the Home Doctor, people responded because there was a real person capable of answering their home repair questions. When Wally was depicted in ads, on radio or on television, there was an actual identity to which customers could relate. It truly didn't matter that Wally couldn't be found in the stores because his personality was large enough to provide the customer with a sense of security and a connection to a real, trusted individual.

You can create a character for your business by reaching way back to the beginning of the book when we defined your business personality. An appropriate voice can emerge from this exercise. With some creative thinking, if a character is appropriate for your product or service, you can develop a name, a sound, a voice and a message.

Testimonials create realities for businesses, too. If they are represented as positive reviews of your business by real customers with real experiences to relate, then they're quite effective. In the case of a celebrated person testifying on your behalf, they must match the profile of the company. You wouldn't want Bill Cosby to endorse your hair-coloring products or Henny Youngman to speak credibly about your tennis racquet. If the person can be easily related to the product, if it's an appropriate match, you can create a great deal of focus and attention on your product by creating a connection between it and someone who is instantly recognized. Clearly this is expensive and the benefits of celebrity endorsements should be weighed relative to the cost. Does the celebrity bring enough attention to your business? Will he or she work on a percentage arrangement? What other companies' products is he or she presently endorsing?

Recently, I saw Mario Andretti, a premier race car driver, endorsing two different products within the same magazine. The advertisements ran within pages of one another. While the goods being offered didn't compete with each other, the message was confusing, and the advertisers must not have checked Mr. Andretti's agenda.

I myself worked on television commercials with Mario Andretti, a charming and talented personality. He was hired to endorse a line of automotive products for a client of mine. His presence was a powerful connection for bringing these products to market. It was an appropriate match because the products were used on automobiles. The celebrity endorsement made perfect sense. We used a person who is highly recognizable within the market we were reaching. His image was bold, his presence was strong and his message was always credible. In this case, the use of his identity created a striking marketing message, and he proved to be an easy person with whom to work. We had even proposed a commercial concept that did not get produced but had a great deal of good humor associated with it. The idea came from looking at Mario himself. Here's a man known throughout the world for speed—long before it became a movie title. We developed a campaign in which a closeup of Mario appears on the screen. He is in full racing gear. The camera is on his head, covered in a highly lacquered helmet. The sounds of a roaring engine are heard. As the camera zooms out slowly to reveal Mario's head and chest, the sounds get louder and the excitement is building. Suddenly, the camera zooms in to reveal Mario seated on a riding mower—as he guns the throttle and leaps forward at about three miles per hour. It's a shame we never got this one in the can.

You're getting ready to create your own ad. The following example is helpful to you because it shows how a commodity product combined with a user-friendly message caused customers to try different products and ultimately buy more.

Something fishy

One of the first clients I signed when I started my agency many, many years ago was a large wholesale/retail fish business just outside of New York City. The owner wanted to promote three aspects of the business—the retail store, the wholesale operation and an adjoining restaurant. He had begun to run pedestrian advertisements that announced the existence of the business to consumers. The ads, as one would expect, stated:

Fresh Fish Right from the Ocean

This was his position statement. It headlined his ads, fliers, menus, signs and billboards. And the response was modest. For one thing, most people already accepted that fresh fish had to come from the ocean. If it didn't come right from the ocean, it wouldn't be fresh. In fact, it might be frozen.

The other reason had to do with intimidation. People would browse past the types of fish, seeing only the price per pound. Some customers would ask for information regarding taste, texture and preparation, but many would stick to what they knew or move on.

My first idea was to deliver a message that was engaging and informational and removed the intimidation factor. "Fresh fish" was a statement without impact and could be used as a supportive concept elsewhere in the communication process. We needed to make a statement that would be heard. The statement was:

The mystery of the sea is solved at Somerset Seafood!

It was supported by a consumer booklet that described each type of fish sold, with a simple illustration, description of taste, serving suggestions and portions per pound. There were little signs that were stuck in the ice next to the fish that reinforced the theme. The employees wore buttons stating: *Just ask...I'll offer a lobster tale!* Thus, the business took on a distinguished life of its own by virtue of seven words. It became the place where the mystery of the sea was solved. Children received *Fish Tales*, a proprietary coloring book that was filled with stories and recipes for the kinds of fish dishes kids would ask Mom or Dad to make. Indeed, we did solve the mysteries of the sea. And we did it with a small budget, small ads and a creative approach.

By offering its customers an advantage (in this case, it was educational and informative), the fish store became more pronounced in the customers' minds. Every business can offer its clientele a distinct advantage, a unique selling proposition that can be expanded into a unique selling program. By taking a single idea and incorporating it into various methods of enhancing the sale, the company becomes far more recognizable in the marketplace and far more credible.

Chapter 14

Nuts and Bolts

Now, let's construct a print advertisement. The following guidelines are for creating a magazine or newspaper ad.

Headline: The banner of your advertisement. It must gain the readers' attention immediately. It can be a question, a statement, a single word...but it must contain vitality. It will often include the benefit of the product or service.

Subheadline: Must support the headline, giving the reader more information and carrying the theme established in the headline.

Body copy: Adds features to the benefits. Sells the idea, informs, educates, provides credible data designed to draw the reader closer to the product or service. It must relate in language, tone and style to the headline and subheadline.

Graphic: Enhances the headline, subheadline and copy. This can be a photograph or illustrated artwork. The graphic must be appropriate and must strengthen the selling proposition by visually supporting the words.

Position statement: The slogan, corporate statement, validation. This is the fingerprint of your ad. It identifies what makes you unique— where your product or service stands in relation to the universe of like products around you.

Call for action: When appropriate, this is a statement or closing line, typically represented in bold typeface. It gives the readers the information they need to order. It may consist of an incentive statement, a toll-free number or a coupon.

Readers like to read headlines. Whether they're accompanied by graphics or not, it's the first thing they see. In the case of a powerful headline and a dynamic visual, the combination is unbeatable. The first few lines of your body copy are critically important. If they don't do their job, the reader turns the page and your advertising dollars are lost. That's why it's so very important that you spend time making sure that the advertising headline does its job well.

Many years ago a global marketer of ultrasonic cleaning systems and solutions for a wide range of industries hired my firm to market its products. One of the most memorable products was a torch fueled by distilled water. The product, called the Aqua Torch, was a safe alternative to traditional welders or soldering tools, which required the storage of pressurized gas as fuel. The major advantage of this product was its unique design, which converted water into gas, thus providing an efficient, adjustable flame for intricate work. It was important for the ad headline to be powerful. We needed to distinguish ourselves quickly and cleverly from the competitor—whose torch was newer and lighter. We decided to use the heavy-duty nature of our product and its nine-and-a-half-year history in the marketplace as marketing benefits.

I looked at what intrigued me about the Aqua Torch and the most obvious aspect jumped right out. It used water to make fire. The headline: *For nearly a decade, we've been building a fire with water.* The photograph showed a bright yellow-red flame emanating from the tip of the torch. A bottle of distilled water was being poured into the torch housing. Fire and water were there in the ad together, and the headline took advantage of *opposites attracting attention.*

The body copy described the advantages of this product. It maintained the theme, the tone and the language of the headline. This is vitally important. A headline needs to be carried into the copy so that the reader maintains his or her interest in the selling proposition. In this case, there was enough intrigue about the unusual nature of fire and water working together to cause the prospect to stop and read further. Don't disappoint the audience by abandoning the headline and allowing the message to go downhill. The body copy for this ad was:

> *Traditionally fire and water are enemies, opposites.*
> *One burns while the other extinguishes the flame.*
> *The Aqua Torch brings these powerful elements*
> *together—producing more heat than imaginable. And*
> *since there's no need for pressurized gas, the Aqua*
> *Torch can be used safely in any work environment.*
> *The Aqua Torch...build your next fire with water!*

Notice how the copy stayed the course created by the headline. The vitality of imagery and language was maintained throughout the entire communication. Copy has to sound like the headline in order to keep the customer from drifting away. Too many marketers assume that a headline is enough, but it's not. Struggle for the right words—from the headline through the copy right on down to the call for action. Build the ad so your reader never forgets your product. It's not easy...but it's a whole lot easier than losing business to the competition.

Your print advertising must address the following questions:

1. Is the message clear?
2. Does the advertisement inform without becoming tedious?
3. Are you asking the reader to do something—think, act, inquire, respond?
4. Does the advertisement alter perceptions, tell something new?
5. Have you created a unique position for your business?
6. Is the offer specific or institutional?
7. What image is being conveyed?
8. Are you giving enough information for the reader to make an inquiry or purchase decision?
9. If you cover the logo and address, can you differentiate your advertisement from every other advertisement in the medium you're using?
10. Will the reader remember the message tomorrow, next week? Why?

Print advertising performs many functions. There is more to marketing than putting a message in front of an audience. Your advertising needs to address the following issues in order to be successful:

1. Your advertisement must create primary demand. The message needs to deliver the customer to your product.
2. If the communication does not sell a product or service directly, it must impose your image on the customer.
3. If your advertisement is in the business-to-business arena, it should gain inquiries and leads for the sales force by offering an incentive for a response.
4. The advertising should help open new markets by creating a message that evolves (contains new aspects of your business frequently).
5. The advertising can guarantee a product or service.
6. The advertising can provide credibility or offer testimonial evidence of excellence.

Surveys reveal that the effectiveness of print advertising is greatly enhanced when the guarantee or warranty is substantiated. Make strong claims, and live up to them! Also, when using testimonials, be sure that they are believable and the credentials of those being quoted relate to the product or service being offered. For example, if your advertisement is for a boat polish, your quoted source should have a substantial background in boating. Deliver the information, and remember that, in this case, the messenger is as important as the message.

When your print advertising won't work well

If your product or service does not live up to its claims...

If your product or service is inferior in the marketplace...

If your product or service is priced higher than comparable products...

If your product or service has no unique selling propositions...

If your product or service has no value-added selling objectives...

...it is imperative that you pay careful attention, when constructing your advertising, to the details that bring power to the message. Without the six essential issues we just discussed, you are greatly limiting your response potential! So, aside from the elements that make up an advertisement, the underlying theme, philosophy and methods of doing business are critical. And continuity of message is also a vital piece of the advertising pie—from headline to body copy... from the call for action to the position statement.

Pitching your tent

An example of continuity between the headline and the body copy is an advertisement for a line of tents sold by the Boy Scouts of America. The distinguishing features of this particular "Adventurer" tent included the strength of the ripstop nylon, the stitching and the warranty. These qualities needed to be conveyed in a way that dramatized the features and benefits without using language that does not cross over into our consciousness...words such as *quality, value.* We had to convey the concept of quality without using the word. By thinking from the other side—approaching the basic benefits to the customer—we decided to illustrate why careful workmanship was important in the production of these particular tents. The ad headline:

> *Adventurer tents keep the weather outside...*
> *where it belongs!*

A photograph depicted two campers peering out from the nylon web in the front of the tent into a torrential downpour of rain and wind. Leaves were flying, tree branches were blowing, but the campers appeared happy and dry. The body copy delivered a message with respect to the headline:

> *It's weather like this that tests tents. And while we*
> *can't control the weather, we can control how it*
> *affects us when we're off on a camping trip.*
> *Adventurer tents are designed to take whatever*
> *nature dishes out. So, through wind, rain, sleet,*
> *hail...you can take comfort in knowing that your*
> *comfort won't be compromised. That's because every*
> *tent is field tested before it's sold. So, we guarantee*
> *that the weather will stay outside where it*
> *belongs...or you'll get all your money back!*

The advertisement also gave the reader the specifications of the product—measurements, accessories and price. The call for action appeared as a coupon for a free catalog and a list of specific retail locations that carried the product.

Another advertisement was designed to sell an ax. In creating the headline, we decided to concentrate on what an ax does best—chop wood. By connecting the benefit to the product, we positioned the ax as superior to similar products. The headline:

> *How much wood would a woodchopper chop if a*
> *woodchopper would chop wood?*
> *It depends on the ax!*

A photograph showed a stack of split wood with the ax resting on a log. The blade of the ax was glistening from the sunlight— illustrating how sharp and majestic this small, powerful tool could be.

By using a playful adaptation of a tongue twister—*How much wood would a woodchuck chuck if a woodchuck could chuck wood*—we delivered a message that stopped the reader because it was recognizable... and intriguing. The body copy continued the theme:

> *Some people have an ax to grind. But not the people*
> *who buy our ax. The Woodsman ax doesn't need*
> *grinding for a minimum of five years. That's because*
> *it's made to stay sharper than any other ax around.*
> *And it's specially balanced—so you hit and split*
> *harder and faster. Woodchoppers chop a lot more*
> *wood when they swing the Woodsman ax. How much*
> *wood would you chop with the right ax? A lot more*
> *than you've ever chopped before!*

Again, the call for action was a coupon for a catalog.

The creative premise is established by your headline. Use the same notion to create the informational message—the body copy— and you're on your way to a professional advertisement. Too often, great headlines lose their authority because they are not followed by copy statements that are as effective. You must pay careful attention to the issue of continuity in order to give your advertisement the lifespan it deserves and the selling power to justify the cost of the media.

Stating your position or assuming your posture?

I have used the term *posturing* because I felt it introduces a marketing concept that utilizes the principles of positioning but has more flexibility. The difference between positioning and posturing is that positioning is rigid and posturing is fluid. Here's what I mean: Once you have established a marketing position (where your product or service stands in relation to the competition), you have a responsibility to uphold that position. Occasionally, marketing positions change. For example, Domino's Pizza's original position was "15 minutes or free." A problem arose when aggressive delivery people attempting to beat the delivery deadline ended up causing automobile accidents. An entire marketing strategy was based upon that 15 minute position. When, for practical reasons, it had to go...so went the marketing position.

Posturing utilizes the same principles as positioning, with one exception: It remains more flexible and more changeable. So, the modified marketing position (posture) that Domino's might have taken was: *Whenever possible, we'll be there in 15 minutes...or less...and for every minute we're over, we'll deduct a dollar*. Does it weaken the selling proposition? Yes, slightly. But it also offers your business flexibility to move off the position if it becomes untenable. The reason I mention it here is because you will be utilizing your slogan or position statement in your ad. Think about it carefully before it becomes a published proclamation.

This statement is your fingerprint, your identifying mark, and it should appear in conjunction with your logo—under it, along its side, over it or as a part of it.

The call for action is just what it states—a statement or device that asks for the sale. In the case of nondirect advertising (an advertisement that doesn't offer a direct response vehicle such as a toll-free number or a coupon), the call for action will not necessarily result in a commitment on the part of the customer to make a purchase decision immediately. But it does require the customer to think about the proposition by virtue of an incentive to respond—free literature, an offer that contains an expiration, a complimentary consultation or information that will result in a sale. Sometimes the call for action is a pronouncement of immediacy: *Act now...Hurry in...While supplies last...Final three days of sale...For a limited time...*and on and on. In any case, it requires the customer to consider the offer and place a priority on the purchase.

Institutional or promotional

When we are selling an institution's image—as opposed to an item and a price—we are offering the reader imagistic messages. Remember "Coke Adds Life"? "You Deserve a Break Today"? "Have It Your Way"? "We Are Driving Excitement"? "A Piece of the Rock"? "Better Coffee a Millionaire's Money Can't Buy"? These are all examples of institutional positions, designed to leave the customer with the company's sense of purpose, not suggesting you go right to the store to buy the product. The message clearly sells the company behind the product, as well as the specific item itself. There is no aggressive call for action in institutional advertising—mostly just the communication of image and brand identity. You will likely use institutional messages when your advertising appears in a noncommercial medium such as a theater playbill or a program for a charitable event. For that reason alone, you need to establish an institutional personality as well as a promotional one. Your image message will be softer, more subtle and more sophisticated. It may develop from our discussion of brand identity in Chapter 15, and it should always offer your best profile.

Creativity is often enhanced by associative thinking. Your image can be helped by associating what you do with what the customer wants, keeping in mind the benefits you offer. Of course, promotional messages incorporate an immediate gratification clause, as the following example suggests.

The greatest copywriter in the world

Jerry Della Femina, an advertising legend renowned for many noted campaigns, told a story that I will never forget. It has to do with creativity in advertising and marketing, and the much sought-after gurus of creative thinking—copywriters! It seems that Jerry got a call from a dear friend in Greenwich, Connecticut, one rainy afternoon. The friend told Jerry to immediately get on a train from Grand Central Station and come to Greenwich where he would meet him. When Jerry asked why, the friend stated that he had found the greatest copywriter in the world, and he wanted Jerry to see his work. Jerry questioned the urgency but admitted that he would certainly travel anywhere to find a truly talented copywriter. His friend again told him to get there as soon as humanly possible. Jerry bolted from his office and headed to Grand Central Station, jumped on a train to Greenwich and, upon arriving in Connecticut, raced off the train to his friend who was waiting by the parking lot.

The friend told Jerry to get in the car and indicated that they would soon see the work of the world's greatest copywriter. Jerry asked repeatedly where they were headed—only to be told that they would be there soon enough. When they pulled into the parking lot of a McDonald's, Jerry was completely bewildered. Again, he asked his friend why they were going to a McDonald's. And again, his friend told him to be patient. They got out of the car, and Jerry followed the friend to the men's room. Completely puzzled, scratching his head, he began to protest when his friend threw open the door and headed for one of the stalls. He opened the door to the stall, and written on the wall above the toilet seat were the words *Stop the war in Vietnam and win valuable prizes!*

Creating your way out of a marketing nightmare

Sometimes you're in the wrong place at the wrong time...or the right place at the wrong time. In either case, you find yourself in a situation that creates marketing misery. That's what happened to a retail jeweler in a start up business in a small midwestern town. The owners, an affable young couple, had inherited a family jewelry business in a small mountain community situated about two hours from a modest-size city. The store was basically on its way out of business, so they decided to create a new jewelry store based upon their own interests, passions and vision. Their interests far exceeded the needs of the marketplace—an area of modest income families with little or no awareness of jewelry trends, designers or major brands. In spite of the mismatch between marketer and market, the couple went ahead with their plans and began to design an elegant gallery of designer jewelry.

They created a distinctive name for the store—one that certainly would have been appropriate for a store on Fifth Avenue in New York City. Then, when their vision was nearly complete, they hired a marketing firm from another state. Based upon the store itself—without taking the market into consideration—the experts they hired produced a program using cable TV and radio exclusively to promote this high-end designer gallery.

Suppose they gave a war and nobody came

That's exactly what happened to our fine, young couple. No one came. First, the couple discovered that the marketing firm had a boilerplate promotional approach to every retailer in the jewelry industry, regardless of the market! Thus, their high-tone communication fell on deaf ears...because the customer couldn't possibly respond to the message.

The look, sound and product presentation all pointed to a customer that didn't exist in their marketplace. They even used inappropriate music—jazzy classical sounds that totally missed the mark. By the time I was aware of their problem, they had spent their entire annual budget—four months into the year.

What we have here is a failure to communicate!

Many years ago, this line was made famous by a character in a movie titled *Cool Hand Luke*. The warden made this statement to Luke, a prisoner portrayed by Paul Newman. Even out of context, it is a classic statement of mismarketing!

The jeweler failed to communicate with the customer. The language, style, tone, product and environment were all products of personal preference on the part of the jewelry store owners. They created a business from their own passions without paying attention to the customers' passion. They couldn't speak to the customers because they were speaking totally different languages. We needed to get back to the basics. The creative approach we agreed upon was conceived to drive people back into the store without making radical changes to the environment itself. We changed the product mix to include lower price points, more popular styles, more silver—and we altered the image to be inclusive instead of exclusive. But we still needed to hear the cash register ring, quickly. In this instance, we altered the game plan from institutional advertising to promotional. The first stage of this program was what we called "The Cinderella Story."

We ran a series of advertisements in the local and regional newspapers. We also developed a target mailing list that included both past customers and new prospects, defined by geography, income and age. The idea was to reinvent the business with a bang.

The first order of business was to educate customers regarding the changes in the store and the new philosophy, which included adding a secondary statement below the store's fancy French name. By doing this, we softened the image: *La Elegance...fabulous jewelry for the families of Allen Township*. The use of the word "families" reduced the snob appeal of the name, yet allowed us to do business without recreating the sign, packaging, business cards and everything else, including yellow page advertising.

The initial promotion, The Cinderella Story, offered three gold and gemstone rings for free to the first three people who came into the store and could fit perfectly into one of the rings. Signs were posted, coffee and refreshments were served, merchandising of many sale items was incorporated into the showroom...and people were lined up to try on the glass slipper.

Because the rings had a retail value in excess of $1,000 each, we were able to attract enough responses to turn this promotion into a local media event, which included a remote radio broadcast, lots of free publicity and a strong showing of new faces inside the store. The jewelers also contributed 10 percent of the day's revenue to the local arts center.

Interestingly, the first woman to fit into the first ring was number 30 on line. It was fun and exciting, and people were turned on by the creativity of the promotion and the significant savings throughout the rest of the store. The same customers who had been afraid of La Elegance because they didn't fit the image created for the business were now comfortable with the store, the people and the product.

As we move forward in producing our marketing materials, we have to stay aware of the relationship between who and where we are relative to our surroundings. If you pull your truck up to a fish market and begin to unload oranges, you're going to be drinking an awful lot of orange juice yourself. What we communicate in our advertising is what our customers want to see and hear. If they're selling fish at the market, sell a larger variety, a fresher catch, a more economical price. Don't sell oranges.

Building your brochure

Most start up marketers need and want to effectively market. The best sources for the making of a brochure are printers, ad agencies, freelancers and graphic design firms—all listed in the yellow pages. Occasionally, this is done before all the rest of the homework has been accomplished. Obviously, I want you to know who you are, who your customer is, where you're going and what you're going to do to get there. Those issues aside, you certainly will benefit from a brochure that gets your attention and keeps you top-of-mind in your marketplace. Good brochures reinforce your position in the community.

What exactly is a brochure? The best answer is that a brochure creates the drama of an advertisement but delivers a more complete sales message that can be retained physically as well as mentally. We also refer to brochures as leave-behinds because they are often used as a reminder of the personally spoken sales message—delivered directly by the marketer. Remember, don't give away the store in your brochure. It is not designed to tell the complete company story. It is designed to entice, sell and inform enough to keep the prospect interested.

Brochures use the same devices as advertisements to attract attention. But because they are printed, they offer options not always available in display advertising. For one thing, brochures can contain a wide choice of colors, paper stock, typography, photos and illustrations, informational messages and response devices. Like any other part of your creative package, brochures must be consistent with everything else you do.

Consistency is a critical issue of communication. All of your advertising and collateral materials must be designed with a consistent look. The power of synergy works when everything you do complements everything else you do.

Accord must be achieved in your selling materials. Think about the way you put your office or home together. Colors complement each other; styles that go together are chosen; there is a harmonious element to your total look. Your collateral materials must maintain this symmetry, as well.

Continuity can be accomplished by paying careful attention to the sequence of issues you are presenting in your brochure. Ask yourself: Is there logic to the material you are developing? You want your customer to read or glance from point A to point B without becoming distracted or bored. Visual elements such as boldface type, large letters, italicized words, graphics and photos must be laid out carefully. Remember, your brochure is your minibook, and like a book, you need to proceed from Chapter 1 to the conclusion.

Focus on your primary selling objectives first. Your brochure must build from the cover to the first page and on to subsequent pages by order of importance. If you lose the reader after the first page, you still want them to get the message. So, front-load the brochure in order to achieve a greater chance of keeping the primary message intact.

Diversity keeps people involved in the material you're presenting. Consider as many different images, statements and ideas as possible in building your case. This may include color changes from one page to another or a graphic element that begins on page one and changes shape on page three. You have a short time to tell your story; be sure to keep things interesting. You don't want laundry lists of words without interruption.

Proportion is achieved by assessing the balance between different elements on the page. You want the combination of words and graphics to balance, so that proper emphasis is given to the complete picture— the ease of the eye to follow the flow of information.

You will need to consult with people in your own circle who may have a background in design. If these people are not available to you, then visit a local printer and ask for help. Most printers employ layout people who can help you with selecting color, size, style and paper and can advise you of costs for the many variables you encounter in producing a brochure.

Remember that color is important in presenting certain products while it isn't necessarily as important in selling others. For example, you should consider the use of four-color (full-color comprised of the four primary colors) if your product is food. Many fashion items as well as household products benefit from being advertised in color. However, black and white or two-color (printing companies will show you a Pantone color swatch book which displays all the available printing colors) is appropriate in advertising that doesn't depend upon the use of vibrant color depiction. Outstanding brochures have been produced, in one or two colors, for hair salons, insurance agencies, pet grooming businesses, parts distribution companies, ice-cream stores, manufacturing facilities, bicycle shops, shoe stores. Ask yourself if color is important in your category, and take a look at what your competitors are doing. The cost differential between one- or two-color and four-color printing is enormous because full-color printing requires color-separated film, which is very costly.

Also, the printer you use should advise you on the use of screens that allow you to create a more colorful brochure without incurring additional expense. The use of screens is a process that breaks up the solid color into variations of that color, thus allowing you to create a multicolored presentation without the use of additional ink.

Research within the marketing field has shown the strength of specific colors in various product categories. Sometimes the simple use of a different color creates a standout brochure. If you're in the automobile leasing business and most of the brochures in your industry are silver or burgundy (strong luxury automobile colors), you should consider producing your brochure in silver and tangerine. Why? Because it will be noticed faster. If you went to the supermarket and saw a large display of tomatoes piled in front of you and one of the tomatoes had a bright green stem, which one would you notice and what would it say to you? You want your brochure to benefit from all of the issues we've discussed prior to this. One of them is getting noticed. Color is one of the elements that can help.

Brochures, like other communication pieces, require layouts. A layout is an arrangement of words and graphics that comprise the contents of the brochure. The best way to begin is to use a pencil and create what is referred to as a thumbnail layout. This is a rough, first draft of your brochure. Here you will pencil in the cover statement, the headlines that appear on the following pages, any graphic elements and copy points. This will become the first stage of your blueprint.

From your thumbnail, you will move on to a comp (comprehensive layout). This next stage of the brochure design will include an accurate size, typestyle, artwork or photography. (Note: You can obtain any subject matter through stock photography companies—simply look under stock photography in the yellow pages. They typically charge a nominal research fee to send you a variety of slides or a CD-ROM that contains many available images. They negotiate charges based upon the use of the photography and also rent stock illustrations. Or you can purchase clip art from art services available through your local printer, so you need not incur huge start up costs for your brochure.) The costs for stock art range from less than $100 for photos and illustrations to several hundred dollars, depending upon how many brochures you're printing and how they'll be used. There are also many freelance services available through printers, design studios and graphic suppliers.

One of the most valuable creative resources for start up marketers is local colleges and universities. Simply call art schools or the marketing departments at local colleges and ask for the names of students who are interested in freelance assignments. There are lots of talented students who will help you develop your artwork, logos and advertising materials. And there are just as many talented copywriters who will work with you on ideas and concepts for your marketing. They will usually work well within your budget and sometimes will offer you sophisticated materials for extremely small fees because they are most interested in seeing their work completed and published.

Now, on to the comprehensive layout, which is your next to final stage in the production of the brochure. Before you begin to set type and create finished, camera-ready artwork (which can go right from disk to the printer), you need to do a "creativity check" for your brochure:

- Does the cover deliver a promise?
- Does the cover gain attention?
- What unique selling proposition is being offered?
- Are you keeping the customer in mind throughout your story?
- Do specifics and technical issues get in the way of the benefits?
- Is there continuity from page to page?
- Does the brochure address and solve the customers' problems?
- Are you asking for a response?

Brochures are an integral part of any business's marketing portfolio. But how they are used is as much a part of the creative strategy as how they are compiled. They lend themselves to distribution by mail, person, kiosks, waiting rooms, reception areas, malls—almost any public place that permits the dissemination of literature. In addition, your brochure is your company's resume. Therefore, you may want to develop a program of direct mail with a cover letter as well as utilizing the brochure in direct person-to-person selling. In any case, the brochure is far more likely to be retained by the prospect than a letter or flier. And the brochure is more tangible and has a much higher perceived value. If you need a direct response, you will have to incorporate a perforated business reply card or publish a toll-free number. When you ask for a response, be sure to make it easy for the prospect to gain access to your company. A toll-free number is better than a postage-paid card, but either will do. Do not ask for a response expecting the customer to do much work or spend any money. Therefore, pay for the response yourself, and be sure that there is a good reason to respond—such as a free sample, complimentary literature, a contest, more information or other incentives. When you use a business reply card with a mailing indicia, you only pay for the postage of those cards actually mailed. Therefore, consider the percentage of responses you anticipate receiving and calculate your costs.

The business letter: If they snooze, you lose

I am not an advocate of standard letters which begin with "Dear So-and-So"! Whoever said letters had to be boring? Someone prominent must have made that statement a very long time ago, because most business letters belong in the circular file.

Start up businesses almost always begin solicitation by letter writing. Many of you may have bought books or subscribed to services that provide you with sample letters. For the most part, I have found that traditional letters receive traditional responses...and very few. Using letters to generate business is economical—just as there is a good reason to consider writing letters to customers who are tardy in paying you. But for the most part, the letters need not resemble those you wrote to your loved ones when you were at summer camp, or in the army, or away at college. In those cases, the recipients had to read them. In the case of business letters, nobody has to read anything.

First, let's dispense with the "Dear So-and-So" and think of our letter as an advertisement. When you begin your typical letter, you usually start with the obligatory polite opener: "Thank you for taking my phone call the other day. I was delighted to have an opportunity to speak with you."

I am going to suggest that we approach letter writing from another perspective: the customer's! The best business letters have headlines that grab hold of the reader's attention immediately. Then, the content of the letter is broken into priorities—from most important to least important—under the assumption that even if the customer doesn't get past the first paragraph, you've already made your point. Therefore, struggle for the headline and the first six lines that succeed it. And if you use a sub-headline, be certain that it, too, grabs the reader by each ear and pulls him or her into the page.

The following letter was sent to a jewelry store's customer list. It was designed to get an immediate response to a sale. The customers were already acquainted with the store but had not made a purchase for at least six months. This promotion was designed to be extremely economical, which is why a letter was the only means of communication. The other promotional dollars were the result of discounting very attractive merchandise. The letter stated:

In the next nine seconds you will save $150, guaranteed!

I have just purchased 112 sea pearl necklaces. They are valued at $249! Once they are sold, I cannot get any more at anywhere near this price. If you call upon receipt of this letter, I will hold one for you with absolutely no obligation. The price: $99! All I can tell you is that this price is below my cost. Why am I making you this offer? Because you are a valued customer and I haven't seen you in more than six months.

The letter contained one more paragraph...but it didn't matter. Of the 300 customers who received the mailing, more than 100 called. Every necklace was sold. The cost of the promotion was the price of postage and letterhead plus a small loss on the product. The results? Customers became reacquainted with the store and strong sales resulted from this isolated group of customers during their visits. The letter broke the rules by appearing more like an ad than a business letter, but the response was far greater than what could have been achieved with standard format and language. The promotion itself was obviously compelling as well, but even a great offer will fail if it's not presented creatively! The outside of the envelope carried the same message as the headline, thus creating a sense of urgency and an assurance that it would likely be opened.

Creating your radio script

Radio is a marvelous tool because it is extremely cost-effective and can build your image beautifully. I'd like to reiterate my earlier claim about radio being the most visual medium available to advertisers and to recall the discussion of visual storyboards—a staple in the creation of television commercials—as a means of developing a radio campaign.

Radio scripts utilize sounds, music and voices and can consist of a donut format (which surrounds the message with music before and after the voice-over), a straight announcement, a dialogue, a jingle or a variation of all of these elements.

Tags are short information bursts that are offered at the end of the commercial message. They act as violators to the rest of the commercial, interrupting the flow to ask for the order or to reiterate the selling proposition. They are typically 10 seconds or less and may repeat a promotional offer or reestablish the position of the company or product.

Because radio requires the listener to remember some aspect of the commercial, keep the contents of the script focused. Begin by creating a divided page, with the left side of the page offering information relating to sound effects, voice talent, use of music. The right side of the page is the actual dialogue, copy, instructions. For example, our script on page 214 is for a real estate development. Note the use of imagery, music and the selection of voices.

Typically your script will run either 30 or 60 seconds. To time a script, speak the parts at a moderate pace and watch the second hand of the clock. You will benefit from establishing time limitations on the use of music. Also, be prepared to embellish or cut copy in order to make the script time-out exactly on the mark. Even though the FCC has deregulated the allotted time for radio commercials, most stations follow strict guidelines and will cut the copy if it runs over. I would prefer that you cut the copy, not the radio station.

Questions about your radio script

1. Do the voices reflect the quality of the product?
2. Does the music enhance the selling message and create the appropriate mood?
3. Do the sound effects augment the imagery?
4. Is the message consistent in tone and language?
5. Does your commercial provide the listener with a believable proposition?
6. Is the nonvisual play (which is really what a radio commercial is) interesting, inspiring?
7. Is the message focused and simple enough to be retained?
8. Do the sound, personality and tone support relate specifically to the target customer?
9. Is it a personal message? (You are communicating to one person at a time.)
10. Does the commercial present a sense of urgency?

Sample script

CLIENT: Horizon's Pasture
Length: 60 seconds
MUSIC: Theme from *A Summer Place* (romantic, soothing, moody, 3 seconds), up and under [*starts loud, then volume is reduced to be heard under the voice-over (VO)*]

VO: (Midthirties male, strong yet soft-sounding)

There's a pasture where you used to play...or dreamt of playing. Now it can be yours.

VO: (Thirtysomething female, sultry voice)

Horizon's Pasture. Thirty-two homesites set high on a hill—in a field of dreams.

SFX [*sound effects*]: Wind

MUSIC: up (3 seconds) and under

VO: Male voice

Come...custom-build your dream home—in a community boasting the area's most prestigious estates.

VO: Female voice

Horizon's Pasture in historic Peapack...now you can set your sights high on homesites that offer a majestic view of the countryside, complete with brilliant splashes of color.

VO: Male voice

Your home will sit on three to four acres of lush property— tucked into more than 150 acres of countryside...away from every conceivable sight and sound...

VO: Female voice

MUSIC: up

Yet less than a half-hour to major highways. It's the best of both worlds.

ANNCR TAG:

Call for a private showing at Horizon's Pasture: 1-800-555-6287. We'll fax you directions and a confirmation of your appointment. That's Horizon's Pasture, 1-800-555-6287. Remember: with only 32 homesites left, don't take too much time to daydream!

Formats for your radio commercial may vary from the use of multiple voice-overs speaking separately as in the example above. The voice-over talent may speak to one another in character, using a dialogue approach. The straight announcer may be used when the message is direct to the consumer. You've probably also heard situational or slice-of-life commercials that present a problem and a solution. Then, of course, there are jingles, which contain the selling message in a musical format. Jingles are expensive and difficult to produce; most start up companies, therefore, may want to begin radio advertising by creating a script and allowing the radio station to produce the commercial.

Your TV storyboard

The advent and increased popularity of cable television have permitted start up marketers to communicate via this powerful medium. If we use industry statistics as a guideline, each American spends more than 1,500 hours per year, on average, in front of the tube. It's a national pastime...and, in many respects, an advertiser's dream.

When you're ready to create your TV storyboard, remember that there are many formats you can use to sell your product or service through television. According to *Adweek* magazine, commercials that used humor ranked highest among both men and women in all age categories—18 to 34, 34 to 59, 59-plus. The second-highest-ranking results were achieved from commercials using children, followed by those using celebrities, real-life situations, brand comparisons, musical formats, product demonstrations, endorsements from experts, hidden-camera testimonials and—last and certainly least—company presidents.

Your television script begins by choosing a theme and a format. The creative process is different from any other in advertising, mostly because you are marrying visual images to words. The principles of promotion remain much the same. That is, you are focusing on the features and benefits of your product or service, while making the most of the medium's vitality: sight and sound!

When you create your television commercial, you are essentially producing your company's movie—in short form. Therefore, you will want to boil all of the wonderful, marketable aspects of your business into a half-minute or a minute. It's not easy, but it should be a great deal of fun.

The storyboard develops from envisioning the situation that you would like to see take place. A marvelous resource for your storyboard and the actual production of the TV commercial is the cable company. Each cable provider has a production staff and facility and will help you produce the commercial for a nominal cost in order to reel you in as an advertiser. The costs may range from several hundred dollars to a few thousand, depending upon how sophisticated and complicated your idea is. Start up marketers should stick to simple, easy-to-produce commercials in order to spend the bulk of the budget on frequency. This does not mean to compromise your message—it simply means that you can do an effective job of communicating through television, utilizing a simple format.

Television storyboards may appear in horizontal or vertical formats. In the case of the horizontal storyboard, the individual pictures appear alongside one another with the action and dialogue described below each picture. In the case of a vertical storyboard, the action takes place from top of page to bottom with video action being described on the left side of the page and audio action on the right.

The next page shows an example of a vertical storyboard without the actual pictures. This concept was proposed to a company that manufactures an all-fruit spread. The idea was to dramatize the fact that this product was made from 100-percent fruit...with a position line that stated: *A Smashing New Way to Serve Fruit!* In the commercial, we used a prop-device—a large mallet.

(Note: Actual storyboards use illustrations of the video action. These are small pictures of the activities taking place alongside the audio portion of the script. Each frame utilized one of the pictures in order to give the advertiser an idea as to what the finished commercial will look like.)

At best, storyboards offer a rough simulation of the finished product and modestly resemble the fully produced commercial. Thus, it is wise to remember that the format of the storyboard is similar to the comprehensive layout of the brochure or advertisement. It is a model to be used for approval purposes only. The creative elements of television include the use of closeups, intimate actions, sweeping visual imagery accompanied by music, sound effects and dialogue. The visual devices include:

Cut. The visual activity ends abruptly and a new shot appears. The first scene is dramatically replaced by another scene. There is no evidence of time changes. The cut is used in order to stimulate the viewer to react and to keep attention focused on the activity.

Dissolve. One scene fades into another. This device is used to indicate movement from one visual issue to another. Typically, dissolves create the perception of some lapse in time.

Zoom. The visual frame becomes smaller or larger with no change in the scene. This is done by a special camera lens that permits the focus

Sample storyboard

Video	Audio
MCU [*medium closeup*] of British male (midthirties)	Talent: Hello, I'm here to talk about Nature's Spread.
Cut to wooden table filled with fresh fruit	Music depicts harvest theme
Dissolve to male spokesman approaching table, lifting large mallet	In order to demonstrate just how fresh Nature's Spread really is...
Cut to medium shot of man lifting mallet over his right shoulder...he turns his face to the camera as he smashes the fruit	SFX: smashing, crashing— wood breaking and splat, squishy sounds
Cut to talent—now scooping the smashed fruit into jars. He is covered with pieces of fruit.	Talent: I've got to talk to the people at Nature's Spread. Surely, there's a far better way to get fruit into a jar. Besides it's awfully wasteful.
Dissolve to man attempting to clean himself off...picking pieces of fruit out of his clothing, hair.	You've got to admit, real fruit's a whole lot better than those sugary jams and jellies. They're like eating lollipops, not real fruit!
Inset of Nature's Spread logo on slide, with type: A Smashing New Way to Serve Fruit...*At the Produce Department of Supermarkets Everywhere.*	Talent: A smashing new way to serve fruit...Nature's Spread.

to remain fixed while the images that appear in the scene are brought closer to the viewer or farther away.

Fade-in. Visual elements fade into focus from a black or blank screen.

Fade-out. This is where the scene fades out into black, creating the belief that time has gone by between scenes.

Wipe. A visual effect that literally wipes away one scene while bringing into play another scene. There is usually no indication of time changing with wipes. Further, the wipe may be from left to right or top to bottom.

Matte. This technique allows the viewer to witness one scene overlapping another. For example, one visual element is depicted in two different environments, as the scene changes.

Start up marketers should depend upon television companies for the first round of creative productions. But you can take your ideas to a storyboard by simply indicating audio and video elements on a sheet of paper, describing each scene in place of using illustrations. Since your commercials will most likely be for your own business, you can develop ideas that will be storyboarded by the production company or cable provider. Also, pay careful attention to the use of music, slides and graphics. Television can be a very intimate medium. Get close to your customers through the images you impose on them.

Much of the creation of your commercial will take place in the editing suite. This process is referred to as postproduction. Here is where technological magic is made. You can sit in the editing room with the technician and make choices regarding the juxtaposition of scenes, sounds and dialogue. You will find that almost anything is possible in the editing process. Let the experts guide you about issues of continuity, pacing, timing, composition and energy. Watch your commercial in the mind-set of your customer, and be sure that you are leaving the viewer with a powerful impression of your business. You have 30 or 60 seconds to make your mark—make each second count.

My brief case about yellow page advertising

The most aggressive marketers in media today are yellow page salespeople. I don't blame them. In fact, I applaud their tenacity. They will tell you what yellow page advertising can do for your business. They will recite sophisticated-sounding research data and stacks of statistics.

Am I opposed to yellow page advertising for start up marketers? Absolutely not! I'm just opposed to a disproportionate amount of money being spent on a medium that is rather limited in its use—especially for certain categories of business. The categories include products and services that are more specialized and require more credible information, such as professional services, jewelry stores, real estate agents, specialty foods, restaurants and companies that are nonurgent-oriented. Yellow pages work well for companies that respond to emergency situations, such as car repair shops, locksmiths and towing services.

Why do people use the yellow pages?

They use them to find products or services in emergencies. They also use them to get phone numbers of businesses with whom they have already done business. But think about how you use the yellow pages in your own business. If you are stuck and need a reference to get you out of a jam, you will go to the yellow pages. If you have a problem finding a particular type of business, you will go to the yellow pages. If your dentist is away and you chipped a tooth, you will go to the yellow pages. Ask yourself if you look to the yellow pages with intent on finding a company that is running a sale or a promotion or if you look in the phone book in order to stimulate ideas for gift-giving.

The fact is that yellow page advertising works well in very specific situations. It is not a substitute for media advertising, direct marketing, promotional messages or image-building. Keep it in perspective and you will find it a useful part of your advertising budget.

Beyond the first few pages, your message is fading

If your yellow page advertisement is not in the first four to six pages of the category you're listed under, your impact has fallen tremendously. Also, the key to yellow page advertising is to keep your message distinctive and your budget priorities in place. I have counseled clients to decrease their expenditures in display advertising while increasing their category listings. In every single case, we spent a great deal less money and got equal or more returns.

How to create your yellow page advertisement

The creation of a phone book advertisement differs from general display advertising. For one thing, your customers are not shopping, they're hunting. When you begin to think about your yellow page message, consider your category and the reasons why your potential customers will look for you in this environment. For example, I have found that health professionals such as dentists, chiropractors and physicians receive a higher amount of emergency calls than regular responses.

The reason is that the yellow pages are the prime reference for re-actionary shopping. Reactionary shopping (otherwise known as "reach-ing") is when consumers have a knee-jerk reaction to a specific issue that needs immediate attention. The yellow pages function magnificently in these cases, but most practitioners cannot maintain a practice from emergency calls. In fact, many of my clients have removed the 24-hour emergency message from their yellow page advertising, opting for simpler, well-positioned messages.

Yellow page salespeople will want to sell you color. It is very expen-sive, and I don't recommend it unless it's offered as an incentive to get you to advertise with a discount price. Color sells—but at far too great a cost when it comes to phone directories.

Try to reduce your yellow page commitment or limit it to a small display ad in your primary business category and bold listings in the other categories that relate to your company. For example, if you're a plumber, create your small display advertisement under the plumbing category. Next, include listings under mechanical contractors, heating and air conditioning, sewer service, and any other complementary category that pertains to your business.

Many years ago, advertisers were encouraged to reference their yellow page listings. It has been stated often enough, but I will reiter-ate: *Referencing your yellow page listing in other media advertising, such as newspaper or radio, is a terrible idea*. It simply invites your potential customers to review the field of competitors. If nothing else, yellow page advertising does offer the consumer many choices in most categories. That's why it's important for you as the marketer to exam-ine the categories in which you will place your business.

You'll find a wealth of ideas just from looking at how inept so many advertisers are in communicating. Simply by going one, two or three steps farther than most of the advertisements in your field, you'll be providing the reader with reasons to read your message. Re-member, too, that yellow pages, unlike other media, are a claustro-phobic environment. Information is crammed together—ads butting up to other ads with no editorial relief. In every other conceivable media environment, advertising is interrupted by other information. In yel-low pages, the advertising is the information. So, you're fighting ex-ceptionally hard to be read and even harder to be retained.

Therefore, you have to arm yourself with stronger weapons, a more developed sense of style and a unique creative approach. This doesn't mean you develop a look that's vastly different just for the sake of being different...but "different" *will* get you noticed.

Here's how I suggest you approach the creation of your yellow page advertisement:

If you run marketing a professional service, use a photo, professional credentials, awards, distinctions, honors and accolades. If you can provide immediate, credible information, you will be given more consideration.

If your product is niche-market-oriented, such as massage supplies (oils, lotions, literature and equipment), you will benefit from defining a singular strength. For example, you will want to distinguish yourself by proclaiming *The Largest Variety of Massage Oils in the Southwest*...or...*The Only Handmade Oak Massage Tables that Weigh Under Fifteen Pounds.*

Let's say you're in the business of teaching driving. After reviewing competitive messages, you recognize that they're all basically the same—*No Embarrassing Roof Signs, Late Model Cars, Door-to-Door Pickup, Low Rates, Parallel Parking Simplified.* Look for the void! In this case, the void is the customers' apprehension and fear. Not one of the advertisements I found in this category in a large directory dealt with alleviating anxiety, and not one spoke of the sensitivity of the instructors. Here's your chance to jump into the pool that has no waves. Create the waves by attacking the issue that no one has spoken about. Most marketers simply emulate the competition. Here you have a chance to outdo the competition.

The ad:

Don't worry...even seasoned drivers
hit a curb now and then!
(photo of president of company)

There are a lot of driving schools that can get you
through the basics. But how many spend as much
time teaching you confidence as they do teaching
you how to parallel park?

Good drivers have skills that go way beyond shifting
into drive and hitting the gas. We teach you to think
about the driving habits of others as well as yourself.
Because, even if you know what you're doing, you're
not alone out on the road.

Safe Driving Associates...instructors who are
sensitive to your needs!

We've discussed the benefits of giving people what's unexpected. You can do that by looking at the competitive messages and providing issues that are absent from them. Most business owners do not really understand that yellow page advertising is based upon the identical principles that apply to all creative messaging...filling a void! If you study the directories, really study them, looking through every conceivable category that relates to your business, you will find a void. Me-too messages always put you in second place.

Power to the patron

You're making claims in all your communications...from print to radio, television to direct mail, yellow pages to billboards. You're running advertising and you're beginning to change the way people feel about you because of your media personality. But be certain to remember you have a nonmedia personality, as well. If you make the claim we just made for the driving school, expect to encounter a few cynics.

People will challenge your claims? Yes, invariably, entrepreneurs are attacked by skeptics and cynics. Ask yourself: When the challenges arise, do you want to win customers or win arguments? You will need to maintain a sense of humor and an aura of goodwill. Any time you appear different, aggressive, bold, exciting or sensitive, someone is bound to challenge you. It may very well be your competition, your customers, your staff. But if what you publish is backed by what you believe, you can dare to be different.

If your store closes at 6 p.m. and a customer shows up at 6:30 while you're vacuuming, do you let him or her in? Ask yourself if the image you're creating externally is upheld internally?

Our restrooms are for anyone who needs them

Remember: Principles are external, values are internal. There are no rules, only guidelines, to doing business—if you look past authority, preconceptions and prerequisites, you force originality. It's like the restaurant owner who posts a sign that the restrooms are not for customers only...they're for anybody who needs them. Your philosophy points consist of a list of how to please the customer—to the exclusion of everything else. They are not written in stone. They're flexible and variable, but mostly they represent your absolute guidelines. If you keep your philosophical beliefs (philosophy points) in your pocket at all times, you can refer to them when you need to make a decision that affects your customer.

Ask 10 people what the purpose of your company is. Create a strategy to accomplish that purpose. Consider that there is a difference between what people say and how they act. I heard a great example of this expressed during a lecture: Ask anyone who lives in Iraq, a country with a democratic constitution, if he or she feels that the lifestyle reflects the management style.

How you market is how you live. People don't always do what they say! These are just two axioms that start up companies must learn quickly.

Chapter 15

Becoming a Brand

Image is everywhere. It's more likely to be a part of your success than almost anything else you do. Sometimes it works like magic; other times it causes instant failure. When I first started my business, I was asked to pitch an exclusive manufacturer of giftwrapping paper in New York City. The company offered the highest-priced products in the marketplace. The lead came from a publisher of a trade magazine for the giftware industry. He made it incredibly easy for me to waltz in and take the business, except that I made a huge error. I sacrificed my image in an effort to get the business.

The publisher had established an identity for my company, explaining that my experience and creativity would be ideal for the gift-wrap company's product line. He established for me a brand identity and image that matched the giftwrap company's own...only he forgot to tell me! So, when I went in to the company, I represented myself in a humble, start up fashion. And like most start up business owners, I was extremely insecure. The quickest way to overcome insecurity is to throw yourself at the mercy of the customer...which is what I did. I offered them the moon for costs that reflected a dirt field. I showed them beautiful examples of my work, but underpriced myself to the point of image-stripping. They told me they couldn't possibly consider doing business with my company because the prices we quoted for producing the materials they needed couldn't possibly do their business justice. I would have worked for *nothing* to get in the door—in fact, that's what I was offering them. They saw through it in an instant and placed the same value on my services that I had offered to them...*nothing*!

We live in a world of labels. We wear them on our butts, our lapels, our arms, our shirts...and we wear them in our psyches, as well. Our labels are our images. Just ask any politician about labels. He or she will tell you that if you don't apply them to yourself, others will do it for you.

Many years ago, I was at a Broadway show called *The Rothschilds*. At the end of the play, a mother is bidding her son farewell as he heads off into the world on his own. Her parting words were: "Son, don't ever forget who you are."

The son replied, "Mom, the world won't let me forget."

Like it or not, the world is full of labels. As start up marketers, we want to apply the principle of labels to our products or services...in a positive, prominent fashion. We want to own a brand!

I attended a rather fancy affair at a prominent catering establishment, where I found myself surfing the buffet before the formal sit-down dinner. When I stopped at a row of chafing dishes, I encountered a twentysomething waiter with serving utensils in hand. As my eyes focused on the luxurious food before me, a young man's voice broke through my trance-like state, "Is that a Nicole Miller tie?"

Somewhat surprised, I looked up at the young man and exclaimed, "Why, yes! I have several." He then explained that he had a half-dozen Nicole Miller ties and absolutely loved them. He also offered that they were purchased by his mother—in anticipation of his pending graduation from medical school. He was so brand-conscious and, more importantly, brand-loyal, that he related to me as a kindred spirit immediately. He also felt compelled to ask me what I did for a living, so that he could better understand how I became a part of the elite Nicole Miller family. I almost slipped and told him that this particular tie was one of a collection purchased for me by my brother. Instead, we spent the next 10 minutes talking about our favorite brands.

Because image is so very significant in marketing, you need to create what the big companies already have—customers with branded behavior.

An example of the power of brand imagery is made evident by a phenomenon taking place in the heart of New York City. The entire group of Broadway theaters has hired a consulting firm to establish a brand for Broadway—not for individual theaters or plays, but for the entire industry of shows on Broadway. The concept is to create a brand image that sells Broadway as a recreational destination. That's what you want to do as well: Sell your brand identity.

Brands exist on many levels, and there are typically only a few brands within each category. We still ask for a Kleenex or a Xerox.

Why? Because brand recognition is stronger than product recognition. Brands do not belong only to products—they often belong to people, as well. Lawyers want to be an F. Lee Bailey; doctors want to be a Michael DeBakey; business leaders want to be a Lee Iacocca; tennis players want to be a Jimmy Connors. And can you name 10 super-rich people—billionaires, not millionaires? Does the name Trump come to mind?

Typically, Donald Trump's name is the first name associated with the image of the super-rich. But there are many super-rich people who maintain a much lower profile than Trump...and have much more money! The difference is brand marketing. Trump has become a brand name for wealth, success and entrepreneurial identity. His name sells so forcefully that his ex-wife is able to use that brand identity to sell books and many other commodity products carrying Trump as the trademark. The equity of a brand is in its image, not its product features.

How do we become a brand? First, by thinking out of the commodity box. Commodities are usually unrecognizable. Brands are instantly recognizable.

What start up companies must do is emulate the methods and the marketing tactics that go into developing brand equity. You have an opportunity to become a brand if you keep your focus on that singular image. A good place to start is understanding the relationship between a brand image and a brand name. A brand image is the result of advertising, public relations and marketing. It encompasses the brand name and overall look of the product.

Brands can emerge from start up ideas. One interesting example of this is Align-meant Inc., a company that targets women who want to change their lives and careers. This market is a wide-open playing field for a company specializing in role and career change. The marketplace is ripe for a brand that will dominate and own this concept. Their position statement is, "Training and Consulting for Creating Meaningful Change." What they offer is guidance from change consultants who help in detailed, realistic transition plans...guaranteed! Does this concept have brand potential? Yes, if it is supported by more specific claims and a focused marketing agenda. This start up company fills a void in the marketplace, and it is far easier to create brand identity when you're first and foremost.

The sound of the name can determine the fame

Let's begin with your company's name. Does it convey the right image? Does it explain what you do? Is it brandable? Look at names such as Tiffany, Cartier, Donna Karan, Calvin Klein, Wrangler, Polo,

Levi Strauss, Izod, Coca-Cola, Kleenex, Xerox, Kohler, Andersen, Kmart, Chevrolet, Range Rover, Pizza Hut, McDonald's, Wendy's, Shoe Town, Prudential, Sears, Timex, Rolex, Nike, Reebok...the list goes on and on. All of these names have achieved brand status as a result of continuous brand imaging in the marketplace. Each of these companies has devoted its selling messages to identifying its name with very unique qualities. To a certain extent, the names become more significant than the products.

You'll notice that in a few cases the name relates to the product being sold, while in other instances, there is no relationship whatsoever to the type of product or service marketed under that particular name.

Typically, names can be broken into five categories:

1. Suggestive names: Jello, Coffee-mate, Crystal Light.

2. Image names: Smirnoff, Movado, Vive La France, Rolls Royce.

3. Easy identification names: Coke, Pepsi, Polly-O, Bud for Budweiser.

4. Fictitious names: Betty Crocker, Uncle Ben's, Jack Frost.

5. Coined words: Whirlpool, Arrow, Vermont Maid, Crest.

It is important to note that when you develop your name and image, you must pay careful attention to the synergy between the product or service and the name. Some companies have gotten lost by introducing products that were not within their image environment. For example, when Black & Decker first introduced small household appliances, the public withdrew immediately. Why? Because Black & Decker owned the tool market, not the household appliance market. There was no transition from one category to another, and consumers could not associate the image-name-brand with anything other than its primary product offering. The public needs time to react to a change in category. If you are well-known in town as a hardware retailer but suddenly introduce a shoe department, your customers will only receive a mixed message. In fact, the confused image will weaken your *primary* business. Keep on track, and when you develop other areas of business, transition them carefully and slowly with explanations and announcements in the media and through direct mail to your existing customers.

Start up marketers must look carefully at the issue of names in relationship to branding...understanding that their goal is to own an identity created by a brand. What intrinsic qualities exist in your product or service that will allow you ownership of a brand? What essential qualities are yours alone? How much money can you devote to developing brand identity and loyalty?

Let's begin by acknowledging that in most start up cases, you cannot provide the kind of economic support that will establish your brand image as a household word in short order. Therefore, your choice of a business name—or new name for your business—is important.

Exercise

1. Does your name tell the tale? Does it include what you're selling in it? For example, with the name "Shoe Town," we immediately know what to expect when we visit the store.

2. Does your name distinguish your business from everyone else in your playing field? For example, a florist that specializes in unusual foliage could be called "Wild Flowers" or "Orchids & Exotica."

3. Does the name use an adjective to reflect how you do business and what you offer? For example: "Quality Electronics," "Superior Lawn Care," "Outrageous T-shirts."

4. Does the name relate to the market with a promise? For example, "X-Its Everywhere"—a travel agency that helps people with phobias related to flying, airport confusion and uncertainties associated with being far from home.

5. Does the name create visual imagery? For example: "Ocean Pacific," "Bluebeard's Castle," "One-Eyed Jack's Saloon," "Moby's Seafood," "Great White Whale Sportswear," "The Black Panther Inn," "The Blue Corvette Dance Club."

Create a list of names that you love, that you feel strongly convey the image of the product or company. Now, describe who the name will appeal to most and why. If your customer is a mature person living in the southern belt of the country, your name should reflect the lifestyle needs of that customer, not your own subjective preferences. If, on the other hand, your customer is a mid-40s baby boomer, you want a name that the customer can identify with—a name that reflects the customer's values, goals, interests and aspirations. Choose your name with great care, because you're on your way to becoming a brand...and your name is the first step to getting there.

When you think about a business name, ask yourself what characteristics the name encompasses. Use a dictionary or thesaurus as a reference, guiding you from the list of names you like to a new list, sparked by synonyms. You can use slang and contemporary dictionaries, as well as *The Trademark Register of the United States* (to see what names exist in the categories that are closest to your business). All are available in the public library.

The perfect name

I was asked to develop a name and brand identity for a start up online service in New Jersey. The company wanted to create a strong presence in the marketplace by promoting easy, economical access to the Internet and proprietary information services covering the state of New Jersey. I offered them the perfect name, a phenomenon which occurs far too infrequently. For reasons that still remain unclear—though I believe they were political in nature—they passed on it. The name was "Enter NJ"—a name that utilized a ready-made image, including the notable shape of the "enter" key on the computer (a symbol already burned into the consciousness of every consumer) and initials to identify where the subscriber was entering. But the online service chose to reject it. Sometimes people look past a perfect fit and accept mediocrity.

There is a firm in San Francisco called Name Lab that develops brand names for companies ranging from automobile manufacturers to food and beverage products to everything imaginable. You can contact the company at: Name Lab, Inc., 711 Marina Blvd., San Francisco, CA 94123; 415-563-1639. You'll receive a brochure describing the process, which includes the use of a computer database of word associations called constructive linguistics. This process enables you to join words together to form new words.

Since many start up companies cannot afford to employ a company such as Name Lab (which offers a sophisticated approach to the development of product and brand names) or to avail themselves of technologically advanced software that constructs names, let's create an imaginary name for a company in order to apply the practical principles we've discussed. Remember, names are just the beginning of the establishment of your brand identity.

Exercise

You are about to open a business that teaches meditation and tai chi (a Chinese form of combat and exercise). You need a name that identifies what you do—but in a way that will give you ownership of a brand. Ordinarily you might think of names such as "The Tai Chi Center" or "Meditation Arts." But what you really need to do is begin your own form of creative meditation, by thinking about the benefits of the service you are providing. One obvious benefit is renewed energy...the result of the meditation process. Another aspect of the service is the spiritual nature of the exercises, bringing mind and body together.

What words might create a brand identity for your business? Begin with "spirit" or "soul." Next, think of "energy." List all of the possible words that can be associated with these essential issues. Now, what can we do to link these thoughts into a name that will be remembered... that operates on more than one level? This process involves looking at what we do and conveying it in a way that plays off existing, familiar sounds and expressions. How about *soul-ar energy?*! "Solar energy" is part of a series of topics that are top-of-mind. By massaging this expression into one that fits your needs as a marketer of a meditation service, you immediately reach people.

Now, we have a name—"Soul-ar Energy...Tai Chi & Meditation for the Body and Soul"! Does it have brand potential? Absolutely.

A very dynamic woman asked me to consult with her. She owns a company that certifies fitness trainers around the country. Basically, she provides this group of people with the necessary credentials to achieve greater profits from their profession. They need to pass rigorous tests in order to assume a more credible posture and increase their customer base. The name of her company is "Pro Fit." This name is brandable because it does several things well. First, it relates to the benefit she provides—she is selling certification credentials that result in profits. Second, it uses the language of the industry in a way that relates to the target market: professional fitness. And last but not least, it ties the benefit to the activity quickly, efficiently and productively.

The same can be said for seminars I deliver titled "Professional Practice Promotion." The seminars are designed to get professionals— doctors, lawyers, accountants—into motion. The name of the seminar series—indeed, the brand—is *Pro Motion...putting professionals into motion*. It's brandable because of how quickly professionals can identify with the concept. First, it says "promotion," the key reason professionals attend the seminar—to promote themselves! Second, it uses a term that relates to the market—"pro"—with action—"motion"! Thus, the name becomes the brand. Can anyone else use it? Not if we protect it with a trademark, which I will discuss later.

Did you ever wonder why the United Parcel Service uses only brown trucks with little identification on them? How about the fact that its name so closely resembles the United States Postal Service? Is this by accident or design? How many people think of UPS as the official parcel service? How many people actually think of UPS as a part of the government? The answers to these questions shouldn't surprise you. United Parcel Service owned the parcel delivery business for many years. One of the reasons was its name and brand image. The brown trucks don't need identification because they have become synonymous with the brand. Not until Federal Express (note the use of the word "federal") took on UPS did the statistics shift. Federal

Express simply provided a value-added concept: *When It Absolutely, Positively Has to Be There Overnight!* This is a perfect example of a brand challenge. It's a question of who's first and who's fastest. I point this out because you, too, will be challenged in your quest for brand ownership. Since Federal Express adopted the overnight position, it has altered its vision to include an international challenge, but its original brand identity is still firmly tied to the "absolutely, positively" position!

Brands exist on a local level as well as a regional, national or global basis. Think about your own neighborhood. Which pizza restaurant does the most business and why? How about a sub shop? What about the dry cleaner? Which video rental business owns your town? What about the orthodontist? Which insurance agency dominates the market? Which real estate company is top of mind? Brand identity is all around you. It's part of your unconscious mind as well as your conscious thought process. Ask yourself why the most popular businesses in your town own your behavior. What makes them special?

Tony owns most of the pie

There are nine pizza parlors in a two-mile radius of my home. My son will only eat pizza from one specific pizza restaurant. At 6 years old, he can easily read the pizza box, and if I bring home the wrong box, he won't eat the pizza. He also will not eat French fries from Burger King or Wendy's or any place other than McDonald's. Tony's Pizza Place owns my son. So does McDonald's. Why? For lots of reasons.

In the case of McDonald's, the answer is simple: exposure! The McDonald's message has been part of my son's cultural experience since he was 2 years old and began to differentiate between words and symbols. The frequency of message from McDonald's to my son was enormous—still is. He was captured and has remained a willing slave ever since.

In the case of Tony's, the brand loyalty is for different reasons. My son has never seen a commercial for Tony's, never read an ad or clipped a coupon. But this particular pizza restaurant has captured him. He loves the free coloring books, crayons, pizza magnets and the friendly pat on the head he gets when he goes there. I love the place because they were the first to offer low-fat cheese on pizzas, the first to offer no-cheese marinara and vegetable pizza, the first to offer stuffed-crust pizza, the first to offer multilevel pizza, the first to offer a menu of brand-name pizza specialties...and the fastest delivery in the area. What did Tony do? He borrowed from the big brands, taking their ideas and going one step further—faster. Then he gave himself an identity by creating a color coordinated interior, exterior, menu, logo, uniforms, hats, napkins. Everything inside and outside the restaurant speaks of branding. Again, he borrowed from the major brands in his field, and he created a brand that has attracted enough attention that there's talk of franchising. Tony isn't a small business owner. He's a large-scale entrepreneur in a small business. There's a vast difference.

Brand Potential Exercise

1. Does your business or business concept provide the customer with memorable images?

2. Have you coordinated the graphics?

3. Do your employees affirm your identity with buttons, badges, hats, scarves, uniforms?

4. Does the product or service name offer special opportunities to the customer?

5. Can the business be cookie-cuttered?

6. Which aspects of the business are likely to remain proprietary?

When Quick Chek Food Stores wanted to create proprietary brands within its 100-plus stores, the concept was to compete with national brands. Why? Because brand loyalty is a powerful force in our country. Survey your friends and family as to their preferences in ketchup, mayonnaise, automobiles, pizza, sneakers, clothing, floor tile, chickens. We buy brands for a variety of reasons. First, because we have a history of brand association. In my house, the only ketchup purchased was Heinz. The only mayonnaise was Kraft. My parents always purchased Chrysler automobiles. Levi's were the jeans of choice. When I left home to go on my own, I carried these brand loyalties with me. Only after many years did I venture out to try other brands that attracted my attention, but they had to fight hard for me to change.

Quick Chek's idea was to create food courts in their rather unusual convenience-type store environments. They're unusual because of their large variety, mainstream pricing, big stores and strong service commitments—policies not necessarily uniform in the convenience store industry. By creating these food courts and incorporating national brands such as Pizza Hut, Taco Bell and Nathan's, Quick Chek used the existing brand identity, equity and loyalty to drive business. *If you build it, they will come!*

In addition to the inclusion of these national brands, the company very intelligently decided to create its own brands. It is important to note here that there is a difference between private label products and branded products. Many companies (supermarkets are a good example) have private label products. These products are usually manufactured by the same companies that market under major labels, but, in the case of private labeling, the cost is different. Private label products are typically sold under a house brand name or the name of the company itself. For example, Pathmark Supermarkets has a whole range of private label products ranging from raisins to milk sold under the "Pathmark" name. They offer the consumer an economical alternative to the national brand, but they don't establish any other selling proposition other than cost savings. And the supermarkets and companies that sell such products usually don't look to create a brand appeal that could potentially be sold outside of their own walls. Private label programs are becoming more popular because the public is more aware of the consistency of quality and the commensurate savings.

Quick Chek's idea went beyond private label products, which it carries under the name Durling Farms, a sister company. In the case of food service, the concept was to establish brands within the stores that could effectively compete with national brands for the customers' attention. Each category was discussed as a separate brand. First, we looked at sub sandwiches, then coffee, then bagels. In each case we tested names with customers. We conducted exit interviews (asking questions of customers as they emerged from the stores), focus groups, telephone surveys, and confirmed brand names and identities before the products were moved into the stores.

Then we began to apply graphic principles to the names in order to build our brand images. In the case of subs, the idea was to build credibility by associating people with product. "Submakers" was chosen as the brand name. The name had an associative image—people. It also pronounced the fact that the product was made fresh in the store, not delivered from a commissary in a packaged state. The brand identity was further developed by strong graphics.

The branding of bagels was done in a similar fashion. The name "Jersey Bagels" was chosen because the chain operates in New Jersey, which is, in fact, a state where bagels became a staple food item many years ago. It is an identifiable brand name, and again, a graphic support system made it more powerful. The name was made more dominant by the use of a bagel graphic incorporated into the logo.

The concept of a branded coffee program resulted in the name "Cafe Ultima." The graphic brand identity was placed on cups, pots, retail coffee packaging, even the creamers, sweeteners and baked goods. It immediately created an upscale image and was expansive enough in sound and appearance that it took on a national look. But the brand didn't end there. The branding concept was supported by a wide range of gourmet-flavored coffees, cappuccino, a large variety of roasts and lots of shakers with nutmeg, cinnamon, cocoa, vanilla and other flavorings. The commitment to the brand went way beyond the name and the graphics. It included all the necessary elements that make brands bona fide.

Another significant creation for the Quick Chek chain was a branded premium ice cream, Durling Farms Premium. The brand was created to compete with the nationally recognized products such as Breyers, Sealtest, T&W and others. The packaging consisted of deep burgundy containers with gold rimmed tops and lettering. The promotion consisted of point-of-sale materials on the freezer doors and in-store cross-merchandising, where references to the product were displayed in various departments. The results: Within the Quick Chek chain of stores, Durling Farms Premium ice cream outsold the national brands in the first year. The branded identity was prominent because it looked and tasted like a national brand, while comparison information illustrated the outstanding attributes of this particular product over the others.

Get your employees involved in branding

All of the support materials that we commonly refer to as premiums and promotions are useful in supporting your branding efforts. For example, use buttons, hats, T-shirts, scarves, bandannas and arm patches to strengthen your branding program. Regardless of your business—retail, wholesale, distributor—you can keep smacking the customer in the face with your brand identity. Whenever we introduce a product for a client, I always recommend that a branded program of premiums be used at trade shows, meetings, company picnics, outings and sales conventions.

When a manufacturer client of mine developed a new technology for its ultrasonic cleaning systems, we carried the brand name into its customer community by offering a variety of giveaways that illustrated the name and logo. It was part of the brand plan. After we developed the name and graphic identity for the Quantrex line of products, we placed it on hats, shirts, Frisbees, balloons...in addition to the advertisements and sales promotion materials. The company's people became the medium that carried the message. The brand identity was everywhere the company or the personnel could be found.

Overcoming a strange name

Each industry has its top brands, but because they are known only to that specific industry, the rest of the world never gets to see them. In the retail jewelry industry, the major brand for business management, consulting and marketing is a company called Scull.

When I was first introduced to the company's representatives, I inquired about the odd name. The answer was simple: Scull was the name of the gentleman who started the company many decades ago. When it was purchased by Joseph Romano, Joe considered the options and chose to stick with the name because of its equity in the retail jewelry trade.

Interestingly, Joe Romano has become the brand since his takeover of the company. I know this because of the comments I hear from jewelers coast to coast. Essentially, Scull is a company consisting of share groups that host institutes in different parts of the country. The purpose is to create symposiums where retail jewelers can share information and receive ongoing counsel and guidance from Scull executives, who are experts in this industry and authorities on all of its idiosyncrasies.

Scull still has significance as a brand, but it is Joe Romano who has the real brand image. I don't believe that Joe consciously looked to shift the brand identity from Scull to himself, but it did happen that way. Joe has become the guru to retail jewelers in every state. His authority has captured the industry, and his ideas and dedication have created a top-of-mind position. When an individual has unusual charisma, energy and enthusiasm, often brand loyalty is given to the individual's image rather than to the company's. In the case of Scull and Joe Romano, this is clearly the case.

Burning your image into the customer's mind

The goal is to become the category reference. This means that in your own start up business or existing business, you need to look at the issues that create categories. Branding means ownership. You have to own the category in order to succeed as the brand. Ownership doesn't mean 100 percent domination. It can mean 20 percent domination, if 20 percent is a higher percentage than any other single player in your category.

Sometimes bigger is better

Stuart left his job with a supermarket chain to buy a small bagel shop near a suburban train station. Aside from the debt service (money owed to the bank), Stuart had to generate more revenue than the previous owner to fulfill his lifestyle obligations. He did many of the right things. His wife left her part-time job and worked in the bagel shop in order to contribute to the business without increasing payroll. He hired high school students to work evenings and weekends. In short, Stuart worked 70-plus hours per week in order to make the business a success. His dream of owning his own business was becoming slightly tarnished by fatigue and flat sales.

Stuart had devoted his time to the operation of the business and to the concepts of business management—food costs, payroll, advertising expenses and on and on—but what he didn't see was the patron. His method of communicating was the same as his competitors'—fliers, newspaper coupons, window signs. And like his competitors, Stuart was selling bagels. While it was true that some of the bagel stores had introduced blueberry bagels, bagel kisses, mini bagels, bagel sticks—no one in Stuart's market had created a brand image. So, when the population within a two-mile radius of Stuart's store thought about buying bagels or having lunch, they chose a bagel shop based solely on convenience or coupons.

Stuart had a wonderful opportunity to become the brand in his community, but he couldn't see how, until one day a truck driver stopped in for a sandwich that he could eat while driving. This man looked at the menu and asked Stuart's wife, Michelle, if he could get a tuna fish sandwich on something other than a bagel since he had to eat in the truck and the bagel sandwich would be messy. Michelle indicated that they only had bagels. The man left. Michelle saw him get in his truck and drive away. She also saw a $6 sale drive away.

What Michelle did then changed the nature of the business and was the beginning of brand thinking. She told the bagel baker to make some bagels without holes...and to make them at least 30 percent larger. He did. The result? A bagel that would not leak when eaten in a car.

For all the years that I have eaten Thomas' English Muffins, the category leader, I have always been frustrated by the modest size of the product. Not until a short time ago did Thomas' introduce Sandwich Size English Muffins. What took them so long? Well, Stuart and Michelle did the same thing. They introduced a sandwich-size bagel with no hole in the middle. They also created a bagel in the shape of a sub roll and another first: a nine-inch traditional round bagel with the trademark hole. They promoted these products and became known as the home of the giant bagel and the no-hole bagel! They achieved brand status and their ownership position took hold.

Branding and ownership can result from simple steps in opposite thinking. Bagels have holes. Stuart's bagels have no holes. By inventing your own proprietary properties, you're well on your way to branding. A quote from an unknown source applies to our discussion here—"I couldn't wait for success, so I went ahead without it." Traditional thinking yields traditional results. Go ahead and think about being first—even if it means being criticized or ostracized. Assume you know more than the next person. Talk yourself into authority and create systems that will sell outside the common thought processes. Becoming a brand is an exercise in entrepreneurial muscle-flexing.

When you're completely satisfied, it's time to retire

There is a good news/bad news scenario with entrepreneurs. The good news is that they're compelled and motivated to strive for more. The bad news is that they're never satisfied. I have met people who tell me they are satisfied with their businesses, that they don't see how things could be improved, or that sales have reached a saturation point. These people illustrate the difference between entrepreneurial thinking and pedestrian thinking.

Branding your business is an outstanding goal. Few will achieve it. Be among the few by remembering the rules.

Branding rules

1. Focus on your name, logo, position statement in media, customer service, telemarketing.

2. Create frequency by utilizing your brand identity in publicity releases, premiums, promotions, giveaways.

3. Be single-minded. Refer to your business by brand name and market position.

4. Always remain loyal to your credo. If the brand becomes identifiable with service-beyond-belief, provide it with constant commitment.

5. Constantly look for line extensions—offshoots of products with additional features and benefits. These strengthen the brand identity and create a more expansive image.

6. Give the brand away. Staples sent customers a $20 gift certificate to get them in the store. Get people to invest in your brand by giving them a sample of what they can expect in a long-term relationship. Remember, if you invest in the brand, customers will invest, too.

Chapter 16

Untangling the Web, Entering the Internet

We hear a great deal about Web sites, Internet marketing, e-mail, cyberselling. What most start up businesspeople don't understand is that marketing on the Internet is similar to marketing on cable television 20 years ago. It's still immature. And it adds little or nothing to your bottom line, in and of itself. Why? Because all of the other elements that will point your customer to your Web site must be in place before you can consider the use of the Internet as a valued part of your marketing mix.

Today, almost every company wants to be on the Internet. Tiny companies, start up companies, one-person companies and middle, large and supersize companies all want their own Web site. What most businesspeople simply don't understand is that no one will find you unless you create a map for them. In other words, all of the principles of marketing must be in place in order to benefit from this form of high-tech marketing.

Representatives of a company that distributes refrigerator and air conditioning parts contacted me about creating a Web site for them. I asked them why they wanted to market the company on the Web. Their answer was that, from what they've read, everyone has to be thinking about Internet marketing as part of their future.

While I agreed that this is an issue that has to be considered for the future, I pointed out that what they were reading was written by individuals and companies who provide the technical expertise to get on the Web. They weren't reading information from marketing people. I indicated that if they expected to simply create a Web site and expect results, they would be better off spending their money on new cars for the sales staff.

Internet marketing is one medium. And it's a very limited medium for most companies. Why? Because no one can tell you who's viewing your message, how often or in what numbers. The creation of a Web site, in and of itself, does nothing for your business unless it's supported by a comprehensive marketing plan. Directing people to your site requires a strategy and has a decided downside. Think about how many companies ran advertisements telling customers to *find us in the yellow pages*. The problem with directing people to another medium is that you're also directing them to your competitors. Therefore, your Web site has to be more powerful, better positioned and markedly more compelling than the other choices in the category.

Remember, the Internet is the most intriguing media toy to come along since the radio was invented. Every era has had its new technology that, it was thought, would radically and swiftly change the way we do business. But radio didn't unify the culture—just as creating a Web site will not allow you to instantaneously market your wares to the outer reaches of the world.

It's fascinating, and for that reason alone, marketers will flock to it without recognizing that using it to its fullest potential requires time, imagination and money. Marketers who want to use Web sites effectively need to do a great deal of homework. It's not as simple as putting your e-mail address on your business card and expecting lots of responses.

Admittedly, Internet activity is going wild. It is estimated that traffic on the information superhighway is increasing between 15 and 25 percent every month. That means that more and more people are surfing and businesses are looking for that action. It's exciting, it's cluttered and it's becoming enormously competitive. For that reason, the creative execution of your Web site must be as powerful as any other form of marketing communications you create.

Don't forget we're mostly technophytes

Remember, at present, most consumers don't know how to access the Internet. Clearly, like programming your VCR, the educational process takes time. The consumer-friendly information is on the way—but it's still a distance away.

When you begin to consider creating a Web site, consider the client-server technology. Servers are high-powered computers. They contain programs that are shared. The Web server is the method of accessing the World Wide Web. And since a server has both hardware and software components—Unix-based at the top, Mac- or PC-based at the middle to bottom—you will need technical consulting before you can really create a professional site. That information precedes the creative consulting necessary to be noticed once you're in place on the Web.

A brief start up review

What you need: A high-speed phone line to connect the server to the Internet. There are two types. T1 lines, which are expensive, can accommodate the most data at the fastest rate. ISDN lines operate at about one-tenth of the speed of the T1 lines, says Stewart Limm of Cyberlinks, an Internet service provider in Voorhees, New Jersey. Hookups through standard telephone lines are available, but they are considered slow and less reliable. According to Limm, T1 lines can be leased for a flat monthly fee. ISDN lines are billed by the minute. That means a Web server running on an ISDN line 24 hours per day will mount high costs quickly. Limm also explains, "Because of the cost issue, ISDN is only good for a user to access the Internet, and that isn't good to establish a presence there."

According to an article by Bob Adams in *Publishing & Production Executive*, February 1996, "Web surfers must use a Web browsing program to access various Web sites. Mosaica is one of the earliest to be developed and is among the most popular. Another widely used program is Netscape's Navigator. Other applications include commercial packages and free applications on the Web."

Essentially any computer can serve as a Web server. In one case, one of Stewart Limm's clients used a Macintosh SE computer as server hardware. "That worked fine because all he was doing was distributing pages and graphics. The speed element is determined by the connection, so you really don't need much processor power unless you're handling databases."

Server software is what permits the computer to field incoming requests for information through the Web and transmit the requested documents back to the person making the request. The following list was compiled by *Publishing & Production Executive* and represents software for starters.

While this list includes some of the sources for start up Internet marketers, it is not a comprehensive source, but rather a random sample, of the companies producing technology for the start up business.

- **Apple Computer:** Apple Internet; Server Solution.
- **Dataware Technologies:** Netanswer.
- **Electronic Book Technology (EBT):** Dynaweb Server 1.0.
- **Navisoft:** Navipress and Naviserver.

- **Folio:** Folio Infobase; Web Server.
- **Scitex:** Internet System 10.
- **Silicon Graphics Inc. (SGI):** Webforce.
- **Starnine:** Webstar.
- **Sun Graphics:** Netra.

Getting past the technical difficulties isn't easy. Even if you're convinced your business needs a presence on the Web, you've got to research the software and hardware suppliers in your area and get some high-tech support. Further, you must evaluate what brand of file server you need. Ask yourself the questions that Bob Adams poses: How much processing power and hookup speed will you require? Who can help you determine your server needs?

There are a great many competent computer consulting firms. A good source for them is your office superstore or computer chain store. Speak to the sales manager of your local chain and get the names of consultants who can begin to answer the questions that will lead you to the Internet. Companies such as Computerland have technical counselors who take businesses onto the World Wide Web. Another good source for help with your technomarketing requirements will come from the vast array of trade shows and exhibits. You will find an ample supply of hardware and software consultants at each of these events. Remember, the technical information you need in order to get you on the Net is only the first step you must take in real-value marketing with your Web site. Because the marketing process within this technology is still incredibly immature, you must approach this part of your overall marketing agenda with caution.

According to Boris M. Krantz, in *Business News New Jersey*, February 1996, "Companies would do well to adopt a skeptical, common-sense approach to marketing on the World Wide Web. Krantz, the principal of a communications firm, insists that companies require their Web advisors to keep the strategy simple. He strongly suggests that companies "get past the gee-whiz-this-is-the-wave-of-the-future mentality. You need to know why you should use the Internet. What is it going to do for you? Will it reach the audiences you want to reach? How will you measure your success?"

Another critical component to your Web site is design. You must approach this in the same way you would initiate the development of a brochure, a catalog, an advertisement or direct mail solicitation. Clearly you wouldn't permit an engineer to design your marketing materials. Well, be certain that a technical person doesn't design your Web materials.

The principles of marketing don't change because of changes in technology—only the means with which we reach the customer changes. Creative strategies still apply.

How many are on the Web?

The number of corporate sites on the World Wide Web is estimated to be far more than 10,000. Open Market, an Internet services corporation in Cambridge, Massachusetts, says that between 50 and 100 business sites are added every day. Straightline International, a New York City company, predicts that 77 percent of U.S. companies will be on the Internet in the next two years. Companies that have no present plans to enter the Net explained that they were taking a wait-and-see approach or were concerned about corporate security issues.

Clearly the number of subscribers is growing at an enormous rate...with 100 million people projected to hit the Internet in two years. This not only adds to the opportunity for marketers but to the confusion and frustration of reaching customers in a cluttered environment that presently leaves technically intimidated people out of the loop.

Using the Net to catch the most fish

According to *Webmaster Report*, a twice-monthly newsletter for Web site managers, fresh content is a Web site essential. *Webmaster Report* writer Anne Bilodeau explains, "Webmasters who load their Web sites with rehashed versions of printed marketing materials could be losing thousands of visitors every week. People who are using the Web are looking for interactive-oriented information, not sales pitches or corporate propaganda."

Peter Bowman, president of Designfx, a consulting firm in Cherry Hill, New Jersey, agrees. "Small businesses should use the Internet as a tool to augment communications rather than a replacement for their current marketing programs. Companies should avoid just publishing their mission statements...because a Web site is potentially much more useful to a viewer if it contains in-depth data, which might be too expensive to include in a newspaper advertisement. Your Web site should be 90 percent information and 10 percent persuasion. Put just enough information to tease the viewer into calling you."

Many companies will ultimately use Web sites to deliver complete product information as well as suggestive information. For example, smaller firms are already looking at ways to translate their catalogs onto their Web site in order to create an easy, economical method of receiving direct orders. How this will work is hard to say. Ultimately, it will be part of every business environment...but when that will happen nobody seems to know.

One way to assess where Web sites are headed is to view those already established by other companies. *Webmaster Report* offers some marketing resources on the Web. These sites are dedicated to online marketing. You can visit these, using the information to model your own site.

Remember, the principle of modeling should be part of your business philosophy. Look at how this new medium is being used and begin to create a file of ideas from the existing materials.

Webmaster Report resources

Internet Marketing Archives: <http://www.gnn.com/gnn/wic/buc.28.html> This site features a searchable index. If you're looking for information on electronic malls, type in "electronic malls," and everything relating to this subject will appear on the screen.

The **Internet Business Journal** <http://www.phoenix.ca/sie> is the online home of Michael Strangelove, a leading authority on issues surrounding marketing on the Internet.

The **HTMARCOM** web site <http://www.bayne.com/wolfBayne/htmarcom> offers links to advertising agencies that specialize in computers and electronics, marketing resources, trade shows and publications.

Dan Janal is the author of the **Online Marketing Handbook** <http://www.anal-communications.com/janal.html>, which offers information about online marketing.

I strongly suggest that you add *Webmaster Report* to your list of information tools in your quest to conquer the newest marketing technologies. You can subscribe to this easy-to-read, interesting and user-friendly publication by contacting Lawrence Ragan Communications, Inc., 212 W. Superior Street, Chicago, IL, 60610; phone: 312-335-0037; fax: 312-335-9583; e-mail: 71154.2605@compuserve.com.

According to Natalie Davis, editor-in-chief of *Business Credit* magazine, a host of services can address the needs of both businesses and individuals, relative to the Internet. In her article "What's in the Net for Me?", *Business Credit*, January 1996, she provides a list (provided here) that contains various services for use on the Internet. She also suggests that your own Internet server can help you to install or purchase the various programs you'll need to use these services.

- **Electronic mail.** E-mail allows you to send correspondence anywhere in the world.

- **Usenet newsgroups.** Right now there are more than 15,000 forums on any topic. You can gain information or provide it to the worldwide group. Many businesses topics have newsgroups of their own, so you can tap into resources that affect your specific industry.

- **World Wide Web.** This represents the graphic interface of the Internet. You can see visuals, graphic presentations and movies from around the globe. You can visit museums in Europe and, with certain software, receive audio messages as well. Businesses use the Web to communicate their products and services.

- **Yahoo, Lycos, Webcrawler.** These services make using the Web faster and easier. They act like a table of contents—you type in your choice of topic, and these search engines find you a list of Websites related to your area of interest.

- **File Transfer Protocol (FTP).** Software exists that enables you to send or receive (upload or download) files to and from sites. Some sites are specific to subject matter, while others deal with a company's own software.

- **Gopher and WAIS.** Services such as these allow you to search the Net for various sites so that you can get information regarding a specific issue. Gopher and WAIS provide you with the information you will need (mainly addresses) to make use of the following: Teinet—a gateway that allows you to connect to other sites and utilize their computers through your own; Internet Relay—a service through which you can chat with others throughout the globe; LISTSERV—a trademarked service that enables companies to automatically send e-mail, press releases or any other material to members of mailing lists.

Note: Business owners and managers must use reliable, credible consultants to sift through the enormous amount of material affecting the Internet. It is the fastest-changing field in the universe; therefore, you have to exercise caution in approaching the development of a Web site. Look at your expenses, and then remember that the creation of a site in order to market your products will be far more costly than you first imagined...mostly because the site itself is the smallest part of your marketing effort.

With estimates that approximately 80 million people use computers in the United States, the Internet obviously has enormous potential for marketers at some point in the future. But circulation figures for computer magazines indicate that about four million people read these publications, indicating that most of the population remains intimidated by the technology and the roads to the superhighway. Therefore, the way we create a marketing program that includes a business Web site is to point people to our site...and then dazzle them once they arrive.

Begin with the business card

I truly believe that as marketers travel into cyberspace, the business card will increase in size from about 2 inches by 1 inch to probably an 8-inch by 10-inch sheet.

This will be necessary because of the increased amount of information we need to convey. The first step in announcing your presence on the Internet is to publish your e-mail address on your business card. Generally, I am not in favor of lots of information on a standard business card, but with the advent of electronic marketing, I suggest you look at a folding card which actually triples the amount of information you can present.

I saw a business card that provided enough information to be called a mini brochure. The cover offered the standard fare—company name, person's name, title, address, phone, fax and e-mail. The upper inside of the card listed bulleted services and the bottom half offered the company's mission statement and position. At first, I was put off, until I realized that the card easily fit into my wallet, business card holder and Rolodex. I also appreciated knowing more about the company, especially since it was referencing its Web site with all the necessary information needed to find it.

Your business card, therefore, is the first method of communicating that you're displaying your message on the Internet. But it's only the beginning.

Everything you do now includes your Internet identity

Once you've made the decision to create a Web site, all of your marketing materials must reference it. Therefore, your collateral materials, advertisements, direct marketing literature, brochures and sales promotions will all direct your customers to your Web site. This means that your Internet marketing program will require aggressive advertising in order to make it work for you. And since your traditional forms of advertising are designed to create an image, soften the market for sales, inform and educate, your Web site must be consistent in look, theme, position and image projection to all of these other elements.

Many of the businesses surveyed consider electronic marketing to be a benefit in helping to solve problems in customer service support. Further, business-to-business marketers use the Net for researching various areas of commerce—viewing customer and market trends, tracking news about specific industries, gathering competitive intelligence—and for advertising their own products and services. Clearly the future is bright for start up businesses to access and disseminate information. It's still critical to understand that before you create a Web site, you must create a marketing plan that will take your customers on the magic carpet ride to your site. Without this ingredient in place, you might as well be selling ice pops in Alaska—nobody will come!

As far as the design of your Web site is concerned, you need to keep content in mind. Colorful graphics will help sell and consistency with existing materials is vital, but content must offer your customer value-added information such as product data, news updates, reference material and documentation. You will need to update your site materials frequently as new sites are added on a daily basis. You must also keep tracking your competitors by visiting their sites every day. If you provide real information to your customers, you will be using the Web site to its fullest advantage. Don't just sell—inform and help.

You can have your customers or browsers register on your site. Get the information you need, such as their names, addresses, titles, jobs and interests. Technology exists to help you gain access to the information that will enable you to follow up inquiries made on your site.

If your location on the Web isn't producing the desired results, you may want to consider hooking into trade association listings or other places that are already popular. Some companies have grouped together to make what appears to be a food-court-like marketing home on the Web.

Once you make the commitment, recognize that, unlike most other media environments, the Web changes as quickly as you post your message. Keep constant vigil over your site—because just when you think you've said what you wanted to say—10 others are saying more!

Chapter 17

Personal Marketing: Power to the People

I can honestly say, with complete objectivity, that the wisest man I have ever met was my father, Samuel Leo Nulman. He died very young, but in the 20 years that I knew him, I learned more about human kindness, human nature and morality than I have learned in the 25 years since his death. His words still keep me on track as a writer, marketing professional and a human being: "Never argue with someone when they're right."

What he said holds true in every situation of life. In business, winning the argument usually means losing the customer. Start up marketers are in a particularly vulnerable position. First, you must become known, gain attention and create a selling platform, not to mention your marketing position and business strategy—all formidable tasks. Beyond these issues, you have to do what most people find difficult: You sometimes have to subordinate yourself for the good of the business. This doesn't mean you become passive or permit anyone to take advantage of you. It simply means that you will learn to adjust your demeanor in the face of particular business situations, especially when you can see the validity of the customers' claims.

Selling is the most essential element of marketing. It requires a great many variables applied to specific situations. When we speak of situational marketing and personal marketing, we are talking about how we approach selling in an era of rapidly changing rules and roles.

"Marketing is the one thing in a company that is too important to delegate."
—David Packard, Hewlett-Packard
founder

Back in the 1950s, every Wednesday evening was spaghetti night, Thursdays were fried fish and Fridays were roast chicken. Those were the days when Mom didn't work and Dad made it home by 6 p.m. for family dinner. The rules and roles no longer apply. Our situations have shifted, and our lifestyles are in flux. Personal marketing means that you create selling propositions that relate to the person's present needs...in specific, substantive ways.

It begins by defining who you are to your customer. As a start up marketer, you must grip the wheel tightly, not allowing anyone else to steer, at least until you're well on your way to your destination. The way you manage your business is the model you set for your employees, whether you have one or 1,000.

If the voice on the phone or the receptionist who greets customers is unpleasant, you're in a losing selling environment. You need to turn the organizational chart upside down—putting the customer at the top and yourself at the bottom. It's the *customers* who drive your business. Your job is to be the chauffeur...looking after their needs and addressing them.

> *"If you can't change the facts, try bending your attitude."*
> —George Eliot, 19th-century
> English novelist

In *Principle-Centered Leadership*, Stephen R. Covey explains that to make enormous leaps in leadership and sales potential, you must change your frame of reference. Changing behavior is simply not enough. He speaks about shifting your management paradigm, which essentially means changing the methods you use to understand certain aspects of reality. For example, if you're married, recall what it was like to be single. Things shift dramatically when your situation changes.

This applies to business in a multitude of ways. If you achieve a new position within your company or become the boss of a start up business, your behavior and methodology of doing business changes because of the new role and the new rules.

One of the examples Covey has spoken of in his lectures related to an incident on an airplane. There was a father with two small children on the plane. Across the aisle was a man who was discomforted by the amount of noise created by the children. He perceived the children as unruly. When he finally confronted the father, he expressed his feelings about the noise. The father explained, apologetically, that his wife had just died, and he was taking the children to visit relatives.

Instantly, a paradigm shift occurred, and the man who was previously upset became a sympathetic observer.

What I mean by recalling my father's words, "Never argue with someone when they're right," is that when you concede that someone else may have a good point or a better approach to solving a problem, you immediately become more credible. By shifting the center of the issue from your side to the other person's, you are actually bringing the person back to you. When you apply this to marketing, it means you are establishing a win-win scenario.

Empower the patron

"Empowerment" is, unfortunately, one of those words that, through overuse, has become greatly weakened. Lee Iacocca, in his autobiography, wrote that his study of psychology was invaluable to him in the world of business. By understanding what motivates people, marketers have an edge in satisfying them. As start up marketers, one of your goals must be to hand the power to the patron. By placing the baton in his or her hands, you have essentially asked the question, "What do you want, and what do you need?"

A friend of mine was interested in buying a service business from a woman in her late 60s. The business had enormous potential but was losing money. My friend researched the marketplace and then researched the owner. He uncovered as many things about her as he could—her interests, hobbies, lifestyle, automobile, partnerships, education. He essentially reviewed her resume through direct requests and more subversive methods of discovering who she was. He did this because he wanted to understand her needs. In the final analysis, he thought he had a good understanding of what she wanted, but to be sure, he did something quite radical. He asked her.

He called her and simply asked her what she wanted from the relationship. Did she want to stay on with the business? Did she want to develop more business under an incentive plan? Did she need lots of money up front? What ensued was a very productive exchange that resulted in her revealing her situation to him. Once he understood her situation, he could develop a pointed proposal that answered her needs.

What situation are your customers in? What are their lifestyles, and how can you create a personal marketing voice that will reach them and touch them? Harvey Mackay, author of *Swim with the Sharks*, said that "goals are dreams with deadlines." You need to know what your customers' goals and dreams are. Regardless of the business you're in, if you know what circumstances affect customers, you can solve their problems.

"How many cares one loses when one decides not to be something,
but to be someone."

—Gabrielle Coco Chanel, French
fashion designer

If you recognize how to use personal charm, sensitivity, humor and goodwill, your start up business will have a decided advantage over the competitors. It's more than playing golf or sponsoring lunches or sending customers premiums and theater tickets. All of those issues are great if they are the result of an overall effort on your behalf to become personal. There are very few people in businesses today who shun the relationship side of business.

Andrew Carnegie, a master of selling, stated, "Take my factories and my money, but leave me my salespeople, and I'll be back where I am today in two years." When all is said and done, marketing is always greatly enhanced by personal selling.

Learn from the smiling goat

I received a letter and a brochure from Smiling Goat, a company that offers music and multimedia services. The outside of the brochure had the words "Smiling Goat" in the upper left-hand corner with nothing else except a small logo at the bottom. The letter was personal in tone and brief.

Aside from the illustration of the smiling goat and the wonderful name, the company did something quite spectacular in terms of personal marketing. The resume of each person in the company was included in the brochure. Smiling Goat was like many other companies soliciting business from marketing and advertising firms, but it truly created a smile on my face. I read the resumes, which included brief personal information, credits and accomplishments, and immediately tossed it into my "keep" file. They had won me over in seconds because they offered me a message that included both the people and the product. And in this particular industry, people's talents are what we're buying.

Remember: *Once your customers know who you are, it's far easier to do business and far more difficult to stop doing business.*

Finding a mentor

One of the best methods of learning when entering the start up business arena is to go beyond the personal and find the person. Each industry has a trade association and many industries have other types of associations that can help you with various issues that are common to smaller businesses. Finding a mentor is not as difficult as you may think. In fact, your own suppliers and customers may be the best place to start. Of course, you can contact the Small Business Administration in Washington, D.C., for information on accessing help for a start up company.

When I started my business, I relied upon two clients for advice. I had confided in both of them that I needed help in specific areas, and they were more than delighted to begin a mentor relationship. To this day, they have remained my mentors. I also asked questions from suppliers, such as printers, designers, consultants—and without a penny changing hands, I entered into relationships that enabled me to learn from seasoned professionals who had put all of the theoretical information to work in the real world. They were always happy to help, and I was always happy to pay for lunch.

By creating these mentor relationships, I was able to test ideas, using people who had great success under their belts as sounding boards. This has proven to be an invaluable resource and one I encourage you to pursue.

Up close and personal: We're moving from mass selling to singular selling...and it feels good

I want to review some issues that we touched upon in various ways throughout this book because we now must think about how we can apply them to driving our business farther and faster. If we think of our customers as individuals, if we create profiles (databases) of them, we will become passion- and performance-oriented in serving their needs. Both consumer and business-to-business markets need to pay careful attention to key issues in relating to the customer as one person to another:

Honesty. There is an intense need for real information. It is communicated in the tone of voice you use, the real testimonials you deliver and the personal commitment you make as a marketer. If you offer a no-hassle, money back guarantee, give customers their money back with a smile and a handshake!

Open-door policy. Be accessible to your customers. Proclaim your accessibility. Don't hide behind a sales force, management team or even a front counterperson. You are your business!

Response to criticism. Every business receives angry letters or phone calls. Respond personally to each and every one. You'll find the most immediate method of disarming the angry customer is a simple apology. It acknowledges that you care, even if you disagree with the issues being raised. If you state that you're sorry the incident occurred or you're sorry the customer feels a certain way, you're creating loyalty that even money can't buy!

Time. It's the most valuable commodity on the face of the earth, and it's what your customers want most. Give them convenience, ease and comfort in procuring your products or services, and you have given them a great gift. I frequent a restaurant that often has lines. But the owner brings a tray of appetizers to the people waiting in line, also offering them complimentary beverages while they wait. Even though he can't make the time pass more quickly, he makes it pass more pleasantly. Give your customers as much joy and ease of doing business as you can possibly create! Remember, technology has erased the waiting process in many industries, but hold onto the personal issues, even if it means e-mailing your customers following each request. Keep it in the first person!

Customized selling. In addition to personal selling, customized selling will be part of your business future. Custom-fit shoes, suits, jeans and gloves are all becoming mainstream. Consumers want the personal touch, and while variety is a keen selling proposition, it is customization that means the most today. Levi's will deliver custom-fit pants from computer profiles that retailers maintain. It's the individual that counts! Don't make the customer fit into your business—make your product or service fit into his or her needs!

Flexibility. Situational marketing means change. While we market to current situations, even these change more rapidly than ever before. I recently read about a manufacturer of modular homes—designed to expand and contract as family needs change. Adaptability and flexibility are large issues. If you only make one size sandwich, you're eliminating the changing needs of the marketplace. One of the most popular delicatessens near my office offers three sizes of sandwiches. The owner told me that he surveyed his customers and found that many women and most children wanted less product between the bread. Thus, he created a category that accommodated the people who frequented his business.

Privacy. Regardless of what you're marketing, your customers' relationship with you is no one else's business. Customers want their privacy protected. This is an emotionally charged issue. Offer them assurances that the information you give them will remain private. Banks, insurance agencies, health care providers, accountants, lawyers, service bureaus, real estate agencies—all must pay particular attention to the ongoing issue of privacy. It has become so significant that approximately 81 percent of small businesses surveyed stated that they would not enter the world of electronic marketing until they had reassurance that their proprietary interests could be protected.

The difference personal marketing can make

I had an occasion to take one of my most valued clients to a special dinner coinciding with his birthday. I spoke to several people in his organization and discovered his passion for French cuisine. I also found out that he had mentioned his interest in a specific restaurant in Manhattan. Fortunately, a good friend in the food industry knew the restaurant and the chef/owner. It was the perfect present for my client...an evening of fine food and wine, a chance to put personal and relationship marketing to work. I immediately called my friend in the food industry and asked for her help. She assured me that the chef would be notified and would come out to our table during the meal in order to buy us a drink and chat. This would clearly make the evening far more special for my client and me.

We arrived at the restaurant and were seated right away. We ordered wine and began what would turn out to be a wonderful evening of relationship marketing, easily weaving personal and business issues into the conversation. Only one thing went wrong. Claude, the chef, didn't make it to our table during our wine, appetizer, entrée, dessert or after-dinner drinks. When I quietly inquired as to his whereabouts, I was simply told that he preferred to stay in the kitchen. In truth, it didn't hurt my evening or my agenda. It only hurt Claude's business. And what could have been a wonderful enhancement to the evening went by the wayside. But the real reason this situation is so memorable to me is that there's a secret side to success that has little or nothing to do with the product—it has to do with the person delivering the product. If Claude had done some personal marketing during that particular evening, I would have remained a devoted fan, patron and referral source. Instead, I remember him only as arrogant and uncaring.

Delivering your message is not enough. Delivering *yourself* is so very vital in making all of your marketing efforts work!

A wonderful method of delivering yourself to the market is through seminars. Every association, chamber of commerce, Kiwanis club, business council and trade group wants and needs qualified people to deliver seminars. Take advantage of these and offer insight and inspiration, and word-of-mouth marketing will carry your message farther than you could imagine.

Chapter 18

Baby Boomers Are Easy to Find...But How Do You Make Them Go "Boom"?

There are more than 80 million people in America today who are between 30 and 50 years of age. You would think this represents a large pool of customers for you. So, why isn't your phone ringing off the hook?

Well, start up marketing is not exactly like Alka Seltzer. You don't pop it in water and watch it fizz instantly. There are times when it feels like no one's out there. The truth is that they're elsewhere—at least for the moment. When I was a senior in high school, the science teacher questioned a student who had arrived 10 minutes late to class. In a voice that signaled his annoyance, the teacher admonished the student, "Mr. Albert, where were you when the class started?" To which the student replied, "Teacher, I was elsewhere!"

Your customers are out there—they're just elsewhere at the moment. Most businesses today have one thing in common: baby boomers as customers. Consider that this category includes men and women from late 30s to early 50s in age, with the majority facing 50 and already feeling the sweat running down their backs. There's a lot of insecurity associated with reaching the half-century mark...and millions are doing it. This is a huge market for most businesses today, representing enormous potential to almost every business category. How do we get them to ring our bell?

A mighty market and a big niche

Boomers are busting out all over. According to the finest minds in market research today, they don't live by the rules of the generations before them. Baby boomers are redefining the way businesses operate. This market has been the most elusive in the history of marketing, yet each and every one of us wants a piece of this enormous body of people.

It doesn't matter what you're marketing—tires, auto parts, clothing, nuts and bolts, home repair services, pet supplies, jewelry, books, coffee—and it also doesn't matter if you're at the manufacturing, distribution or retail end or if you're selling to consumers or other businesses. This generation has penetrated every corner of the marketplace. Is it a niche or an entire group of niches?

Understanding what this market needs and wants will help you define your start up business. First, if you're creating a business, you will need to know what quirky characteristics baby boomers possess. First, they have broken every rule in a short span of time. Remember, this is the generation that turned its back on status, personal appearance, grooming and traditional values. And while it's taken a longer time for this market to mature, it's maturing more gracefully. Baby boomers celebrate life with greater exuberance than the previous generation. They are dedicated to staying young, even when they're fearing turning old. But in a very real way, you can make your cash register ring by paying attention to the issues that are so much a part of this generation's thinking.

Niche marketing

Your business has an opportunity to own a piece of this market if you really take the time to understand the concept behind niche marketing. We've discussed target marketing, but niche marketing goes one step further. Once you've targeted who your product or service appeals to demographically, you refine that process by uncovering why it appeals to them psychographically. The concept is to create a strategy that, in some cases, may fragment your overall message and redefine it for the niche market.

It is better to create a multitude of niches within your own company than to offer a broader, more unified approach of doing business. Why? Because you will be perceived as having expertise in specific areas...and when you're smaller, you can service your niche market better.

This has become known as "micromarketing"—segmenting your product or service categories to fit micromarkets. In the case of the baby boomer, if you've got a product or service to sell, tailor it to fit this customer's decidedly idiosyncratic behavior.

The great adventure

Ex Officio is a leading designer and manufacturer of a clothing line defined as "adventurewear." As a start up business created by a young entrepreneur, Ex Officio was named to *Inc.* magazine's list of fastest-growing private companies. The president, Joe Boldan, and his partner, Rick Hemmerling, expressed that once they had established their reason for being, they shot up toward success.

They began by designing their own line of fishing shirts, but soon recognized that the market was too narrowly defined. So, they expanded into a more generic category called "adventurewear"— including pants, shorts, vests, jackets and tote bags. Today, a decade since its inception, the firm offers more than 50 items...in varying sizes, colors and styles. And while the partners recognize that they have created a niche business, it's a mighty big niche. Not all of their customers care about climbing, hiking, fishing, boating or biking, much less adventures into the outback. But the market niche and focus have created a powerful presence for the firm in the marketplace. The products are designed to look good and be functional—a baby boomer's dream.

The company is now recognized as the definitive adventure clothing company. What began as a narrowly defined niche business has become broader-based with new opportunities for expansion. Interestingly, its market consists of men and women between 35 and 55 years old with an average income of about $70,000...the biggest niche market in our country today. *Boom!*

Offer instant gratification

According to researchers in product marketing, baby boomers want immediate reaction and gratification. That's one of the reasons that this market has not been as responsive to direct mail as other niches. Traditional direct response communications don't offer immediacy, even with toll-free numbers. If asked to do too much in terms of responding to a solicitation, the baby boomer turns off. Giving these customers what they want also means giving them information and access to your goods quickly and easily. So, if you want to reach them, use incentives, coupons, memberships and discount policies, and make the process of completing the sale painless.

Think about the product categories that appeal to a group of people who are reaching real maturity while trying to hold onto youth. What can you offer them? They're disappointed because they've saved less money than the generations before them. They're highly mortgaged, highly leveraged and worried about their own health and their children's well-being. They're experiencing traumas associated with the death of parents and their teenagers' behavior. And they're taking a hard look at mortality.

Researchers suggest that baby boomers are likely to return to the products associated with childhood—the warm fuzzies that remind them of their youth. They want to go to summer camp again...but there's no one to write home to in many cases.

For marketers, the critical issue in relating to the baby boomer niche is providing comfort and reassurance, not fear. While fear has been a traditional marketing tool in many industries, such as insurance, it doesn't work with baby boomers because they tend to go into denial. One example I read told the story of a life insurance company that had relied upon anxiety-producing messages that created a fear response. Their advertising message posed the question, "How will your family survive once you're gone?" Their direct marketing was considered quite successful, with a 1½-percent response. After considering the new rules associated with the baby boomer niche, the advertisement illustrated an environment of serenity with a grandfather playing with the grandchild. According to the article, their response was 10 times higher than what they received by posing the fearful question.

According to the Bureau of Labor Statistics' 1993 consumer expenditure survey, baby boomers spend 20 percent more on cosmetics than the national average. This is the hippie generation—who wore ragged clothing and long hair as the uniform of the generation, and proudly so! But they've changed, and you need to define and refine your marketing to reach their new psyches.

For example, an orthodontist near my home decided that the baby boomer niche represented a viable secondary market for his practice, the primary market being teenagers and young adults. He recognized that baby boomers are vitally interested in personal grooming and appearance, so he developed a program for mature people who could benefit from orthodontia—primarily for aesthetic reasons, not health benefits. In order to do this, he created a niche image, complete with niche hours to accommodate this market. Further, he offered consultations at the prospect's place of work, doing this on his standard day off. Then, he announced free seminars where his assistant would illustrate the dramatic differences that could be achieved with orthodontia. He did this with computer imaging, highlighting the present or before picture with the future or after picture.

This doctor created a new category for his practice. And considering the number of people in this particular niche, it was a mighty profitable move. Today, he owns the adult orthodontia marketplace— adults between 40 and 50 who want to look good and are willing to pay for it if it's made easy and accessible.

The mere size of the market has caused baby boomers to become a spoiled generation. Businesses had to pay attention because it was, after all, a *boom*! Who wouldn't pay attention? Think about how this generation has changed the marketplace and consider the categories that have been created or supercharged by the boomer generation:

- Adventure travel.
- One-price car dealerships.
- Plastic surgery.
- Running and walking shoes.
- Cosmetics for men.
- Environmentally friendly products.
- New conveniences, such as meal delivery services.
- Massage therapists who visit offices.
- Fast-food restaurants creating new menu items.
- Recreational vehicle manufacturers designing for boomers.
- Harley Davidson designing motorcycles for business executives.
- Sailboats and motor yachts.
- Bottled water.
- Personal trainers.
- Fold-away fitness equipment.
- Exercise clubs.
- Electronic memo books.
- Personal fax machines.
- Cellular phones.
- Books on tape.

As a start up marketer, you can look at a vast array of products and services that will accommodate this huge niche market. And you have an opportunity to create your own category without tampering with your existing business.

Chapter 19

Ready to Market: How About a Marketing Plan?

Creating your marketing plan should come after you've wrestled successfully with all of the issues we have discussed. Essentially the marketing plan is your road map to the treasures we call success. But like all plans, it is only as good as the implementer. I've seen too many mission statements and marketing plans remain under wraps—in drawers or on shelves—forgotten and unrealized.

Understanding your customers' needs, defining your role in serving those needs and positioning yourself in the marketplace are far more critical than a well-written marketing plan. Therefore, the plan you create must correspond with all of the information you have gathered about your customers and your competition. From your marketing plan, you will be able to develop offshoots that include all of the issues of communications and achieving identity through advertising.

Components of the plan

Goals. This defines your reason for being in business. It may include financial gains, sales volume, gross profit or projected increases. Beyond the monetary goals, you may include broader goals as well. For example, you may want to increase the number of employees, broaden the amount of products you carry, increase the varying types of services, expand into foreign markets, create a retail division of a manufacturing facility or open a direct mail component of your business. Next, examine your personal goals and incorporate them into your plan. These may include quality time with your family, vacations, a boat, new cars, renovating your home or sending the kids to summer camp. It's important to include all of the goals that you associate with your business. It helps define your reason for being and it stimulates the motivational side of your being.

Objectives. Here you refine your goals to include specific issues that are important to you and your business. Your objective may be to own 23 percent of the market in your business community. Another objective might be to acquire your chief competitor within five years. Perhaps your objective is to create two new product categories each quarter for the first three years. Your objectives are targeted goals.

Opportunities. What opportunities exist for your business? Examine the market for voids, unusual trends that you can take advantage of and competitive weaknesses. Thoroughly review the trade publications that are dedicated to your industry. If you own a pizza restaurant, get a subscription to *Restaurant News*. Learn what innovative thinking is taking place among your suppliers and peers. Develop opportunities based upon all of the information and all of the models available to you.

Strategy. What steps will you take to achieve your goals and objectives? Perhaps you need to finance a new piece of equipment in order to stay ahead of the competition. Another strategy might include outsourcing employees in order to gain accelerated growth. You may need to hire a marketing consultant to increase your presence in the marketplace. You may also need to apply for a line of credit to finance more advertising. Your strategy will be multifaceted and doesn't require you to specify details until you begin to put each program into place.

Position. Outline your company's strengths. Define your market position relative to your competitors'. Detail the major issues that you will need to exploit in order to achieve your goals and objectives. Who are you, and where are you going in the market?

Obstacles. List obstacles and ideas to overcome them. Years ago when Spam wanted to reenter the marketplace with advertising, they had to overcome a major image problem. There were misperceptions regarding the product—that it had fillers and wasn't really ham. The company faced the obstacles and overcame them by communicating how fundamentally good the product was...that it could be grilled, fried, baked, breaded, barbecued. They overcame the obstacles by communicating and altering previously held beliefs. Look at your potential obstacles and begin to create solutions.

Situational analysis and research. When the marketing plan has gaps, sometimes research is necessary. There are many companies that provide survey information, statistical research and customized data gathering. You can locate these firms in phone books under market research or contact the American Association of Advertising Agencies in New York City (see page 85 for contact information). Research of your market may not require sophisticated analytical study. It may be as simple as contacting the trade association in your field and asking for help.

What we're after is the pertinent information regarding your industry. What's happening to product movement, service issues, sales trends, innovations in technology, environmental issues and industry projections?

The creation of your marketing plan will lead you to ask yourself a great many questions. This is one of the primary benefits of developing such a document. You'll be raising many issues that will need consideration. Look at your plan and reflect on your own situation. If you're in a start up mode, you will need to define your economic needs. Remind yourself again and again that you're in a learning process and that you will stumble and fall a few times before you begin to sprint. The marketing plan you create is flexible. It will change—in fact, it should be reviewed at least twice a year, updated and refined. You should also create a six-month checklist that evaluates your progress in relation to the plan.

Checklist

1. Have you closed in on any of your goals? Are you achieving them? Which ones? What issues created success? What failed?

2. Have your objectives changed? Which ones have been accomplished?

3. Have you taken advantage of established opportunities? How have you used innovation and ingenuity to create new opportunities? What has happened in your own market relative to your competition?

4. Has the strategy worked? Which steps toward your goals and objectives resulted in gains? What can you now add to your strategy to propel you forward, faster?

5. In what ways have you supported your market premise and position? Have you defined who and what you are? Are you constantly reviewing the competitors in the marketplace in order to refine your position?

6. Which obstacles had to be overcome? What issues didn't you anticipate becoming an obstacle? What's left to overcome? How do you anticipate breaking down remaining barriers to your success?

7. What have you learned that has helped you? What situation exists now that didn't when you began? How has your industry changed? How has your own business changed since you created the plan?

I want you to create an addendum to your marketing plan. This will incorporate issues that should be broken down and identified within the context of the plan. The purpose is to keep yourself reminded of the plan itself and the results of successfully executing it.

Addendum

1. Examine the value-added aspects of your selling proposition.

2. Outline the methods of communicating your strengths.

3. Define your brand identity.

4. State, in one sentence, your marketing position.

5. Review how your competitors view you.

6. Which customers do you presently have, and which ones do you still want?

7. What specific components are necessary for you to dominate your market?

Once you've put your plan to use, reviewed it at least twice a year, redefine it, share it with friends, family, employees. Infuse it with as many new ideas as possible. Only then will it become a living, breathing document that takes on a defined role in your business future.

Chapter 20

Copyrights and Trademarks

The difference between trademarks and copyrights is that trademarks identify the products or services of a specific company and distinguish them from competitors, while copyrights protect literary, creative or artistic works (also called "intellectual properties")—not the names the works are marketed under, but the works themselves.

Most of your marketing materials can be copyrighted—including the packaging, advertisements, brochures, labels and direct mail literature. You can either apply to the copyright office yourself or engage an attorney to apply for a copyright. Once you receive it, you must affix, on the copyrighted material, the © symbol followed by the year of first publication and your company name.

If you plan to use copyrighted materials in the promotion of your business, you should get permission from the copyright holder. You can also consider joining the Copyright Clearance Center, which enables you to reproduce certain published materials without having to get permission from individual publishers.

Your trademark protects your product or your service—not the literature that communicates these issues. A trademark is literally your mark of trade, identifying you as the sole owner of a particular product or service identity. There are trademark attorneys in every community, and the cost for a simple trademark is between $200 and $700. Once you have established the trademark, you will want to look for any possible infringements.

Companies who infringe upon others' trademarks have to be caught before they can be stopped. In my own community, a retail jewelry business began to offer franchises called "Jewelry Repairs R Us"—using a backwards "R." I saw their billboards everywhere, and then I noticed they were gone. Why? Because Toys R Us (reverse R) reported them for trademark infringement. Suddenly, Jewelry Repairs R Us became Jewelry Repairs *By* Us. If left to their own devices, many businesses will look to benefit by association. In this case, the distinction between jewelry and toys caused little or no confusion, but apparently there was enough concern on the part of Toys R Us to ask the jewelry company to cease and desist.

Once you have established your trademark, your goods or services are legally protected. According to the American Association of Advertising Agencies, you can lose your rights in a trademark, under federal law, when "any course of conduct of the registrant...causes the mark to lose its significance as an indication of origin."

Trademark registrations are renewable. Therefore, if used properly, you can own the trademark forever. But as pointed out by the AAAA, if the mark becomes generic rather than specific, it loses its designation as an exclusive property. They give the following example: When Otis Elevator Company owned the "escalator" trademark, they used it in conjunction with a reference to their elevators—a generic designation. By failing to distinguish the escalator's trademark identity from a generic term, Otis helped establish the premise that the escalator had become generic.

How to properly use a trademark

Always use the generic name for the product or service in conjunction with the trademark. Ask yourself if the trademark being used in promoting the product can be omitted from the sentence—without losing the meaning.

Proper: *Mow your lawn with a Toro mower.*

Improper: *Mow your lawn with a Toro.*

In the improper example, the sentence doesn't make literal sense without identifying the product. Without the use of the word "mower," people might assume that Toro was a generic name instead of a specific product. This is what happened with the Otis escalator.

Trademarking is risky business...and it requires finesse. Think about trademarks that have become generic and have lost their ability to maintain trademark status. The AAAA offers the following examples: aspirin, cellophane, celluloid, kerosene, lanolin, linoleum, milk of magnesia, shredded wheat, thermos. Astonishingly, these were all trademarks until they became associated with generic categories.

Mostly, trademarks lose their vitality and become generic through improper presentation, communication and advertising. Therefore, you must be careful to keep your trademark specific—through proper use of labels, advertising and public relations. Always use your trademark in your communications materials. This includes product labels, packaging, coupons, sales promotion items, advertisements and the like.

Once you have registered your trademark, simply use the ® symbol. It is the simplest form of trademark identification. Prior to registration, you can indicate that the product is a trademark of your company by using a footnote at the bottom of the text, or you can use the symbol ™ for brand names or ˢᴹ for service marks. Be certain, though, to contact an attorney if you have any questions regarding trademark identification or use.

Start Up Marketing Summary

Start up marketing should feel like turning the key on the ignition switch. It's an exhilarating experience—putting your business into overdrive. And it can be accomplished through dedication and hard work. Probably the most significant aspect of marketing, and one which is emphasized throughout the book, is the idea of differentiation. It is incumbent upon you to create your vision—holding steadfast to the principles of your *position*. By defining who you are and who you are in business to serve, you have already begun to step on the accelerator.

Keep reminders of your goals, visions and attributes in front of you and your people at all times. Make certain that every member of your organization maintains your identity and offers your message at every conceivable opportunity. When you go to McDonald's, you hear a little message that each and every employee is drummed into asking you: "Would you like fries with that burger?" This illustrates the concept of motivation.

Marketing communications *is* complex...but the simplest things can also create uncommon experiences. If your business agenda includes simple suggestive sales techniques such as the one illustrated above, or if you create an environment that is cohesive and team-oriented, your marketing materials will be supercharged.

"A wise man will not communicate his differing thoughts to unprepared minds, or in a disorderly manner."

—Benjamin Whichcote, 18th-century writer

It is your responsibility to communicate your strengths, ever mindful of your customers' preferences. If you do one without understanding or knowing the other, you are risking your opportunity to capture the marketplace. Marketing begins in your mind—with your vision and your dreams. It becomes a reality the moment you commit to a plan and expose your message publicly.

Remember, too, that once you proclaim your business identity, you are responsible to uphold it. Be sure that your message is correct...that it reflects your true identity and is not an image without substance. You have a choice to make. You can rub the sticks together and build a small fire—enough to keep you warm. Or you can create a blaze that will set new standards in its glow. The difference is in how you approach your marketing and how often you reassess your thinking and the conditions of the market.

"Hear the other side."

—St. Augustine, early Christian
theologian

Listen carefully to the market and to your customers. They will tell you what they want. Start up marketers have a wonderful opportunity to create powerful impressions because they don't need to overcome imperfect pasts. Know the customers, and create your position or posture from what they tell you. Own the market by becoming the most responsive, innovative, learned, entrepreneurial-minded business in your world. Examine the rules and break as many as need to be broken. Discard what isn't working and think about new ways of doing the same things. Your competitors will be watching you if you're inspired. But they won't catch you if you're first.

Remember: Entrepreneurs see limitless opportunities. The rest of the world only sees limits!

The Marketing Glossary

The following is a selective glossary that is designed to expand your marketing vocabulary. When you enter a start up marketing situation, you will be better armed with the language of the marketplace, and you will have more authority with the media!

ADI (area of dominant influence)—a term that identifies the primary market for a particular medium. In television, it refers to the stations that receive the most viewers.

Artificially new—a product or service that appears to be new by virtue of updating or changing the packaging, name or other cosmetic aspects of it.

Balance—the relationship between elements in an advertisement so that the visual appeal is complementary to the message.

Blind headline—a headline that does not indicate what the product or service is until the reader gets to the body copy.

Blitz schedule—an intensive start up campaign that front-loads the communication program. This could consist of three advertisements in the same issue of a magazine, introducing the company or a specific offer.

Boutique agency—small or freelance creative services company. It offers production services but usually not media placement, marketing counsel or a full range of services.

Brainstorming—idea-generating meetings between peers. No agenda, criticism or evaluation is necessary...just an exercise in pushing the envelope as far toward the edge of the table as possible.

Brand name—the name and graphic identity of a specific product or service. The identifying symbol that buoys a product higher than those around it.

Breakout merchandising—when a company offers products that are atypical for the business. An example would be a hair salon that sells snack items or a florist selling jewelry.

Budget—the prioritized plan of spending for a business. Typically broken into line items pertaining to specific issues such as advertising, merchandising, inventory, sales commissions and cost of goods.

Bulk mail—third-class, high-quantity mail programs.

Business-to-business advertising—communication between companies as opposed to consumer advertising. This typically takes place in industry or trade journals, literature or direct marketing.

Campaign—a well-coordinated advertising and marketing effort that is planned and executed over a specified period of time. This establishes continuity and creates prolonged identity.

Canned advertising—materials prepared by a manufacturer or distributor and disseminated to retailers for use in local media.

Circulation—the number of homes or individuals being reached by a particular medium. In broadcast (radio and television), this applies to the homes in the station's broadcast range. For print media such as newspapers or magazines, it is the actual number of copies sold or distributed. In outdoor advertising, it is the anticipated traffic count or gross impressions during any given part of the day.

Combination rate—a discounted rate paid by an advertiser who commits to running space in various publications owned and operated by the same company. This usually represents a substantial savings over individually placed advertisements.

Competitive strategy—a marketing program that identifies the strengths of one product or service over the competing brands.

Comprehensive—a tight layout that closely resembles the finished advertisement.

Consumer advertising—promotional messages directed at the general population.

Consumer goods—products or services for individual or family use.

Contract rate—a media rate that permits the advertiser to take advantage of a discount by committing to either frequency (number of advertisements in a year) or lineage (quantity of space).

Cooperative advertising—the arrangement between manufacturer and dealer/distributor/retailer to share in the cost of promotion. Typically manufacturers will pay their share of a circular, flier or advertising program in order to have their product featured as part of the sales message. Many start up companies overlook co-op possibilities that could greatly contribute to or enhance their promotional programs. Retail or distribution companies can include a manufactured product in an advertisement and greatly reduce the cost of the advertising or receive an allowance or discount on purchases from manufacturers in lieu of shared advertising costs.

Copy block—the text of an advertisement.

Copy testing—testing techniques that evaluate the effectiveness of an advertisement or campaign before it is published.

Corporate advertising—also known as institutional advertising; promotes the company rather than the products or services.

Corrective advertising—sometimes required by the Federal Trade Commission, advertising that corrects previous misleading or false claims in print.

Cost effectiveness—producing the largest number of prospects at the least cost.

Coverage—in broadcast, the number of homes that are within a radio or television station's reach. In outdoor advertising, the number of cars that pass a particular location during a 30-day period.

CPM (cost per thousand)—the cost to reach 1,000 prospects. In print media, you can determine the cost per thousand by using the following formula: *CPM = cost of advertisement x 1,000 ÷ circulation.* For broadcast media, the formula is: *CPM = cost of a single unit of time x 1,000 ÷ number of homes reached by a part of the day or program.*

Creative strategy—the defining creative methodology used to create awareness and incite responses. Includes market position, brand identity, communication platform—presenting *how*, *what* and *why* issues.

Cume—the net cumulative audience. This refers to the number of people exposed to a single broadcast program or to an entire commercial schedule over a four-week period.

Cumulative audience—the number of people exposed to a medium over a specified period of time.

Demographics—identifying factors regarding population. Includes age, gender, income, marital status, location, occupation, ethnicity, home ownership and any other factors that segregate the market by categories.

Depth interview—process of getting customers to talk without fear of criticism. They can divulge real concerns, likes and dislikes and give substantive reasons for their feelings.

Diffusion—how a new product or service is accepted into the marketplace within a specific period of time.

Direct marketing—any form of communication that is produced by the marketer and delivered directly to the customer. This may include mail, television, radio, outdoor media, Internet, interactive online services, telemarketing.

Drive time—the parts of the day when most of the marketplace are in their cars. Radio stations use this as their premium selling time—typically 6 a.m. to 10 a.m. and 3 p.m. to 7 p.m.

Duplication—the number of prospects who are reached by more than one of the media choices within a mix. For example, if your advertisement appears in *Better Homes & Gardens* and *McCall's*, your duplication will be quite high because many of the same readers receive both publications.

Empirical method—a testing program for determining the best use of advertising dollars. Typically, this requires running the same advertisement in different markets to determine the strength of the market and the message.

Federal Trade Commission—established in 1914, this regulatory agency controls unfair practices and monopolistic methods of business.

Flighting—a method of scheduling a communications program on radio and TV that involves advertising over a period of time with voids of one to three weeks between announcements. Research has indicated that advertising that is "flighted" will, in spite of the voids, be perceived as constant by the consumers. For budgetary purposes, you may run a four-over-six schedule on radio, which means you will pay for four months' worth of an advertising program, but spread it out ("flight" it) over a six-month period so that there are gaps within the total time period.

Four-color process—printing process that produces real, full color by using the four primary colors—red, yellow, blue and black—in varying combinations and concentrations to obtain a wide range of color variations.

Frame of reference—the forces that affect people's perceptions. They may be cultural, social, political...and they influence the way in which people react to marketing messages.

Frequency—the number of messages that are communicated within a given period of time. Radio, for example, is a high-frequency medium. It requires repetition in order to penetrate the minds in the marketplace.

Full run—refers to an advertisement that runs in all of the markets of a particular medium. For example, you can purchase spots in regional editions of *The New York Times* or you can expose your message to the entire paid circulation if you choose a full-run program.

Full-service agency—a company that provides complete marketing and advertising services, such as marketing consultation, media planning and placement, creative production, research, public relations, scheduling, writing, graphic arts, TV and radio and direct marketing.

Gaze motion—the way that people's eyes move during reading. Typically people see right-hand pages first, which is why so many advertisers battle for the upper-right-hand position on a page.

Gross audience—the total number of people exposed to a medium.

Gross impressions—the figure that refers to the whole audience delivered by a media program.

Gross rating points (GRP)—a figure that represents 1 percent of the total audience within a specified market or geography. This is applied to both radio and television media.

Horizontal advertising—refers to advertising by a trade association or group of companies within the same industry—designed to promote the entire industry, thereby benefiting all who participate. It is a cost savings method of promoting.

Horizontal publications—publications for people engaged in a specific function that is prevalent across various industries—for example, *Plant Manager*, which appeals to plant managers in various industries.

Industrial advertising—advertising of products or services that are used in the production or marketing of other products or services.

Innovators—refers to entrepreneurs who break most of the traditions and rules in order to create a new category or means of marketing.

Insertion order—a form sent to the media that reserves space or time, offering specific terms and conditions, such as run dates and position on the schedule or within the print environment.

Inserts—also known as freestanding inserts, these promotional materials are produced by the advertiser and then inserted into publications, either blown in or bound in.

Institutional messages—image-oriented messages designed to enhance the identity of a company, not a product. For example, when Monsanto advertises, it is selling the image of the company and illustrating how it is part of a process that ultimately benefits the consumer.

Layout—the rough concept and arrangement of materials within a given promotional piece. Advertising layouts consist of headlines, sub-headlines, body copy, position statement, borders, logo, etc.

Lifestyle marketing—issues that affect a marketer's decision to create a specific message. This refers to the way in which the target group lives—what opinions they have, how they travel, what type of vacations they go on, how many cars they drive, the kind of food they eat...information drawn from demographic data.

List broker—a person or company that rents or sells mailing lists. Usually a list broker can produce a list for any conceivable category.

List compiler—a company that compiles lists of names and sells them to list brokers or direct to customers.

Logo—the identifying symbol that trademarks a company. This may consist of typography, a symbol or a combination of both.

Make-good—a free placement of an advertisement used to replace one that ran incorrectly, was unreadable or was placed at the wrong time. The publisher issues a make-good for any mistakes that are the result of his organization.

Market—the body of people who are in the buying arena.

Market potential—refers to how much sales activity a product or service can sustain in a given market.

Market segment—the divided territory in which a particular group exists. Companies segment the market in order to prioritize their customers and make their marketing efforts more directed and efficient.

Marketing—the system of bringing a product or service to market. Includes advertising, public relations, merchandising, research, media, personal selling and sales promotion.

Marketing mix—all of the issues that go into marketing a product or service. This includes product, price, distribution, promotional plans and methods of communicating.

Marketing research—the data derived from conducting research into consumers' buying habits, specific issues that affect the marketplace, competitive products and price sensitivities, and the many other factors that will result in a more targeted communications effort.

Mechanical—the finished camera-ready artwork, ready to be published or printed.

Media (sing. *medium*)—method of reaching the marketplace; includes print, broadcast or electronics. Typically refers to vehicles through which entertainment or information issues reach the public—such as newspapers, magazines, radio, television and on-line services.

Media mix—the program that utilizes various media in order to reach customers during different parts of the day and in various aspects of their lifestyle.

Merchandising—a program that delivers a sales message at the point of sale or within the sales environment. Includes point-of-purchase displays, signs, shelf-talkers (small signs affixed to the shelf where the item is displayed), window signs, banners and posters.

Motivational research—applying psychological principles in an effort to understand why people buy and their habits and preferences.

Narrowcasting—the manner in which radio is segmented into different groups of listeners, each with its favorite types of music and programs.

National advertising—advertising paid for by the manufacturer or producer of the goods or services.

Network radio—a group of stations carrying the same programming, though not necessarily the same advertising.

Objective budgeting—the establishment of a marketing budget by analyzing marketing objectives and placing a performance/value relationship on each piece of the agenda. This is a method of prioritizing areas of business, giving higher promotional dollars to higher priority issues.

Open rate—a noncontract rate for newspaper or magazine advertising. It is the highest published rate because no frequency or space commitment is being made by the advertiser.

Optical center—the site on an advertisement that is usually about two-thirds from the top. Statistically, it is shown that the eye gravitates to this position, thus marketing designers use this as a pivotal point in the design of a communications piece.

Package inserts—promotional materials that may be packaged in the shipment of goods or stuffed into invoice mailings.

Package plan—many media companies offer specific plans at discounted rates. If an advertiser commits to a plan, it receives a certain frequency for a reduced cost.

Paid circulation—differs from circulation of certain types of publications that are sustained by advertising alone. Paid circulation publications are audited by the Audit Bureau of Circulation (ABC) and can only announce the number of readers who actually pay to receive the publication. This is the most valuable circulation within the arena of printed material.

Pass-along readership—a method of promoting the expanded circulation and life a printed publication may receive from secondary sources. For example, a magazine may have a circulation of 100,000 but claim a readership of 300,000 due to the fact that it projects at least three readers per copy within a household, an office environment or a waiting room at an office of a dentist or other professional.

Percentage of sales budgeting—the most utilized principle of budgeting. This is figured out by applying a percentage of gross sales to marketing. The American Association of Advertising Agencies has a list of industry averages by SIC codes. SIC refers to Standard Industrial Classifications, but it lists every conceivable industry from retail to manufacturing.

Point of purchase (POP)—messages that are posted at purchase points. Very often, they are produced by manufacturers and given to retailers to promote the product at impulse points, such as the checkout counters in stores or near registers at supermarkets.

Positioning—the single most important element in marketing. It identifies where your product or service falls in relation to the competition. It also identifies how the customer perceives the product in relation to the universe of similar products. The issues that affect positioning may include specific creative images, pricing, packaging, branding, perceived value, function and design.

Poster—typically 30 by 40 inches, a colorful presentation that can be hung on a wall or near product displays.

Posturing—similar to positioning, but more fluid. This is a company's pronouncement of its objectives. The primary difference from positioning is that posturing a product may consist of using a variety of characteristics to create an identity as opposed to one or a few. For example, if you position a product by price or size alone, when market conditions shift, you may lose that position and need to redefine yourself. Posturing, on the other hand, relates to various selling benefits and features, so that if one becomes untenable, you can more easily maintain the posture.

Premiums—incentive materials designed to keep your product or service top-of-mind with your customers. These giveaways can be as mundane as a refrigerator magnet or as high-tech as a talking business card.

Primary data—essential information gathered by a company in direct contact with customers. This may be accomplished through interviews, personal surveys, mailings, diaries, telephone conversations and focus groups.

Primary demand—the demand created by a marketer for the product; the highest priority issue a marketer offers to the consumer.

Prime time—in television, the hours between 7:30 p.m. and 11 p.m.

Private label brands—the proprietary house label under which products are marketed by a retailer or wholesaler. For example, A&P's Eight O'Clock Coffee.

Product life cycle—stages of a product's life: 1) infancy or introductory stage when the product is immature in the market; 2) youth or high-energy growth stage when the product is in an accelerated mode; 3) mature or stable stage when the product holds its position; and 4) old age stage when the product shows sign of decline.

Professional promotion—promotional activities such as advertising and public relations from members of the professional community to consumers. This is a more subtle form of solicitation than general promotional programs because professionals are bound by certain ethical and legal restrictions. Even if they're not, they're judged by peers and associations when they appear too aggressive in communicating to the marketplace.

Promotional mix—the combination of elements a company uses in promoting its business. For example, direct mail, personal selling, advertising and publicity.

Psychographics—the psychological portraits of customers, developed for use in predicting consumer behavior and response. It goes beyond demographics and sociographics, reaching into the psychological factors that affect people's decisions.

Puff words—the overused, underabsorbed words that have lost their meaning—words such as "quality," "value," "service," "best," "finest" and "most popular."

Pull marketing—a strategy designed to pull consumers into the sales environment by directing advertising to the customers in order to attract them to the dealer. In other words, manufacturers will often communicate with customers to create demand and deliver them to the sales agent.

Push marketing—a manufacturer's strategy to incentivize the retailer to push its product—through co-op advertising or other incentives.

Rate base—guaranteed circulation upon which advertising rates are based.

Rate of adoption—the length of time it takes for a new product or service to be accepted in the marketplace.

Reach—how many people are exposed to a marketing message.

Reader service card (bingo card)—a prepaid postcard bound into magazines (both trade and consumer) that features the entire list of advertisers and a method for the readers to receive information regarding any advertised product or service. Typically readers simply circle a number that corresponds to an advertiser, and the publication forwards the cards to the company, which can follow up with a phone contact or by sending requested literature.

Reassurance value—designed to alleviate buyer's remorse, a method of providing post-purchase assurance to customers that they've made the right purchase decision. This can be done by follow-up phone calls from the advertiser or by mail.

Regional marketing—exposing your message to a specific region rather than the full circulation or audience of the medium you're using. This is especially useful in launching a new business—by testing a medium before you commit to its full audience.

Retail advertising—the communication by an individual company designed to bring customers to specific locations for the purchase of specific advertised products.

Rotary plan—a term that applies to programs in outdoor advertising. This plan moves the same poster to different locations over the course of a specified period of time. It can also apply to rotating various messages to different billboard locations.

Roughs—unfinished layouts, designed to give an overall impression of what finished artwork will look like.

Sales potential—the percentage of a market that a company can expect will try its product or service.

Sales promotion—nonmedia-oriented sales and marketing materials, such as brochures, leave-behinds, flip-chart presentations, videos, slide and sound presentation and across-the-desk binder materials. These are communication devices that promote the sale of the product and enhance the advertising campaign.

Sample—a representative portion of the market.

Selective marketing—appealing to a specific market segment. This type of marketing will be more prevalent as technologies permit us to capture and manage database information.

Self-mailer—a direct mail vehicle that contains a self cover and does not require an envelope. The address of the prospect appears on the piece itself.

Service mark—a symbol or name used in selling services.

Share of market budgeting—modeling your budget after a company that already owns a piece of the market. You can usually obtain this information by speaking to the media and asking what a particular company is spending or how frequently it advertises.

Short rate—the prorated difference in cost between what an advertiser contracts to spend in a medium and what is actually spent. For example, if you sign a 12-time contract with a magazine in order to take advantage of a frequency discount, but you only run 10 issues, the magazine will charge you the appropriate rate for a 10-time schedule, billing you the difference, since you did not achieve the frequency discount. Likewise, a rebate is offered if the advertiser contracts for 12 issues and actually runs advertisements in 14 issues.

Slogan—same as a position statement, but usually accompanies the logo and serves as a signature to the advertisement or communications vehicle. This is essentially your company's thumbprint.

Sound effects (SFX)—audio devices used in radio advertising or audiovisual presentations.

Speculative campaign—you may request this from freelancers or advertising agencies when considering doing business with them; it's a method by which the creative resources team offers you a speculative look at what you can expect from them. It may consist of an advertisement or a series of promotional pieces—a direct-mail flier, a radio commercial, a TV storyboard or a logo design.

Spot radio or television—local market advertising within a defined geography.

Starch rating—calculation of the number of reader responses within certain issues of publications.

Statement stuffer—a promotional piece inserted into credit card statements or bills sent out to customers.

Stock creative—may consist of music from a stock library, photos, illustrations or clip art that can be used by advertisers for a fee. It is available from a variety of stock sources listed in phone books.

Storyboard—the words and pictures depicting a marketing message before an actual commercial is produced.

Surplus inventory—a virtually unknown phenomenon that exists in the publishing world. Many publications, such as trade and consumer magazines, newspapers and even direct mail companies, have unsold advertising space for a specific issue. The discounts can range from 20 percent to more than 50 percent, and you will only know about them if you ask and become part of a select list of advertisers who will make a marketing decision to buy the space on very short notice.

Take-ones—postcards that are offered for free and usually contain a promotional or incentive offer. They are torn from a pad displayed on buses, in train stations, at mall kiosks or in supermarkets.

Target market—the most likely consumers of a particular product, identified by the marketer based upon a variety of information—demographic, psychographic, research and statistical data.

Teasers—typically, small space messages that appear before the opening of a business or in conjunction with some significant new announcement. They are designed to titillate the market without giving away information. They tease the customer in an attempt to create a high level of curiosity, so that when the real information is delivered, the interest is intense on the part of the consumer.

Test marketing—the process of testing a product's appeal in various markets before a rollout takes place.

Thumbnails—the first rough stages of an advertisement or brochure.

Trade advertising—advertising that is placed in trade publications and communicates between businesses such as wholesalers, distributors and retailers.

Trade name—a name that is used for commercial purposes by a company promoting products, services or people.

Trade show—an industry event designed to display wares to potential buyers. Typically manufacturers or distributors exhibit at shows, with the end user in attendance as the customer. Trade shows are an ideal forum for start up companies looking to develop new product or service ideas.

Trademark—the registration of a name and symbol, providing for exclusive use.

Traffic—the number of people who respond to marketing information and promotional activities.

Unit of sales budgeting—a variation on the percentage of sales budgeting method. This requires that a specific monetary amount, rather than a percentage of sales, be committed to each unit.

Vertical publications—usually refers to trade publications. A vertical publication covers an entire industry—for example, *Industrial Equipment News*, which targets the entire industrial business arena and deals with issues relating to all of the varied concerns of industrial manufacturing.

Voice over (VO)—in audio presentations or television, when an actor's or speaker's voice is heard but the person remains unidentified.

Index